Dr. Ryker

BROTHERS PARADISE

A Novel

by:
Grace Maxwell

Brothers Paradise: Dr. Ryker/Grace Maxwell — 1st edition

ONE

Ginny

I'm three rounds into my darts game, and my aim is getting better. That's either proof that I'm finally relaxing or that I've crossed the invisible line between buzzed and dumb.

The dart lands just shy of the bullseye. I smirk, turning toward my friend Kara Bishop, except Kara is no longer on the barstool beside me. She's across the room, giggling in the arms of Elijah Caldwell, one of Paradise's finest.

Figures. One flash of a badge and a square jaw and she's reenacting a scene from a country music video.

I sigh and wave off the bartender when he glances my way. "Water, please," I call. "Heavy on the ice, light on the judgment."

I don't do drama. And I definitely don't do Paradise men.

That's a rule I've stuck to since I moved back a year ago, and I have the self-respect to keep it. Mostly.

I just need to sober up before I order a rideshare. It's late, but not too late, and Mikey's is tame tonight. Just a few locals at the bar and the usual town gossip brewing over pitchers of cheap beer.

Then he walks in.

Ryker Paradise.

The door doesn't creak, the music doesn't stop, but it might as well. He's got that kind of presence, like the room takes a collective breath, unsure whether to be annoyed or impressed.

He's tall, confident, and unfairly hot. His dark hair is a little tousled, his jawline looks like it's never heard of insecurity, and his smile is the kind that gets women pregnant.

I turn back to the dartboard and pretend I didn't notice.

He's not for me. Too smooth. Too pretty. Too...Paradise.

Besides, I've already made one impulsive choice tonight by coming out by myself. I don't need a second.

"You're either aiming for the bullseye or trying to kill someone. Should I duck?"

His voice is behind me, low, teasing. I curse inwardly as I feel the corner of my mouth twitch.

I let the next dart fly. It hits a solid red ring. "Depends. You planning on making yourself a target?"

He steps closer. I can smell him now—clean soap, something warm like cedar. He's wearing a Henley that hugs his arms in all the wrong ways. Or right ways, depending on the level of alcohol in my system. "Only if you promise to go easy on me."

I glance at him. Big mistake. His eyes are a stormy blue and completely amused.

"Ryker Paradise," I say, like his name is a warning.

"Ginny Dempsey," he replies. "I was starting to think you were avoiding me."

Of course I was. Everyone knows what happens when a Dempsey gets tangled up with a Paradise. Drama. Scandal.

Reputations ruined. And I'm fresh out of patience for small-town headlines with my name in them.

I arch a brow. "Starting to think? You're slower than I thought."

He laughs, deep, warm, and way too charming.

I turn back to the board and toss another dart. This one misses. *Damn it.*

"You know," he says, stepping up beside me, "we could make this interesting. Loser buys the winner a drink?"

"I've had enough drinks for tonight."

"Then how about a bet?" The corner of his mouth turns up.

There it is. That Paradise grin.

And despite every reason not to, despite the warning bells clanging in my head, I feel my mouth move. "You're on."

He grins like he's already won. "All right then. Closest to the bullseye."

I hand him a dart. "Try not to embarrass yourself. You Paradise boys like to do that."

He laughs again, but there's a flicker of heat behind it. I've poked the bear.

Ryker takes his time. Lines up. Throws. It lands just outside the center.

"Not bad," I say, ignoring the flip in my stomach. "But not great either."

He shrugs. "Mediocrity looks good on me."

I step up and throw without overthinking. The dart lands, just outside his mark. "Damn."

He raises a brow. "Looks like you're buying the first round of whatever we're betting."

"I thought it wasn't a drink wager."

"It wasn't." He steps closer. "But I'm open to suggestions."

The way he says it sends a shiver down my spine. Not dirty. Not innocent either.

"Are you always this cocky?"

He grins. "Only when I know I'm right."

"Right about what?"

His eyes move to mine, steady and smug. "That you've been watching me since the moment I walked in."

I scoff, but the heat crawling up my neck betrays me.

"It's okay," he says, softer now. "I've been watching you too."

I laugh. "You think very highly of yourself."

"No," he says. "I just pay attention."

Something about the way he says it pulls me in. I've learned to brush off attention that feels performative or possessive. But this? This feels different. Like he sees me, really sees me.

I hate it.

I love it.

"You're not my type," I blurt. He's the kind of guy I've spent years avoiding. The kind that burns bright, then burns out. I've had enough ashes in my life. But damn it, something about him makes me want to throw logic out the window and chase the fire anyway.

His mouth tips into a smirk. "What is your type?"

"Safe. Boring. Uncomplicated."

He steps closer. "Good thing I'm none of those things."

I exhale, low and shaky. I should walk away. Call my ride. Go home and eat a cold grilled cheese sandwich and forget any of this ever happened.

But I don't.

Because Ryker is heat and pressure and the kind of trouble I crave. Maybe I need a little trouble tonight.

"I'm not sleeping with you," I say, though I might be lying.

His eyes darken. "Then let's play another round."

"Darts?"

He leans in, and I feel the warmth of his breath against my cheek. "Flirting."

I should stop this. I should care that he's a Paradise and

I'm a Dempsey, and this whole thing has *town scandal* written all over it.

But I toss the dart anyway. It lands a fraction closer to the bullseye than last time. I smile, but I don't turn around. I know he's still behind me. I can feel him.

"Not bad," Ryker murmurs, like he's impressed. Or turned on. Maybe both.

I straighten, my skin tight with awareness. "Are we still playing or just pretending it's about darts?"

His chuckle is warm. Dangerous. "That depends. Are we still pretending you're not interested?"

I finally face him. "You want honesty?"

"Always."

I take a step closer. So does he.

"I think you're insanely attractive," I say, watching his pupils dilate just enough to catch it. "But you're also trouble. You've probably slept with half the single women in this bar."

He lifts a shoulder. "Exaggeration. Maybe a third."

That earns him a snort. "See? Trouble."

"Maybe," he says. "But the good kind."

He's close now. Too close. But the part of me that usually pulls away isn't moving. "You're not what I need," I whisper.

"No," he agrees. "But maybe I'm what you want."

God help me, he's not wrong.

His gaze drops to my mouth, then lifts again. He doesn't move, doesn't touch me. He's waiting — for permission or for me to run.

I do neither.

"I don't do messy," I tell him.

He nods. "Then we'll keep it clean."

I arch a brow. "Doubt it."

"Dirty can be fun too," he says with a grin that should be illegal. "If you trust the person you're getting dirty with."

The air between us snaps taut. My pulse hammers. My mouth is dry.

"Say it," he murmurs.

"Say what?"

"That you want me."

My brain offers some sort of feeble protest, but my body's not listening. I lean in, our noses nearly touching. "What happens if I do?"

He smiles. "Then I stop waiting."

Ryker shifts position, hiding me from the crowd at the bar. His hand slides up my thigh. "Are you wearing underwear?"

I laugh, tossing my head back. "Wouldn't you like to know?"

His hand slides under my skirt, fingers finding the heat through my panties. "You're so wet for me."

I shut my eyes and let him take me away. His fingers are like magic.

"What do you want?"

"You," I whisper.

He steps back and reaches for my hand. I look around, and no one seems to be watching us. He leads me back to the private party room that has a pool table.

The door shuts behind us, and he locks it. I don't want to think about how he knows about that. Instead, I want to see if he's half the man I've made him out to be.

He leans down. His lips touch mine, and it's fire. The kiss ignites something within me, an urgency that pulses with the rhythm of my racing heart. His hands frame my face, and I melt against him, surrendering to the heat that envelops us.

"Tell me what you want," he breathes against my lips.

"I want…" My words falter as his thumb grazes my cheek. "I want you to fuck me. I don't want a relationship with you, though. I don't even want a repeat."

His smile is feral, predatory. "Then let's make it unforgettable."

With that, he spins me around, laying me back on the felt of the pool table. I can feel his breath on my neck, each exhale a promise of what's to come.

He brushes a strand of hair from my face. "Tell me to

stop," he murmurs. "And I will."

I swallow hard. "Don't stop."

His mouth crashes into mine, and everything after that is heat and hunger.

His hands roam along my sides, exploring every curve. I arch into his touch, craving more friction. Just as I think I have him figured out, he pulls back slightly.

"Are you ready?" he asks, daring me to say no.

I nod. "More than ready."

In an instant, he's on me again, lips crashing onto mine. His hands find the hem of my skirt, fingers inching up my thigh. I gasp, heat pooling in my belly. With a snap, he pulls my panties off and puts them in his pocket. He pushes me back on the pool table as his fingers dive into my heat.

I gasp, the sensation electrifying as he explores. The room fades away until it's just him and me, lost in this moment of raw desire.

"Is this what you wanted?" he murmurs, as if he knows exactly how to unravel me.

My fingers scramble for purchase on the edge of the pool table, grounding myself amidst the spiraling pleasure. "Yes," I breathe. "Don't stop."

There's a devilish glint in his eyes. "Oh, I won't."

And with that promise hanging in the air, he plunges deeper, making my head spin. I can feel tension building inside me like a coiled spring.

"Look at you," he whispers, as if reading my thoughts. "So ready to let go."

His fingers move faster now, coaxing soft gasps and moans from my lips.

"Come all over my fingers so I can lick them clean."

The command sends a jolt of heat surging through me. My body responds, surrendering to the crescendo within. "Ryker," I mumble, stifling a moan.

But it's futile. I cry out as my pleasure unfurls, echoing against the walls of our secret sanctuary. I arch my back, granting him access to every part of me he desires.

"Just like that," he murmurs. "You're so beautiful when you're lost in it."

Something inside me shatters, restraint further dissolving as I plunge headfirst into ecstasy. My body quakes as waves crash over me. I'm swept away by a current that's impossible to fight.

His blue eyes glimmer with triumph, but he doesn't stop there. He bends down and laps up my climax, sucking my clit. The sensation is electric, a jolt of fire igniting my skin. I grip the edge of the pool table, my body trembling as he devours me, his mouth bringing me to the brink of another wave. My breath is ragged, punctuated by soft cries that spill from my lips against my will.

"Ryker," I gasp, feeling heat rise from the pit of my stomach once more. "Please…"

He pauses just long enough to look up at me. "Please what?" he taunts, reapplying pressure with his tongue that sends shockwaves through my core.

"Don't stop," I plead. "I need —"

Before I can finish, he dives back in. His tongue dances, coaxing me toward an edge I didn't know existed. I arch into him, losing myself in the sensations that ripple through my body. He wraps his hands around my thighs, holding me steady, as if he knows this ride is going to be wild.

He lifts me up and undoes his belt. *Holy shit.* His cock is huge. He pulls a condom out of his pocket and rolls it on. "Ready for me to really rock your world?"

I'd roll my eyes if I didn't entirely believe him. He turns me around and bends me over. He begins to push in, and it's tight.

I gasp at the sensation, every inch of him stretching me, filling me. This is what I wanted, a connection of our impulsive desires.

"Damn, you feel incredible," he growls. He grips my hips, anchoring me as he thrusts deeper.

Each movement sends ripples of pleasure coursing

through me. "Ryker," I moan.

His breathing turns ragged. "Just like that," he grits out as we find a rhythm.

Eventually, he drives into me one final time, his body going tight before shuddering hard with his release. His grip tightens, and he makes a low, guttural sound as he comes deep.

But he isn't finished. After a moment, he begins to move again, adding his fingers to the mix in a way that sends my lit-up nervous system into overdrive.

"That's it. Let go for me," he urges.

I can feel the weight of his body against mine, a beautiful balance of control and abandon. My climax crashes through me in sharp, breathless waves, my cry muffled against my arm as he drapes himself over me.

Finally, we're both spent, tangled together, breathing hard. "God, that was good," he murmurs as he presses hot kisses along my neck. "Shall we take this back to your place?"

"Can't," I manage between breaths. "I have a friend staying with me."

"How about my place?" He lifts me off the table, and his hand finds my breast and then my nipple.

I can't think when he does that. "Okay, that's fine."

What the hell am I doing?

He tucks himself away with a wicked grin and reaches for my hand. "Let's get out of here. Your car's safe here, but you're not, at least not with me."

My mouth falls open. I should stop. I should say no.

But instead, I let him lead me out the back door.

TWO

Ryker

Six months later

Sunday night dinners at my parents' house are my favorite family ritual. Every week, without fail, me, my three brothers, my little sister, and their significant others gather around the table for a meal, usually prepared by Mom. Sometimes, there's a little business or a little drama, but it's a good chance to catch up. Sometimes, our uncle and cousin join us as well, but tonight, there's no Max or Zach. That makes the dynamic even more casual.

Tarryn barely lets Dad finish his steak before she leans forward, wine glass in hand, and drops a bomb. "The pinot vines in block nine, right along the Dempsey border, aren't thriving. The canes should be thick and rich, even while they're brown, but there, they're thin, patchy in color, and shriveled like they gave up before winter even set in. It's the only block pulling from the shared well. Could be stress...but it doesn't feel right."

Tarryn doesn't even try to sugarcoat it. She never does. That's her thing, cutting straight through the crap. That's what makes her the right person to take over Paradise Hill Family Estate Winery when Dad finally retires. The land has been in our family for eight generations, and it's been a vineyard for three.

Our oldest brother, Kingston, raises an eyebrow, already calculating ten steps ahead like he always does. "Do you think the Dempseys are sabotaging us?"

"No," Tarryn says slowly. "I think they're doing something that's affecting our side. Whether it's intentional or not, I don't know yet."

These vines are new, and we've had some minor issues already. That area used to be a plot of peach trees. They were a remnant of the fruit our family enjoyed long before we started the vineyard. We kept them to lure pests away from the vines and bring a splash of color to the vineyard each spring. For a while, they thrived, their blossoms drawing visitors and their fruit selling alongside our wine. But after losing most of our pinot vines to smoke two years ago and last year having a disastrous late frost, we needed to replant. Tarryn and Elise realized the slope of the plot was perfect for young vines, and that promised a more profitable harvest.

"Elise and I tested everything. It's not the drip system, and it's not mildew," Tarryn continues, answering all our questions, some before we've even had a chance to ask. "Not phylloxera either. It's something else. The symptoms don't match anything common. And it's only happening near the Dempsey line."

The table is quiet. No one moves. No one dares name what we're probably all thinking. It wouldn't be the first time the Dempsey family has tried something with us. Every generation has its drama. Ours has been land and water issues.

I could reach out to Ginny to get her take on it. But I can't bring her into this. I'd like to think just talking to her wouldn't make the problem bigger, but it very easily could.

"Let's not jump to conclusions," I say, though my gut is already churning. "We need proof before we start another war."

Everyone nods and seems to think on that a moment.

Then our brother, Greyson, stands to head out, effectively ending the discussion. He's on call at the hospital, and Trinity, his wife, is nearing her due date, so his mind is clearly all over the place.

Once we've said goodbye to them, my other siblings and I linger around the table.

"I'm just checking," I say, looking between Beckett and Kingston. "You guys going to this baby shower thing next weekend for Trinity and Greyson?"

Beckett makes a face like he bit into a lemon. "Do we have to?"

"It's a shower hosted by our *mother*," Tarryn says, arms crossed like she's ready to fight all of us at once. "You're going. There will be tons of people. Their friends. Brunch food. Games."

Beckett lets out a low grunt. "Yeah, I'm not exactly interested in sniffing melted chocolate in diapers."

"Too bad," Tarryn fires back. "You're going. All of you."

Kingston lifts a brow and shrugs. "I'll bring a bottle of whiskey and a deck of cards. We'll hang out in the back."

I grin. "Now, that's a baby shower I can get behind."

The following morning, I take my coffee from my office and walk across the courtyard to the hospital. The pediatric practice Mom and I run is closed today, but I still have rounds in the pediatric wing. A little girl with a broken wrist is waiting for me, and I've got three consults before lunch. Then it's back to family business this afternoon. We're having the annual report on how Paradise Hill did last year, and Tarryn will be analyzing our situation and making suggestions for the future.

I know she's nervous, but Tarryn's killing it at the vineyard. She's got the kind of leadership that makes people sit up and listen.

Inside the hospital, as I walk past the mural in the hallway — the one Ginny told me looks like a kindergartener went wild with finger paints — I catch myself smirking.

I haven't heard Ginny's voice in months, other than inside my head. I've seen her in town a few times, but we haven't so much as waved at each other. Still, I don't know how to get her out of my system.

Half a year, and I can't shake her. The leaves turned, we did the crush for last year's harvest, the holidays have come and gone, and now, snow's frosting the edge of the world. But the impression Ginny left behind after one night together? Still there. Still bleeding. Like something in me never quite scabbed over.

That was a wild, whiskey-slick, heat-of-summer mistake. I've told myself this so many times. But that lie doesn't hold up, not when I'm alone in the dark, not when I smell something sweet and floral that reminds me of her hair, not when I catch myself looking for her every time I walk into Mikey's.

Ginny Dempsey.

I should've known better. Hell, I did know better. She's a Dempsey, which makes her off-limits in every way that matters. But I didn't walk away. I didn't stop when I should've. And now, I'm stuck with this itch under my skin that hasn't stopped since the second she walked out of my house and didn't look back.

She's bold. Sharp-tongued. Trouble.

And I want her like she's the only cure for something broken in me.

I reach the pediatric wing with a few minutes before my first patient. I scroll through lab results that aren't urgent but give me something to do besides think about Ginny.

I've been with plenty of women. Casual, uncomplicated, drama-free — exactly the way I like it. But Ginny wasn't like any of them. She got under my skin fast, left claw marks on the inside of my chest, and then vanished like none of it ever mattered. No texts. No calls. Not even a "thanks for the orgasms."

I move quickly through my appointments, checking charts, adjusting treatment plans, and offering reassuring words to patients. The steady rhythm of the work keeps me focused, but once the last case is signed off, my mind shifts to the afternoon ahead and the family meeting that's bound to include some fireworks.

Normally I'd beg off, claim a packed clinic schedule or a flu outbreak, but this year, I don't have that luxury. Dad wants all of us there. And since Tarryn's basically running the damn place now, there's no way I'm letting her go in without backup. Especially with Zach and Max in the room.

Uncle Max, my dad's brother, always seems like he's about two steps away from a hostile takeover. Zach's his son, and that guy's a snake in work boots. The kind that smiles while he plants poison. Neither of them wants Tarryn in charge, but she's earned it ten times over. She's the one holding everything together, and she's still barely getting the credit. There have been so many positive outcomes in the last year, but if given the chance, I know all those two will want to talk about is whatever problem Tarryn has identified in block nine.

I send her a quick text.

Me: You've got this. Don't let those assholes get in your head.

Me: Show them why you're the boss.

She doesn't reply right away, but that's fine. She's probably pacing the barn, going over her notes for the tenth time. I know her. She'll go in composed, firm, no-nonsense. But under it all, she'll be bracing for impact.

After a quick trip back to my office across the way, I leave the hospital behind, the city giving way to open road as I drive my Armada to the vineyard. Crossing the bridge, the water below glints cold and hard in the winter light, the air sharper on this side of the bay. By the time I turn down the winding drive toward the vineyard, the noise of the hospital has faded, replaced by the quiet pull of home.

The vineyard is quiet this time of year. Frost clings to the bare vines like cobwebs, the lake in the distance still and silver under the low winter sun. It's peaceful.

For about five seconds.

I spot Max's truck. And Zach's beat-up sedan, parked too close to the manager's spot, like he's already staking a claim.

Great. Let the games begin.

I head for the house, and Mom's kitchen smells like something sweet as I enter, probably something she made. I round the corner just as Beckett reaches across the counter to steal a kiss with his fiancée, Sadie.

"Afternoon, lovers," I say, loud enough to make them jump.

Sadie laughs and swats at Beckett. "You're early."

"I was hoping to score some lunch, but it looks like you've already cleaned up, and I wasn't invited." I glance at the empty plates stacked neatly by the sink and the wiped-down counter. "Rude."

"We were doing some wedding planning with your parents," Sadie says, brushing a lock of hair behind her ear. Her cheeks are still pink.

"Ah." I lift my brows at Beckett. "So when's the big day?"

"Just before the crush," Mom says, stepping into the kitchen from the hallway like she's been waiting to chime in. "We were going over the timing this morning, and I believe they've settled on August twenty-fourth." She looks to Sadie for confirmation, and she nods, taking Beckett's hand.

It's perfect, that window of calm that's not really calm at all. The vineyard pulses in the heat, lush and beautiful, the vines heavy with fruit that won't be picked for a few weeks. Tourists flood the valley, soaking up sun and wine, but it's that sliver of time—hot, heady, and on edge—when everything looks peaceful, even as it's all waiting to explode. There's something about it. Charged. Romantic, even.

Damn, I'm still thinking about Ginny. I clear my throat. "That's the best time of year out here. The vineyard looks like a painting. You picked a good date, Sadie."

"Thanks," she says. She and Beckett exchange a look, and he hugs her close.

Then Beckett grabs an apple off the counter and tosses it in the air. "You up for drinks after basketball tonight?"

"Always." I grin. "Assuming you don't pull a hammy, trying to keep up."

He snorts. "Dream on."

I head for the coffee and pour myself a full mug from the percolator. The espresso machine looms in the corner like a spaceship, all gleaming chrome and blinking lights. Fancy as hell. But this? This pot on the stove is where the good stuff comes from. Strong, rich, and just the right amount of bite.

Mom eyes me as I take the last of it. "You always finish the pot."

Dad walks in just in time to hear her. "That's because he's the only one around here with real taste."

I raise the mug in salute. "Finally. Someone gets me."

Dad claps me on the shoulder as he passes. "You ready for the recap meeting?"

"As I'll ever be."

He gestures for us to follow, and we all trail him out the door and over to the administrative offices for the vineyard.

The boardroom in the barn next door smells faintly like oak and old wine, and the air has a buzz to it — a little tension. It's the kind of atmosphere where one wrong word will light a fuse.

Tarryn's already inside, standing near the head of the table, a tablet in one hand, notes in the other. She looks sharp — crisp button-down, tailored slacks, and low heels instead of her usual scuffed boots. It's not flashy, but it's a signal. She's not here to be overlooked.

I sink into one of the chairs near the end of the table, far enough to watch the whole scene but close enough to jump in if

Max tries anything slick. Beckett slides into the seat beside me.

I look over at Tarryn again. I'm so damn grateful she loves this place because the rest of us bailed. Me, Greyson, Beckett, Kingston, we all found our calling in medicine, like Mom. Pediatrics, trauma, cardiology, and orthopedics. Not exactly helpful when it comes to running a multimillion-dollar wine operation. But Tarryn looks at those vines and sees her future. And she's made it work. More than that, she's made it thrive.

That's always been a bitter pill for Uncle Max.

He's never said it outright, but we all know he blames Dad. For leaving. For chasing Mom out to Vancouver Island for a year before they were married. For coming back and still getting to be the one to inherit the family business. Max believes this should've been his after that. And maybe it should've been.

But now that Dad and Max are close to retiring, Tarryn is stepping up. And she's earned the right to handle every inch of this ground. She's got plans. Big ones. Dad just keeps putting off stepping down because Max still hasn't retired like he was supposed to—last month, actually.

A low *whir-whir-whir* outside breaks through my thoughts.

I don't even have to look. *Kingston*, arriving by helicopter, as he likes to do. He lives about nine miles away as the crow flies, across the lake on five hundred acres of prime grape-growing Paradise real estate. The drive takes over an hour, so he usually flies. He built a mansion big enough to host a world summit. Said it was for his wife, but she left before they even poured the foundation. These days, he lives alone in that palace and shows up here when he feels like it. He has a "friend" in Vancouver he's been visiting more and more lately.

My guess? It's only a matter of time before he trades the lake house for the city. He's an orthopedist, but he developed some minimally invasive joint-replacement techniques and made billions, so he's wealthy in his own right.

Beckett snorts. "Right on cue. Kingston had to take his helo in for a checkup today."

The helicopter blades grow louder before cutting off abruptly. Five seconds later, Kingston walks in, all tall, moody energy in a black wool coat with his sunglasses still on, even though we're inside.

But he's here. And I'll take it.

Kingston nods at Tarryn, and then takes a seat at the opposite end of the table, keeping his coat on like he's not planning to stay long. "Let's get this over with," he mutters.

Tarryn raises her chin. "Glad you could make it."

With that, she steps up to the front of the boardroom like she owns the place. She kind of does. The screen behind her lights up with the first slide of her PowerPoint—clean, sharp, and branded with the vineyard's updated logo, and in moments, she's in full CEO mode.

"Let's start with last year's numbers," she says.

I lean back in my chair, arms crossed, watching the room. Watching them. Max is pretending not to care, but he's already tapping his pen like a fuse is burning. Zach looks bored.

Tarryn dives into the cost-cutting initiatives first— refinancing the warehouse expansion, renegotiating supplier contracts, shifting some distribution to a leaner model. She's not just cutting fat, she's building muscle. Efficient. Scalable.

She clicks to a new slide and gestures toward the bar chart. "Despite setbacks from the fire and frost over the past few years, we've pushed through. And now, we're nearly out of the red. Thanks to some aggressive recovery, we're tracking toward one of the strongest years on record."

That gets a few raised brows.

"And yields?" she continues. "Despite the downturn in pinot, it was exceptional. We've adapted well to the newer vines, and Elise believes this may be one of our best vintages."

Max shifts in his chair. "And the screw tops?" he grumbles. "Those make us look cheap."

Before I can roll my eyes, Greyson speaks up from across the table. "Actually, all of the top winners at the International Wine Festival last year used screw tops. It's a preservation decision, not a prestige one."

Tarryn doesn't even acknowledge Max's comment. They've had that argument before. "Elise and I are heading back to Paris in three weeks. This year we're competing with the Chardonnay, the Merlot, and a red blend Elise developed with her father. Interest has already been pouring in. Elise has been approached by competitors in both France and California. They're trying to steal her," she adds with a grin.

"Maybe she should go," Zach says, tapping the table. He leans forward, smirking. "We don't need a vintner anyway."

Tarryn takes a deep breath. "We don't just grow grapes, Zach. We make wine. And if we want to grow beyond selling bottles out of the tasting room and government liquor stores, we need someone whose job is wine. Not farming, not tradition— craft. That's what a vintner brings. Control, consistency, and vision."

He scoffs. "What a waste. And now, we're running a restaurant and a wine club? What's next? More fridge magnets in the gift shop?"

Tarryn smiles. A dangerous smile. "Great segue, Zach," she says. "Let's talk about how those fridge magnets are keeping this vineyard afloat."

She clicks to the next slide. "The Paradise Grill now carries a typical three-week waiting list for dinner reservations. A week out for lunch. We've been contacted by Michelin. We may be in the running for the first Michelin Star in Black Bear Valley."

Mom makes a quiet sound of delight. She pushed hardest for the grill. I glance over, and she's glowing.

"And the tasting room? The gift shop?" Tarryn continues. "Sadie's helped grow our Barrel Society to almost four thousand members in less than six months. That's four thousand VIPs who've prepaid for wine, special events, and exclusive tastings."

Tarryn's locking in future sales now. That kind of foresight? Dad never had it. Max sure as hell doesn't. And Zach's blinking like he just found out she's smarter than he is. That is a surprise to no one else.

She moves to another chart. "So yes, wine sales are strong. But these so-called distractions? They're now nearly equal to wine revenue. That's not a side hustle. That's a second revenue stream."

There's a beat of silence. Then Dad stands, slow but proud. And starts clapping.

One by one, we join him. Me, Beckett, Kingston, Greyson. Even Sadie, off to the side, lights up with pride. Eventually, Max and Zach rise too, grudgingly, but they do it.

Whatever they came here to derail? Tarryn just steamrolled it.

I wonder if Ginny would've smirked, called it badass, and kissed me for backing the right team. She's the kind of woman who respects a strong play. She would've called it a power move, smirked at Zach's dumb face, and then whispered something wicked in my ear just to watch me squirm.

But she's not here. I don't see how she ever could be. And it doesn't matter anyway because who knows if I'll see her anywhere again. I wonder if she ever thinks about that night. If she's just as wrecked and pretending otherwise.

THREE

Ginny

I push open the door to the Black Bear Winery gift shop and enter the world of cedarwood candles and barrel-aged port. For a second, I let myself breathe it in. The comfort of familiarity. The calm before the inevitable storm.

The bell above the door jingles behind me as it closes. We've only just opened for the day, but I can already feel tension in the air. Sharp. Heavy. Ready to snap.

I begin by surveying the glass display near the register. My jewelry—bright gemstones wrapped in silver or gold—glimmers under the lights, and there are several openings in the arrangement. A smile tugs at my lips. The peridot and aquamarine wrapped in gold have clearly been popular. It's a strange, fluttery feeling, knowing people are actually buying something I made. I make a mental note to order more stones and make more before the offerings get too picked over.

I look up as my oldest sister, Sera, enters through the back door from her office down the hall. Her face is pinched tight in that way she gets when she's trying not to scream. She doesn't even look up as she walks in. Sera's next in line to take over the family vineyard, right behind our grandmother, who still runs the place with an iron fist, as she has since our grandfather died, before I was born.

My dad, Henry, was supposed to take over at some point, but something happened years ago—something no one talks about. All I know is he was cut off completely, and Gran never looked back. Once the family cuts someone off, it's like they vanish. You don't call. You don't visit. You don't even say their name. If you do, you risk being cast out right alongside them. Alaric made sure to keep in touch with Dad, but my sisters and I have been more cautious. I haven't really spoken to Dad in years.

"Morning," I offer carefully, stepping past a new display of locally made jam in jars shaped like wine barrels.

"You're late," she says, though she doesn't seem particularly bothered. She's still not looking at me. "And I'm going to murder someone. Just haven't picked who yet."

I arch a brow. "I vote Max Paradise."

She finally glances up, her mouth twitching. "Not a bad choice."

I slide around the counter and drop my bag. "So, what's the latest?"

Sera leans her hands on the register like she needs to physically brace herself. "The well servicing blocks one-hundred one through one-hundred forty has a problem."

"Wait, the pinot vines?"

She nods. "This time it's worse. We brought in Alvarez's team to check it, and they think the aquifer's been overdrawn. Gran's convinced the Paradise family did it on purpose."

I fold my arms. "It's winter. Their vines are dormant. They've already blown out the irrigation lines. There's no way they're draining anything right now."

"Try telling her that," she mutters. "Alvarez said Tarryn's newly planted parcel must have tapped into a different section of the well, and it's redirecting flow."

"That's...not how water tables work." I want to laugh it off, to tell her Gran's just looking for another war to fight. But a part of me hesitates. What if it is connected? What if Ryker knows something and isn't telling me? I mean, how could he tell me since I haven't looked him in the eyes for the last six months? But was he playing me when we got together that night last summer?

That all seems ridiculous, but logic has never stood a chance in this family. Especially when the name *Paradise* is involved.

The feud's been alive longer than any of us—eight generations of bad blood. Started when both families came to the valley. The Paradises set up the general store, and my family were fur traders and eventually ended up with grapes. The Dempseys and the Paradises have been at each other's throats ever since, fighting over land, water, awards, and whatever pride is left to claim. And they've dragged the entire Black Bear Valley in with them.

Now, the well's dry, so of course that's who gets the blame.

I glance out the window at the tasting patio beyond the vines, now mostly bare in the winter chill. "Have we looked into drilling deeper?"

Sera gives me a flat look. "Gran wants to take the fight to the Paradise city council. She said, and I quote, 'they stole from us, and they're going to pay'."

"Oh good." I sigh. "War. That's always productive." I grab an apron and loop it over my head. While it's quiet, I may as well fold tea towels and stock honey sticks. We still get about a dozen people in the store every day this time of year. It helps that we have an internationally acclaimed pinot noir and syrah.

Sera hands me a clipboard. "Do you think you could handle things while I call the water district?"

"Where's Josie?" I ask. She's my other older sister and also our vintner.

"We have a vat that isn't cooperating, and she's working on that."

Josie won gold at the International Wine Festival last year, and she'll be defending the title next month, but she remains hands-on around here. No job is too dirty for her.

"I have you covered," I assure Sera, looking at the to-do list I made before I left last night. "And if I see Max or Zach Paradise lurking in the bushes with a garden hose, I'll take one for the team and tackle them."

She smirks. "Just don't date any of them, okay?"

I stiffen slightly but keep my tone light. "Please. Not a chance."

They've all heard the rumors. In a town this small, of course someone saw me leave that bar with Ryker Paradise. I'm not about to admit it was toe-curling, amazing, and the best sex I've ever had. Ryker's face flashes through my mind—cocky smile, dark eyes, the way he made me forget everything, even just for a night.

I shake it off. That was six months ago. A mistake.

And I'm not making it again.

Sera returns to her office, and I busy myself lining up the bottles of olive oil. When I reach the last one, I stare blankly at the label, my fingers tight around the glass.

I wasn't supposed to end up back here.

When I left Paradise, I swore I'd never return. I went to university to get a marketing degree, and I graduated with just enough ambition to pretend I had a real plan. I found a job with a boutique marketing firm in Vancouver—scrappy, creative, and always one client away from closing its doors. But I didn't care. I was building something. I had my own apartment, a fiancé, a future.

Jeremy McQueen. The name still makes my stomach turn.

He was charming, successful, just the right amount of rugged to impress my family and my social media followers. We'd been together almost two years. I thought I was done searching. He proposed to me at a fancy restaurant, and we were busy planning our future.

Until his birthday.

I left work early to surprise him. I had his favorite cake, his favorite bourbon, and balloons, even though he always said they were too much. I walked into our apartment, full of love and celebration, and found Jill Delaney naked in our bed.

My best friend. On her knees. Giving him a very different kind of birthday present.

I didn't scream. I didn't cry. I didn't even speak. I just left.

Five hours later, I was parked outside the Black Bear Winery tasting room with nothing but the suitcase in my trunk and humiliation clawing at my throat.

I had no backup plan. No apartment. No dignity. And the company I worked for couldn't guarantee my continued employment. So I just came home.

So yeah, I'm back in Paradise. Not because I want to be. Because I had *nowhere else to go.*

And if one more person tells me it's a blessing in disguise, I might throw a bottle of raspberry balsamic at their head. I didn't come back here for redemption. I came to forget.

But so far Ryker Paradise is the only person who's let me do that.

I move on to the next task and my phone buzzes just as I finish rearranging the display of handmade soaps.

Sadie: Drinks after work? You in?

It's a weeknight. Odd. Unless Sadie's matchmaking again... But I don't hesitate. I'm always up for an evening out.

Me: Hell yes. Where?

Sadie: Mikey's. 6:30?

Of course. Mikey's.

My stomach tightens. That's the place where I let Ryker Paradise talk me into a bet on darts…and then a visit to the back party room. The pool table. God, the pool table. And as if that wasn't enough, I let him take me home, where we christened his kitchen counter, his couch, the shower. We never even made it to a bed.

I press my lips together and shake off the memory. I give Sadie a thumbs up and slip my phone back into my apron pocket.

The door creaks open behind me, and I don't have to turn around to know who it is.

"Put the phone away, Genevieve," my grandmother snaps. "You're at work."

"I already did," I say softly. No need for her to hear me.

She's wearing one of her usual wool skirts and a cardigan that looks like it's survived three generations of Dempseys and a lightning storm. Her lips are pressed into a line so tight it's practically a wrinkle. She's gripping her purse strap like she wants to strangle someone with it.

"What's wrong?" I ask, dreading the answer.

She mutters something under her breath. All I catch is *Paradise*.

Of course.

She marches toward the office, a storm cloud in orthopedic shoes. I let her go. There's no reasoning with her when she gets like this.

I used to think I didn't care, that her cold shoulder didn't bother me. But the truth is, it feels like being twelve again, trying to prove I belong in a family that only loves you when you play by their rules.

She pretty much stopped speaking to me altogether the moment she saw Beckett Paradise and Sadie Calloway walking off the Dempsey cottage porch together months ago. Never mind that they were in the middle of a crisis—Sadie's and my best friend from high school, Rosie, had just died, and someone was hunting Sadie. None of that mattered to Gran. Only that she was hiding at my place. And more than that, that a Paradise had stepped foot on Dempsey land.

Around here, that's not just a faux pas. It's practically an invitation to joust.

There's a clause in the original town charter, written back in the 1800s when this valley was nothing but dust, gold fever, and bad tempers that says any Paradise found trespassing on Dempsey property could be shot on sight.

And somehow, it still holds. In the sixties, a judge chose not to prosecute our grandfather when he shot and killed a Paradise on our land. That story plays on repeat in my head every time Ryker so much as looks at me.

The whole thing is one tangled mess of hate and pride and history that nobody seems interested in unraveling. And honestly? I'd rather set the whole damn feud on fire and watch it burn. But that's not how things work in Black Bear Valley. Not when you're born into a name like mine.

I'm busy all day rearranging and restocking, waiting on customers, and ordering new items I think will sell well. Mom started the gift shop at Big Bear Winery, and it's always been her project. When I came back, Gran asked me to take it over, but sometimes, I wonder if Mom truly meant to step aside. Because every time she stops by, she rearranges whatever I've changed and scolds me like I don't know the first thing about selling wine trinkets.

That makes today mostly an exercise in futility, but thankfully Gran stays away, so I don't have to deal with her on top of everything else. Before I know it, I'm rushing out the door. If I hit the traffic lights just right, I won't be late.

The second I step into Mikey's, I spot them. Sadie, smiling and waving, and Beckett, relaxed with a beer in hand. I suppose that's not a huge surprise — they are engaged — but next to him is Ryker, his brother, all dark smirk and sin-stained memories.

My body locks up, ice and fire colliding in my veins. I hate that I still react to him like this, like I haven't spent six months trying to bury that night under a hundred reasons why it was a mistake.

I shouldn't care that Ryker's here, shouldn't feel like the air's been knocked out of me. But there he is, like a debt I'm still paying interest on.

Oh hell.

Sadie rises from the booth and comes toward me, her dress swaying like she's floating on air. She's glowing. And dammit, that makes it hard to be annoyed.

"He doesn't bite," she says, looping her arm through mine.

Behind her, Ryker leans back in the booth, arms stretched wide. His eyes meet mine, and a flicker of heat travels way too quickly through my bloodstream.

"I do," he calls, "if she asks nicely."

I pretend I didn't hear that. Pretend my pulse doesn't jump. Pretend I don't remember exactly how that cocky mouth felt on my skin.

"Subtle," I mutter.

Sadie gives me a look. "Are you going to behave?"

"Depends. Are you playing matchmaker?"

She doesn't answer, just drags me toward the booth. "You two are going to be seeing more of each other."

I snort. If she only knew how I've been working to avoid that.

Beckett and Ryker stand as we reach the booth, and Sadie and I slide in. Ryker sits beside me — way too close for someone I'm trying to forget. His thigh brushes mine, and my body betrays me instantly. I remember everything. His hands, his mouth, the way he looked at me like I was the only thing in the world.

I cross my legs tightly and focus on the drink Sadie has waiting for me.

"Okay," Sadie says, bouncing a little. "We have a favor to ask."

I brace myself for a setup. Maybe a double date. Maybe a new guy Sadie's found for me who's "*not like the others.*" That's what she always says. But nothing prepares me for what comes next.

Beckett grins and puts his arm around her. "We want you two to be in our wedding."

I can feel my eyes widen. "Wait, what?"

"Together," Sadie says, practically clapping. "Maid of honor and best man."

Ryker snorts. "What, Caleb too busy?"

Beckett laughs. "He'll be there, giving Sadie away. He's her brother, so that seems right. But anyway, I always thought it'd be you standing beside me."

Ryker is silent a moment, and then he nods. For a beat, the cockiness fades. "Of course. Count me in."

I look at Sadie, her eyes full of hope and excitement. I can feel my resistance cracking. She's been through so much. The car accident that took her parents? It wrecked her. Changed her. For a long time, she was just…floating. But now, she's anchored, happy and whole.

All because of Beckett.

And I have to support that, so yeah, I'll do it. Even if it means standing next to the man who makes me want to scratch his eyes out and rip his clothes off in the same breath.

"I'm in," I say finally. "But if this one misbehaves—"

"I'll behave," Ryker says, voice low. "Unless you don't want me to."

I ignore him again, but I'm burning. And this time, I don't know if it's anger or something far more dangerous.

With that settled, Beckett and Ryker head toward the bar, and I finally exhale. Ryker makes it impossible to think straight.

Sadie nudges me with her elbow. "I guess maybe I should have asked you this first. You gonna be okay at a Paradise wedding?"

The question lands softly, but I feel it like a punch. I push past all my old instincts, all the beliefs I was practically raised on—*We don't cross the property line. We don't trust them. We don't mix blood.*—to get to my answer.

"I'm not doing this for Beckett or Ryker or any Paradise," I tell her. "I'm doing it for you. You deserve a beautiful day and a fresh start. And I can't wait to go dress shopping."

Sadie's eyes get a little misty, and she wipes them with a laugh. "Okay, no crying at Mikey's. I'll save that for your speech."

We both laugh, and she leans forward, lowering her voice.

"I think I want a big dress," she whispers. "Like, poofy. Ballerina energy."

"You'd rock it," I say. "But we'll go try everything. You might surprise yourself."

She grins. "True. What color do you want to wear?"

I smile into my glass. "I'll wear whatever color you want me in. Chartreuse? Neon pink? Bring it on."

She laughs and opens her mouth to say something else, but the guys return, each with a fresh round. Beckett slides in beside Sadie and hands her a drink. Ryker sets one in front of me, then drops back into his spot at my side—too close again.

I've barely gotten my hand around my glass before I feel it.

His hand. On my thigh. Fingertips warm, slow, like he's got all the time in the world to remind me what it was like the last time we were alone.

My breath catches, but I don't give him the satisfaction of looking his way.

"You up for a game of pool?" he asks.

I turn my head and meet his eyes. "Never again."

He grins like I just gave him a challenge instead of a hard no. And maybe I did.

But if he thinks I'm falling into that trap again, he's wrong. Then again...my pulse says otherwise. And that's scary. Because I already know what it's like to fall into bed with Ryker Paradise.

I don't think I'd survive it twice.

FOUR

Ryker

"Thank you both," Sadie says, looking across the booth at me and Ginny toward the end of the night.

"Yeah, we promise not to be too difficult," Beckett assures us.

Something lodges in my throat—surprise, mostly. Maybe a little pride. We don't do a lot of mush in our family, and I never expected to be anyone's first pick for something like this. Not even my own brother's.

"Hell yeah," I say, high-fiving him. "You're stuck with me now."

Beckett laughs. "Wouldn't have it any other way."

I lean back in my seat, heart thumping. *Best man*. Huh.

That means wedding planning, more meetings, tastings and fittings and dinners…and more time with Ginny.

I glance at her next to me, where she's been forced to be all night. She's mid-sip, totally unaware that she's the best part of this gig. For once, I don't mind all the wedding crap. Not if it means getting a few extra hours in her orbit.

Sadie and Beckett stand and slide out of the booth, tossing their napkins on the table like they've just wrapped up a five-course meal instead of two rounds of fries and a couple of beers. I wave them off when they reach for their wallets. I've got the bill. I do own the place, after all. Mikey was ready to let it go, and I needed an investment. Not many people know that, and I'm fine keeping it that way.

Sadie looks over at Ginny. "You good?"

Ginny nods, barely. Her spine's straight, her expression neutral, but I can tell she's debating whether to bolt.

Beckett slaps my shoulder on the way out. "Try not to say anything completely inappropriate for five minutes."

"No promises," I call as they head for the door.

And then it's just me and her.

Mikey's hums around us—pool balls cracking, beer bottles clinking—but all I can hear is her breath as she exhales slowly, like she's bracing for something. Or trying not to want it.

I look over at the dartboards. There's one open. "You up for a round?"

She lifts an eyebrow. "Of darts? Didn't I already tell you never again?"

"I meant karaoke. Thought I'd serenade you with some Bon Jovi."

Her lips twitch. "God, no."

"Then I suppose it will have to be darts. Seems we're going to be spending some time together, so we might as well be friendly, right?"

She gives me a look. "Yeah, because that always goes so well for our families." She sighs, like she's already regretting this. "Fine. One round."

I rise to grab the darts from the bar and hand her three. "What should we bet?"

She spins one of the darts between her fingers, and her eyes cut to mine, dark and unreadable. "You already took my virginity," she says.

I blink. "I did?"

The corner of her mouth lifts, slow and wicked. "Just kidding."

A laugh bursts out of me. "Jesus, woman. You're dangerous."

She shrugs, all innocence and sharp edges. "Winner picks the prize."

"Winner's choice?" I ask, stepping into position beside her. "You sure about that?"

She lines up next to me, brushing her shoulder against mine. The contact is brief but electric, like the air between us shifted.

"You scared?" she asks softly.

"Terrified," I murmur. Because yeah, she could wreck me, and I think she knows it.

I throw first. Bullseye. Her eyes widen. She didn't expect that.

"Your turn."

She steps forward and tosses. Just off-center. "Lucky shot."

I scoff. "You keep telling yourself that."

We fall into a rhythm—throw, tease, taunt. The distance between us shrinks with every exchange, tension curling around us like smoke. I forget the bar. I forget the damn game. All I see is her, Ginny Dempsey, with her razor wit and guarded eyes, daring me to look closer.

On the final throw, she sinks a triple twenty.

I let out a low whistle. "Damn. Didn't think you had it in you."

She walks toward me, slow and deliberate, her smirk firmly in place. "You just got beat by a Dempsey."

I don't move. I don't breathe. "Twice now," I murmur. "And I'm not even mad about it."

She stops in front of me, close enough that I can smell the citrus in her shampoo. Her chin tips up, defiant, but her eyes dart to my mouth for a moment. "I'm not collecting my prize tonight," she says, and her voice isn't as steady as she probably wants it to be.

"No?"

"No."

I step in closer. "So what is the prize, winner?"

Her eyes move past me, toward the back of the bar. The private room waits in shadows, half-hidden behind a velvet curtain like a dare. I remember how it felt the last time we were back there, her lips on mine, her breath warm against my neck, her fingers gripping my shirt, like she couldn't get me close enough.

My voice drops low. "Wanna go back there?"

She tilts her head like she's weighing her options, but I can already see the flicker in her eyes. That fire's lit. The question is whether she'll let it burn.

"Are you always this predictable?" she asks.

"Only when I'm dying to see if lightning can strike twice."

She bites her lip, and I feel it like a punch to the gut. "It can't," she says.

But she doesn't step away.

Instead, she lifts her chin, eyes sweeping the row of pool tables against the far wall. "There are plenty of pool tables here," she says. "I'd rather beat you at pool in front of all of Paradise."

I grin. "So you want to humiliate me publicly now?"

She tosses a glance over her shoulder, already walking. "Only a little."

I follow her to the farthest table tucked in the corner, not minding at all. Not when she's walking like that, hip-sway confident, knowing damn well I'm watching.

She reaches for a cue stick and chalks the tip, like she's done it a hundred times before. There's something hypnotic about the way she moves, like she's in control of the whole room and doesn't care who knows it. Maybe she brought me back here to remind me I don't hold all the cards.

"Let's lag for it," she says, grabbing two cue balls from the rack and handing me one.

"Fair." I roll the cool weight of it in my palm, then take my stance behind the head string. "You know the rules?"

She turns and shoots me a look. "I grew up in this bar. Don't insult me."

We shoot at the same time. I intentionally overshoot just enough to let her win, though the competitor in me twitches at the loss. Her ball bounces off the foot rail, drifts back smooth as silk, and stops inches from the head rail. Closer than mine by a mile.

She raises a brow, satisfaction practically radiating from her. "Looks like I win."

I chuckle, unable to help it. "Again."

She meets my gaze with one that's cool and unreadable, but there's heat there too, banked and controlled, the way a wildfire waits for the wind.

The real question isn't stripes or solids. "What game are we playing?"

That's what I want to know. And not just about pool.

"I'll let you pick something," she says with a smile.

I let the silence stretch. "Strip pool."

She freezes, cue stick in hand. "Strip pool?"

I nod. "For every missed shot, one article of clothing comes off."

She just stares at me. No smile. No sarcasm. Nothing but that unreadable expression that makes it impossible to know if I've crossed a line or opened a door.

And then, just barely, the corner of her mouth curves. "Set it up," she says.

My eyebrows shoot high. "Seriously?"

"Eight ball," she says. "Let's go."

I rack the balls fast, but my hands aren't steady. It's hard to focus when she's bending over the table like that, stretching in those jeans, the curve of her waist begging for my hands. Her hips sway just enough to make me forget how numbers work.

She lines up the break and sends the cue ball flying.

Crack.

Two solids drop instantly. Clean. No hesitation.

Shit.

She circles the table, smooth, confident, eyes on the layout like she's working a puzzle. Then, another shot. And another. Four shots in, the only balls left on the felt are mine. I'm not just turned on. I'm impressed.

I haven't even lifted my cue.

She straightens, cue stick propped casually against her shoulder, and plants her hands on her hips like she's staking a claim. Her smile blooms wide. "The winner gets to choose."

I lean against the table, letting my gaze drag down her body and back up again. I'm not even trying to hide it, though my heartbeat's punching through my ribs like it's trying to reach her.

"So I've heard," I tell her. "What do you want, sweetheart?"

Ginny tilts her head. Her eyes stay focused on mine, but there's something in them now, something less playful. "I want to go home," she says quietly. "Alone."

I blink, not sure I heard her right. Not after that look in her eyes. Not after the way she just worked me over like a fantasy in motion.

I push off the table, slow and deliberate. "You're missing out."

She smiles, just a hint, but it's enough to wreck me. "I know from experience that's probably true."

That twists something inside me I didn't expect. Not lust, or not just that, anyway. It's a rejection, but it feels heavier. Like I lost something I didn't even know I wanted until she put it back on the shelf.

I step closer, enough to feel her warmth again. "Then what's stopping you?"

She shrugs. But it's not flippant, it's defensive. Like she

can't let herself soften for one more second. "I'm not in the right place for anything now," she says. "Not even a casual...scratch."

I study her—the calm mask, the dry wit, the confidence that shines through everything she does. Underneath it there's tension. Maybe regret. Maybe fear.

"Just figured we could help each other out," I murmur. "Nothing complicated."

She huffs a quiet breath, somewhere between a laugh and a sigh. "How could it not be complicated?"

"It worked out last time," I tell her. "And I should know. I'm allergic to complications. Hives and everything."

That earns a genuine smile, but then she shakes her head. "If I'm ever in a position to have an itch scratched," she says softly, "I'll call you."

I cross my arms, not quite ready to let this go. "Promise?"

She steps back, walking toward the door in reverse, her gaze still tethered to mine. "Nope." She picks up her purse and gives a lazy wave as she turns.

The door swings shut behind her, leaving me standing with a pool cue in my hand, a scoreboard that screams loser, and one hell of a craving that's not going anywhere.

Not for a long, long time.

Now that Ginny's gone, I can't find much reason to stick around, so a little while later, I head out too. The drive to my house should take ten minutes. I'm on track to make it in seven. My mind is whirling.

She's a Dempsey. Every second I spend wanting her is one more step toward a choice my family won't forgive. She's exactly right. How could it not be complicated? Why doesn't that seem to matter?

Every second, I'm chewing on the same damn thought, *What the hell am I doing?*

Ginny Dempsey. She's got a mouth like a blade and a body that won't quit, but it's more than that. It's the way she looks at me. Like she's already decided I'm trouble but can't help circling anyway. And I know she's trouble too.

I guess I want to find out how much.

I blow out a breath and shift lanes, my headlights carving through the curves that hug Black Bear Lake. The water's dark and smooth, reflecting the moon like it's trying to stay neutral in this town. Too bad nothing else is.

I grew up hearing her last name spit like a curse. And now, I'm thinking about her mouth for all the wrong reasons. I drag a hand down my face as I turn in to my driveway, gravel crunching beneath the tires. The lights of my house flick on as I hit the remote, casting shadows out the windows. Everything's quiet. Still.

Unlike my brain.

If anyone in my family even suspected what went down in that bar tonight, they'd be supremely unimpressed. Tarryn would lecture me. Beckett would shake his head — though maybe he wouldn't be surprised. Kingston would…disappear on his high horse.

Maybe I should focus on that.

But being careful has nothing on the way Ginny made me feel tonight. Like I'd finally met someone who could keep up. Push back. Throw fire and not flinch when I throw it in return.

She didn't walk away with just the win tonight — twice. She walked away with something I didn't know I'd put on the line. I thought I wanted another night, one more hit of her fire. But now I'm not so sure. Maybe what I really want…is to matter.

I hate how much I enjoy being with her.

I shut off the engine but don't move. Just sit there in the quiet, hands loose on the wheel, her voice still echoing. *"If I'm ever in a position to have an itch scratched, I'll call you."*

Yeah. And if I were smart, I'd block her number instead of waiting for that day to arrive.

But I won't.

Because I already know, if she called me, I'd pick up on the first ring.

I've learned that pediatrics is most often a carousel of colds, coughs, and crying kids on repeat. I've also learned I don't mind it. The noise, the pace — it keeps things moving, keeps my head out of everything else, even the things I should probably be dealing with.

But today, the moment I push open the door to exam room three and catch the look from Mel, my medical assistant, I know this is going to be a different sort of Monday.

"New patient," she says quietly, stepping out of the room to intercept me. "Six years old. Foster placement. Nonverbal since the transfer. Possible signs of trauma. Just came from the Ministry of Children and Family Development's care last week."

Mel's seen plenty over the years — hell, we all have — but the cases that come with the word *trauma* hit differently. Especially when the kid can't — or won't — speak.

I nod once, jaw tight. "Thanks, Mel."

She gives me a sympathetic look, then disappears down the hall, leaving me alone at the threshold. I take a breath, reset my posture, and step inside.

The boy is tiny, smaller than most six year olds, sitting stiff and guarded on the exam table. His knees are pulled to his chest like armor. His socks don't match. His hair is a little too long, curling over his ears, and there's a scab healing above his left eyebrow. I make note of it automatically, but my focus stays on the way his eyes avoid me completely, head turned just enough that I can't catch even a hint of expression.

In the corner stands the foster mom, Jocelyn Ward — tired, late forties maybe, with kind eyes and a cardigan that's been tugged at one too many times.

"This is Eli Stone," she says. "He's… He hasn't said a word since he came to us last week. Eats okay. Sleeps…okay. But sometimes he just sits like this for hours." Her voice wavers, and I see the fear in her eyes, not fear of the boy, but fear she's not enough to help him.

"Hi, bud," I say gently, crouching so we're at eye level. "I'm Dr. Ryker. Heard you've had a rough few weeks."

He doesn't move. Doesn't blink. Just sits there, small and still, a knot of tension barely breathing.

Then, when my voice dips a little too low, too close to some memory I'll never know, he flinches. Just a twitch of the shoulder. Barely anything. But enough to make my gut clench.

Shit. Whoever hurt this kid didn't just leave bruises. They left ghosts.

I look back at the foster mom, who's watching me like I might have the magic answer. I don't. But I know how to take my time. I know how to show up.

And I know this boy needs me to be something he doesn't expect.

Safe.

I back off a step and grab a tongue depressor from the counter, holding it like a lightsaber. "Are you a Star Wars fan?" I ask, keeping my voice light. I make a few slow sound effects, waving the stick through the air. "Wom, wom, wom…"

Still nothing. No smile. No movement. Just his dark eyes fixed on a spot somewhere past my shoulder, like if he stays frozen long enough, the world might forget he's there.

I turn to Jocelyn again, and she lifts her hands in a helpless shrug. "I don't know what he likes yet," she says. "I've only had him a few days. He's…sweet. But quiet. Just like this." She gestures to the boy. "He wets the bed every night and screams sometimes in his sleep. Won't let me tuck him in. He doesn't speak, but he hums sometimes. Not like a tune. Just…a sound."

"Mind if I try something?" I ask.

"Not at all," she says, stepping aside but not leaving the room. I respect the hell out of that.

I cross to the toy bin in the corner, digging through the collection of battered plastic figures and worn board books until

I find what I'm looking for, a soft, lime green plush dinosaur with floppy arms and a goofy grin.

"Okay," I say, turning back around. "Dr. Rex here is going to do the exam today." I make my voice gravelly and ridiculous. "I'm the best dino doctor in the business. *Rawr.*"

There's a flicker, just the faintest shift of attention. Eli peeks up for a second. His eyes dart to the dinosaur and then drop again. He relaxes a little bit.

But it's something.

I step closer and gently place Dr. Rex on his knee. "I need to check your tummy, but only if Dr. Rex says it's okay. Can you lie back?"

Eli uncurls his body without taking his eyes off Dr. Rex. I guide the plush dino's arms to lightly pat Eli's abdomen, keeping my movements slow. He flinches at first—a muscle-twitch of defense—but doesn't pull away. When I sense he's steady, I shift slightly and do the real exam with my fingers.

No bruising. No distension. He's underweight, but not dangerously so. I note the slight muscle tension in his abdomen, a common symptom of stress. Guarding.

His eyes still don't meet mine, but I can feel his shoulders soften, though only a little bit.

When I'm done, I offer him the dinosaur. "Dr. Rex says you're pretty brave."

Eli still doesn't say anything. But he reaches for Dr. Rex. He clutches the dinosaur tight.

For some reason, my mind flutters to Ginny. I wonder what she would say to a kid like this. Something blunt, probably. Honest. But she'd see him. I know she would.

I rise and step over to Jocelyn, lowering my voice. "His silence could be selective mutism triggered by trauma or instability," I explain. "It's not uncommon after a major transition, especially in kids who've been neglected or harmed."

She nods. "What can I do?"

"Routine," I tell her. "Keep things calm, predictable. Keep offering him choices—small ones, like what to wear or which snack he wants. That gives him control without pressure. And if he makes a sound, even a hum or a laugh, just go with it. Don't push for words. Let him come to them on his own. Eventually, I'll give you a referral for a psychologist, but I think just getting used to the new environment will go a long way for now."

She exhales, looking over at Eli. "Thank you."

"You're doing great. Really. I'd like to see him again in a few months to see how things are coming along."

Eli is still clutching Dr. Rex like the thing's magic. "He just needs to feel safe," I add. "Once he knows no one's going to leave — or hurt him — he might surprise you."

Her eyes mist up a little, and she wipes them quickly. "Thank you."

"Call me if you need anything. Seriously." I write my personal cell number on the notepad and hand it to her. "And keep the dinosaur. Sometimes having a sidekick helps."

She smiles. "Thanks, Dr. Ryker."

I nod and turn back to the boy.

"It was nice to meet you, Eli. I'll see you next time," I say confidently.

He doesn't respond, but he's still holding the dinosaur. And he watches me leave the room. That's enough for today.

After the door clicks shut behind me, I settle against the hallway wall, letting my head fall back against the cool plaster.

Mel rounds the corner, nearly bumping into me. Her brows lift. "You okay?"

I nod automatically, but it feels like a lie. I rub the back of my neck, trying to shake it off. "Yeah. Just didn't expect to —" I cut myself off. "That just got me a little, that's all."

Mel studies me for a beat, then hands me the next chart without another word. "You've got a big heart under all that sarcasm," she says as she continues down the hall. "Don't worry. We won't tell anyone."

I huff a laugh, but it's half-hearted. My feet stay planted a moment longer, the chart loose in my hands, my mind still back in room three. That kid cracked something open in me. I felt something that didn't come with a punch line or a coping mechanism. It felt real and human. Complicated, not something I usually involve myself with, as Ginny and I have discussed.

I find myself wanting to tell her about this, talk it through the way I might with my family, one of my brothers. She'd get it, not just the kid and his struggles but the feeling and weight of it.

And yeah, maybe that's insane. She walked out on me last week with no more than a carefree wave. But even then, I sensed more beneath the surface. She's someone who could handle the mess underneath my mask if I ever let her. Or if she ever decided it was worth the trouble.

But she's a Dempsey, my brain immediately counters. *How could that happen?*

FIVE

Ginny

I drop the same stemless wine glass twice before I realize I've been stacking them in the wrong place. *Sip Happens*, the label reads. No kidding.

It's been a week since I walked away from Ryker at Mikey's. Seven days of replaying our conversation on a loop, of trying not to think about the way his voice slid over my skin like warm honey, or how his hand felt when it grazed my lower back, all heat and promise. I've spent every one of those days reminding myself that walking away was the smart thing. The right thing. Why would I pick a fight with my entire family when I've just come back to town and begged for their mercy?

I mean, I'm not here because this job is my dream. I'm here because it's something. It pays the bills, gives me a place to live, and keeps my grandmother from breathing down my neck. And I suppose it's good to help out at the vineyard, even though my family's drama has never been what I wanted.

But if my grandmother finds out I so much as flirted with a Paradise, all hell will break loose. Gran would have a meltdown, and not the dramatic, throw-a-fit kind. The kind that ends in exile and icy silences and my key card being deactivated before I even hit the parking lot. I'm already dreading telling her I'm in Sadie's wedding.

I text my brother, Alaric. He's about the sanest one in this bunch.

Me: Hey. When you have some time, can we meet up?

Ric: How about tonight?

Me: Sure. Name the time and place.

Ric: Chinese at my house. I'll order in.

Me: You're speaking my language! Kung pao for me, please.

I slip my phone back into my apron and my thoughts wander. Ryker isn't just a bad idea. He's a beautiful risk I can't afford. And yet...the pull is still there. He feels dangerous in the exact way I crave, and I don't think that's just about my family. I've given love more than a few chances, and all I have to show for it are mistakes that still sting. Letting go with Ryker might actually be freedom — being seen, being wanted — not for what I represent, but for who I truly am.

If I let myself experience that, though, I'm not sure I'll know how to walk away. And that's the problem. I can't afford to want that. Not from him. Not from anyone. My ex, Jeremy, taught me that.

I move to stack the glasses in the right spot and force myself to focus. Inventory is off again — big surprise. Mom was in last night, and she rearranged everything. We have a difference of opinion on the best setup for the store, but since now I'm in charge, I put things where they seem to sell best. Then she changes them back. It's just another way I wish I felt more in control here. Mostly I still feel like a pawn in someone else's game.

The bell above the door chimes, and I turn my smile toward a couple of tourists asking about olive oil tastings.

Good. Better this way. Safe. This is a path I know how to tread.

When I've sent them on their way, the door swings open again, and this time it's not tourists. It's my sister Josie, her long strawberry-blonde ponytail swishing behind her as she breezes in.

"You're a million miles away," she says, glancing at me as she pulls a gumdrop from the sample bowl near the counter. "What's going on in that head of yours?"

I shrug. "Inventory's off again. Mom was here, so chances are she put things away somewhere I can't find."

Josie arches a brow. "Uh-huh. That the kind of inventory that wears scrubs and a cocky smile?"

I look up sharply. "What?" But I already know. It's one of the joys of living in a small town. Nothing is ever a secret.

She smirks but lets it go. *Thank God.*

I change the subject. "How's the well?"

Josie sighs and hops up on the edge of the display case, as if she doesn't know I hate that. "Still dry. Dormant vines don't crumble in your hands," she says. "These aren't sleeping. They're gone. We're talking about hand-watering in the spring. Depends on how long this wet winter holds out. Maybe we'll be lucky."

"Forecast says more rain," I say, folding tissue paper around a candle. "So maybe you'll catch a break."

"Maybe." She gives me a long look. "You sure you're okay?"

"Fine." I don't even look up. "Go bug Sera. She loves feelings."

Josie snorts, and just as she hops down, the bell above the

door rings again. My heart sinks the moment I see her — our mother.

Monica Dempsey glides into the gift shop like she's waltzing into a gala, wearing a vintage scarf and oversized sunglasses. She looks around like she's never been here before, then brightens when she sees us. She blinks like she's coming out of the dark as she puts her glasses on her head. Her gaze darts around the space, a beat too long on every shelf.

"I thought I was working today!" she says, sounding breathless and vaguely confused.

"You're not," I say, carefully calm. "We talked about this last week. You said you were thinking of stepping back."

"Oh, right." She waves that off, as if it's all a delightful misunderstanding. "I am thinking of retiring. But I haven't decided. I'll go mad if I don't have something to do." She looks around the gift shop again. "Why did you move things around? It took me hours to get it back."

"I have it this way because it creates better flow."

"When did you decide to pick up a jewelry line? Gilded Grape? Who is this?"

"It's mine. Gran said I could sell it here if I gave the store forty percent."

She shakes her head. "If it's okay with your gran, that's fine, but the store was better the way it was."

Josie gives me a sympathetic wince and ducks out the side door like the damn place is on fire. Traitor.

My mother makes a little humming sound. "You rearranged the jam display."

"Yes."

"I liked it better the way it was."

She walks over and starts shifting jars back into their original formation, completely undoing the project I spent an hour on this morning. I press my tongue to the roof of my mouth and try not to snap.

It's not worth it. It's never worth it.

"Customers flow through the store better this way," I say,

hoping logic might carry the day.

She doesn't answer. Just keeps rearranging like I'm not even here. After a moment, she starts in with her usual commentary. "You know, you should have the more colorful labels at eye level. That's what catches people's attention. No one buys the buried ones."

I nod. "Okay."

"I just want to help," she adds, her voice thin and fragile now.

"I know." I force a smile, the one I've perfected over years of swallowing my frustration. "Thanks, Mom."

Inside, I'm screaming. There's a version of me that flips the jam table and tells her to get the hell out. But that version never made it out of adolescence. This version just nods and waits for the moment to pass.

I'm about to lose it—my jaw clenched, fingernails biting into my palms—when my phone buzzes in my pocket.

Sadie: You up for Vancouver or Toronto for dress shopping? Thoughts?

My fingers hover over the screen. I should say no. I would prefer never to return to Vancouver, and Toronto is a bigger investment. But I don't.

Because some part of me wants to say yes. Just once.

Me: I'm fine with wherever you want. With enough notice, I can plan around it. It's your wedding, so it's your call.

The response is instant.

Sadie: You're the best. Beckett and I also want to have you and Ryker over for dinner sometime to go over a few wedding things. You in? It's going to take a while to figure out the schedules.

I stare at the message for a beat. Dinner. With Beckett and Ryker. My stomach flips, but not in a bad way. I should say no. I should invent an excuse. But I've agreed to do this. It's not her fault I have no self-restraint where Ryker is concerned.

Me: Sure. Sounds good.

A second later, another message lights up my screen.

Ryker: This wedding stuff will be fun.

My heart jumps like it always does when it's him. My stupid, reckless heart.

I roll my eyes so hard it's a miracle they don't fall out of my head. But a smile tugs the corner of my mouth anyway. Stupid, charming, too-hot-for-his-own-good idiot.

I tuck my phone away and turn back to the shop, only to find my mother still frowning at a pyramid of jam jars like it personally offended her.

"Sadie asked me to be her maid of honor," I tell her.

"That's nice. Who's she marrying?" She moves over to rearrange the scarves it took me hours to fold.

Breathe in. Breathe out. "Beckett Paradise."

Mom stops and looks at me. "And you'll be in the wedding?"

"Yes."

"Your grandmother isn't going to like that."

I sigh. "She's my closest friend, and I want to do this."

"Just tell your grandmother before she finds out."

I nod. That's why I want to see Ric tonight. I'll get his take on how to *tell* her without asking for permission. Because if I ask, she'll tell me no.

Mom is now pulling boxes out and putting away the stemless glasses I just arranged. "These never sell in the winter."

I let out a slow breath and remind myself it's not forever. Nothing is.

When I step through Ric's front door that evening, I'm pleased to find it already smells like ginger, soy, and garlic. His house feels like a pocket of calm in a world that's spinning too fast—warm lighting, overwatered plants, and a lived-in couch covered in dog hair even though he doesn't have a dog anymore. Miles Davis hums low from the speaker in the kitchen.

"Hope you're hungry," he calls. "I ordered enough to roll us both out the door."

I kick off my boots and head in, already feeling lighter. "You always order too much."

"It's a talent," he says, grinning as he dishes out my usual— extra spicy kung pao chicken, beef and broccoli, and low mein with pork. He sets it on the counter with a pair of chopsticks. "You okay?"

I slide onto the barstool and inhale deeply over my plate. "Yeah. No. I don't know."

He doesn't push. Just hands me a spring roll and waits.

"What's going on with you?" I ask, deflecting.

He frowns, confused. "What do you want to know?"

"This isn't a therapy session for me. I wanted to see how my big brother is doing. You moved back just before I did and haven't even faked interest in someone local."

His face goes still, guarded. "She didn't want this," he says after a long pause. "Didn't want small-town life. You can't take the city out of some women."

"Why didn't you stay in Vancouver?"

"I stayed in Vancouver as long as I could, but once I finished school, I couldn't ignore what was happening here. There was no one else. Gran cut Dad out, so I knew someone had to come home and support Seraphina. But Liz didn't want this life, and I couldn't ask her to give up everything for something I can't walk away from."

"So she didn't come with you," I say quietly.

He shakes his head. "No. And I didn't ask her to."

My heart hurts for him. I've been so caught up in my own problems, I hadn't noticed how much he's still carrying. "I'm sorry, Ric."

He shrugs, but I can see the tension in his shoulders. "Some things don't work out. Doesn't mean they didn't matter."

I reach across the counter, resting my hand over his. "You deserve more than waiting around on something that already ended."

He nods but doesn't answer.

We eat in silence for a while. I've always felt like I could breathe around Ric, maybe because he never asks me to be anything other than exactly who I am.

Halfway through my plate, I set my chopsticks down and stare at the chicken, like it might offer me some kind of divine answer. "I have to tell Gran something, something she might not like."

He chews slowly, watching me with that therapist face that used to drive me crazy when we were younger. "Okay…"

"It's…complicated."

He waits.

"I'm going to be in a wedding," I say finally. "Sadie's wedding. She's marrying Beckett Paradise."

There it is. The surprise in his eyes, quickly masked. "Oh."

"Yeah," I murmur, dragging a hand through my hair. "Oh."

Ric sits back in his chair. "So when you said this was a thing Gran might not like…"

"She might kick me out like she did Dad and never speak to me again. And I don't even think she'd miss me."

"Ginny." His voice is gentle but firm. "Dad and Gran had a complicated relationship. Just remember, you're doing this because Sadie's your friend."

"I know," I whisper. "But that's not going to matter to Gran. All she'll see is the groom's last name." My fingers tighten around the edge of the counter. I try to imagine telling Gran—her mouth pressed into a thin line, disappointment hanging in the air. "She already thinks I'm too soft," I tell him. "Too willing to forget. She looks at me and sees everything she hated in Dad—his kindness, his blind spots. Like loving people makes you reckless." I shake my head. "If I tell her I'm standing up at a Paradise wedding, I don't know what she'll do."

Ric rests his elbows on the counter. "Then tell her why it matters. That it's not about the name, it's about Sadie, about friendship and showing up when it counts."

I swallow hard. "And if she kicks me out?"

"Then she does," he says. "But that's on her. You've been jumping through her hoops since you were ten. You left once, and maybe she's realized you're more than able to do that again."

I look up at him, eyes burning. "I just don't see how she can get past this. She's spent her whole life being angry at them. And it's not like I don't get it. She lost a close friend, and Granddad lost his sister because of the Paradise family."

"You know it's not that simple," Ric counters. "Granddad's father was the one who killed her."

"But that doesn't matter to Gran." I shake my head. "In her mind, the entire Paradise family is guilty by blood. That's the part that doesn't seem right."

He nods. "Yep. All that shaped her for good and bad." He reaches across the counter. "No matter what she does, I'll still be here. No matter what."

I squeeze his hand. "Thanks, Ric."

"Always."

SIX

Ryker

It's Saturday afternoon, and I'm spending it on a tasting with Beckett and Sadie at Paradise Grill. I arrive ten minutes late, which means I'm right on time by my standards. Sadie texted that they're already seated just as I was parking. I spot Beckett first — dark suit, stiff posture, classic him. And next to him, is her.

Ginny Dempsey.

She's wearing a dress that does not belong in this town unless the goal is to ruin men. Her auburn hair's half up, half down, like she couldn't decide whether to behave or misbehave. God help me, I hope it's the second option.

I slide into the seat next to her. "You're in my spot."

She doesn't flinch. Just lifts a brow and takes a sip of wine. "You're late."

"I like to make an entrance."

Beckett clears his throat like he's warning a toddler. Sadie glares at both of us and gestures to the lineup of appetizers. "Focus, children. We're tasting, not flirting."

Ginny stabs her fork into a roasted pear salad. "I can multitask." She chews thoughtfully and turns to Sadie. "I told Gran I'm going to be in the wedding."

The table goes still.

"What did she say?" Sadie asks.

Ginny shrugs, trying to play it off. "I didn't ask for permission. I just told her — more of an FYI situation. She gave me that look. You know the one."

Sadie winces. "Yikes."

"But she adores you," Ginny adds, smiling now. "You and Ric practically kept me out of jail in high school."

Sadie snorts. "Please. You flirted your way out of every detention and half the town's speeding tickets. Ric and I just follow your mess."

"Should I be asking if your new family is okay with me in the wedding?" Ginny presses, looking over at Beckett.

He answers before Sadie can. "They don't care."

I school my face, because that's not entirely true. They do care. Not because of Sadie's choice in bridesmaids, but because of the fallout we're bracing for — the judgment, the whispers, the lines being crossed. But Beckett's too good a guy to put that weight on Ginny's shoulders. And he would never upset Sadie about it.

We go through grilled prawns, steak bites with chimichurri, and a butternut squash ravioli that's so good I might propose to the chef. Beckett makes polite noises of approval. Sadie's taking notes like it's a tasting for the Queen.

She sets her pen down and dabs at her mouth with a napkin. "Oh, did you see the family vineyard chat this morning?" she asks, like it's no big deal. "Last night the syrah took a gold, and they gave our pinot ninety-two points at the International Wine Festival."

I glance at Ginny. "I did see that." Sadie has to know I did.

"That's fantastic." Ginny smiles graciously. "The more award-winning wines we can get here in the valley, the better we all do."

"Do you know how Black Bear did this year?" Sadie asks.

"Josie called late last night and said another gold for our pinot and for the red blend."

I nod along, pretending I'm listening, but I'm not. Not when Ginny keeps twirling the stem of her wineglass like it's more interesting than anything else on the table.

But it's the cake that does me in. Three options — Vanilla almond, chocolate truffle, and one with Champagne and berries that tastes like a damn love letter written in sugar and silk.

"Holy hell," I mutter after a bite, shaking my head.

Ginny closes her eyes and lets out the softest, most satisfied hum I've ever heard. It's not loud. It's barely there. But I feel it like a hit to the ribs.

I nearly choke.

Sadie kicks me under the table, hard enough to make me jerk. "Behave," she hisses, shooting me a pointed look.

I sit straighter, schooling my expression. "What? She made a noise. I'm just reacting to the environment."

Ginny opens one eye. Her lips quirk, just slightly. "You should see what kind of noise I make over crème brûlée."

Shifting in my seat, my pulse thuds through my body. I'm not sure if she means that or if I even care. Because now I want to hear it. And now, I'm picturing things I have no business imagining at a cake tasting in front of my brother and his fiancée.

Ginny reaches for another bite, her fingers brushing mine where they rest near the tray. That simple touch short-circuits something inside me. I steal a glance at her. She doesn't meet my eyes, but her lips twitch like she knows exactly what she's doing.

I clear my throat and stab my fork into the next option, trying to focus on cake instead of undressing her with my eyes.

Not flirting. Just advanced dessert appreciation.

And if that's the story I've got to tell myself, so be it.

When Beckett shifts forward to talk to the chef about guest

counts and timing, I take my shot.

I shift closer to Ginny until my shoulder brushes hers. Close enough that she can probably smell the citrus from the beer I barely touched. Close enough that if she turned her head, her lips would be just a breath from mine.

"You're going to wreck me, Red. And I think you know it," I murmur.

She doesn't flinch. Just licks a crumb off her thumb, slow and deliberate. "You keep acting like I'm not used to the burn."

Damn.

Before I can answer, Sadie lets out a dramatic gasp about the steak entrée we had—something about the pepper crust—and the moment vanishes like smoke in the wind.

Ginny reaches for her water. I do the same.

But under the table, her knee finds mine. And lingers.

I could shift. Should move. But I don't. I sit here like a man holding a lit match, waiting for it to burn down to his fingers.

The rest of the afternoon moves in a blur. We vote on dinner options, sample one last wine pairing. Pretend we're all very serious about wedding logistics when every part of me is focused on the woman beside me and the way she hasn't once looked my way since dessert. She's cool. Effortless. Untouchable.

Except for the knee.

When the tasting wraps, Sadie pulls Beckett into conversation with the chef again, giving me exactly ten seconds of space.

Ginny stands and slips her purse over one shoulder.

"You keep looking at me like I'm some kind of bad idea," I say, rising beside her.

She doesn't miss a beat. "You *are* a bad idea."

I grin. "Then why are you smiling?"

She shrugs, eyes cutting toward me with heat I feel in my bones. "Because bad ideas make for fun nights." Then she turns and heads out, hips swaying like a dare.

I'm supposed to be wrapping things up—thanking the staff, getting the timeline from Sadie—but Ginny's slipping away. Not out the front, but down the side path that leads behind the restaurant, toward the row of wine barrels the Grill uses for storage.

She pauses once to glance back, just long enough for me to catch the invitation in her eyes.

And I follow. Of course I do.

Because I've never been great at walking away from temptation. Especially when she's wrapped in a sweater dress and smells like peaches and danger.

I say goodbye to Sadie and Beckett, and once I'm out the door, no one sees me follow. No one calls my name. The world shrinks to the sound of my heartbeat and the path Ginny left behind. The air shifts the moment I turn the corner.

It's quieter back here—muted sounds from the dining room fading behind the wall, the wind in the vineyard beyond, the sky blushed with the last light of sunset. The barrels are stacked in neat rows, towering and solid, their wood aged and sun-warmed. And Ginny's there, tucked in the shadows between two stacks, her back against one, arms loosely folded.

She doesn't say a word. Just watches me.

And I watch her right back.

"Thought you said I was a bad idea," I murmur, closing the space between us.

"I did."

"You always lure bad ideas into dark corners?"

Her lips twitch. "Only the ones who follow me."

She hesitates, just for a breath, like she's fighting herself. But then she steps closer, and I know she's lost that battle.

That's all I need.

I crowd her back against the barrel, my hands braced on either side of her head. Her breath hitches, but she doesn't flinch. Doesn't pull away. Her eyes move to my mouth, then back to my eyes, and I kiss her.

Hard. Deep. Like I've been waiting years instead of months. She melts into me, her hands fisting in my shirt, dragging me closer. I slide her winter coat off her shoulders and move one hand to her waist, the other into her hair and tilt her head to get a better angle. Her lips are soft and hot, tasting like sparkling wine and rebellion.

My tongue slides against hers and she moans, the sound vibrating through me like a match strike.

Her body arches into mine, and suddenly, it's not just a kiss. It's a tangle of limbs and want. I grip her hips, pull her flush against me, and press her against the barrel, letting her feel every ounce of what she does to me. "Jesus. You're driving me insane," I whisper against her mouth, my forehead resting against hers for a beat. "Tell me you want this."

"I don't," she says, breathless.

But her hands are still on me. Still pulling. Still clutching.

I search her face. "Liar."

Her fingers slide into my hair, yanking me back into another kiss, this one slower, deeper, like she's memorizing the taste of me. My hands slip beneath the hem of her dress, tracing the smooth skin of her thighs. She lets me, for a beat. Just long enough to spark hope.

Then she pulls back.

Her breathing is uneven. Her lipstick's smeared. She looks like a fever dream.

"This isn't anything," she says. "It can't be."

I blink. "That felt like more than nothing."

She straightens her dress. "It's not."

"You sure about that?"

She steps around me, not meeting my eyes. "I don't do complicated either. Not right now. This wedding is complicated enough."

"But you do me?"

She pauses, then looks back over her shoulder. "Yeah," she murmurs. "That's the problem."

And then she's gone, walking back toward the restaurant like nothing happened, like my mouth wasn't just on hers and her body wasn't pressed against mine like we were the last two people on Earth.

I sink back against the barrel and stare at the sky, trying to catch my breath.

"This isn't anything."

She said it like a fact.

But every nerve in my body is still lit up. Because she almost let me in.

And almost? Almost is a hell of a drug. It's the kind of thing that makes a man chase a woman who already said no. And worse, it makes him believe she might change her mind.

SEVEN

Ginny

I should be concentrating on the inventory, but Mom is back in the store again today, and that has put me on edge. Still, my inability to focus is not entirely her fault. My brain's stuck in a loop I can't escape. Ryker's smirk. His fingers skimming my thigh under the table. The way he looked at me like he knew every dirty thought in my head because they were in his too.

What was I thinking at that tasting? This is reckless, and I know better.

I don't need useless distractions, and I certainly don't need to pick a fight with my family. Not when the vineyard's got problems and our well's running dry.

Sera walks into the gift shop a few minutes later and pokes around a bit before coming over to see what I'm doing...or trying to do. "You're quiet," she says after I fail to greet her or start conversation.

I tilt my head toward Mom, and Sera nods. "I could use your insight on block one-hundred-and-one," she says after a moment. "Can you get away to come look?"

I look over at Mom. "Can you manage this for a bit?"

We haven't had a customer all morning. I shrug into my winter coat and follow Sera.

"Of course," she says. She's still rearranging my work, and I'm sure that will keep her occupied for a while.

Sera and I pile into her truck and head out to the edge of our property that abuts the Paradise land. The sun hits these vines just right, and this is where we grow the grapes for our best red wines.

Sera glances at me from the driver's seat. Her dark hair is pulled into a tight ponytail, her face bare except for the sunblock she always wears. "What's up? Mom driving you crazy?"

I shrug. "I'm always quiet before I've had enough coffee."

She snorts. "You're brooding. There's a difference."

I don't answer. The farther we drive from the main road, the bumpier it gets, tires crunching over gravel as we climb the ridge toward the corner of our property. Across the property line from this block were rows of peach trees, until the Paradise family decided they wanted new pinot vines just under two years ago.

"I'm really excited for you and Josie," I tell her as we approach. I should try to make conversation. "Gran must be overjoyed with the big win this week."

Sera shrugs. "I'm not sure she believes it helps our sales. She made a snotty comment about the money we spent *going* to the festival."

"How can she be so dense?" I protest. "Josie's going to be on the national news. That will bring in buyers from all across Canada and probably the U.S. and the rest of the world."

She shrugs. "That's Gran."

Sera parks near the edge of the bluff, and we get out, squinting against the glare. The well cap is intact. No signs of damage or wear, just silence.

Rows of grapevines stretch out in the morning light, their twisted trunks still bare and lifeless, buds tight against the woody canes as if reluctant to wake. The soil beneath them is dry and cracked, and the few emerging leaves are pale, tinged with yellow. Across the property line, the Dempsey vines stand thick and steady in their winter rest.

Sera pulls out the dipmeter and lowers it into the well. It works like a fishing bobber, unwinding the line until it hits bottom. The device lets water in as it descends, so when she hauls it back up, it shows how full the well is. After a wet winter, the water level should be rising as the groundwater replenishes. She checks the reading, then notes the level in her logbook. "No change?" I ask.

She shakes her head. "It hasn't changed. I had the guy from Okanagan Drilling out earlier this week. He thinks if it's not changing, it might be rerouted."

"Rerouted?"

"Blocked. Buried. Sabotaged. Take your pick."

I swallow hard. "Do you think it's them?"

Sera doesn't say anything for a beat. "They're the ones who gain if we fail."

They being the Paradise family. The people we've spent our whole lives competing with. The people we've blamed for everything from lost contracts to our parents' divorce.

The people who gave birth to Ryker.

That makes my stomach twist. Because I don't think it's them. I know it's not them. But saying that out loud feels like a betrayal.

"You okay?" she asks.

"I don't know." I crouch beside the wellhead and press my palm against the rusted pipe. It's cold.

I close my eyes for half a second, trying to focus, but all I can see is Ryker's stupid crooked grin. My mind echoes with the heat in his voice when he talks about "scratching an itch." He makes it sound so easy. Like there's no history. No worry. Just chemistry.

But all of *this* is a warning label I keep trying to ignore.

"Sooo, Ryker Paradise, huh?" Sera says suddenly, like she's pulled the thought straight from my head.

I jerk my hand away from the well. "What?"

She shrugs. "You're not as sly as you think."

"I'm not anything with him."

"Yet," she mutters.

I shoot her a look, but she just grins and walks back toward the truck.

"Why would you think that?" I call after her.

"Come on. All of Paradise is talking about you two right now."

My heart stops. "What? Why?"

"You were flirting pretty hard down at his bar."

"His bar?"

"Yeah. He owns Mikey's."

"Wait. He owns Mikey's? When did that happen?"

"Mikey's wife got half in the divorce, so Ryker stepped in and bought her out. Obviously, Mike still runs it."

I stare down at the dry earth for another second, then stand and dust my hands off on my jeans. "There's nothing going on. We've just had some meetings. He's the best man, and I'm the maid of honor in Beckett and Sadie's wedding."

"You know Gran is going to demand that you back out of that."

I shrug. "I've already told her. Sadie's my best friend. I can't control who she marries, and honestly, Beckett's really good for her."

"What did Gran say?"

"Not much. I didn't ask for permission. I just told her."

Sera whistles. "Gran much prefers you to ask permission."

"This thing between our families needs to stop. It's getting ridiculous."

"Max Paradise ruined our parents' marriage."

"Don't you think Dad had a hand in that as well? He

cheated with Max's wife. Sure, Max went out of his way to make sure Gran knew, but if Dad had kept it in his pants, Max wouldn't have had anything to say."

Sera's jaw tightens. "Yeah, well, Gran sees it differently. And you know how she gets when she feels threatened. This thing with the wedding isn't over, Gin. She'll make it ugly."

"Then let her. I'm tired of pretending everything's black and white. Ryker isn't Max."

"No. But he's got the same blood. Same last name. Same swagger." She arches a brow at me. "Just have a plan because Gran is going to go apeshit when she learns it has gone beyond you being in Sadie's wedding."

"It won't," I say too quickly, but my face gives me away.

"So there *is* something," Sera says.

I hesitate. "No. Not really."

"*Not really* sounds like the kind of thing people say when they're already in trouble."

I sigh and look off toward the ridge. "It doesn't matter. It can't go anywhere."

"Because of Gran?"

"It's more than that. It's everything," I say quietly. "I don't trust myself anymore. I have no idea what I want or what I need. My taste in men is crap. And on top of that, we're standing at a well that was probably sabotaged, and everyone thinks Ryker's family's behind it. Our grandmother calls them snakes, and I've been kissing one like I forgot who I am."

"She'd probably feel better about any other last name. Why would you tempt fate like this?"

I swallow hard. "I thought leaving my family behind when I moved out and then went to university proved I could stand on my own. But somehow, I ended up with nowhere to go and came back." My voice cracks. "Because I still need the Dempseys, but I want to be me as well. Now, I'm stuck trying to figure out how to be part of this family without thinking like Gran. Without letting her define me."

Sera's face softens, but she doesn't say I'm wrong.

Because I'm not.

My phone buzzes in my back pocket.

Sadie: Still up for dress shopping in Vancouver next month? Also, Beckett and I want you and Ryker to come over for dinner next week to talk wedding stuff.

Before I can even process it, another message pops in.

Ryker: This'll be fun.

I close my eyes a moment, and despite everything, I can feel this pulling me right back in. He's impossible. Charming. Infuriating. And exactly what I tell myself I don't need. But I'm smiling anyway.

Somehow, I get myself into the passenger seat of Sera's truck, and we wind back toward the vineyard offices.

"Well?" Gran is outside the main house when we arrive, her hands on her hips and her rain boots caked in mud.

Sera gets out first. "We dropped the dipmeter, and it's measuring the same."

Gran turns her frustration to me. "You think I don't know how Ryker Paradise thinks? How that whole family operates? They're already sending in their sons to cozy up. I see what's happening, even if no one else has the guts to say it." Her eyes narrow. "Mark my words, this isn't an accident."

My throat tightens.

Ryker doesn't feel like the enemy. Not the way he touched me. Not the way I wanted it. But this barrier between us is real, and crossing it feels like treason.

"Go tell your mother to go home." Gran points me inside.

Sera raises her eyebrows but doesn't say anything.

Eventually, Gran storms toward the back offices. When the door slams, I finally breathe.

"We just have to figure out how they're doing it," Sera says softly.

My phone buzzes again.

Ryker: Still thinking about last night? I can't stop. And I don't want to. Why did you leave?

My heart stutters. I shove the phone into my pocket and head back to the gift shop. This has to stop.

EIGHT

Ryker

I'm half a mile into sweating out last night's beer on the elliptical when my phone buzzes. I almost ignore it — it's my one damn day off — but the text tells me I can't.

Tarryn: Urgent — lab results. Come quick.

That's all it says. No context. No explanation. But if Tarryn says urgent, it is. Which means something's really wrong.

Cutting my workout short, I take the world's fastest shower and fire up the Armada, tires spitting gravel as I reverse out of the driveway. It's barely nine, and the sun is already stretching long across the hills, casting that golden glow over the vines. Normally, I'd admire it. Today, it just pisses me off.

As I drive, my mind races through possibilities — bad infestation of leafhoppers? Contaminated rootstock? A fungus flare-up? But we've been on top of everything this year. Precise irrigation. New cover crop rotation. We even doubled up on soil testing for the new pinot block we planted last spring.

Block nine. The one down on the southern property line.

A bad feeling curls low in my gut.

Fifteen minutes later, I'm jogging across the gravel lot toward the barn, my hair still damp. Tarryn's waiting like a storm cloud, arms crossed, lips pressed tight. She holds up a manila folder without a word.

I take it and flip it open. The second I scan the numbers, my stomach drops.

Root rot and the emitters are corroding. The soil pH is off. And the cover, which should be thriving in winter, is brown. Our newest pinot vines are dying.

"No," I mutter, flipping to the next page like it'll magically change. "This can't be right. This is block nine? What rows?"

She nods. "Thirty-six to forty-five. All the plantings from last spring. We're losing them."

"Could it be the grafted vines we got from the grower?"

They have a guarantee, and they'll replace them, if that's the case.

"No. And before you ask, it's not the drip system either."

I look past her shoulder toward the trellis lines dipping gently up the hill, beyond that is Dempsey land.

"Jesus." I run a hand down my face. "That's a sixty-thousand-dollar loss. Maybe more if whatever is affecting our grapes spreads." And that's not just dollars. It's the block we chose specifically because we knew the grapes just over the line on Dempsey land had won big awards. And now, it's rotting from the inside out. *Pretty damn poetic.*

"I had the lab run it twice," Tarryn says. "It's not a mistake. And it's not frost. Or underwatering. This looks like contamination."

I snap the folder closed, rage bubbling. "From what? Fertilizer? Herbicide drift?"

"This isn't anything they've seen before," she says with a

sigh. "It could be sabotage."

The word hangs between us.

"But we share the well in that parcel," I note. "What affects us affects them."

Tarryn's nod is slow. "Yeah. And we noticed they had someone out to look at the well recently. Their vines don't look like ours, but they're not in top form either, I don't think."

"You think they'd kill our vines and sacrifice their own in the process?"

"I'm not saying that."

"No. But you're thinking it," I counter.

Her silence says enough. Our families have both done worse over the generations.

I swallow hard. It was bad enough when this was just business, just vines and family rivalries. But now, it's not.

Because I've seen Ginny Dempsey smile in the dark like she forgot the world hated us being in the same room. Yet now, I'm staring at damage that might've come from her family's side of the hilltop. And I can't stop wondering. She doesn't have a lot to do with the agriculture. She's running the gift shop. If someone told her, would she warn me? Would she even know? Would she care?

I want to believe she doesn't know. That this isn't her fault. But if someone on her side did this, if this was intentional, then maybe there's still something to this feud. And every moment I spend thinking about her — or worse — is a mistake.

Tarryn and I stand lost in thought until footsteps crunch across the gravel behind us.

Zach rounds the corner of the barn, wiping his hands on a rag. His face brightens when he sees us, like he's just stumbled across old friends, not cousins who know he's been gunning for their jobs since the day he was demoted from the tasting room to the fermenting warehouse.

"Hey," he says. "You two look serious. Everything all right?"

"Just looking over some numbers," I say, closing the

folder. No need to invite him in.

Zach nods, glancing toward the barn. "I was hunting down the clipboard with yesterday's brix readings. Thought maybe it got misfiled."

"Vineyard logs are on my desk," Tarryn offers. She sounds friendly enough, but not open. "Have you checked there?"

"Heading there now. Just figured I'd swing by since I saw you out here."

Tarryn gives a polite smile. "Appreciate it. Let me know if anything looks off."

He grins and tosses the rag over his shoulder. "You got it. Always happy to help."

Zach glances at me over his shoulder as he goes. "Rumor has it you and Ginny Dempsey are a thing."

My spine stiffens before I can stop it.

Tarryn's head swivels toward me, eyes wide. "Seriously?"

I lift both hands. "No. She's the maid of honor, and I'm the best man in Beckett and Sadie's wedding. That's all it is."

Zach smirks. "Bar talk says otherwise. You two weren't exactly subtle at Mikey's the other night."

Tarryn shakes her head. "I thought you hated her."

"I don't hate her," I mutter.

"I won't tell my dad," Zach says with a wink. "But fair warning, if he finds out, he'll lose his shit."

I give him a look. "Your mom had an affair with Ginny's dad. He has zero room to judge anything."

Zach shrugs. "Never stopped him before." He heads off toward the crush pad like he didn't just drop a grenade in the dirt.

I didn't want this to get complicated. But it already is. Every choice I make now feels like stepping into a trap, one I might've built myself.

Every move I make with Ginny—every glance, every smirk, every second too long in each other's orbit—is being noticed. Catalogued. Whispered about.

Stupid small town.

One wrong move and I won't just be the idiot who slept with the enemy. I'll be the one who handed our family's greatest grudge a front-row seat to our implosion.

"I'll give him this," I murmur. "Zach knows how to stay useful."

Tarryn scoffs. "He's trying to show he belongs here."

"Or that he can run the place better than you can."

She stares out at the vineyard. "Let him try. We'll still be standing when he's done."

I watch him go, my jaw clenched. "Why's he even still here?"

She exhales. "Because he's family. And Dad doesn't want the fight with Max."

"He stole from the damn till. Fired Sadie because he felt threatened—"

"I know."

"—and now he's poking around like he's waiting for the right moment to strike. Stirring shit about Ginny being in the wedding. Making veiled threats about starting drama like it's sport."

Tarryn's voice drops. "Zach's a problem, but Max is the one pulling his strings."

"It wouldn't surprise me if he had a hand in this." I motion toward the vineyard. "Getting both families riled up again, reigniting the old feud—it's exactly the kind of chaos he thrives on."

She tilts her head, considering. "I'll talk to Dad. Fill him in on everything, including what Zach just had to say."

I look down at the folder again, fingers tightening around the edges. "If someone's trying to bury this vineyard—"

"They won't," she says fiercely.

But it seems to me someone already has a shovel in the dirt.

NINE

Ginny

Tarryn Paradise is in full wedding-planner mode, which is both terrifying and impressive.

She has a clipboard in one hand, a latte in the other, and a Bluetooth headset that makes her look like she's about to lead a TED Talk on high-stakes event coordination.

"Okay," she says, spinning on her heel in boots that are far too cute for mud season, "we've got three options for ceremony locations. All different vibes. All stunning. Ready?"

Sadie gives a little clap. Beckett gives a grunt that I think means yes.

Ryker stands next to me in the Paradise tasting room, his shoulder brushing mine like it's an accident. It's not. I know it. He knows it. And the fact that we're not acknowledging this just adds to the tension.

"Lead the way," I say, trying not to swivel my head endlessly, taking it all in. It's not often that I have the opportunity to experience the Paradise Estate vineyards firsthand. It was bad enough being at their restaurant the other night. Now, I'm actively trying to stop myself from thinking of this as enemy territory.

The first location is up by the west garden, near a row of peach trees. There's a view of the lake in the distance, and the vines will stretch toward the horizon like green ribbons for the wedding. Tarryn explains the seating capacity, where the string quartet would set up, and how the sun will hit the altar at the golden hour.

"I mean..." Sadie looks around. "That's kind of perfect."

"It's a little soft for us, though, don't you think?" Beckett asks, glancing down at his phone like he's hoping a surgery will materialize and pull him away.

I smirk. "You want something less...picturesque?"

"Maybe something with less pollen," he says.

We move on. The second option is a small clearing just off their barrel room, shaded by massive oak trees and framed by wine casks stacked artfully in the background. Rustic, moody, a little more intimate.

"I like this," Sadie says. "It feels more...real."

Ryker dips his head toward me. "You into moody weddings?"

I don't look at him. "I'm into people minding their business."

"Feisty," he whispers.

I bump his arm with my elbow, but I'm smiling, and he knows it.

Beckett looks around. "I'm open to other venues too. Doesn't have to be here."

I catch the flash in Tarryn's eyes before she smooths her expression.

"Just not Black Bear," he adds with a smirk. "That'd be...awkward."

My jaw tightens. Sadie shoots him a look, and Tarryn goes very still.

I shrug. "We don't do weddings. Not our brand. Don't worry. You're safe from scandalous cross-vineyard competition." My jaw aches from the smile I'm faking.

Ryker tenses beside me like he's about to say something, but I cut him off with a smile. "I'm just here for moral support," I assure them. "And cake tastings."

"Speaking of support," Ryker says as the others get absorbed in the seating capacity and details of this option, "you leaned into me on that hill. Should I start charging a shoulder fee?"

"I tripped on a root."

"Sure you did."

Once Tarryn has finished her spiel, we walk over to the third location—a wide-open lawn, framed by wildflowers and overlooking Black Bear Lake. There's a gentle breeze, and even Beckett stops scrolling.

Sadie breathes it in like she's imprinting the scene on her memory. "This might be it."

"It's got space for a tent," Tarryn offers. "Room for dancing. Easy access for vendors. And it's close to the kitchen in case of emergencies."

"Like running out of bubbly?" I ask.

"Exactly," Tarryn agrees.

As they discuss layout options and backup plans for rain, my gaze drifts back to Ryker. He's already looking at me.

"What?" I ask.

"Nothing." He grins. "Just think this wedding's gonna be fun."

"With you around? It'll be chaos."

He shrugs. "Same thing."

I shake my head, but I'm still smiling when I turn away.

If anyone notices how close we stand, how his hand lingers a little too long when he passes me the clipboard, or how my gaze drops to his lips every time he smirks, no one says a word.

But our chemistry is only getting harder to hide.

"I've set up appointments with several dress shops," Sadie says, shifting gears after a minute. "I think we should all go." She looks at Tarryn. "We'll make it fun. Dress appointments, Champagne, a little nightlife in Vancouver. A fun weekend in the big city."

"Maybe the guys should come along," Beckett muses. "Turn it into a whole thing."

Tarryn smirks. "What? You afraid Sadie's going to meet someone else and trade up if you're not there to hover?"

Beckett looks properly offended. "No. I just think it'll be fun. And we wouldn't be with you all day. It's not like you're dragging us through every bridal shop."

"You never know," Sadie teases. "We might."

"Then I'll sneak out to a hockey game with Ryker."

Ryker grins but doesn't comment. His shoulder brushes mine again, and I'm starting to feel like my skin logs every point of contact before my brain does.

Tarryn looks at Sadie with a gleam in her eye. "So, where are your appointments for dresses?"

Sadie brushes her hair over her shoulder. "A few different boutiques."

"Is one of them Bisou Bridal?" Tarryn asks.

Sadie's eyes widen. "Yeah. I mean, I have them on my list, but everything's couture. Probably out of my budget."

Beckett's head turns fast. "Then we'll adjust the budget."

Sadie gives him a look. "Babe—"

"I don't care what it costs. If they have the dress you want, I'll manage it."

That silences the group for a beat.

I always knew the Paradise family had money—hell, they own Paradise—but Beckett just said that like dropping twenty-five grand on a dress was nothing.

And Sadie, for her part, is still blinking like she heard him wrong. "You're ridiculous," she says softly.

Beckett shrugs. "You're worth it." He pulls her in and kisses her.

It's quiet again, and I pretend to scribble something in my notebook just to keep from reacting too obviously.

Tarryn clears her throat. "All right. Dates. I hear you're looking at the end of summer, before the crush?"

Sadie nods. "Yep, August twenty-fourth, six months away. Gives us time to pull everything together."

Beckett nods. "Speaking of pulling everything together, let's circle back to the shopping trip for a second. I've got a connection at the Rosewood Hotel in Vancouver. I'll get some rooms, and while you guys go dress shopping, we'll find some other stuff to do. Then we'll have evenings to hang out."

My blood goes cold. The Rosewood. Of course.

"Have you ever been to the Rosewood?" Sadie asks.

I paste a smile on my face and nod like that suggestion doesn't make me want to crawl out of my skin. "Yeah. A couple of times. It's a great place downtown."

My ex-best friend, Jill, is a sales manager there. She knew my coffee order, cried when I got engaged, and then decided my fiancé looked better in her bed.

Sadie must see something in my expression because she lifts an eyebrow. But she doesn't push. Thank God. Sadie has no idea that I know the Rosewood Hotel entirely too well. Is it too late to change my mind about this trip?

Tarryn turns toward me. "Maybe you can come up with some ideas for while we're there. Fun things to do in the city. You used to live in Vancouver, right?"

"Yeah," I say. I clear my throat. "I can come up with a few things."

I can feel the dread seeping in. If I had my way, I'd never set foot in that city again. Too many memories, too much betrayal, and far too high a chance of running into people I'd rather forget.

But I'm the maid of honor. So I'll go, and I'll smile.

Ryker leans closer, lowering his voice. "You okay?"

"Totally fine," I lie.

He doesn't push, just watches like he sees through me. Like he always does.

I feel hot and cold at the same time. How is that possible?

Tarryn checks her watch. "I've got a vendor call in ten. Let me know what you decide on the location. I'll hold your wedding date for all three for the next week." She gives Sadie a hug and waves her clipboard. "We're on track. Don't screw it up."

She turns and struts off, her boots crunching on the gravel.

Beckett glances at his phone. "I should head back to the hospital. There are a couple post-ops I want to check in on." He gives Sadie a soft kiss, the kind that makes you feel like the world's still a little good. "Let me know if you need any help, and I've already cleared my calendar to make sure I'm free for Vancouver."

"Thank you," Sadie says with a warm smile.

Ryker claps Beckett on the shoulder, and they walk toward the main house. Ryker glances back, and his eyes meet mine. He winks.

It's just a glint of mischief, but it hits me square in the chest.

Butterflies. Stupid, fluttering butterflies.

I'm relieved he's leaving, frankly. I need a minute without his heat trailing behind me, every breath I take.

"Are you sure you're okay with going to Vancouver?" Sadie asks once we're alone.

I nod and give her hand a squeeze. "This is your party. It's your call. I'll go where you go."

She smiles. "You're pretty great at this whole maid-of-honor thing."

I grin. "Don't get used to it."

We walk back to the main parking lot together where Sadie hugs me goodbye and heads for her car. I walk the other way to my own car.

Now that I'm alone, my mind takes full advantage of the opportunity to freak out about the Vancouver trip. The moment

I walk through the doors of the Rosewood, I know I'll feel her presence. That overly bright smile. The perfume she always wore. The way she held my hand as I cried, swearing she didn't mean to sleep with him, that it just happened.

That wound hasn't fully healed. And now, I'm supposed to walk into her domain, smiling, helpful, a vision of bridal support?

I exhale hard as I spot my car. Then I stop. Ryker's resting against the passenger-side door, arms crossed like he's got all the time in the world.

"You stalking me now?" I ask.

He grins, slow and sure. "Just making sure you didn't need help getting out of your head."

I step closer before I can talk myself out of it. "What are you doing here, really?"

He doesn't answer. There's something in his eyes—not cocky, not smug. Just...open. Like I'm not the only one scared of how far we've already gotten into this mess. He steps forward, cups my face, and kisses me.

It's not rushed or frantic. It's steady. Certain. Like he knew I'd let him.

And God help me, I do.

I kiss him back, my fingers curling into his shirt, his body warm and solid and familiar in a way that terrifies me.

When he finally pulls away, I'm breathless. I know this is reckless. Family explosions aside, every step closer to him peels away another layer of the armor I've built to keep the past from bleeding into now. But I'm tired of guarding myself like a locked gate. And it seems it doesn't matter anyway. Vancouver has come to find me.

"Is this an invitation?" I ask.

"It is my day off," he says with a nod.

"Just this once," I whisper. "I'll go home with you."

His thumb traces the corner of my mouth, eyes burning into mine.

Surely, we've both realized this isn't a one-time thing. If it was, we'd be done with it by now.

This is the beginning of something we might not survive.

TEN

Ryker

Some days gut you.

I knew it was leukemia the second I saw her blood panel. I hoped I was wrong, hoped the lab made a mistake. Hoped for anything but what I had to say.

She's six. She still thinks Band-Aids fix everything.

Her parents went quiet when I said the word, the kind of silence that feels like screaming. Her mom gripped the armrest so hard her knuckles turned white. Her dad blinked too fast and wouldn't look at me.

I walk them through the next steps. Referrals. Blood work. Oncology. I say all the right things because I have to, but it doesn't matter. No one hears you when you're the guy who's brought the earthquake.

My day continues after that, and so does theirs, but I keep

thinking back to the moment I had to tell them. They're changed forever, and I can't shake that.

By the time I finish my shift, I'm exhausted and jittery. I wish the usual basketball with my brothers wasn't canceled tonight. Going home feels unbearable. The silence, the thoughts—I can't face any of it. I need noise. A distraction. Something that won't involve people asking me how I'm doing or looking at me with pity.

It's been three days since I saw Ginny during—okay, and after—the venue planning meeting at our vineyard. When I reach my car, I pull out my phone and type a message.

Me: Drink at Mikey's?

I stare at it for a second. Ginny doesn't owe me anything. And this is probably a bad idea. She left my place without a goodbye the other day, and I'm fine with that. We're supposed to be casual—scratch-an-itch casual, not text-on-a-bad-day casual.

Still, I hit send.

I toss the phone on the passenger seat and start the engine. The sun's setting behind the hills, painting the sky in fire and cotton candy, but all I see is that little girl's face. Her tiny fingers wrapped around the exam table paper like it could anchor her.

My phone buzzes. I pick it up at the next red light.

Ginny: Sure. I'm already halfway there.

I blow out a breath, feeling ridiculously relieved. What I should feel is stupid. This was never supposed to be anything more than a release valve for pressure I didn't want to name. But in this moment, I know what I want isn't a distraction. I want her.

Beyond our combustible chemistry, she seems to get me in a way I can't explain. Doesn't push. Doesn't hover. She lets me be, which is exactly what I need tonight.

When I walk into Mikey's, she's already at the bar, a bottle of cider in front of her, her long auburn hair glowing under the overhead lights like fire.

She turns as I approach, and our eyes meet. In an instant, I forget all over again why I ever thought being near her was a bad idea.

"Hey," I say, sliding onto the stool next to hers.

"Hey yourself." She takes a sip, studying me. "Rough day?"

I nod. "One of the worst."

She doesn't ask why. Just flags Mike and orders me a beer.

God, I needed this. And I needed her.

Ginny doesn't look at me directly. Not at first. She watches me through the mirror behind the bar, studying from a safe distance. Her fingers trace lazy circles around the base of her bottle.

"So," she says casually, "when did you buy the bar?"

I look at her reflection, arching a brow. "Who told you?"

"My sister," she says, turning to look at me, rather than the mirror. "She said you bailed Mike out after the divorce."

I shrug. "It wasn't a big deal. He didn't want to sell to strangers. I didn't want the place to close. He's still running it. Most people don't even realize it changed hands."

She lifts her bottle and nods like she's impressed. "Huh. I always thought the Paradise family was a little more...ruthless than that."

I laugh under my breath and take a sip of the beer Mike delivers. "Yeah, that's a myth. We're not all wine-soaked villains plotting world domination."

"Shame," she says, and her mouth curves into that half-smile that always gets me.

She takes another sip from her bottle.

"Which one is that?" I ask.

She turns the label to face me. "Paradise Brewery, the mango flavor," she says. "Was my drink of choice last summer. Still is, I guess."

"Sweet and dangerous," I murmur.

She arches a brow. "Just like me?"

I don't answer. She already knows.

We sit in silence for a minute, but it isn't awkward, just easy. Familiar in a way it shouldn't be.

Then she says, "So...why'd you text me?"

I swallow, my fingers tightening around my beer. What I'm about to say proves I wanted something more than a distraction this evening. "I had to give a family some bad news today. Little girl. Leukemia."

Ginny's face softens. "Ryker..."

"I went into peds to avoid that kind of thing. Thought I could fix more than I'd have to break." I shake my head. "Days like today make me feel like I was lying to myself."

She shifts and bumps my shoulder. I catch the faint scent of citrus and sunshine. "I'm so sorry."

I nod, not trusting myself to say anything else. The knot in my stomach hasn't loosened all day.

"What can I do?" she asks. "To make it better?"

I look over at her. "You're already doing it. Just being here is enough."

Her lips part, like she's expecting something else. Like she thought I'd say sex. I usually would.

Truth is, I need that too. The escape. The burn. But I won't ask for it, not this time. Not like that.

Ginny finishes her drink, scoots the bottle across the bar, and slides off the stool.

"I'm gonna hit the ladies' room," she says. "Meet you at your car?"

I blink. "What?"

She gives me a look, pointed, amused, a little wicked. "Your car."

Then she disappears down the hallway, leaving trouble in her wake.

It takes me a second to catch up.

My beer's still half full, but I toss some bills on the bar anyway and wave at Mike. "'Night."

"'Night, Doc," he says, barely looking up as I head out into the cold.

The wind off the lake slices through my jacket, biting sharp at my neck. I stalk across the parking lot to my Armada, unlock it, and slide inside. The leather's cold against my skin, and the interior still smells faintly like the pine-scented detailing from last week's wash.

A few minutes later, the passenger door opens, and Ginny climbs in. Her cheeks are flushed, hair wild from the wind, and she's grinning like she knows every thought in my head.

She buckles in and eyes the dash. "Big vehicle, Paradise. Overcompensating for something?"

I smirk. "When you're six-five, you don't fold easily into a sports car. Plus, I wanted something big enough to fit me and my brothers without having to amputate anyone's knees."

"Practical and luxurious," she says, running her hand over the console. "Very on-brand."

I glance at her, feeling a little…something. I'm not sure what. I'm not entirely in control of this situation. "You ready to go home?"

"Actually…" she says, drawing out the word like a dare, "I was thinking maybe we could take a drive. The lookout over the lake might be nice."

I turn to face her, raising an eyebrow. "The lookout? As in, the old make-out spot?"

She shrugs, all innocence. "Is that what it is? Huh. I must've forgotten."

I laugh, but my chest tightens with anticipation. "And what exactly are your intentions, Red?"

She doesn't answer. Instead, she reaches into her coat pocket and pulls out something small and black. She places it in my hand—silky, soft.

Jesus. They're her panties.

I look up, stunned, and she just grins. "Drive, Ryker."

My fingers tighten around the fabric. "You're gonna kill me."

She smiles. "Not tonight."

I practically floor it out of the parking lot, and she laughs, kicking my heart into an even higher gear. I chill out once we reach the street, and we drive in an electric silence for a few moments. I keep realizing how badly I've needed someone like her.

As requested, I stop the car at a secluded part of the lookout that has a fantastic view of the lake and valley, even at night. Once I put it in park, I turn to her, and our lips meet.

Her mouth is warm, and the world outside fades until there's nothing left but us. After a few minutes, she looks at me. Meaningfully.

I haven't had sex in a car for a long time, but I think I'm still limber enough. I release the seat back until it's almost completely horizontal. I unbutton my fly and pull my pants down to my thighs. My cock stands straight. "It's all yours to do with as you please."

She takes it in her hands and strokes me. I relax into her touch. "So many options."

She licks the head, and I have to shut my eyes to keep from shooting my load down her throat. The heat of the moment, combined with the thrill of the unknown, heightens every sensation. The feel of her hand on my cock, stroking me to the near-bursting point, is almost too much to bear. I grip the headrest behind me, my fingers digging into the leather as I try to maintain some semblance of control.

"Ginny," I groan, a plea and a warning all at once. "You're killing me."

When I open my eyes she looks up at me, and I know she's feeling it too. Slowly, she moves up to brush her lips against mine, her hand never stopping its ministrations. "I told you...not tonight." Her voice is a husky whisper against my skin.

Unable to resist any longer, I wrap my fingers in her wild hair and guide her mouth down onto me. She moans over me, a primal sound that sends shivers down my spine. Her warm, wet mouth envelops me, her tongue swirling around my tip before she takes me in until I'm hitting the back of her throat.

"Fuck!" I exclaim. My hips buck involuntarily as she begins to bob up and down, expertly alternating between long strokes and teasing flicks with her tongue.

I've always known Ginny had a way of making the mundane extraordinary, but this—this is something else entirely. The car feels too small, too confined for the intensity blossoming between us. I can barely think straight as I watch her, entranced by her confidence, the way she relishes her task.

"Damn," I breathe, gripping the seat tighter.

Her gaze flickers up to meet mine, and she speeds up, driving me toward the edge. I fight to keep my composure as the rhythm of her mouth destroys everything rational in me.

"This is..." I can't finish the thought as she swallows, sending a wave of pleasure crashing over me. I know I'm close. Too close. "Ginny! Slow down...please." That last part slips out not as a command but as a plea for mercy, yet it only broadens her mischievous smile.

"Oh, but Paradise," she teases, leaving me gasping for breath. "I thought you liked it fast."

Before I can respond, she dives back down, taking me in completely, and I feel myself unraveling. My body betrays me as I lose control, a rush of heat surging through my veins.

"God...Ginny!" My voice cracks, struggling against the tide of bliss washing over me.

Before I make an ass of myself, I pull her off, reach for my wallet in the center console, and pull out a condom. "I only have one."

"Challenge accepted." She gives me a salacious smile.

"You sure?" My voice is rough. I don't want to stop. But I want to be fair to her as well.

When she nods, I roll on the condom, but for one fragile second, I hesitate. Despite everything we've said, this feels like more. Like a promise I can't take back. I lift her onto my lap and push up into her.

As she envelops me, a jolt of electricity courses through

my body. She sinks down slowly, and I can barely contain my groan as she stretches around me. The sensation is overwhelming, a mix of heat and pressure that sends my head spinning.

"God," I whisper, gripping her hips as she settles fully, her warmth an abyss I never want to escape.

Her eyes sparkle with mischief. "You okay there?"

"More than okay," I manage. "You feel incredible."

With a wicked smile, she begins to move, gradually picking up the pace. Each rise and fall sends shockwaves through me, through both of us, based on the look on her face.

I'm lost to the moment as she rides me with abandon. The car rocks slightly with our fervent movements, and she runs her hands over my chest, nails grazing my skin, leaving trails of fire in their wake.

"Harder," she gasps, and that single command unleashes something primal inside of me. I grip her waist tightly and thrust upward, meeting her descent with force.

The sound of skin slapping against skin fills the enclosed space, and her eyes roll back in pleasure. Each thrust drives me deeper into the haze until all I can think about is the way her body moves against mine, how perfectly we fit together.

"Just like that," she gasps. "Don't stop."

I grip her hips, feeling the tension build with every thrust. "I'm close," I warn her, struggling to keep my voice steady.

"Me too," she manages between gasps, her walls tightening around me.

My heart races as I feel that familiar edge approaching. With one final thrust, I push us over the precipice. Fire ignites in my core as I release inside her, filling the condom with everything we've built up in this cocoon of pleasure.

"Ryker!" she cries, her climax crashing over her. Her body convulses around me, squeezing tightly as she rides out the waves of ecstasy.

I pull her close as we come down from the high, our breaths mingling in the confined space. She rests her head on my chest. "I want you to come home with me."

"That's playing with fire," she warns.

I rake a hand through my hair, still tasting her on my tongue. I know it's a bad idea. But I still want her, and I hate how much that truth burns.

My phone pings, and I ignore it. But then come several more consecutive pings.

"You're blowing up," Ginny teases.

I reach for my phone.

Greyson: It's a boy!

Greyson: Theodore John Paradise, born at 8:12 p.m., 8 lbs. 1 oz.

Greyson: Trinity was amazing, and both are doing great.

A grin cracks through my haze. "Another generation of Paradises is born. Greyson and Trinity had their baby."

Ginny smiles, but it doesn't quite reach her eyes. "Sounds like you're going to the hospital."

I nod, but the moment stretches, heavy with everything we aren't saying.

If this were something else, I'd take her with me. But instead I'll repay her kindness by abruptly dropping her off. She gave me exactly what I needed tonight.

ELEVEN

Ryker

The Paradise family has spent the whole weekend focused on baby Theo. Greyson and Trinity are exhausted but glowing, and I can't blame them. Theo is perfect. I've checked him over a dozen times. That's the perk of being a pediatrician in the family. He's strong, healthy, and stubborn already. He's going to do great in this world.

Now, with a new week started and the new-baby haze fading — at least for me — I head to the vineyard after my morning in the clinic. I've come looking for Tarryn. I want her opinion about coming out about Ginny. But I've checked the tasting room, the office, and even the damned bottling line, but Tarryn's nowhere to be found. *Figures*. The one time I actually need to talk to her — really talk to her — she's vanished.

I duck into the barrel hall. It's cooler here, though the air is thick with humidity. Rows of barrels stretch out like a maze, the lights overhead casting long shadows that make everything feel more cavernous than it is.

My boots echo off the concrete as I cut through toward the vat room. If she's not checking barrels, maybe she circled back to sample progress from the new steel tanks. Tarryn's meticulous like that. Always chasing perfection. But as I reach the threshold, it's not her voice I hear.

It's Dad and Max.

I pause just inside the doorway, staying in the shadows for a beat. They're hunched over one of the large fermentation tanks, wine thief in hand, glasses on the metal worktable beside them. Max's posture is tight, irritated. He's in a mood, arms waving like he's swatting at flies only he can see.

"It's not balanced," Max says. "You can't bottle it like this."

Dad takes a slow sip, swirling his glass like he's got all the time in the world. "It's evolving. Give it time."

"If Tarryn blended it, I trust her palate." I smirk and stand against the doorframe, arms crossed. Same fight, different vintage.

Max looks over, his gaze narrowing. "Look who decided to show up."

I lift a brow. "Didn't realize I was expected." I nod toward the glass in his hand. "That the new syrah?"

Dad motions me over. "Try it. See what you think."

He pours me a taste, just enough to coat the glass. I swirl, sniff, take a sip.

It's young. A little sharp on the finish. Not quite ready, but the bones are there. Good structure. Fruit's forward. A little more time and it'll open up beautifully.

"Tarryn's work?" I ask.

Dad nods. "She adjusted the percentages two weeks ago."

Max's jaw tightens. "She's not infallible."

"No," I agree, letting the wine roll across my tongue one more time before swallowing. "But she's winning awards for her blends."

Dad sighs and pinches the bridge of his nose like we're giving him a migraine. "Enough. Jesus. We're supposed to be making wine, not fighting with each other."

I take another slow sip, just to annoy Max.

He scowls, but he doesn't say anything else. Probably knows he's outnumbered, or maybe he senses I'm not in the mood to trade jabs. My thoughts are already moving back to the reason I came. Tarryn's not in here either. Which means I need to move on.

I set the glass down. "Have either of you seen Tarryn?"

Dad nods toward the back doors. "She took off toward the lake as we got here. Said she needed some air."

Of course. The one direction I didn't try. Classic Tarryn — the water always makes it right.

I give a nod. "All right. Thanks. I'll go find her."

Max scoffs. "What's so important you need her now?"

I look back at him, but I don't answer. It's not his business. And frankly, I wouldn't trust him to hold my water bottle during a jog. He's been lingering around the vineyard more than usual lately, sniffing around reports and asking questions, like he's suddenly interested in how things run. It doesn't sit right. He's supposed to be on the way out.

Dad's still watching me too. Not suspicious exactly, just curious. His brow pulls together, like he's trying to read the subtext.

I head out before he can say anything else.

As I step outside, the sun disappears behind a bank of clouds, and the air is crisp with that early-spring chill. The cold works its way under my collar, and I pull my jacket tighter. I shove my hands in my pockets and head toward the lake.

Once I get closer, the wind comes off the water hard, tugging at the trees, slipping icy fingers down the back of my shirt. I duck my head and keep going, passing the equipment shed with its old line of tractors and rusting sprayers we never quite get around to replacing. There's a faded orange Kubota that still runs but smells like oil and regret. I step around it and follow the edge of the building, using it to block the wind.

But then I hear a voice.

I slow my steps and angle toward the side of the barn, keeping to the shadowed edge where a stack of old harvest crates blocks the view. The wind whistles through the metal siding, masking the sound of my boots as I edge closer.

It's Zach.

He's tucked just behind the corner of the shed, one hand braced against the weathered frame, the other clutching a phone to his ear. He's talking fast, his voice low but urgent. "I'm telling you, it's a liability issue," he says. "If it gets out, the entire operation's at risk."

I freeze.

Operation? Liability? *What is he up to?*

He glances over his shoulder, paranoid, like he can feel eyes on him. I shrink back into the shadows, heart thudding against my ribs. He doesn't see me.

"I'm not saying it was sabotage," Zach argues, voice tight. "But it doesn't look good." A pause. "If someone saw it…" his voice dips. "Yeah, I know, but it wasn't supposed to go this far." Another pause. "No, I didn't say anything. I've kept my mouth shut. But if they find out—"

Silence again. Then, almost reluctantly, he says, "Fine. I'll handle it. But this is the last time."

I pull in a breath and hold it as he ends the call and shoves the phone into his back pocket. He stands there a second, muttering under his breath and kicking the gravel. But he's pale. Shaky. Whatever this is, it's enough to rattle him, and Zach's not easily rattled.

I take a step back, then another, moving carefully around the crates until I'm out of sight. Only then do I let myself breathe.

My pulse is pounding, adrenaline rushing through me with nowhere to go. I came here looking for my sister. Now, I feel like I've stumbled into something I have to decipher. I don't know who Zach was talking to. I don't know what operation he meant, or what he's worried about being discovered.

But I know this wasn't harmless venting.

If we're talking contamination, misreporting, liability...this isn't just a family problem. It's a business-ending kind of problem. A legal one. And if Max is involved? That takes it to another level.

I keep walking toward the lake, but my pace has slowed. My mind's not on finding Tarryn anymore. Not fully. It's back behind that barn, stuck on Zach's voice.

Whatever it is, he's hiding it. And that alone is a problem. But it's more than that. He's scared. And if Zach's scared, this isn't some clerical error or harvest misstep. This is something worse.

I round the bend in the path that snakes toward the lake. The wind kicks harder here, sweeping up the slope. The lake glints like polished steel beneath the clouded sky, waves choppy against the dock.

I spot Tarryn standing at the lake's edge, her figure still and small against the vastness of the water. She's got her arms wrapped around herself, chin tucked down against the wind. She doesn't move when I approach.

"You look like you're trying to get pneumonia," I say, stopping a few feet back.

She glances over her shoulder. "Did you see Dad?"

"Yeah. And Max." I step up beside her, breath misting in the air. "Still arguing about the syrah like it's the end of the world."

"Sometimes, Max's criticism is too much."

"I'm sorry. I tasted it, and it was young, but I think it'll be excellent."

She nods, and we stand in silence, the wind swirling around us.

I came out here to talk to her. I still want to. But now, I don't know where to start.

Do I tell her about Ginny, or do I tell her what I just heard behind the barn, that Zach's covering something up and it might already be too late? She's already out here by herself. Maybe she doesn't need to be burdened with either right now.

She tips her head toward me, probably reading something in my posture. "Are you okay?"

I shrug. "Define okay."

"That bad?"

I let out a long breath and stare out at the restless waves. "I came to see you today to talk to you about...Ginny."

Tarryn lifts a brow. "Oh?"

"Yeah." I rake a hand through my hair. "We've been...sort of seeing each other."

Her other brow joins the first. "Zach was right. And here I thought you were just learning the fine art of subtle longing."

I huff a laugh. "It's complicated."

Tarryn crosses her arms. "Dating a Dempsey? Complicated? Color me shocked."

I smirk despite myself. "It's more than complicated, actually. It's risky — to her, to me, to the whole family."

She narrows her eyes, not out of judgment, more like calculation. "So why are you telling me and not Dad, who can protect you from Max? Because we all know that's who the problem is."

I shift my weight, staring down at the dock's worn planks. "Because I needed to tell someone who wouldn't immediately call me a dumbass or run to Dad so I can hear a lecture about optics and fallout." I look over. "And because I think I really like her. She's sharp, honest, impossible to pin down, and she doesn't care that I'm a Paradise. Or at least she doesn't want to." I rake my hands through my hair. "This is dangerous for her as well, but she sees past the name, the legacy. She sees me. And I didn't realize how much I needed that."

Tarryn's quiet for a moment. The breeze lifts a strand of her hair, and she tucks it behind her ear. "Then hold on tight. Because if she's the one, she's worth fighting for, especially when it gets messy."

I nod slowly. That's helpful. I'm glad to hear her say that, to have at least one of my siblings on my side. So that should feel more clear. And I think it would have, before Zach.

I chew the inside of my cheek, pulse kicking up again. "There's something else. I overheard Zach on the phone on my way out here. Behind the barn. He was hiding, whispering. Said something about liability and how it's not supposed to be like this. He agreed to take care of something one more time."

Tarryn's brows pinch together. "You think it's related to the issues in block nine?"

"I don't know. Maybe." I shake my head. "It didn't sound small. He said, 'It doesn't look good'."

Tarryn turns toward me, her stance stiff. "What doesn't look good?"

"I don't know. It seems like he's doing something for someone."

Her gaze drifts back to the lake, but I can tell she's running calculations behind her eyes. "You think it's Max?" she asks. "I also wouldn't be surprised if Zach was involved in that mess with the Tremblays that Sadie got mixed up in last summer."

"I guess betting money he doesn't have would be up Zach's alley." I shrug. "I don't know who'd scare him into silence, though."

"Zach doesn't scare easy," she agrees. "He's a lot of things, but not panicky. If he's scared —" She breaks off and exhales sharply. "This could get ugly for the vineyard. His last name is Paradise, and whatever he does affects all of us."

"Already feels ugly," I say. "And I don't know what to do with it."

Tarryn nods, her lips pressed into a thin line. "No one else hears about it until we know more, okay?"

"Agreed."

She hesitates, then adds, "And Ryker?"

I raise my eyebrows.

"If you're serious about Ginny, be careful. And not just because of the family crap. Sadie told me she moved home after a nasty breakup. If she's not ready, there might be no path forward for you."

"I know." I nod. "Believe me, I know."

Tarryn rests her shoulder against mine, her face sharp with worry. "We need to keep our eyes open," she says quietly, like the wind might carry her voice too far.

"Okay."

I came out here looking for clarity. A sense of direction. Instead, I'm walking away with more questions than I started with.

But at least now I'm not holding them alone.

TWELVE

Ginny

The next Saturday morning, there's a knock at my door long before the sun even thinks about rising.

I crack it open, squinting into the dark. Ryker stands on my porch, grinning like it's noon and not an ungodly hour of the morning. He's here to pick me up for the airport, and he's a morning person. I hate morning people.

"Good," he says, stepping inside without waiting for an invitation. "You're awake and dressed. I was worried I'd have to carry you to the car. Not that I'd mind."

"I'm barely conscious," I mumble. "Flirt later. Coffee first."

He holds up two cups. "Already handled. One's black, one's sugary and sinful. I wasn't sure which version of you I was getting."

I snatch the sugary one like it's a life raft. "The one who

doesn't speak full sentences until caffeine hits."

Ryker moves closer, his voice low and annoyingly chipper. "Guess I'll have to find other ways to wake you up."

I narrow my eyes. "Try that before I've had coffee, and I'll throw this at you."

He chuckles, taking a sip from his own cup. "You say that like it's not part of the thrill."

I roll my eyes, but the coffee's already working its magic. My shoulders loosen. My brain starts catching up.

I slip on my shoes by the door and reach for my overnight bag. Ryker grabs it before I can.

"I've got it," he says.

"Chivalry before sunrise. Impressive."

He holds the door open for me, and I step out into what cannot possibly be the morning. The stars are still out, the world quiet in that sacred, sleepy way.

As we walk toward his SUV, he glances over. "I know you're tired, but are you okay?"

The question is gentle. Not prying. Just…there.

I nod, then shake my head. "I don't know. It's weird. Vancouver used to be— My whole future was there. And now, I'm going back for dresses and Champagne toasts and pretending it doesn't sting."

Ryker's hand brushes mine. "You don't have to pretend with me."

The words fill me with warmth. "I know," I whisper.

It's quiet as we climb into the SUV, and I rest my head against the window. But now, I don't feel like I'm heading into something alone.

We pick up Tarryn next, and she's exactly as expected at five in the morning—fresh-faced, perfectly dressed, and carrying the largest monogrammed travel mug I've ever seen. She's got caffeine for days.

She slides into the backseat with the grace of someone who's never tripped over a power cord or panicked while packing. "You're late," she says, even though we're not. "I had time to finish my serum routine *and* clean out my inbox."

Ryker groans. "Remind me why I'm voluntarily spending a weekend with you?"

"Because I'm delightful," Tarryn says sweetly.

We pull into short-term parking at the airport just as the first blush of sunrise hits the mountains. Sadie's already there, standing outside the terminal with her suitcase, bouncing slightly on her toes.

She beams when she sees us. "Oh my God, we're doing this! We're actually doing this!"

I manage a smile, but my heart pulls tight. *Vancouver.* I remind myself again that it's a big city. I'm not going to run into anyone I know. The odds are microscopic. Practically nonexistent.

Still, as we all walk toward the terminal, I keep my head down and my hood up, just in case.

Sadie throws her arms around me anyway. "Thanks for coming," she says into my shoulder. "Really."

I hug her back. "Wouldn't miss it."

And for a moment, I let that be true. This trip is about her. And maybe it's also about me moving forward. I shouldn't be scared to go to Vancouver. I did nothing wrong.

The flight isn't even long enough for beverage service, but that doesn't stop Tarryn from treating it like a red-eye to Paris.

She drops into the window seat beside me, pops in her noise-canceling earbuds, and slides on a silk sleep mask. "Wake me when we land," she mumbles.

Within thirty seconds, she's dead to the world, exuding luxury and mild judgment even in unconsciousness.

I glance across the aisle. Ryker's watching me with a smirk, like he's been waiting for the moment Tarryn checked out.

"You two bunking together?" he asks, tipping his chin toward the sleeping beauty next to me.

"Yes," I whisper. "But she's probably packed six outfits for a two-day trip. I can't compete with that kind of energy."

"That's too bad. It would have been more fun sneaking

around without being caught." He chuckles, and then moves in slightly. "So...be honest. You think Beckett and Sadie are trying to join the mile-high club back there?"

I glance over my shoulder. They're seated directly behind us, whispering and smiling like no one else exists.

"Probably," I say without hesitation. "She's been glowing since she got to the airport. They may already be members, or they're applying for elite status."

Ryker laughs, and I feel it skitter down my spine. "I mean, if they're in, we might as well give them credit for the referral," he murmurs, eyes glinting.

"Keep dreaming," I say, sipping my water like it's spiked.

"I do," he says, looking at me.

I roll my eyes.

The flight is over in a blink. One minute we're crossing the Strait of Georgia and the next the wheels touch down with a thump and a short bounce that startles Tarryn awake.

She lifts her sleep mask with a sigh. "Did I miss anything interesting?"

"How could anything interesting happen when you're asleep?" I ask. "So...no."

Two black SUVs wait for us outside baggage claim, polished and silent and probably stocked with bottled water and breath mints.

Beckett gestures vaguely toward one. "The guys can take this one," he says. "We're going to...check something out."

"Golf," Ryker adds, entirely too casual.

Tarryn narrows her eyes. "Golf? As in grass, balls, and bad fashion in the rain?"

"Exactly that," Beckett says, already opening the car door. He gives Sadie a quick kiss. "We'll meet you back at the hotel tonight."

"Suspicious," Tarryn mutters as the guys climb in and disappear like a pair of overgrown golden retrievers.

I shrug. "At least we get the fun part."

"Damn right we do," she says, linking her arm through

mine and high-fiving Sadie. "Let's find Sadie a dream dress and me something that says 'sexy, supportive sister-in-law, and I'm available.'"

I laugh as we climb into our own car, bridal bags and coffee orders ahead of us, and absolutely no sign of our past behind us.

Not yet, anyway.

The bell above the door jingles as we step into Aimee's Bridal. Sadie has a long list of appointments this morning, and this is the one she's most excited about.

The store is scented with lavender, soft music plays from hidden speakers, and everything—from the curved racks of gowns to the tufted chairs and pale pink walls—feels like stepping into a cloud. A very expensive, mostly white cloud.

"This is the place," Sadie says, her eyes sparkling. "I called Aimee last week. She has the dress." She takes my hand. "The one that looks like something a ballerina would wear."

"It's very poofy," I confirm. She's had the picture saved on her phone for weeks now—a massive tulle skirt, soft sparkle, and sweetheart neckline. It's pure magic. Or so she thinks.

Aimee greets us, warm and bubbly, like an old friend you actually want to run into. "You must be Sadie," she says, taking her hands. "I pulled the dress this morning. It's even better in person."

She leads us into a private dressing room the size of my childhood bedroom. A soft blush rug covers the floor, and the three-way mirror looks like it belongs in a royal dressing suite. I settle into a tufted chair just outside the curtain while Sadie disappears inside with Aimee.

Moments later, the curtain rustles.

Sadie steps out, and my breath catches—for all the wrong reasons.

Oh. No.

The massive tulle skirt overwhelms her. The bodice squeezes her large bust, and the girls look like they're about to pop. Her face says it all before she even opens her mouth.

"Is it everything you hoped for?" Aimee asks, her voice full of cheer.

"Um…" Sadie manages, smoothing the skirt over her hips, hips that now appear to rival a small tractor. "Just…give me a second."

Tarryn's jaw drops, but not in awe. I try to cover my reaction, but I know my eyebrows give me away.

"Oh," I say carefully. "It's very…fluffy."

"I look like a cupcake," Sadie laments, turning toward the mirror with a sigh.

Tarryn tilts her head, trying to find something redeemable. "Like a…generously frosted one?"

Sadie laughs, but it's halfway to a sigh.

The dress she's obsessed over makes her look like she's been swallowed by a bridal piñata. It's not the one. Not even close.

She turns again, catching the full three-sixty view in the mirror near the platform. The bodice pinches just enough to create rolls she doesn't have, and the skirt? Less romantic ballroom, more runaway pastry cart.

"I look like I weigh three hundred pounds." Sadie sounds like she's going to cry.

I wince. "Maybe it's the angle?"

"It's not the angle," she deadpans.

Aimee, bless her, doesn't argue. She simply disappears and returns with another dozen options. Tarryn jumps in like she's starring in her own *Say Yes to the Dress* spin-off.

A sleek off-the-shoulder gown catches Sadie's eye first. She slips into it, and when she steps out, there's a collective hush. It's elegant—simple lines, structured fabric, a subtle shimmer when she moves. Red-carpet-worthy.

But it's not her.

She keeps tugging at the neckline, unsure whether she's supposed to feel sexy or strangled.

I can tell the moment she decides. It's a beautiful dress...just not her dress.

Next is a lace-covered gown that clings in some places and floats in others. It has long illusion sleeves and tiny pearl buttons that trail all the way down the back. The train fans out like something from a storybook. I feel like I should be barefoot in the forest, carrying wildflowers, reciting vows under an arch made of driftwood.

"It's giving off woodland elf vibe," I say.

"Sexy elf," Tarryn corrects, popping a chocolate-covered almond into her mouth.

"Still not it." Sadie sighs.

And then—

"This one," Tarryn says, holding up a gown like it's Excalibur.

It's fitted all the way down, mermaid style, with a dramatic flare at the hem and delicate beading that catches the lights. "Just trust me."

Sadie hesitates.

It's the kind of dress that leaves nothing to the imagination. It's going to cling like it was poured on.

She crosses her arms. "That's a lot of dress."

I grin. "You won't know until you try."

Back in the dressing room, Sadie shimmies into it slowly, carefully, letting the fabric slide over her skin. She reports that it's heavier than she expects—thick and structured, like armor and lingerie had a secret lovechild.

The dress hugs every inch of her—hips, waist, chest—like it was made just for her. Her curves are front and center. The neckline dips low, but not too low, and the beading catches the light like a constellation stitched across her skin.

Still, when she steps out, her arms fold instinctively. "It's too tight," she says. "I look like I'm worried Beckett is going to dump me."

Tarryn scoffs. "You look like a knockout."

"I look like white trash playing dress-up."

I roll my eyes. "You're a bride who knows what she wants. Which, for the record, is rarer than a groom who remembers to RSVP."

Sadie glances back at the mirror, uncertain.

The silhouette is dramatic. Bold. It demands attention. It's nothing like the poofy princess dress she thought she wanted, but somehow…it works. She looks fierce. Feminine. Strong.

From the corner, Aimee smiles. "You're glowing."

Sadie doesn't argue. She presses a hand to her stomach. It's not nerves. Not doubt. It's…something else. "I don't hate it," she says, voice low.

Tarryn claps. "Okay! We're documenting the moment. Hold still. Or don't. Actually, twirl."

She spends the next ten minutes snapping every possible angle of Sadie on the platform. High angles, low angles, over-the-shoulder, mirror shots, laughing shots, dreamy gazes. By the time she's done, Sadie has blushed a deep pink.

"We've got other appointments," Sadie says with a last look in the mirror. "We should keep moving. I still have to get out of this thing. I'm not going to forget what it looks like, though," she calls over her shoulder with a laugh as she returns to the curtained area with Aimee.

Once Sadie has returned to her street wear, we grab lattes from the café next door and walk a few doors down to Bisou, a boutique so chic it makes Aimee's feel like a mall store. Tucked between a vegan bakery and a luxury consignment shop, Bisou smells like white roses and money, the kind of place where you don't ask for prices. You just whisper yes and pray your credit card doesn't burst into flames.

Tarryn's in her element the second we step inside. She starts flipping through racks with the bridal stylist assigned to Sadie. "This. This. Definitely this."

She hands me half a dozen gowns, and the stylist immediately takes them to the dressing room. The boutique only carries sample sizes—meaning they're designed for someone who hasn't eaten since 2017. None of them are actually going to zip around Sadie.

In the dressing room, Sadie stands under fluorescent lights in her bra and underwear, surrounded by lace and satin somehow molded to her body with a complex system of pins and clips. From the back, she looks like a puzzle someone gave up on halfway through. But from the front...

Her mouth falls open as she stares at herself in the mirror. Her eyes get a faraway look, but then I watch her reel herself back in. She turns and takes in the rear of the dress. "I look like a toddler playing dress-up."

I peek in from the side and snort. "A toddler with a killer rack."

She twists, trying to see all angles at once.

"Obviously they'll get you one that fits correctly," I point out as a clip pops loose and a flap of silk droops over her hip. She still looks amazing. "You just have to use your imagination for a moment."

Tarryn pops her head in through the curtain like a proud stage mom. "It's couture. You look fantastic."

Sadie groans. "I look like I'm trying too hard."

"That's the point," Tarryn says with a shrug. "Trying too hard means you care."

Sadie raises an eyebrow. "Or it makes people think I'm marrying Beckett for the money."

Tarryn smirks. "Please. That dress says you belong at his side, not because of what he has, but because of who you are. Do you like it?"

After a moment, Sadie nods, almost as if she's embarrassed to admit it.

In an instant, Tarryn's dialing her phone.

"Tarryn, don't—" Sadie hisses, but it's too late.

She angles the screen toward us like she's unveiling the

next contestant on *The Bachelorette.*

And there she is. Vicky Paradise, in full midday Saturday glory.

"Mom," Tarryn coos, "tell me Sadie doesn't look drop-dead in this."

Sadie stands awkwardly in the center of the dressing room, surrounded by three-way mirrors and a sea of abandoned tulle. The dress she's wearing makes her look radiant. Not like the ballerina princess she thought she wanted to be, but something infinitely more sophisticated and fabulous. This dress is *her*, even if she doesn't quite believe it yet.

She waves shyly at the screen. "Hi, Vicky."

Vicky's eyes light up. "Oh, sweetheart," she croons. "You're stunning. That neckline? Divine. Your figure? Perfection. You look like a *Vogue* editorial."

Sadie blushes and glances at me like she's not sure what to do with the compliment. Vicky is a force, the kind of woman who can pack a fundraiser hall, calm a room full of parents, and diagnose a toddler on sight. She makes you feel lucky just to be standing in her orbit.

"She does look amazing," Tarryn agrees, smug as ever. "And wait until you hear the best part. This baby is just forty-two thousand dollars."

Sadie seems to choke on air. *"What?"*

My eyes widen, but Tarryn nods. Yep. Forty-two thousand. Not including alterations. Or emotional trauma.

Forty-two thousand dollars.

I swallow hard, trying not to let my expression crack. I've always known the Paradise family had more money than my family, but this is *a lot* more money. Their whole world is polished and bright and expensive. I know what it's like to make something priceless. But I've never felt less valuable.

Tarryn grins like a game show host unveiling a luxury prize package.

Vicky doesn't even blink. "Well, of course it is. That lace is handmade. See the detail along the bodice? And those pearls are

South Sea. Very rare, very elegant. I'd love to buy it for you, Sadie. It would be my honor. You'll be absolutely radiant walking down the aisle in it."

Sadie's mouth opens, then closes. She fidgets, fingers toying with a clip near her hip as she looks in the mirror again. "I just… I don't know what people are going to say."

"That you look like a goddess," Tarryn responds, fussing with the train.

Vicky's tone shifts, the glamour fading into something softer. "I was very close with your mother. You know that. And I know she'd want you to have this. She would've loved this dress for you."

This is a dress that will be worn once. It's more than some people make in a year, more than Sadie used to make in a year. I can see how acutely aware of that she is. But I'm pretty sure bringing up her mom did the trick.

The room goes still. Sadie's gaze drops to the floor. Her arms fold around her waist, not like she's hiding, but like she's holding herself together. When she finally looks up, her eyes are glassy.

"Okay," she whispers. "Yeah. Okay. I would love to wear this dress. Thank you."

Tarryn lets out a squeal and throws her arms in the air. "We have a dress!"

Sadie blinks like she's still in a daze but then smiles. It's soft, but real.

And for once, I don't roll my eyes at the drama. Because, in that moment, everything feels right. I have to smile too. This? Every second it took to get here and every second in Vancouver was worth it. This is what it's about.

The magic, the memories, and the people who remind you that you deserve them.

Then, as if someone flipped a switch, the attention turns to Tarryn and me.

"We still need a dress for the maid of honor," Tarryn declares with a dramatic sweep of her hand, "and one for me."

But suddenly I'm not thinking about the dress or the Champagne or the room full of mirrors. I'm thinking about Ryker. And how being here, surrounded by dresses and promises, makes me realize how much of my heart I've opened to him, without noticing until now.

THIRTEEN

Ginny

After spending most of the day in and out of bridal shops, we have three dresses ordered—one for Sadie, one for Tarryn, and one for me. When we finally get back to the hotel, my cheeks hurt from smiling, and my head is pounding from too much caffeine and too many opinions. There's only so much tulle a girl can take in one day.

Tarryn stretches like a cat the second the elevator doors close behind us. "I need a hot bath, a bottle of wine, and a nap. I didn't sleep at all last night."

Sadie yawns behind her hand. "I'm crashing too, and Beckett and I have dinner plans with one of his medical school friends."

They're already halfway into planning tomorrow's boutique list and arguing about napkin colors again by the time we reach our room.

"Do you have a preference?" Tarryn points to the two queen-size beds, and I shake my head.

She opens her bag and brings out her noise-canceling headphones and her sleep mask. "Don't worry about me. I can sleep through anything."

She lies down, and I'm stuck trying to figure out what I want to do. Though it's probably the safest place for me, I don't want to stay in the room.

I grab my key card and scoot out the door. I've always loved the hotel bar here. They make my favorite gin and tonic. It's purple.

Downstairs, Prophecy is dim and cozy, all low lighting and velvet booths—the kind of place where people keep their voices low and their distance respectable. The bartender doesn't ask questions.

Perfect.

Exactly what I need.

I slide into a booth in the back corner, as far from the main area as I can get without actually hiding behind the liquor shelf. The velvet upholstery sinks beneath me as I settle in and tug my sweater around my ribs like armor. I let out a long breath.

For a full minute, I don't move. I just sit.

I let the low hum of conversation wash over me, the soft clink of glassware, the occasional rustle of a cocktail napkin or a laugh from another booth.

No more dresses, no more decisions. Just ice in a glass and a quiet stretch of space that's all mine.

I pull out my phone and stare at Ryker's name, thumb hovering.

I told him we'd found dresses earlier after he sent a picture of him and Beckett standing with a medical school friend and his brother.

I tap out a message.

Me: At the bar in the hotel—Prophecy. Tarryn's

sleeping.

Three dots appear almost instantly, then vanish.

Then reappear.

Then vanish again.

Before the message comes through, the server sets a tall glass in front of me. An Empress gin and tonic, extra lime. Clean, crisp, and exactly the way I ordered it.

I take a long sip, savoring the cold bite and the way it spreads through my body like a slow exhale.

"Ginny?"

I freeze. The voice is familiar—and one I never wanted to hear again. I look up, and there she is.

Jill.

Of course.

Perfect hair, glossy and curled just enough to look effortless. Perfect skin, lightly bronzed and not a pore in sight. Perfect teeth in that perfect smile that once made me feel lucky to be her friend.

And she proudly doesn't work weekends, which made me think it was safe to come down here. My stomach nosedives, taking the rest of me with it. Every muscle locks, fight or flight thrumming in my blood.

"Wow, it is you!" she says like she's spotted me at a farmer's market and not blindsided me in the place I came to be alone. She walks over without hesitation, all sunshine and fake sincerity, and plants a manicured hand on the edge of my table like we're catching up after yoga and brunch.

I sit up straighter, my heart pounding behind my ribs. "Jill."

She has the audacity to look genuinely happy to see me. "Oh my God, you look amazing. I've been meaning to reach out again. I know I already apologized, but... Seriously, I never meant for things to happen that way."

Sure you didn't. You just happened to fall on top of my fiancé naked and repeatedly.

"I was promoted to head of sales, and I'm working a party this evening," she says like we're old friends bumping into each other on vacation.

I don't respond. I don't trust myself to.

"What brings you to the Rosewood?" she asks brightly.

I open my mouth, trying to keep my tone neutral. "I'm here wedding dress shopping—"

But I don't get to finish.

Because a warm presence slides into the booth across from me, calm and confident, his cologne familiar and grounding.

Ryker.

He doesn't say anything. Just settles in, one arm draping across the back of the booth. Like he's been here the whole time.

And for a second, I'm stunned into silence because he came. Right now, that feels like the most important thing in the world.

I blink, startled and weirdly relieved. "Hey."

He nods in greeting, then turns his head toward Jill. "Hi there."

She falters for a half-second, clearly not expecting anyone to join me, let alone someone like him. Ryker's presence is the kind that fills a room. Strong jaw, broad shoulders, voice like low thunder when he speaks.

"Oh," I say quickly, pushing past the lump in my throat. "Ryker, this is Jill. Jill, this is Ryker Paradise."

Jill's perfectly sculpted brows lift, her eyes narrowing with interest. "Paradise? Like those Paradises?"

He tilts his head, lips curving in a slow, almost teasing smile. "Probably."

Her expression shifts instantly from surprise to recognition to something resembling approval. And something else. Calculation, perhaps. Can she fall on him over and over too?

She turns back to me with a little gleam in her eye, like we're sharing some delicious secret. "I'm so happy for you. Engaged already? Wow. That was fast."

My lips part, confusion flickering. "What?"

She waves a hand between Ryker and me like she's connecting dots that don't exist. "You two. I just assumed since you're wedding dress shopping…"

I freeze. My mind races for a reply, something to defuse the implication without giving her more power. But before I can open my mouth, Ryker's voice slides across the table.

"She's got that whole ethereal-glow thing going on," he says. "Hard not to notice."

"I just went shopping myself." Jill casually extends her hand, and there it is, the ring Jeremy gave me. The one I hurled at him when I caught them together.

"You and Jeremy?" I croak.

"Yes. We haven't set a date yet, but he kept asking, so I finally gave in."

"Congratulations."

"You better protect yourself," Ryker says, looking right at her. "Jeremy has a habit of sleeping with his fiancée's best friends."

Jill stiffens like she's been slapped.

Her mouth falls open, and I turn to her with a saccharine-sweet smile.

Then Ryker reaches across the table, lacing his fingers with mine. His thumb strokes the back of my hand and just like that, I feel anchored. I glance at him and smile, the real kind, full of quiet gratitude. I'm so damn glad he's here with me.

Recovering, Jill clears her throat and pastes on a smile. "Well, I'm sure you're over all that." Her gaze moves back to Ryker, sharpening like a hawk's. "I mean, Jeremy and I — We're in love."

Ryker doesn't react. Doesn't even blink.

I lift my glass and offer the most hollow toast of my life. "Congratulations," I say. Calm. Neutral. Perfectly polite. Because the last thing I'll give her is the satisfaction of knowing she still gets under my skin.

Jill takes a small breath and straightens her shoulders, trying to reclaim the moment. "Drinks are on me," she announces like she's doing us a favor. "You look like you're a Johnny Walker Blue man. Neat, right?"

Ryker lifts a brow, intrigued. "That sounds good."

Jill always knew everyone's drink. Always knew how to make people feel seen. It was quite a gift before she used that talent like a weapon.

She winks like it's a compliment. "I thought so."

She waves and struts over to the bar in heels that probably cost more than my half of the rent when Jeremy and I lived together. I watch her speak to the bartender, still smiling like she won something. Then she looks over her shoulder and waves one last time.

Then finally, mercifully, she's gone.

I exhale slowly, sinking into the booth like someone just cut the tension wire running down my back.

Ryker looks at me. "You okay?"

The server delivers Ryker's drink.

I nod. "Now I am."

Ryker raises his glass to me, his eyes glittering with mischief. "That was fun."

I glare at him, though it's half-hearted at best. "You just told my ex-best friend we were engaged."

He shrugs, entirely unbothered. "Well, she slept with your fiancé. I figured we were making up stories now."

I press my fingers to my temples and groan. "You're impossible." Then I laugh. I can't help it. Because that felt a little bit like winning. It didn't erase the betrayal or stitch my dignity back together, but it gave me a moment. A small, delicious taste of payback. And Ryker handed it to me like a gift with a smirk and a shot of top-shelf whiskey.

Ryker swirls the Johnny Walker Blue in his glass, slow and deliberate, eyes on me over the rim. That damn panty-melting smirk is back, full force, laced with trouble.

Then he puts his elbows on the table. "So," he says, "if you really want to get even, we could have wild, crazy sex tonight. You know, really sell the fake fiancé story."

I bark out a laugh, though my pulse skips at the idea. It's all banter. All bravado. Except that it's not.

"Is that your idea of support?" I ask, trying for sarcasm, but my voice dips a little.

He shrugs, lazy and self-assured. "Just being a team player."

I tilt my head, studying him. "You think that would help me work through my unresolved emotional trauma?"

He grins. "Absolutely. I have very therapeutic skills. Highly recommended."

I shake my head and pretend to be unimpressed, but my lips betray me. They're already curving. I can feel the tension slipping off my shoulders, replaced with something else. Something electric.

The kind of energy that comes before a kiss that changes things.

"Well then..." I swirl the lime in my drink. "We'll see if you can talk me into it."

His smile shifts, goes from cocky to something darker. Hungrier. "Challenge accepted."

The air between us thickens, and everything else fades — the buzz of the bar, even the sting of old betrayal. All I feel is him. The way his gaze anchors mine. The way his presence settles into me like gravity. Like he's not just sitting across from me, he's already in my blood.

Forget Jill. Forget Jeremy. And forget everything that came before this moment.

Tonight, I'm all about Ryker Paradise. Because fake fiancé or not, he's the only thing going for me in this mess of a weekend.

FOURTEEN

Ryker

I clocked the way her shoulders relaxed the second Jill left the bar. Ginny kept her expression neutral, but I know enough by now to realize it's a mask.

"Tarryn's called it an early night," she says, looking at her phone. "And Beckett and Sadie are off having dinner with a buddy of his from med school. It's just you and me."

I arch a brow. "Dangerous combination."

"Should we take our drinks upstairs?" she asks.

"We could," I say. "But it's stopped raining. Do you want to get out of here? The sun won't set for a bit. Maybe rent a bicycle and ride over to Stanley Park before it gets dark?"

That gets me a real smile, one warm enough to melt the tension in her posture. "Sounds like a date." She fingers her glass and bites her lip.

"You can call it whatever you want," I say, standing and

jerking my chin toward the front door. "Come on. Let's get out of here before someone ropes us into something else."

Ten minutes later, we're outside the Rosewood, helmets in hand, scanning the row of rental bikes.

"I feel like I should warn you," Ginny says, straddling a bright blue cruiser with a basket. "I used to ride the seawall almost daily for my workout, so I take it pretty fast."

"Good," I say, selecting a bike of my own. "I ride like I've got something to prove."

Our transaction complete, we take off through the edge of downtown and snake our way into Stanley Park. The wind off the water is crisp and cool, the city buzzing behind us as we dip into the quiet shade. It's beautiful out here—trees towering overhead, the scent of cedar and ocean mixing in the air, the path curving along the edge of the bay like it was built just for us.

Ginny glances over her shoulder as we ride, her hair whipping in the breeze, and for a second, it's easy to forget all the crap we're trying to outrun. We're just two people. Moving. Laughing. Free. And damn if I don't wish I could freeze time right here.

"Hey!" she calls back. "You still with me, or am I losing you?"

I pedal harder to catch up. "Not a chance. I'm just pacing myself. Wouldn't want to humiliate you."

She laughs, and the sound settles inside me. We follow the curve of the seawall, Ginny just ahead, legs pumping. She points to the seaplanes in the harbor, circling overhead before they skim the surface and land in a spray of water.

"They look like they're barely touching down," she says as we pause, our bikes side by side. "I forgot how majestic it is here."

"Yeah," I say, watching one dip low, wings tipping. "It's like they're dancing."

She glances at me. "That's unexpectedly poetic for you."

I smirk. "I contain multitudes."

She laughs, then pushes off again, calling over her

shoulder, "Race you to the totems!"

Our tires hum against the path. She's fast, faster than I expected, but I've got longer legs and more stubborn pride.

Still, I let her win.

Just barely. She jumps off her bike with her arms raised in victory. "I am the queen of speed."

"Only because I let you be." I brace myself on the handlebars, catching my breath.

She points a finger at me. "Liar."

"Believe what you want," I say. "I was distracted by the view."

She snorts. "Smooth."

We wander toward the collection of towering totem poles nearby, vivid with color and history. She falls quiet, studying each carving with a reverence I hadn't expected, her fingers brushing over the names and stories etched into the plaques.

"They're beautiful," she says. "You ever think about how much these mean to people?"

"You can feel it," I agree. "Like the past is still breathing through them."

She looks over at me, seeming surprised again. "Multitudes."

I grin. "Told you."

We return to our bikes and loop around the park, detouring along the waterfront where couples walk hand in hand, kids zip past on scooters, and the world feels...normal. Peaceful. Like we're a couple whose families haven't hated each other for generations.

"Let's take a picture," she says, pulling her phone from her pocket.

I raise a brow. "You sure? You might want plausible deniability after this afternoon."

She grins. "Just smile, Paradise."

We pose with the harbor and mountains behind us, one with me pretending to fall off my bike, one with her flashing peace signs and sticking out her tongue, and one where I loop my arm around her shoulders and she laughs, leaning into me without even realizing it.

That one's my favorite.

As we scroll through the shots, she shakes her head. "We look like idiots."

"We had fun, so who cares? We're not worried about the Black Bear News running the photo."

"True." She laughs again, eyes squinting from the sun, cheeks flushed. "This was…nice."

"Yeah," I say. "It was."

We're quiet for a second, watching the waves roll in and the city glint gold in the distance.

Then she turns to me and nudges my arm. "So…dinner?"

"A date with food too?"

She rolls her eyes. "Don't push it."

But she's still smiling when we turn our bikes back toward the hotel.

And this time, I don't let her win.

We return our bikes just as the rain starts again, and we scoot into a small noodle house.

"I hate it," Ginny says randomly over dinner.

I'm not sure if she's talking about the girls cackling at the next table, the rain, the traffic, Vancouver. "Hate what?" I ask.

"The gift shop. It feels like a cage." I must still look confused because she adds, "At the vineyard. I feel like I'm dying in there, stocking jam jars and arranging scented candles like it's my life's calling. And any changes I make, my mother comes in and undoes them."

"That's surprising," I say. "I feel like you'd have good ideas."

"My mother doesn't think so." She sighs. "But I do know what works. In the meantime, I know how to fake it. I have a degree in marketing, and I worked four years at a firm I actually liked. But being part of the family business isn't me. What I really love is making jewelry and seeing people wear it."

"So…why'd you leave Vancouver? I get breaking up with

Jeremy, but you didn't have to move home."

She sighs, and I squeeze her hand. "I didn't come back because I missed the vineyard," she says. "I had to leave because I'd made my life all about Jeremy. Jill was my only friend outside of work. His friends were my friends, and I couldn't stay in that situation." Her voice cracks just slightly. "I had nowhere else to go."

My jaw tenses. "That's brutal." I want to go back in time and rip that guy out of her life. She didn't deserve that kind of isolation. No one does. But I know she doesn't want sympathy. So instead, I just give her my time. Without strings, without pressure. Just space to breathe if she wants it. "I'm so sorry, Ginny."

She shrugs, but it's defensive. "Yeah, well. Lucky me. I traded one mess for another."

We're quiet for a second. "You know, I was at the last Black Bear Valley Wine Consortium meeting. They're planning a major expansion, trying to turn the whole region into a destination, like Napa or the Columbia Valley."

Her eyes widen. "Seriously?"

"Dead serious. They're looking for fresh ideas. Smart leadership. I think it's part time, so you could still work on your jewelry business."

She doesn't answer, but her brows draw together like she's already calculating next steps. I let the silence stretch, hoping she fills it with possibility.

After a moment, she looks up. "I know the wine business. And I'm good at marketing. Do you know someone I should talk to?"

"Marc Warner," I tell her. "He's the director. He'd take a meeting. Especially with someone who knows the area and has actual strategy experience."

She kisses my cheek, quick but warm. "Thank you."

We linger over dinner until the plates are cleared and the candles burn low. By the time we step outside, the night air is cool and quiet, and the walk back feels shorter than I want it to.

As we approach the hotel, I grin. "You know, I have my own room."

She lets out a low laugh. "Tarryn would figure it out in about thirty seconds."

"She might," I say. "But she might also understand."

She looks like she's trying not to hope too hard. And maybe I'm trying not to care too much. But something about this moment feels like it matters.

Ginny presses her lips to mine. It's not rushed or desperate. It's intentional. She pulls back, but her gaze lingers. "Goodnight," she whispers. "Thank you for a lovely evening. I've got something I need to do."

She disappears into the hotel, leaving me with my heartbeat running wild and a smile I can't shake.

FIFTEEN

Ginny

By the time I get back to my room, my legs are starting to feel pleasantly sore from the bike ride and my heart is still fluttering from Ryker's kiss. I've barely stepped inside when I smell something savory—like sesame, ginger, and grilled meat—and find Tarryn sitting cross-legged on the bed with three open room-service plates spread out around her.

"I thought we agreed on self-control so we can fit in our dresses," I say, amused.

She pops a bite of something into her mouth and shrugs. "I'm giving notes to the chef at Paradise Grill. Consider this restaurant espionage."

We both laugh.

"Where were you?" she asks.

I flop onto the other bed. "Ryker and I biked around

Stanley Park. Had dinner after. It was…"

"Cute?" she offers.

I shake my head. "Fun."

She hums.

There's a knock at the door.

Tarryn raises a brow. "Expecting someone?"

"No. More room service?" I ask as I get up. I crack the door open, and every good feeling from the past few hours vanishes.

Jeremy.

My mouth goes dry. "What the hell are you doing here?"

"Ginny. Can we talk?"

"No." I step out and pull the door shut behind me. "What is there to say? Except maybe congratulations. Jill told me you're getting married." I turn to go back in, but the door has closed and locked, and I don't have my room key.

"I made a mistake," he says. "A huge one. I shouldn't have—Jill—"

My stomach twists. "Shouldn't have slept with my best friend? No shit." I knock on the door and silently beg Tarryn to run and let me in.

"I know. And I've regretted it every single day." He pulls me close, and his lips skim my neck. It always drove me crazy.

Does he think nothing has changed between us? I push him away and glance down the hallway, needing an escape. That's when I see Ryker.

He's coming off the elevator, laughing at something on his phone, but then his gaze lifts and lands on me and Jeremy in the hallway.

His smile fades. He doesn't stop, but the shift in his eyes punches me in the gut.

Then he's gone.

He thinks…what? That I asked Jeremy here?

Guilt swells inside me, though I've done nothing wrong.

"I want to fix things," Jeremy is saying. "We were good together. We can be again."

"No." My voice is hard now. "You don't get to rewrite

history."

"Come on. Don't tell me you haven't thought about us. About what we had."

"I've thought about how much of a coward you are. How you gaslit me for months, saying I worked too much while you were sleeping with someone I thought was my friend."

"Gin—"

"Go," I snap.

He doesn't move. "I'm not giving up that easy."

"You can't fix this. I'm serious, Jeremy. Leave."

"I still love you."

I close my eyes. This is a nightmare. "That would be more believable if you weren't engaged to the person you cheated with." I turn and knock again. Sharp. Loud. Willing Tarryn to hurry.

Jeremy moves closer. "Remember Santa Barbara? That wine festival you begged to go to? You said it was the happiest you'd been in years. You don't just throw that away."

"Stop. You're the one who threw everything away."

Tarryn finally opens the door, and I slip in, closing the door firmly behind me and leaving Jeremy outside. Thankfully, he doesn't knock again.

"I take it that was your ex?" she asks as I brace against the door a moment.

I nod and move to drop onto the edge of the bed. "Jeremy."

"And who's Jill?"

"My ex-best friend," I say bitterly. "It was his birthday, and I found her giving him a blow job. They were naked in our bed."

Tarryn grimaces. "That's horrible."

My laugh comes out bitter. "Jill works in sales here at the hotel. She saw me when I went down to the bar." I shake my head. This is so ridiculous. "She asked why I was in Vancouver. I said wedding dress shopping, and before I could explain anything else, she assumed I was engaged. That's when Ryker sat down. He played along as my fiancé to save me. I guess Jill must have reported the good news to Jeremy."

Tarryn looks completely baffled. "That sounds like Ryker," she says. "But also…not."

My brows lift. "What do you mean?"

"He's a doctor, so of course he's caring—stepping in to help is who he is. But I know he's also careful…because you're a Dempsey."

I nod, and my stomach tightens. "And now he saw me in the hallway with my ex. I'm sure he'll believe the worst."

She shifts forward. "You don't owe Ryker anything. He's not your boyfriend, and your family would lose their minds if you were to date him."

I twist the corner of the duvet between my fingers, but it doesn't help my pounding heart.

He's not my boyfriend. He was never supposed to be anything to me. But he makes me feel seen, not just useful. He seems like he truly cares. Losing that? It would confirm everything I fear about myself, my judgment.

Ryker Paradise has touched every inch of my body. I've had his mouth, his hands, his full attention, and I've craved every second of it. We've been sneaking around for weeks now, stealing moments that blur the line between casual and something dangerously close to real.

And today? We biked through Stanley Park, talking, laughing, flirting like the rest of the world had faded away. We didn't sleep together. We just enjoyed each other. It was easy. Natural. Joyful.

Until I opened the damn door and found Jeremy standing there like a ghost from the life I barely escaped.

And Ryker saw it. I told him I had something to do, and he now thinks it was meeting up with Jeremy when it was really just an excuse not to go back to his room.

The look on his face was awful. It wasn't anger. It was hurt. And I hate that it matters. I hate that my first instinct was guilt, even though I've done nothing wrong.

Except maybe feel too much for someone I swore would never mean anything, because he can't. But he does.

"You don't owe him anything," Tarryn says again, still watching me.

No. But I want to explain. I want him to know Jeremy means nothing, that I'm not looking back.

But then Tarryn adds, "It's not like you two were ever going to work out, right?"

And that gets my attention.

Because no one knows what's been happening between Ryker and me. Not Tarryn. Not Sadie. No one. And hearing her say that, like it's just a fact, like it's inevitable, crushes my heart a little.

We're not supposed to work.

But that doesn't stop the way I feel when he looks at me. It doesn't stop the way my skin still tingles from the way he kissed me outside Mikey's, or how we can't seem to keep our hands off each other when we're alone. It doesn't stop the way I miss him when he's not around.

"I don't want him thinking I'm still involved with Jeremy," I murmur, staring at the carpet. He's about the only thing in my life right now that feels real.

Tarryn shrugs. "Then tell him."

I hesitate.

She doesn't know what she's asking me to do. Telling Ryker how I feel means admitting I feel something, that I've crossed a line I said I never would. And that terrifies me almost as much as the idea of losing whatever this thing is between us.

But I don't want to let this go, and I certainly don't want him thinking I don't care at all.

I stand for a long second, heart pounding like I'm about to walk into a war zone.

"You going?" Tarryn asks.

I glance toward the door. "I'm...thinking about it."

She arches a brow. "That usually means no."

I don't answer. Because walking down the hall to Ryker's

room is too obvious. And risky. Especially with Tarryn right here watching me. But I can't let that be the last thing he remembers about me tonight. So I get my phone from the nightstand and sit back on the edge of the bed, typing out a message.

Me: Hey. That wasn't what it looked like. Jeremy showed up without warning. I didn't invite him here, and I didn't want him here. Just...in case you were wondering.

I stare at the message for a solid minute before hitting send.

Tarryn is talking about dessert or something from the menu, but I can barely hear her. My eyes keep flicking back to my phone.

Three minutes pass.

Then five. Nothing.

My pulse picks up, panic creeping in around the edges. What if he thinks I'm back with Jeremy? What if this thing between us was always more to me than it is to him?

I'm about to type another message when my screen lights up.

Ryker: It's okay. I figured that's who it was. No big deal.

I exhale sharply. My shoulders drop.

But then another text buzzes through.

Ryker: I only looked away because I didn't want it to be obvious I wasn't staying with you. Didn't want to make it worse for you.

Of course he would think about that. About me.

I bite back a smile, a flutter working its way to my heart.

Me: Thank you.

Me: Seriously. That was really thoughtful. Even if you

looked like you wanted to strangle someone.

His reply is quick this time.

Ryker: Never said I didn't.

I grin, tucking the phone into my lap before Tarryn can catch the look on my face.

"Everything okay?" she asks.

"Yeah," I say. "Everything's fine. My sister had a question about the gift shop." I roll my eyes.

But things are more than fine. I'm filled with relief, gratitude, and the warm ache of something real. Even if no one else can know it.

Tarryn stretches and lets out a groan. "Okay, I need to shower before I eat any more of this," she says, waving a hand over the half-eaten plates.

I nod, trying to play it cool. "Go. I'll guard the dumplings."

She grabs her things and disappears into the bathroom. A moment later, I hear the water running.

As soon as I'm sure she's not coming out anytime soon, I grab my phone and slip out onto the small balcony. I could wait. Should wait.

But I don't want to.

I hit Ryker's name and bring the phone to my ear. This isn't just about hearing his voice. It's about letting him hear mine—shaky, unsure, still willing to try.

He answers on the second ring.

"Hey," he says.

"Hey." I press a hand to my stomach, trying to calm it. "I just... I wanted to hear your voice."

There's a pause. Then, "Yeah?"

"You pretending not to know me in the hallway? That was—" I lower my voice. "Really hot."

He chuckles, the sound like gravel and heat. "You liked

that?"

"Too much."

Another pause. Longer this time. "You didn't look like you liked it."

"I didn't. Not at first." I shift in the chair, thighs squeezing together. "But now that I know why you did it? It's doing all sorts of things to me."

"Tell me."

God. His voice is like smoke and sin through the phone.

"I keep thinking about the way our eyes met before you looked away," I whisper. "Like you were holding something back."

"I was," he says. "Every instinct I had told me to walk over and clock that guy."

My breath hitches.

"But I didn't," he continues. "Because I knew you didn't want a scene. And because if I touched you in front of him, it would've been a different kind of fight."

"Ryker..."

"Tell me what you're wearing."

I glance toward the bathroom door to check that the water's still running.

"T-shirt. No bra. Panties I'd take off if you were here."

A deep growl vibrates through the phone. "Say that again."

"I'm wet," I whisper. "Because of you. Because you looked at me like I was yours and you were swallowing it down."

"You are mine," he says, voice hard. "You know that, don't you?"

My thighs clench tighter. "Prove it."

A pause. "Come here now."

My pulse skips. "Are you serious?"

"Dead serious," he says. "You want me? You've got me. Ten minutes."

I set the phone down, heart pounding. This isn't just about need. It's about trust. And about everything I haven't said out loud yet but might be ready to show.

Maybe, for once, I'll stop running from what I want.

SIXTEEN

Ryker

It's just after midnight when I hear the quiet click of my bedroom door closing. I don't even have to open my eyes to know it's her. Ever since we returned from Vancouver two weeks ago, Ginny has been coming to me in the middle of the night. She moves like a whisper — barefoot, careful, the way someone moves when they're used to not being noticed. But I notice. Every time. And she's always gone before the sun rises. She leaves her car at home and takes a rideshare over.

The sheets shift and the mattress dips slightly as she crawls into bed beside me. I pull her in without a word, her head finding the space just under my chin like it belongs there.

Like she belongs here. She keeps her visits quiet, like we're something shameful, like being caught would cost her. And I'm sure it would. Evelyn doesn't forgive betrayal, particularly not from her own blood.

That thought should scare me. Hell, it does.

No one knows about my true feelings for Ginny. Not Tarryn. Not even Ginny.

But this thing between us? It's not just sex anymore. At least not for me.

If I lose her, it won't just hurt. It'll hollow something out inside me, leaving me empty.

I don't know when it changed. Maybe it was the first night back after the trip, when she showed up at my door in one of my old baseball shirts and nothing else. Or maybe it was the way she made my bed her home without asking, the way she rolls toward me in her sleep, fingers tangling in my shirt like she's afraid I'll vanish if she lets go.

Or maybe it was way before that, and I just don't want to admit it.

But no matter when it started, now I've got a problem. And that problem is Ginny Dempsey.

Not because of who she is—not really—but because of who I am. My last name might as well be gasoline and hers a lit match. Everyone in this damn town knows it. We're not just on opposite sides of a feud. We are the feud.

Still, I can't stop.

I should. But every time I let her in... And when she leaves, I stare at the empty space beside me, wondering how the hell I'm supposed to go back to the way things were before.

I shift slightly, brushing a strand of hair off her cheek. She sighs in her sleep and curls closer, like she knows I'm thinking too much again.

I've always had flings. Short-term things. Fun, easy, forgettable.

Ginny's none of those.

She's sharp and bold and funny. She doesn't just see me. She sees right through me. I want her to.

I close my eyes and try to will the thoughts away. But her body is warm against mine and her breath is steady and soft on my neck, and all I can think about is how I already know this is a lie.

I'm in trouble. And I don't want out.

I need to talk to someone. I know where Tarryn sits on this, and the only other Paradise who would possibly understand is my mother. We're meeting about the practice tomorrow, and maybe I can add this to the agenda as well.

After a full day of seeing patients, I've joined Mom in her office at our clinic for a meeting. I sink gratefully into a chair in her sitting area, and we talk through our current patients. Some of them started with me, but several are transfers from her caseload, as she continues to pull back, and she graciously answers all my questions. Eventually, it seems like we've been through everything, but she's still looking at me expectantly. I don't know what else to say.

Mom studies me for a long beat, eyes narrowing the way they used to when she knew I was lying about sneaking cookies before dinner. "Ryker," she says softly, "what's really going on? I understand you had a leukemia diagnosis last month. It doesn't get any harder than that. I promise."

I run a hand through my hair and exhale. I've danced around it long enough. I could lie, say I've just been tired, blame work or the weather. But she's always seen through me. And if I want something real with Ginny, I can't keep hiding her.

"I'm seeing someone," I say. "Ginny Dempsey."

Her brows lift. "You're dating her?"

I nod slowly. "It started…casual. Just a hookup."

She takes a sip of her coffee and doesn't say anything.

"But it's not that anymore."

She stays quiet, waiting.

"I didn't mean for it to get serious. But it is. At least for me.

She gets me in this weird way, and I don't have to pretend with her. And yeah, I know it's risky — I know the history — but when I'm with her, none of that seems to matter. Until it does."

"How long has this been going on?" Mom asks.

"It started a while ago, but it's only gotten serious since we went to Vancouver. We spent time together. And every night since we've been back, she's come to my place. No one knows."

She sits back, processing. "And you think this is more than just a phase?"

I look her square in the eye. "Yeah. I do. And I don't care what Max or Dad thinks," I add quickly, but the words feel thin even as I say them. "Actually, that's a lie. I care. They're going to lose their minds when they find out."

"Especially Max," she says. "It's not really public knowledge, but the reason Max and Chereen broke up was because Chereen had an affair with Ginny's father before Zach was born."

I stop short and stare at her. "Chereen slept with Henry?"

She nods. "I think they were both trying to get back at their spouses."

My stomach drops. All this time, I thought Max's hatred was about land and legacy. But it's not. It's personal. The Dempseys are a constant reminder of his biggest humiliation. Which means coming clean isn't just risky. It's explosive.

I think back over what I know, piecing in this new information. So Chereen, Max's wife, had an affair with Henry, Ginny's dad. Then they broke it off, and Zach was born. Chereen left Paradise not long after that, never to be heard from again. And Henry must have been banished after Evelyn found out about his affair. This is a huge part of the generational drama in our families. No wonder our parents despise each other and have bred mistrust among everyone else.

Mom presses her lips together. "Chereen and Henry were never in love." She closes her laptop. "But Max never forgave him for what happened. He's always blamed Henry for breaking up his marriage. And you dating Henry's daughter? That's a powder keg. Especially with Zach so…involved."

Something about the way she says it gives me pause. But she doesn't explain, and I don't press.

"He'll use Ginny against me. Twist this. Turn it into proof that I'm not loyal to the family."

Her mouth tightens. "You've always been loyal. Don't let Max make you think otherwise."

"But what if it doesn't matter?" I say. "It won't if everyone thinks I'm sleeping with the enemy. Even if she's not the enemy. She's just…Ginny."

My mom nods slowly, then reaches across the table and covers my hand with hers. "You don't get to choose who your heart breaks for. But you do get to choose whether you fight for them. And if this is real, you fight for it. But you do it with your eyes open. Because you're right. There will be fallout."

"I know. You just want more grandchildren."

She laughs. "I'm so transparent. But really, I want my children to be happy. I watched what happened with King and was crushed when it all fell apart. But I'm so glad Greyson and Beckett have found their forevers. I hope you, King, and Tarryn do too."

"And you want more grandchildren."

"I'm a pediatrician. Of course I do. But I'm serious when I say you need to be smart about your relationship with Ginny. And don't let anyone—*anyone*—make you ashamed of how you feel." Her grip tightens. "I'm proud of you," she adds.

I swallow the lump rising in my throat. "Thanks, Mom."

She smiles gently. "And for the record, I always liked Evelyn's granddaughters more than her wine."

I bark out a laugh, surprised by the rush of relief that floods my body.

"Bring her on Sunday," Mom suggests. "Max and Zach won't be there. You and Ginny can tell the family yourselves and control the narrative before Max spins it into something it's not."

Tarryn's going to see this coming. My dad probably won't. But either way, once the truth's out, there's no going back. And I can handle their anger, just not losing Ginny.

"Are you sure?" I ask Mom.

"Positive."

"Thanks for your support."

She stands and pulls me into a hug. "I love you, and I want nothing more than your happiness. And honestly, if this puts this Paradise-Dempsey crap to rest, all the better."

I hold on to that hope, for a future where Ginny and I can stop hiding. But even with Max and Zach gone, Sunday's going to be a battlefield. If this blows up the way I think it will, someone's going to bleed. I just hope it isn't Ginny.

SEVENTEEN

Ginny

For once, I wake up nestled in Ryker's arms. I like being here with him. I hate having to rush off before it's even morning. But today I have an interview with the wine consortium and he has the day off, so I get to sneak out of here later. For once, I'm not rushing out the door.

His arousal pushes against my bottom. I shift playfully to provoke him.

"If you keep doing that," he whispers, "I might lose my self-control."

I grin. "I enjoy it when you lose control." And maybe that's the problem. Every time he gives in, I fall a little deeper. I turn and roll toward him. "Good morning."

"I like that you didn't sneak off this time." He reaches for my breasts, and his touch sends electricity coursing through me. There's a wild intensity in his gaze that makes my heart race.

We've been careful. Always. But this time, when he reaches for the drawer, I stop him. Not because I'm reckless, but because I trust him. Because I want to feel everything. Him. Us. Nothing between. He searches my face like he's making sure, and I nod once, steady. This is a choice. My choice. "I haven't been with anyone but you since I left Jeremy."

His eyes soften. "I haven't been with anyone else since we were first together."

I gasp. "That was over nine months ago."

"Yes. For over nine months."

"Are you good with no condom?"

"Yes." He smiles and strokes his hard cock.

"What are you going to do about it?" I tease, biting my lip.

A challenge ignites in his eyes. "Oh, I have some ideas."

In a swift motion, he flips us over, pinning me beneath him. The weight of his body feels delicious, sending a rush of heat through me.

He lowers himself, his breath warm against my neck as he whispers sweet promises of what's to come. My hands find their way to his shoulders, pulling him even closer as I arch my back instinctively, craving more.

His lips brush mine before deepening into something fervent and consuming. Every nerve ending blazes as we lose ourselves in each other.

He pulls back, dropping the sheet from his shoulders. I open my legs for him, and he runs his fingers up my slit. "I love how wet you get for me."

I gasp as his fingers glide over my most sensitive parts, teasing and tantalizing. "More," I breathe, urging him on.

Ryker smirks and slides a finger inside me, and I moan at the sensation. "Is this what you wanted?" His voice is low, almost a growl.

I nod, lost in the rhythm of his thumb strumming my clit. "Yes! Just like that!"

He adds another finger, stretching me as the pressure builds within. My breathing quickens.

"I want you," I beg, the words tumbling from my lips like a secret I've been holding too long. "I want you to touch me, to make me feel everything."

His lips crash against mine in a fierce dance that speaks volumes. His hands grip my waist. "Say it again," he murmurs against my lips.

"I want you," I breathe.

He shifts his weight, bringing his body flush against mine. When he pushes inside me, I swear my eyes roll to the back of my head.

"Good," he replies. "Because I intend to show you just how much I feel the same."

He locks eyes with me as he rocks slowly in and out. His hands glide down my sides, tracing paths across my skin, deepening the claim he's already made.

He finds his way back between my legs, fingers teasing and coaxing me closer to that blissful edge. Every caress is exhilarating and maddeningly sweet.

The way he looks at me, equal parts hunger and satisfaction, makes my pulse pound.

"You have no idea how much I want this," he murmurs.

Heat spreads through me like wildfire. My fingers clutch the sheets beneath us, twisting the fabric in my fists as I surrender. Shockwaves of pleasure spiral through me. My climax builds, and my body shakes.

"Can you feel it?" he whispers. "Can you feel how close we are?"

"Yes!" I cry out, my voice cracking with urgency.

He pushes his dick deep inside me.

"God, you're perfect," he murmurs.

"More," I plead. "I need more."

A wicked smile curves his lips, and he obliges, picking up the pace as he drives into me. Each thrust reverberates through me like a drumbeat until we are one, lost in an ocean of sensation.

"Just like that..." I moan, meeting his movements, pushing us closer and closer to the edge. The friction between us is exquisite torment, every thrust unraveling me, dragging me deeper into bliss.

He leans down to capture my lips again, swallowing my cries as they escape into the space around us. The pressure coils inside me, tight and relentless, like a spring pulled to its breaking point. I gasp, arching beneath him.

"Look at you," he growls between ragged breaths. "So responsive. So damn beautiful."

"Don't stop," I beg. "I'm so close."

His hand slips between us again, fingers circling where our bodies are joined. The deep fullness of him inside me and the precise pressure of his touch sends waves crashing through me, each one more powerful than the last.

"I'm about to come," he gasps, focused on where we move together, his pace growing frantic.

"Yesss," I whimper, teetering on the edge of release.

His mouth meets mine, and the world falls away. It's not gentle. It's desperate, consuming, a kiss that sears straight to my core. His hands tangle in my hair, pulling me closer until there's no space left between us, just heat and hunger and the raw ache of wanting.

Every nerve lights up. Every part of me responds. My toes curl, my fingers dig into his shoulders, and a moan escapes — shameless and broken — because this kiss doesn't just wreck me. It undoes me. It's the kind of kiss that leaves me ruined for anyone else.

My climax slams into me, fierce and all-consuming, stealing the breath from my lungs as I shatter beneath him. He's right behind me, groaning my name as he loses himself. It's not just intense, it's soul-shaking. Earth-tilting. And as we collapse together in the aftermath, I know I'll never forget the way this felt, like everything inside me just broke open and bloomed.

I collapse against the pillow, chest heaving, skin damp with sweat, too shaky to move. My body still hums — electric and over-sensitized — as Ryker stretches out beside me. He seems entirely satisfied and entirely too casual, as if he didn't just rewrite my entire existence in under ten minutes.

I can't feel my toes. In a good way.

He doesn't say anything, just throws his arm across his eyes, like he's catching his breath too. The room is quiet except for the fan spinning overhead and the low creak of the old bedframe adjusting under our weight.

Holy hell. I close my eyes, trying to come down from the high, but it's useless. My mind is already spinning because this isn't normal. Not just the sex. God, the sex. Jeremy was good. We were good together. Comfortable. Familiar. Safe. But this? With Ryker? It's like stepping off a cliff and finding out I have wings.

He touches me, and I forget every good reason to stay away. I'm floating somewhere between bliss and delusion, and I need to get my feet back on the damn ground.

I keep calling it casual. Keep pretending I'm in control. But if that were true, I wouldn't be this afraid. This is supposed to be simple. Physical. Temporary. Yet I'm knee-deep in something I can't control.

Ryker shifts, pulling me into his side like he can hear my thoughts. "I could get used to this," he mumbles. He runs a hand down my spine and presses a kiss to my temple. "I told my mom about you."

My whole body stiffens. "What?" I sit up, eyes wide. "Ryker, you did what?"

He blinks like I've slapped him. "I told her about us. That we've been seeing each other."

"You weren't supposed to tell anyone," I snap, dragging the sheet over me, as if there's some reason to be modest now. "This is a secret. That was the deal."

"She won't tell anyone," he says, like that fixes it. "She's just…happy for me."

I stare at him, heart thudding. "Happy for you? Ryker, this isn't—" I break off, exhaling hard. "It's not a thing. We're not a thing. We can date other people."

His expression shifts, not hurt exactly, but something closes behind his eyes. A door I didn't mean to slam shut.

He sits up too, brow furrowed, the sheet around his waist. "Then what are we doing? Because this feels like more than just sex."

"Why does it matter?" I deflect, forcing a laugh that doesn't quite land. "We're having fun. That's all this is."

"Is it?"

"Yes." *It has to be.*

He watches me like he's trying to figure out if I'm lying.

I don't even know anymore.

"I want us to be together. You're not a dirty secret. I think you should come to Sunday dinner at my parents'," he says finally. "Just once. We can tell everyone."

My stomach drops. "No," I say quickly. "I can't. I won't."

I still remember what happened when Josie caught me texting a Paradise cousin in high school. She didn't speak to me for a month. Gran made me help in the cellar all summer. These days my sisters might understand, but Gran never will, and they'd never risk their futures by crossing her.

He flinches. But telling his family means telling my family. My grandmother. Yeah. That's not going to land gracefully with her in any light.

I pull him close and kiss him before he can say anything else—soft, lingering, distracting. "Can we not do this right now?" I whisper. "Let's talk about it later. When we're not naked."

"Ginny—"

"Please?" I beg, gently placing my hand on his chest. "Just…tell your mom not to say anything. Okay?"

He exhales and nods. "She won't."

"Good." I slide out of bed, searching for my clothes. "I should get back to the caretaker house," I say as I shimmy into my jeans. "I have an interview with Eric Warner today."

His brow arches. "Black Bear Consortium?"

"Yes. The Black Bear Valley Wine Consortium." I reach for my shirt, then lean over and kiss him once more. "Wish me luck."

"Good luck," he murmurs, though there's something tense in his voice now.

I dash out the door and don't look back.

By the time the rideshare drops me at home to get ready for my interview, I'm sweaty, frustrated, and two seconds away from screaming into the empty air.

I didn't plan on snapping at Ryker. I didn't walk into his house last night thinking we'd argue in bed. I thought I'd head out this morning with that glow he always leaves me with — high on him, heart still pounding from everything he makes me feel.

But then he opened his mouth. *"I told my mom about you."* Like it was no big deal. Like we're the kind of couple who makes announcements. Who goes to family dinners and gets asked to bring dessert. Who sit next to each other at the long Sunday table with matching wine glasses and inside jokes.

But we're not. We can't be that. Not when I'm a Dempsey and he's a Paradise.

Telling his mother is one thing — wrong, but manageable. But wanting me to show up and smile at Sunday dinner? That's a whole different beast. I'm not just sleeping with Ryker. I'm treading the edge of a fault line that could split the valley in two.

My grandmother already believes the Paradises are behind the well issue. She thinks they're trying to ruin us.

And honestly? I'm not sure she's wrong. I know it's not Ryker doing it, but it wouldn't be the first time someone in that family tried something. But the Dempseys are resilient.

That stretch of land is where our award-winning grapes come from. The vines there feed off the well, and if the water doesn't return this season, we could lose the harvest.

And what do the Paradises do? They take down a peach orchard and plant a new block of grapes. Pinot, of all things. The thirstiest damn grape on the market. They knew exactly what they were doing when they laid those rows. It's either a declaration of war or proof of how little they think of us.

So how the hell do I explain Ryker to my family?

I can already see the look on Gran's face if I show up with him on my arm. Shock first. Then fury. Then that tight, cold silence she uses when she's plotting our death.

My mom wouldn't say anything at all. She'd sip her wine and pretend it wasn't happening, then gossip about it for months.

Sera and Josie would demand a full health check and possibly a blood sample.

And Addie... My youngest sister, Addie, would just tell me I'm a fool.

And maybe I am.

Because despite what I said this morning, I still want him. Even knowing all that.

Because when I'm with him, everything is clearer. Quieter. Easier. The war between our families feels like it could be ancient history, not the reason I've spent the last year rebuilding trust with people who think I ran away when things got hard.

That afternoon, I arrive at Dot's Diner early for the interview. I tilt my head back against the seat while I wait and close my eyes.

My phone buzzes in my pocket.

Ryker: Sorry about this morning. Good luck with your interview! You're going to knock it out of the park.

I stare at it for a long moment, my thumb hovering over the screen. But I don't answer.

I tell myself this is some statement of independence, proving to myself that I'm still okay. That I don't need him.

But even if I don't text him back now, I'm sure I will later.

Because I don't know how to let him go.

EIGHTEEN

Ryker

As I pull into my parents' drive for the Sunday family dinner, my gaze catches on the rows of vines stretching toward the lake, their skeletal arms dotted with the first signs of life.

It's late March, the time when everything stirs awake. Tiny buds peek through, fragile and full of promise. This is when we all hold our breath, praying the frost stays away so the vines can settle into the season.

One hard freeze could undo it all. I grew up watching this dance between hope and risk, knowing how much rides on timing and temperature. Even now, those buds feel like a heartbeat, one that belongs to all of us.

I love this season of the year. It's a miracle every time.

I've barely shut my car door behind me when I hear the crunch of tires on the gravel drive. Greyson's SUV pulls in. The back door swings open, and Trinity climbs out with a massive tote bag slung over one arm. In seconds, she has a wriggling baby in the other.

"We're here," she announces like she just crossed a finish line.

"Barely," Greyson mutters, rounding the front of the car. His shirt's streaked with something that might be formula, and one of his shoelaces is untied. "We forgot the pacifier. Again."

"I told you to put one in the glovebox," Trinity says through clenched teeth as she adjusts the bag on her shoulder.

"Didn't we have, like, four of those things?" he fires back.

"None of which are currently in this car."

"All right, hand him over," I say, stepping in as Mom appears behind me.

"I have spare pacifiers in Theo's room," she assures them.

Mom has turned the old housekeeper's room into a makeshift nursery in hopes that she'll have plenty of time with Theo and, eventually, other grandchildren, I'm sure. She may be sorry.

Trinity sighs in relief and passes Theo to me. His tiny face is scrunching like he's about to lose it.

"He needs to be changed," Trinity says, practically tossing the diaper bag inside when we reach the front door. "And I think I sat on a burp cloth that used to be clean but is now…definitely not."

Without missing a beat, Mom takes the bag and the reins. "Come on, sweetheart. Let's get him sorted." She collects the baby from me, and Trinity follows her into the house, already unbuttoning the top of her blouse.

I wave as they go. Greyson rests against the porch rail and scrubs a hand down his face. "Tell me it gets easier."

I smirk. "You've seen the charts, right? Sleep deprivation peaks at six weeks, and he's what—five?"

"Five weeks and three days," Greyson says. "But who's counting?"

I clap him on the shoulder. "You're doing fine. You just

look like hell."

He huffs out a tired laugh. "Thanks. That helps. I've actually considered faking an emergency and going to the sleep room at the hospital for just one uninterrupted night."

"I won't tell Trinity."

He shakes his head, and we go to the living room. I can hear Mom cooing in that high, ridiculous baby voice she only uses for her grandchild. Dad's pouring wine. No one blinks twice at all the activity.

This is how my family works. Someone drops the ball, someone else picks it up. No questions, no guilt. Just instinct.

I follow Greyson into the kitchen, watching him automatically check the monitor even though Theo's just two rooms away.

He catches me watching. "I'm not paranoid. I'm just..."

"In love with a tiny dictator," I finish for him.

Greyson cracks a real smile. "Exactly."

It doesn't take long before Mom is back at her post, working on the dinner, the scent of beef stew and couscous filling the air. "Trinity and Theo will be out shortly. She's going to nurse him and hope he settles down for a nap so she can eat some dinner."

"Thanks, Mom." Greyson gives her a side hug. "We really appreciate everything you and Dad have done."

Dad grabs Greyson for something to do with one of his vats, and as they head out to the warehouse, I stick around with Mom.

"Hey, sweetheart." She wipes her hands on a towel and walks over, pulling me into a hug. "Where's your guest?"

I shake my head. "She's not coming."

Mom doesn't ask why. She just holds on a moment longer, then pats my back and pulls away to look up at me. "Have patience," she says softly. "It's hard for her too."

I nod, throat tight, not trusting myself to speak. She's not wrong. Being here, surrounded by the people who love me, should feel good. But all I can think about is how much I want

Ginny to see this, see us. Not the feud, not the gossip or the expectations, just family. But she's not here. I hoped she would decide to take a risk, give this a chance, but she's not ready to change her mind. And hope, like those buds on the vine, is fragile, and too much frost can kill it.

"She said to tell you thank you for the invitation," I manage.

Mom smiles gently. "She'll come around. If she's anything like you, it just takes a little time and someone stubborn enough to wait her out."

I let out a breath, trying to chuckle. "I can do stubborn."

She gives me a nod. "That's my boy."

Dinner's almost ready. I take my usual seat, but tonight, it feels different. I wonder if it'll always feel like something's missing now.

And if Ginny never feels ready for this... I don't know what that means.

Mom disappears into the kitchen, and I'm about to grab a drink when the front door swings open with Tarryn's usual flourish.

"There you are." She kicks off her boots and shrugs out of her jacket. "Took you long enough."

"Nice to see you too, T," I say, brow raised. "You planning on saying hi or just passing judgment?"

"Both." She crosses the room and gives me a quick hug. "Hi. Now go pour yourself something strong. You'll want it."

That gets my attention. "Why?"

She grins. "Because when Kingston lands, I need you in the library. All four of you. Me, you, Beckett, Greyson, and our golden boy jetting in from the city."

I frown. "You want a full sibling summit?"

"Correct."

"What's going on?"

Tarryn shakes her head. "Not until everyone is here. I don't want to repeat myself."

"Tarryn."

"Nope."

She pats my cheek like I'm five and moves toward the kitchen. "Go pretend it's a normal Sunday night for Mom's sake. I'll come find you when it's time."

I watch her disappear into the kitchen. My stomach knots. Whatever this is, it isn't dinner-table gossip.

Kingston's boots echo down the hallway as he arrives. His duffel bag drops to the floor with a heavy *thunk*.

"Sorry," he says. "I was in the lab and lost track of time."

Tarryn doesn't even blink. She's already halfway down the hall, tossing a sharp, "Library. Now," over her shoulder.

We exchange glances. Beckett lifts a brow, Greyson sighs, and I just follow. When Tarryn's like this, it's easier to comply than question. She's been this way since she was born. We're used to it.

Once we're inside the library, Tarryn closes the door, but she doesn't move. Her fingers tremble slightly as she crosses her arms. She takes a breath. "I think Zach is sabotaging the vineyard."

The words land like a rock in the middle of the room.

Kingston blinks. "You think Zach is doing what now?"

Tarryn shifts her weight, chewing her lip before answering. "Look, I know how it sounds. But I've been watching him. Things are not right. Today, I discovered two barrels missing from the cellar." Her voice wavers for just a second. She presses her hand against her chest, like she's trying to steady her own heartbeat. "I've been documenting everything," she continues. "Little things that don't add up. His timecards. Tank temperatures. Where he's working and when." She looks around at us. "And Ryker overheard him having a weird phone conversation weeks ago. That's when I first started really keeping track."

"Are you sure you're not just looking for a scapegoat?" Beckett asks. "Zach's been working double shifts. That doesn't scream saboteur."

Greyson tilts his head. "Why haven't you told Dad?"

"Because I don't have anything real. Not yet. I wanted more before I said anything." Her hands flex, curling into fists, then opening again. "But it's starting to feel like waiting could be worse."

Beckett edges closer. "And you're sure it's not just paranoia?"

"I'm not sure of anything," she snaps, then immediately softens. "But something's wrong. I can feel it. And if we wait too long, we won't just lose the vines. We could lose a lot more than that."

The door swings open before anyone else can speak.

Mom.

She scans the room, her expression sharp. "What's going on in here?"

Tarryn's breath catches. "We were talking about some things at the vineyard," she says, voice lower now. Controlled. But I can see her swallowing hard.

"What things?" Mom presses.

Tarryn looks at us like she's hoping for backup, but none of us moves. She draws a slow breath and forces the words out. "I think Zach's been messing with the vineyard. On purpose."

Mom stares. "Messing with—? Are you serious?"

Tarryn nods, hands clutched tightly.

Mom's face twists in disbelief. "No. If you're talking about sabotage, we're not doing it in here. Come to the table. Tell your father."

Tarryn opens her mouth as if to object but seems to think better of it.

We follow in tense silence.

Dad is already seated with his daughters-in-law when we arrive, sipping his wine, oblivious to the storm walking toward him. He looks up, brow furrowed. "What's all this?"

"Tarryn has something she wants to say," Mom tells him.

Tarryn's throat bobs as she swallows, and she looks like she might bolt. But she doesn't. Instead, she squares her shoulders and steps forward.

"I think Zach is undermining the vineyard. Quietly. On purpose."

The room freezes.

"I've been noticing small inconsistencies," she continues, her voice more breath than sound. "Missing barrels. Water levels that don't match usage. Equipment being tampered with. He's always in the wrong place at the wrong time, and his timecards don't line up."

Dad stares at her, unreadable. "Do you have proof?"

She hesitates. "Beyond what I've told you, no."

"Tarryn..."

"I overheard a phone call two weeks ago," I chime in. "Zach was saying something about liability, about how this wasn't what he signed up for. Then he said he'd cover it one more time."

"I know how serious this is," she says, her voice rising. "That's why I haven't come forward until now. But something's not right. I can feel it. And I'm done pretending it's all coincidence."

Dad sits back, jaw clenched. For a long while, he stares at the floor like his thoughts are too heavy to voice. His shoulders slope, not from age but from something deeper — disappointment, maybe. Or guilt.

"Zach's a good kid," he mutters finally. "Eager. Green as hell, but..."

Beckett crosses his arms. "What he did in the tasting room, trying to sabotage Sadie, wasn't a mistake. It was a spotlight on his character. This is who Zach is, and trusting him isn't an option."

Dad exhales, rubbing the back of his neck. "Damn it." He looks around again, like he's hoping someone will argue. Hoping we'll tell him he's wrong.

But no one does.

"I'm not wrong." Tarryn's voice breaks. "I might not have hard evidence yet, but I'm not."

Finally, Dad sighs. Then, to my surprise, he reaches across

the table and takes her hand. "Then document everything. Quietly. You understand me? Because if we bring this forward without proof, it could split this family—and this vineyard—down the middle."

"I will," she whispers. "I already have a list started."

His grip tightens. "Good. Keep going."

She nods, lower lip trembling, but she's holding it together.

That's enough for tonight, though. We sit down for dinner, everyone takes a collective cleansing breath, and then it's loud in the best way.

Soon, Kingston and Beckett are trading sarcastic jabs about who Mom loves more. Greyson's already halfway through his second plate, and Trinity has laid down on the couch after managing some semblance of a meal for herself. She snores softly while Theo curls against Mom's shoulder. Tarryn keeps swatting Kingston's hand every time he tries to steal a bite from her plate. The wine is flowing, the food is delicious, and for a while, the tension from earlier melts into laughter and sibling antics.

"Honestly," Mom says, looking around the table with misty eyes and a smile that's all heart, "having all my children home feels like a miracle. I wish I could bottle this up and save it for the quiet nights."

"You mean the peaceful nights," Dad teases, lifting his glass.

"Don't pretend you don't love the noise," she shoots back, and he chuckles.

She reaches across and touches Kingston's wrist. "Even you, troublemaker. I'm glad you're here."

"I feel attacked," Kingston says, dramatically placing a hand over his brow.

Tarryn rolls her eyes. "Please. You live for attention."

"You say that like it's a bad thing."

Greyson nearly chokes on his wine.

Sadie and Mom are laughing so hard, I worry they're going to fall out of their chairs. I laugh along with them and try again to shake off Ginny not being here. She isn't ready. I know that. Still, it stings.

A little while later, the others are in the kitchen helping Mom with dishes—or pretending to, anyway—and I step out on the back porch for some air. A beat later, Tarryn joins me, leaning on the railing beside me with a mug of tea.

She bumps her shoulder into mine. "Mom said you were bringing a guest. So...where is she?"

I sigh. "Not here."

"Ginny bail on you at the last minute?"

I glance out at the vineyard, the rows of vines stretching into the night. I know she's fishing for information, and she's the perfect person to offer a fresh perspective, but I don't want to bring her into my drama. She has enough on her plate. "It doesn't matter."

Tarryn nods slowly, sipping her tea. "You okay?"

"Not really." I drag a hand through my hair. "But I'll get there."

"You can always talk to me."

I look at my little sister. She's only ten months younger than I am, and we're as close as twins. I know I can trust her. "Ginny's not ready for anything. Doesn't want to go public."

Tarryn raises a brow. "And you do?"

I nod once. "Yeah. I do."

"That's gotta be hard."

"It is," I admit. "I get it. Her family would lose it. Ours might not be thrilled either. But I'm tired of sneaking around like we're doing something wrong."

"Does she care about you?"

"I think so. But caring and being willing to go nuclear with your family over a guy? Different things."

Tarryn exhales, setting her mug on the railing. "You should talk to Sadie. After her parents died, she and Ginny were really close, and they thought of her as family."

I look over, surprised. I knew that about Sadie, but I guess I forgot. She was always Caleb's little sister to me, and he's best friends with Beckett.

"Sadie's been through the wringer with people trying to tell her what to do with her life," Tarryn continues. "She might be the only one who can help Ginny see that living for other people's expectations is a losing game."

I glance back through the window, where Sadie's laughing at something Beckett said, wiping her hands on a dish towel.

Yeah. Maybe Tarryn's right. I nod. "I will. Thanks."

When we go back inside, the house has started to settle into its usual Sunday-evening lull. The dishes are done. The wine glasses are mostly empty. Soft music drifts in from the living room where Beckett and Kingston are arguing about some old hockey stat, but I slip into the side hallway and catch Sadie just as she's pulling on her coat.

"Hey," I say quietly. "Got a minute?"

She tilts her head and smiles. "Of course."

I gesture toward the office just off the hall, and she follows. Once the door shuts behind us, I take a breath. "I wanted to ask you something. About Ginny."

Sadie's smile fades a little, her expression softening into something more thoughtful. "Okay."

"I want to see more of her. Like, openly. Not sneaking around or pretending we're just friends in front of everyone."

Sadie rests against the desk, arms crossed. "Does Ginny know that?"

I nod. "I've told her. She's not ready."

Sadie's gaze drops to the floor, turning something over in her mind. Then she says quietly, "She's scared."

I nod. "I figured. Evelyn is a force. But I don't understand exactly what she's scared of. She went out on her own once before…"

Sadie exhales. "Your families are everything—your identity, your roots. And Evelyn? She doesn't hesitate to cut people off. Being with you puts a lot on the line for Ginny. Yeah, she left once, but it didn't go so well. Now, she works at the vineyard. She lives there. Her sisters are her support system. You're asking her to risk all of that, to walk away from the only safety she's ever known." She breaks off, looking thoughtful again.

I wait, giving her space.

"She grew up in chaos," Sadie says. "Her parents...fighting was basically their only means of communication—loud, public, constant. It felt like they thrived on the drama, and they didn't care who got caught in it. Her dad cheated, her mom struck back, and holidays were full-on warzones. They'd split and get back together a dozen times a year, and Ginny was always stuck in the middle. I kept my distance, but I saw how hard it was on her. When she finally left, she didn't have much support, just her sisters. She was isolated. And when her world fell apart, coming back home couldn't have been easy."

My breath catches. "That's a lot."

"It was." Sadie meets my gaze. "And Evelyn... She doesn't yell. She controls. Ice instead of fire. Everything has to revolve around the vineyard. Ginny was practically raised to believe emotions are a liability and loyalty only counts if it's to her grandmother."

I whistle softly. "Evelyn's not exactly a charmer."

"She's terrifying," Sadie admits. "And she's still Ginny's biggest challenge. Evelyn won't accept Ginny having a life outside of Black Bear. And Ginny's always said she'd never get married, never have kids, never bring anyone into the dysfunction she was raised in."

"But she got engaged," I point out.

Sadie's eyes dim a little. "Yeah. And he cheated on her. With one of her best friends. Just like her dad did to her mom. So she doesn't know how to trust anyone anymore, how to believe a relationship won't end in betrayal or power games, or even how to trust herself and her own judgment."

I shift back, processing it all. "So that's what I'm up against."

"She's not trying to push you away," Sadie says gently. "She's trying to protect herself. And maybe protect you too."

I nod slowly, my jaw tight.

"She's also scared of losing her place," Sadie adds. "Right now, she's completely dependent on the vineyard. She hates the gift shop, hates the politics, but it's all she's got. If she loses Evelyn's support, she has nothing. No income. No home. No fallback."

"She's been looking into the Wine Consortium, and she has her jewelry business."

Sadie smiles faintly. "Yeah. If she gets that job, it might be what changes everything. It would give her some independence. Something of her own. Some options."

I shove my hands into my pockets. "Then I hope like hell she gets it."

"Me too," Sadie says. "Because you're not the problem. You're the first good thing to happen to her in a long time. I really believe that."

That knocks the wind out of me. All this time, I thought I was chasing her. But maybe she's been carrying this weight, trying to protect me from what she believes about herself. Maybe what she needs isn't space. It's someone who stays.

She's spent her whole life watching love implode. No wonder she doesn't trust it. But I do. I trust us. And that has to be enough until she can trust it too.

"Thanks," I say.

Sadie smiles again. "Don't give up on her yet."

"I'm not going anywhere."

NINETEEN

Ginny

Sadie texts me on Monday morning, just after eight.

Sadie: Brunch? My treat. You pick the spot.

I stare at the screen, thumb hovering. There're a million reasons to say no. Awkward doesn't even begin to cover being friends with the Paradise family's newest soon-to-be in-law. She's practically royalty in the very vineyard my grandmother swore to crush.

But…it's Sadie.

My best friend. My history. The girl who used to sneak into my room with a bottle of root beer and peanut M&Ms after every one of Evelyn's meltdowns.

Me: Match Eatery 9:30?

She sends back a thumbs-up and a heart.

By the time I get there, she's already grabbed a corner booth. Two coffees sit on the table—mine looking exactly how I take it, like no time has passed at all.

"Still go heavy on the cream?" she asks, nudging the mug toward me with a grin.

"Some things never change," I say, sliding in across from her.

She watches me over the rim of her cup. "You look good."

I huff a laugh. "You look better."

We order and talk about safe things. The weather. The bakery down the street that's selling moon-shaped croissants. Beckett's sudden obsession with patio heaters. It's easy. Comfortable. Like slipping into a favorite sweater I forgot I still had. We say nothing about Ryker. Nothing about the vineyard. But he's here anyway.

Our eggs benedicts arrive, and I'm mid-bite when she finally breaks the silence we've both been tiptoeing around.

"I miss you. And I know you're helping with wedding stuff. But I miss having real talks, just hanging out together."

I blink. "I miss that too."

"I know me marrying Beckett makes things complicated…" Her voice softens. "But it doesn't have to be one family or the other. You don't have to pick sides."

I shake my head. "Tell that to Evelyn."

"Forget Evelyn." Sadie puts her elbows on the table. "You get to choose your own life. And hey, this isn't even just about me and our friendship. If you want Ryker—and I mean really want him—you're allowed to build something that doesn't revolve around your family's grudge."

My eyes widen, but I don't say anything. Everyone knows everything around here.

"You don't have to do it all at once," she adds. "Just…let someone stand beside you while you figure it out."

I look up at her, my heart swelling. Sometimes, I forget

what a good friend she is. Maybe that's the part I've been missing. I've spent so long holding everything on my own that I forgot what it's like to have someone in my corner.

When we leave the café, she pulls me into a hug. "Ryker's completely gone for you, Ginny," she tells me. "The Paradise boys don't fall easy, but when they do, it's the real thing. He'd move mountains for you. Burn the whole world down if he had to. If there's even a part of you that wants that, take the chance."

Sadie's words from this morning are still echoing in my head as I swirl the wine in my glass over dinner, pretending to be fascinated with opening up the young cabernet Jonas ordered.

One thing I didn't mention during our breakfast is that yesterday afternoon, I ran into Jonas Goodwin at Steaming Mugs. It had been years since I'd seen him, and he asked me to dinner. I heard what Sadie told me this morning, but yesterday, I was convinced I needed to get Ryker off my mind, so I said yes. Not to mention, I'd prefer that people in town think I'm seeing Jonas, not Ryker.

And now, here we are. Jonas is the kind of man I'm supposed to want — kind, friendly, not a Paradise. And across the table he's animated, charming, and absolutely not the man I can't stop thinking about.

Damn you, Ryker.

I take a sip and smile when I'm supposed to. Jonas is sweet. Tall, clean-cut, and with warm eyes that make people feel safe. He's a local cop now, a former hockey player, and apparently a hero too. He's just finished telling me how he helped Sadie get safely through her ordeal with the Tremblays. The story should be riveting. This is a perspective I've never heard on the matter. But my mind keeps drifting.

That smirk that drives me crazy. Those hands that know exactly where to touch. The man I swore I wouldn't fall for, but I did anyway.

"...it was harrowing, honestly," Jonas says, pausing as our meals arrive. "There was a lot happening behind the scenes that most people didn't even know. Sadie kept her cool, but I could tell she was terrified. You remember her from high school, right?"

"Yeah," I say, blinking back to the present as I scoop a bite of risotto. "Sadie and I lived together for a couple of years in this terrible apartment downtown. We were kind of infamous for our parties—cheap wine, too many people, music until the police would come."

Jonas grins. "That's right. I wasn't cool enough to be invited," he teases.

"They were never planned. People just showed up. My older brother, Ric, got us the apartment, since both of us needed a place to live."

Jonas nods. "In those days I was busy playing hockey. I thought I was going to be the next Wayne Gretzky or Gordie Howe. But I was never really that good."

"Do you still play?"

"Sure. There's an over-thirty league at the rec center. We may be a little slower, but it's great exercise, and we play other teams around the valley. What do you do these days, outside of working at the vineyard gift shop?"

"I'm creating a jewelry line. It's mostly a hobby, but I sell at the gift shop and at Tanya's Collectables." I don't have the heart to tell him I also spend way too much time with Ryker Paradise.

"Nice!" he says with real enthusiasm. "Is that one of your designs?" He points to my neck.

I'm wearing a delicate gold-wire wrap with peridots and aquamarine. I touch my necklace. "Yes. It's one of my favorites."

"I've seen people wearing those around town. You're very talented."

"Thank you. I love it, but so far it barely compensates me

for the time I spend on it. I guess at least it's a hobby that pays for itself."

He laughs. "My hobby is a money suck."

"What, hockey? How much equipment does one man need?"

He laughs. "No, I also have a boat."

I nod. "Ah, isn't that a hole in the water to throw money into?"

He joins me laughing. "You know what boat stands for, don't you?"

I smile. "Break out another thousand."

He high-fives me across the table.

Ryker doesn't own a boat. He sails borrowed yachts and has friends with lakefront mansions. Jonas has calluses and boat shoes. Ryker has cufflinks and a big bank account. I didn't think that stuff mattered until now, until I realized what it meant to be around someone who has to work for every little thing.

He takes a sip of wine. "So…I'm glad to see you, of course, but what brought you back to Paradise? You always swore you were going to leave and never return."

I hesitate, swirling the cab in my glass. "A nasty breakup." I shrug. "I didn't want to stay in Vancouver after that, and I didn't know where else to go."

He nods like he understands, and maybe he does. "Well, it really is good to see you again. You look…happy."

I raise a brow. "Do I?"

He gives me a sheepish grin. "Okay, maybe content? Curious? Slightly tense?"

That earns a real laugh. "Closer."

Jonas sets down his fork. "I've got a little girl, you know. Her name's Maddie. She just turned six."

The shift is gentle but unexpected. "Oh," I say, surprised. "I *didn't* know you were a dad."

"Yeah. Her mom's Amy Simmons."

My jaw drops slightly. "Amy? From our class?"

He chuckles. "The one and only. We were…not exactly

meant to be, but we're good co-parents. She's in Calgary now, married to a guy who works in oil and gas. I see Maddie as often as I can. We FaceTime almost every day."

"That's really sweet."

And more than a little intimidating. Ryker never talks about kids, not other people's kids or even if he wants to have a family one day. He's a pediatrician, so he must like kids, but I don't know. Seeing Jonas so openly proud of his daughter feels like stepping into another life entirely, one I'm not sure I'm ready for.

"She's got my sense of humor and Amy's bossiness," Jonas says proudly. "Wears glitter boots with dinosaur T-shirts and corrects my grammar regularly."

"She sounds amazing."

"She is." He pauses. "You want kids?"

I blink at the question. It's not one I've let myself think about seriously in years. I can barely untangle my own thoughts, let alone imagine raising someone else.

"I used to say no," I admit. "But now...I don't know. I think I just want something that's mine. Something that doesn't belong to the vineyard or the Dempsey name or whatever expectations everyone's decided I should live up to."

Jonas nods thoughtfully. "That makes sense."

He doesn't make it weird. Just lets the silence settle, warm and easy between us. And still, my mind drifts back to Ryker, who drives me crazy. He has this impossible way he looks at me, like I'm the only thing he wants in the whole damn world.

I force another bite of risotto and try to focus on the man in front of me. Jonas is safe. Kind. Everything I should want.

I set down my fork and edge forward, trying to meet him halfway. "So...Maddie. What's her thing? Dinosaurs? Dance? World domination?"

He chuckles. "All of the above. She wants to be a paleontologist one day and a princess the next. Yesterday, she told me she was going to build a glitter volcano and make it erupt over her school."

I grin. "Sounds like a solid career plan. I'd subscribe to her YouTube channel."

"She's got personality, that's for sure," Jonas says with a soft smile. "Every time I see her, she's changed a little. Grown up more. It kills me to miss so much, and she's only six."

"That must be really hard."

"It is. But it's worth it. Being a dad changes everything. Your priorities shift. You want to be better — for them."

He doesn't say this to impress me. He means it. And I feel myself soften, just a little.

Jonas finishes his wine and sets the glass down, rolling it between his fingers like he's deciding whether or not to say what's on his mind. Finally, he looks up. "Can I ask you something?"

I brace myself. "Sure."

"What's it like...being back in the middle of all this?"

I raise a brow. "Define 'all this'."

He gives me a look. "You know what I mean. The Dempsey-Paradise mess."

Ah. There it is. I shrug, trying to be casual. "So far it's quieter than I expected, honestly."

Jonas folds his arms. "Yeah. That's what worries me."

"Evelyn is always annoyed about something, one Paradise or another. When I moved out during high school, she was in a rage about Max Paradise." My stomach tightens. "You think something new is coming?"

He nods slowly. "It's always been like this — years of peace, then boom. Someone says something or does something, and the whole town's taking sides again. Neighbors stop speaking. Businesses suffer. Kids get pulled out of sports teams. It's stupid. And ugly."

I look down at my half-eaten meal. "Sounds about right."

"When I was a rookie cop," he says, "there was a fight outside O'Shea's. Max Paradise and your Uncle Franklin nearly went at each other with beer bottles. We had to break it up before it got bloody."

What a mess. "That tracks."

"It always starts with land or water or money, but it never ends there. It gets personal." He pauses. "I don't think most people even remember how it started anymore. They just inherited the grudge."

"Yeah." My voice is quieter now. I know. My great grandfather eight generations back got swindled when he sold his pelts to their great grandfather eight generations back, and it exploded into land, livestock, and water disputes — and murders. "It's like family currency."

Jonas studies me. "And you're okay being back in the middle of that?"

I pause. The honest answer? *No. I'm not.* Especially when I'm sneaking around with a person who would make every Dempsey ancestor roll in their graves.

But I just shrug. "I'm used to it."

He doesn't press, but his eyes linger for a second longer than I'd like. As if he's trying to figure out what I'm not saying. "Look," he says, "I'm glad things are calm right now. But if this is just the quiet before the storm…I worry about what happens next. There have been deaths in both families, and the fallout pulls in the entire valley. My grandmother still talks about an unsolved murder from back in the day. It all comes down to the family feud. I just want more for you than that."

That steals my breath a moment, because he's right. That's exactly where I am — caught between loyalty and resentment, history and desire, family and whatever the hell Ryker and I are. Or were. Or could be. I want more than that for myself too.

I force a smile. "Thanks, Jonas. I hope maybe we've evolved to being less toxic if that's what we can call it."

"Just be careful," he says. "If something's brewing, I don't want to see you caught in the crossfire."

I nod and reach for my wine. Little does he know, I'm already right in the middle of what could be the next match to blow things up.

After a little while, the server clears our plates.

Jonas smiles. "This has been a lot of fun tonight."

I nod. "Thank you for getting me out."

"I've been teaching myself how to cook. Maddie says my eggs are 'not disgusting anymore', which is high praise. I don't think you're quite over that boyfriend in Vancouver, but when you are, maybe you'd like to come over, and I can cook us up a good meal."

Suddenly, I'm relieved, not because I don't like Jonas, but because I think I just want some friends, and this gives me an out, even if it's not particularly accurate.

"That sounds perfect," I tell him. "Thank you."

"So, what's next for you?" he asks. "How are you going to get your jewelry to turn more of a profit?"

"I'm not sure," I say with a sigh. "Right now I'm mostly stuck behind a register at the vineyard gift shop. Not exactly what I pictured when I moved home."

"You're too smart for that," he says immediately.

I blink. "Thanks."

"Seraphina mentioned that you were looking into something with the Black Bear Wine Consortium?"

"I had a meeting, yeah," I admit. "An interview. I'm hoping they have something where I can actually use my brain and experience. But they may not want a Dempsey, because the valley does have more than two hundred other vineyards that have nothing to do with my family."

He shrugs. "Well, it's not your fault who you're related to. Surely, they'll see what you have to offer."

The words are so simple, but they land heavy. Kindness always does when you're not expecting it.

I smile. "Thanks. Most people don't see it that way."

"I've been on enough calls with families falling apart to know blood doesn't guarantee anything." He gives me a pointed look. "It's who shows up that matters."

I nod. "Thanks for saying that."

We step out into the chilly spring night, leaving behind the sounds of clinking glasses and soft French music as the restaurant door swings shut.

Jonas walks me to my car, his hands in his pockets, the dark sky with pinpricks of stars above.

I unlock the car door, then turn to him. "Thank you. For dinner. And for being...patient."

He smiles, a little wistfully, I think. "I had a great time."

I nod, meaning it, even if it doesn't feel like enough. "Me too."

He tilts his head, studying me with that calm, steady gaze. I'm sure it's the way I flinch when he moves toward me, the pause before every answer. He's putting it all together, I can tell.

"Does the guy on your mind deserve you?" he asks.

I swallow hard. "Probably not."

Jonas chuckles softly. "Most of us don't. But when you're ready — really ready — promise you'll let me take you out again?"

I smile, grateful once again for his kindness. "I promise."

He opens the car door for me like the gentleman he is, and I slide inside. As I drive off, I can see him in the rearview mirror, hands still in his pockets, watching me go.

When I get home, the caretaker house is dark and quiet. I kick off my heels in the entry and lean back against the door.

I was a lousy date.

Jonas deserved better than half of me, better than distracted smiles and forced conversation and a heart tangled up in a man I'm trying so hard to forget.

But what if Sadie was right, and it's worth the risk? I wake up craving the heat of his skin, the press of his body against my back, the sound of his voice when he says my name in the dark. No one else has ever made me feel both treasured and ruined at the same time.

I cross my arms and close my eyes. I don't know how to stop wanting him, but I don't know how to move forward, either.

I think about what Jonas said, that things have been a little too quiet between the families. Everyone's waiting for the next explosion.

I stare at my phone for a full minute before finally typing.

Me: Went out with Jonas Goodwin tonight. Thought you should hear it from me.

The dots appear right away. Then disappear.

My heart pounds. I try to walk away from the screen, but I don't make it three steps before the phone rings.

I stare at his name, adrenaline zinging through me. I screwed up. I should have told him over the phone. Or why did I tell him at all? It's not like that was the start of something. But now, I have to answer.

"Hey," I say, my voice low. "You okay?"

Ryker exhales. "Now, I am."

I press the phone tighter to my ear.

"I know I shouldn't have called," he says. "I told myself I wouldn't, that I'd give you space. But I'd already been staring at my ceiling for an hour, thinking about the way you looked in my bed two nights ago. And then I got your text."

I close my eyes. My whole body tightens.

"I'm not trying to make this harder for you. I just…needed to hear your voice. Even if it's you telling me to fuck off."

I let out a breath that's almost a laugh.

"Was he good enough?" he asks after a moment.

I pause. "He was…safe."

Ryker's voice lowers. "You and me? We're never going to be safe. But we could be worth it." When I don't respond, he adds, "Was it serious?"

"No." I put my feet up on the coffee table. I have to be honest. "Just dinner. No spark."

He exhales. "Then why go?"

"Because whatever's happening between us is dangerous. We both know it. And I don't know what to do with it."

"Dangerous?" he repeats.

"Jonas brought it up tonight. He's waiting for the town to explode. Ryker, we'll be the match that lights the fire again if this gets out."

"I don't care if they burn down the whole valley," he says. "I'm not giving you up just because our families can't get over something."

"Well, I do care." My voice cracks. "I'm not willing to be the reason things explode again."

"You're not the reason. They are."

"That doesn't matter when the fallout hits everyone we love."

"So what, we just give up? Walk away?"

"I'm saying…I don't see a way forward. Not right now."

"But I do," he says. "And I'm not letting this go."

I blink fast, willing myself not to fall apart. "Don't make this harder."

"I'm not trying to. I just want you to know, when you're ready to stop pretending this doesn't mean something, I'll be here."

TWENTY

Ryker

Mondays at the clinic usually mean ear infections, runny noses, and a physical or two. In fact, that's what most days mean. Pediatrics is predictable, but I like the noise, the pace, and the patients. And things are always moving.

I press the stethoscope to a toddler's chest, something I've done a million times before. Which is good, because my mind isn't entirely here. It's stuck on Ginny, on her date with Jonas and the way she's so easily handed our future over to a decades-old feud. Since when do we let other people decide who we're allowed to love?

I spent the whole damn weekend trying not to care.

It didn't work.

A particularly loud squawk from my patient gets my head back in the game, and I manage to keep her from leaping off the exam table. We finish up her wellness check without incident, and after handing her a sticker, I walk out to see what's next on my schedule. *Eli Stone.*

I finish logging my notes and then pause just outside Exam Room 2, exhaling slowly and attempting to collect myself.

It's been nearly three months since Eli's first visit, when he could barely look at me and Dr. Rex the dinosaur saved the day. I've received a number of cautious updates from his foster mom, Jocelyn, and it seems it's been several weeks of quiet progress.

He still has no words. But there's been no regression, either. Which, in his case, counts as a win.

I knock lightly and push the door open. "Hey, buddy."

He's on the exam table, same spot, same posture—knees tucked up, arms tight around the lime green dinosaur he left with last time. But he's not staring past me. He's watching me walk in.

That's new. I like it.

Jocelyn gives me a tired smile from the chair. "He didn't want to miss his appointment," she says, like it still surprises her. "Woke up asking if it was today. I mean, he didn't say that, but he brought the dino to breakfast. That's his way."

I nod, keeping my tone light. "Dr. Rex makes a good calendar."

Eli's fingers flex over the stuffed dinosaur's arm, but he doesn't look away.

I step closer and crouch down to eye level. "You mind if I sit next to you?"

No answer, of course. But he doesn't shrink back either.

Progress.

I perch on the edge of the table, giving him space. "Is Dr. Rex ready for round two?"

Eli gives the faintest nod. Barely there. But it's real.

I keep everything slow. Calm. Just like last time. And when I check his abdomen, he doesn't flinch. He's still guarded, but not like before. Once I've finished, he looks me in the eye. Not for long, but it lands.

Jocelyn clears her throat. "He hummed in the car this

morning," she says softly. "It wasn't much. Just a little sound. But he did it on purpose. I could tell."

I glance over. "That's huge."

She nods, and her eyes glisten. "I haven't pushed speech therapy yet. We're working through play therapy and drawing. He started coloring eyes on all his people last week."

Eyes. That's what's been missing in his drawings. He was erasing them. Avoiding them. Now, he's putting them in.

"He trusts you," I say, mostly to her, but Eli's still watching me. "That's the foundation. You keep giving him consistency and time, and he'll do the rest. I think he's ready for some one-on-one with a therapist. I'm going to do a referral for you. My staff will be in touch with the details."

She nods. "Thank you."

I pause before adding, "No meds yet. Right?"

"Not unless you tell me it's time."

"It's not. He doesn't need to be numbed. He needs to be seen."

She takes a deep breath and exhales like she's been tense since the moment she walked in.

I turn back to Eli. "You're going to meet another friend of Dr. Rex. First, I've got a new sticker stash in the cabinet. Want to check it out?"

This time, he doesn't look at Jocelyn. He just nods.

And I see it, barely there dimples at the corners of his mouth.

He's smiling.

I pull out the bin, and he picks a sticker—Spiderman. He presses it carefully onto the belly of his dinosaur.

As they leave, Jocelyn squeezes my arm. "You're good with him," she says. "He listens to you."

"I think it's the dinosaur," I say with a wink, but her gaze doesn't waver.

"It's you too. Thank you."

They disappear down the hall, and I stand there a second, the image of that almost-smile lingering like sunlight.

I grab my computer and make a few notes, but my thoughts drift again. I want to tell Ginny about this. A month ago, Eli wasn't talking or looking at people directly. She'd understand what that smile meant. Because even if she won't admit it, she's the kind of person who'd get teary-eyed over a kid like Eli.

Damn it, I want more than this cold war we're stuck in. I want a chance to see what we could be, without letting everyone else's history decide for us. But wanting more doesn't change the facts. And right now, wanting her is like trying to hold onto smoke.

I run a hand through my hair as I head back to my office and shut the door, but the usual sense of calm I feel in this space doesn't come. I should be reviewing labs or tackling my inbox, but I can't stop picturing Eli's face as he clutched that dinosaur, that flash of a smile. I do need to find him a referral for therapy.

I drag a hand down my face, sit at my desk, and spin my chair toward the window. There's one name that keeps circling in my head — Alaric Dempsey, who also happens to be Ginny's older brother.

He's a brilliant psychologist. Respected. In-demand. One of the best in the valley for trauma work, especially with kids. But he's also a Dempsey.

I stare at my phone, jaw locked. It shouldn't matter. But it does. I guess that's the point Ginny keeps trying to make. *Damn it.* I have to put my money where my mouth is, I suppose. If I want her to make her own decisions without considering family ties, I have to do the same.

And besides, this isn't even about me. It's about Eli. And Eli deserves the best regardless of my family baggage.

I scroll through my contacts. Alaric's number has been there since he returned to Paradise last year. We've crossed paths professionally a few times. Mutual referrals. Nothing personal. Always cordial.

I hit call, and he picks up on the second ring. "Dr. Paradise."

"Hey, Alaric. How are you?"

"I'm doing well, thanks. It's a surprise to hear from you."

"Yes, well, I have a professional request." I clear my throat. "My patient, Eli Stone, is six years old and was placed in foster care three months after coming out of Children and Family Development's custody. Severe anxiety. Selective mutism. He's not on meds, and I'd like to keep it that way."

"I'm familiar with Eli," Alaric says. "What can I do for you?"

"Oh…" I stall. I wasn't expecting him to be so direct or so informed. "I think he's ready to meet with a therapist, but drugs aren't going to fix what he's dealing with."

"I agree…"

I wait, because I feel like he's deciding how much to say.

"He watched his mother get beaten up," Alaric says finally. "By his father. Repeatedly. The last time…she was unconscious. Broken ribs. Dislocated jaw. Eli was the one who called 911. The dispatcher stayed on the line with him for six minutes before help arrived."

I sit back, staring at the wall. Some of that was in the paperwork they sent over, but not all of it. My throat thickens, and my hands curl into fists. "And his dad?" I ask.

"In custody. Pending charges," Alaric confirms. "The mom's still in the hospital recovering. Multiple injuries, old and new."

"So this wasn't the first time it got bad."

"No. And it wasn't just her." He pauses. "We believe Eli was abused too. He has signs of previous rib fractures, and anxiety symptoms consistent with direct exposure."

The fury is instant. It burns through me like acid. I hate these cases, and not just because they're difficult to treat. But because I can't understand them. I don't get how anyone, let alone a father, puts his hands on a woman. On a child.

I let out a slow breath, trying to keep my voice even. "Eli needs more support."

"I agree," Alaric says. "I can get him into a trauma program I run at the clinic. It's one-on-one time, and it's covered through the foster system with the right paperwork."

"What do you need from me?" I ask.

"Referral just needs your signature and a note on his chart. I can send the form over."

"Done. Send it now."

"I will." He pauses. "He's a good kid. Hurt but good. You're doing right by him."

I nod. "Thanks. And…" I pause. "Thanks for taking the case. I know you've got a full roster."

"I make room when it matters."

We end the call, and I stare at the phone. Alaric Dempsey, a guy I want to hate on principle, gave a kid a fighting chance without hesitation. And somehow, I knew he would. Change has to be possible. Maybe the lines our families have drawn in the sand aren't as unmovable as we think.

I rub the back of my neck. After a moment, the paperwork arrives electronically, and in a few strokes, I finish the referral. I'm happy to do it. Hell, I'm honored. It feels good to be part of helping someone, to get them the expertise they need.

I don't know how long I sit at my desk after the referral's sent. I need to shake this. I need air. I need —

Her.

I find my phone and stare at her contact. Ginny Dempsey. Still saved under Bullseye Bait, the nickname I gave her the night she beat me at darts.

Coward. That spurs me to tap out a message:

Me: Hey. Just checking in. Been thinking about you. A lot. Hope you're okay.

I stare at it, then add,

Me: Miss you.

Then I wait.

Five minutes. Ten. I check my signal. I check the time. I

check her other social media. Nothing new.

My pulse trips. I should've called instead of leaving her alone all weekend. I told Sadie I wasn't going anywhere, and I should've done better.

I close my eyes, then do something possibly even dumber. I call her.

It rings once. Twice.

Then her voicemail picks up, and I freeze at the sound of her voice.

"Hey, it's Ginny. Leave a message or don't. I probably won't check this anyway."

I let out a breath and wait for the tone. "Hey. It's me." My voice cracks, and I don't bother hiding it. "I, uh... I had a tough case today. I can't tell you his name, but you'd like him. He doesn't say much, but he's strong as hell. He's got this stuffed dinosaur he won't let go of, and today, he looked me in the eye."

I pause, eyes stinging.

"I referred him to your brother. He's good. I mean, I always knew he was, but I think he's really going to help him. When I spoke to him, it felt like we were on the same team."

Another pause.

"Anyway, all I could think was how much I wished I could tell you that. In person. How much I wish you could be here when I need someone to talk to. Not as a secret. Not in the dark."

I bend forward, elbows on my knees, voice low and raw.

"I miss you. I miss your laugh. Your smart mouth. The way you look at me like you already know what I'm thinking. I miss the version of myself that exists when I'm with you."

I swallow hard.

"I don't want to hide you. I know I've told you that, but I'm saying it again. I like you too damn much to pretend this is something it's not. And I hate that our families—this ancient bullshit—gets to decide what we're allowed to feel."

I sit in the silence for a moment.

"But at the same time, I understand your fears, and the risk it is for you to spend time with me. I don't expect you to call back. Just… I needed you to know."

I hang up and drop the phone on the desk like it burns. I put my head in my hands, the weight of everything pressing down—Eli, Ginny, this whole damn war we didn't start but somehow still have to fight.

And for a second, I let it hit me. All of it.

Then I pull myself together. Because I have patients, and I can't fall apart.

But God, I wish I didn't have to do this alone.

Maybe I said too much. Maybe I should just let her go. But I couldn't, not without telling her the truth.

I meant every damn word.

TWENTY-ONE

Ginny

The tension in my shoulders winds tighter with every step toward the door. I've avoided Ryker all week, not because I wanted to, but because I don't know how to handle the way his message fractured the wall I keep trying to cement around my heart.

Gran has called a family dinner tonight at the main house. We all hope she's going to announce her retirement, but I know we'll never be that lucky. My fingers tighten around the flowers I brought for her, a peace offering I hope might soften the sting of whatever's coming.

When I arrive and go inside, the long dining table stretches before me, seating divided by allegiance. Blood may bind us, but tonight there are battle lines, and I worry I've got no army to back me.

On the right side are my brother and sisters—Sera sits

ramrod straight, flanked by Ric and Josie. Across from them are Aunt Georgia's kids—Dylan with his ever-calculating eyes, Kaitlyn sipping her wine, and Logan, all quiet observation. They watch the room like they're casing it.

At the far end, clustered together, are Aunt Eleanor's boys—Scott, Mike, and Eric. Bigger, bolder, and louder. They don't bother hiding their ambition. They think the vineyard is theirs to win, and they're not wrong to think Evelyn might hand it to the one who plays her game best.

No one speaks as I sit. They're all waiting for Evelyn to speak first.

"Finally," Sera whispers as she kisses my cheek. "Gran's been pacing. She's in one of her moods."

Josie shoots me a look—hopeful, nervous. She's wearing her boardroom best, even though this is just dinner, which tells me everything.

At the head of the table, Evelyn Dempsey sits like a queen in judgment. Regal. Ready to strike. She lifts her glass of cabernet with the kind of practiced grace that makes your back straighten just watching her.

Her eyes land on me like a gavel falling. "Genevieve," she says. "I see you've managed to join us after all."

"Wouldn't miss it." I extend the flowers toward her. "I saw these and knew you loved gerbera daisies."

She doesn't reach for them. "You can give those to Lucia."

The housekeeper is right behind me, and she lights up as she takes them from me. "These are lovely and will look great in the vase on your grandmother's desk."

Gran doesn't look at her, just keeps glaring at me. But they haven't started eating, so I'm really not that late.

Dinner is a slow-burn form of torture. Each course is more elaborate than the last, each bite harder to swallow than the one before. Conversation moves between business updates and polite commentary on the vintage we're enjoying, but no one is really listening.

Gran hasn't said a word about retiring. She's letting the

anticipation sit like a trap, spring-loaded and waiting.

Every time she clears her throat, Sera's posture stiffens. Each time Gran lifts her wineglass, Josie straightens like she's preparing to give a speech. And I sit here, chewing through roasted lamb, knowing I'm just a placeholder at this table.

When Gran finally sets down her fork and dabs her mouth with her napkin, the room stills.

"Genevieve," she says, locking her gaze on me again. "How is the gift shop?"

I want to fling my wine in her face. I want to tell her the shop keeps the lights on in the tasting room she never sets foot in. But instead, I smile like it doesn't matter, like she hasn't just reminded everyone I'm nothing more than a souvenir clerk.

The disappointment on Sera's and Josie's faces is immediate and unfiltered. This is not going to be her retirement announcement.

I lift my glass. "Busy."

"Good," she replies crisply. "Idle hands lead to poor decisions. Some of us understand what it means to carry responsibility."

A direct hit.

I don't flinch. I've played this game too long to let her see the bruise. But it still hurts.

Whatever tonight is supposed to be, it's not a passing of the torch. It's a reminder of who's still holding the reins. Gran's gaze cuts away from me like I've been dismissed. Whatever I am, whatever I've become isn't worth her energy anymore.

Her interest shifts to more pressing matters. "The well serving block one-hundred-and-one has a problem," she announces. "The vines don't seem to be maturing like the rest. How is the hand watering going?"

Josie clears her throat. "We're seeing some buds, but not what we see in other areas of the vineyard."

"We share the well with Paradise Hill, and they seem to be having the same issue," Sera adds.

"The Paradise property," Evelyn cuts in. "Convenient,

isn't it? Their new pinot vines that aren't ready for wine making are struggling. And our award-winning vines are dying. And we're supposed to believe that's nature?"

My stomach feels like it's folding in on itself.

Gran presses on, fury crackling beneath the surface. "Our attorney is combing through the original water rights agreements. If they diverted the flow, if they tampered with the source, we'll bury them in litigation so deep, they'll be lucky to keep a single bottle on the market."

Josie quietly sets her glass down. It makes a soft clink against her plate, but it sounds deafening in the silence that's taken over. "Do we have any proof?" she asks, voice careful and respectful.

"Not yet," Gran says. "But I've already ordered soil and moisture samples from both parcels of land. If I can show a pattern—any correlation between our loss and their sudden surge in the other blocks beyond the well—I'll draw the line myself in front of a judge."

She's ready for war.

Sera swallows hard. "What are you thinking?"

Evelyn sits back, her fingers tapping the stem of her wineglass. Her eyes glint. "If they want to siphon what's ours, then we ruin the fruit they stole it for. Their grapes beyond the well are thriving. Let's see how well they survive if those start showing signs of blight."

She's talking about sabotaging the Paradise Hill grapes. My cousins Scott, Mike, and Eric are enthusiastic and obvious in their support. But my stomach drops like it's free-falling off a cliff. She's not talking about retaliation or legal action. She has no proof. She's talking about sabotage. Criminal charges. Ruining people's lives, and she's looking around the table like she expects volunteers.

There are laws that protect vines. She could face fines of up to a hundred thousand dollars each, and in this area, we plant about five hundred vines per acre. She won't do the work herself, so if they catch any of us doing it, we could be criminally prosecuted for mischief or trespass. And the cherry on this ice cream sundae? The Paradise family could sue us civilly, and we'd lose everything.

Josie chokes on her water. Sera's eyes go wide.

My hands curl in my lap, nails digging into my skin.

"They'd retaliate," Josie says, voice tight. "If we're wrong, if this escalates—"

Evelyn cuts her off with a look sharp enough to draw blood. "Then we remind them why you don't cross a Dempsey. We've survived phylloxera. Drought. Recession. Theft. We're still here. Still standing. Because we don't blink when someone tries to steal what's ours."

Then, as if pulled by a string, her gaze swings back to me.

Direct. Cold. Unflinching.

"Assuming everyone at this table remembers which side they're on."

The words echo inside me long after Evelyn moves on, spearing a piece of lamb with the same calm precision she uses in business.

Sera tries to shift the mood, mentioning the upcoming Black Bear Valley Wine Consortium event in town. "We need to finalize who's attending," she says. "There's a talk on regional marketing trends and another on vineyard tech."

Josie nods. "I think we should all go. It's good optics. Shows unity."

My cousin Dylan swirls his wine in the smug way he has when he's about to make a point. "I heard the Paradise family is sending Ryker."

I freeze, wineglass halfway to my lips.

"He's never come to these things before," Dylan continues. "Wonder why he's suddenly interested in vineyard operations."

I force a little laugh. "He's...probably just trying to be supportive. He's got opinions about everything."

It's meant to be casual, throwaway. But the moment the words leave my mouth, I feel the temperature in the room drop.

Dylan narrows his eyes. "Do you know him?"

My fingers slip against my wineglass. *Shit.* "I mean, everyone in town knows of him," I rush out. "He's kind of hard to miss."

"Mmmmm..." Dylan sits back slowly, eyes still pinned on me.

Evelyn's fork stills on her plate. "That's interesting," she says coolly. "You seem to have quite the informed opinion for someone who hasn't lived here in years."

My throat tightens. "I just meant he's got a reputation." I smile. Too wide. Too rehearsed. "Kind of a big personality."

Evelyn picks up her glass of wine, takes a sip, and sets it down with care. "Big personalities are rarely worth the trouble they cause. Especially when they're not our problem to fix." Her eyes meet mine, calm, poised, and lethal. "It's best not to speak too freely about people who have no place at this table. Even in passing. We wouldn't want anyone mistaking divided loyalty for misplaced affection."

Sera looks uncomfortable. Josie studies her plate. Dylan still looks smug. He planted a trap, and I jumped right into it.

I sit here, pulse roaring in my ears, wondering how much I gave away. One more slip, and it likely won't just be suspicion about me.

If it comes down to them or Ryker, I'm no longer sure which side I'll choose. That's why I keep trying to buy myself time. But I've already exiled myself to no-man's land. And for what? I'm denying myself the comfort of Ryker, but clearly, I've lost the trust of my grandmother...if I ever really had it.

So what's the point of all this? I can't sit here much longer pretending I'm someone I'm not. I don't know what comes next, but if I don't make a choice soon, someone else will make it for me.

TWENTY-TWO

Ginny

After Gran nearly declared war on the Paradises, dessert is served like nothing happened. The clink of silverware and quiet hum of conversation almost makes us seem like a normal family.

But I know better. The air here turns cold fast.

"—and you wouldn't believe the nerve of this guy," Mike's saying, his voice loud enough to cut through three side conversations. "Shows up at Ryker Paradise's front door like it's the damn Four Seasons."

I glance up, confused. Mike's grinning, proud of himself, the way he always is when he knows he's holding something toxic.

"Who?" Josie asks, brows pinched.

Mike winks. "Ginny's new ride. Dropping her off at Ryker's place at one in the morning. And not just once, either.

Regularly."

My head jerks up. My brain scrambles to process it — how he knows, how long he's been watching.

Eyes swing to me. Accusing. Eager. Hungry.

And I realize too late, this wasn't a slip. It was an ambush.

The table stills. Even the fire seems to crackle more quietly.

"What are you talking about?" Evelyn asks, her voice sharp.

I feel myself go cold.

Mike shrugs, all innocent. "Just saying what I saw. A black Beemer. Late night drop-offs at Ryder Paradise's home. I was out night-fishing last week, so I saw it happen. Same car the week before. Figured we were all pretending not to notice, but I guess I broke the spell."

My heart collapses on itself.

"Have you been seeing Ryker Paradise?" Gran's voice is no longer just sharp. It's lethal.

"I —" My mouth opens, but no sound comes.

She pounds the table. "Tell me he's lying."

"I'm not," Mike chimes in again. "I've got the timestamped security-cam footage from the shop to prove it."

Josie groans. "Mike, what the hell — ?"

Sera steps in. "Can we just take a second before we start tearing into each other?"

But the look on Gran's face says the moment for second chances is long gone. "Is it true?" she asks again.

My throat tightens. I don't answer. I can't. I don't need to. She already knows.

"You've been sneaking around with Ryker Paradise." Evelyn rises slowly, her chair scraping across the tile like a warning shot. "After everything this family has done for you. After everything they've done to us. You choose him?"

My heart beats double time. Heat floods my cheeks. I feel like I've been dragged to the center of the table and put on trial.

I push back my chair and stand too. "This feud? It's ancient. It's a waste of everyone's time. You don't even know if the Paradise family is behind the problem with the vines, yet you want to go to war with them."

"You think this is about ghosts?" Evelyn's voice rises. "You think this is something we all just decided to keep going out of boredom?" Her eyes flash, fixed on mine like a vise. "They stole our land. The northern ridge? It belonged to us. Your great-grandfather had the deed. But Chip Paradise — he forged a claim. And don't even get me started on what they did when your grandfather passed. Trying to tell me they had a deal about the land. *No.* They've made sure we're still deep in this feud. And you are playing with the enemy."

I blink, stunned.

"He strong-armed it from the county registrar when I was a girl," Gran continues. "Your great-grandfather died trying to fight it in court."

I shake my head, barely recognizing the woman in front of me. "That was before I was even born."

She slams her palm against the table. "And then they killed my sweet Mabel, your grandfather's sister."

That knocks the air out of me.

Josie gasps softly.

The room tilts. My fingers go numb. I've heard about drunken arguments, whispered accusations but never anything like this.

"They ran her off the road," Evelyn says, her voice cracking now. "It was one of those damn boys, Max and his brother, showing off. Racing the ridge road like it was a game. She never stood a chance. They got off with nothing. Called it a tragic accident." She spits the words like poison.

My breath catches. No wonder she's so angry. "I'm sorry that happened. I truly am. But Ryker wasn't alive then either."

Evelyn's voice turns bitter. "And yet every single time we rise, every time we get ahead, they find a way to knock us down. The well. The vines. The deals that suddenly fall through. You don't think they're behind it? You think they're just lucky?"

Tears sting my eyes. "I think Ryker is a good man."

Her eyes blaze. "Then you're a fool."

Silence.

Just the crackle of the fire and my racing heart.

"You want to love him?" she sneers. "Fine. But not under this roof. You don't get to have both. You can be a Paradise or a Dempsey. You don't get to straddle the line."

My throat closes. "You're making me choose?"

"I'm not," she says, jaw tight. "You already did."

I want to scream that I didn't. That I don't understand how I feel or what I want yet.

But deep down, I know she's right. I've made my decision. And I think it's the one I've been trying to make my whole life — not them, not him, but me. I choose myself, what I want, and a future that actually has something to offer besides pain and old grudges.

TWENTY-THREE

Ryker

Sunday dinners at the Paradise house are usually loud, messy, and half a step away from a food fight. But tonight, we haven't gotten to that portion of the program yet. We're still lounging in the living room, where Tarryn and Sadie are deep in discussion on the couch.

I'm sipping a cab franc blend I haven't tried before. It's nice. And I'm trying to listen to Max argue with Dad about a new irrigation system in Dad's office. But my focus keeps drifting to the ladies here in the living room.

"...if we stagger the releases—maybe small-batch quarterly drops—they'll feel exclusive without actually having to limit supply," Tarryn says, pulling out her phone and turning it toward Sadie. "We can track engagement and loyalty through the app."

Sadie nods. "We can gamify the points system. Members

who attend more events, share content, or reorder faster climb tiers. They're not just wine drinkers. They're ambassadors."

They're talking about the Barrel Club, our subscription-based wine loyalty program, but it sounds more like a masterclass in marketing psychology. My sister and future sister-in-law have somehow turned a group of casual wine drinkers into raving, loyal superfans, people who pay extra to feel like insiders.

It's brilliant. And terrifying.

Because I'm not sure I understand how they pulled it off. And I hate not understanding something. I hear heavy footsteps, and then the front door slams shut. Max isn't happy.

"They've got waitlists for exclusive harvest dinners," Dad mutters, clearly eavesdropping too now that he's finished with Max. "One woman cried when she got bumped to the top tier."

I blink. "Cried?"

He shrugs as he sits next to me. "Apparently her husband gave her the membership for their anniversary."

I glance back at Sadie and Tarryn, who are now laughing about something involving barrel-shaped candles and branded robes. They're a powerhouse team, the kind that makes you want to work harder and smarter or get out of the way.

I should have focus like that for pediatrics and the staffing shifts we've got coming up at the clinic. Mom talks about retiring like it's right around the corner, but the truth is, I'm not ready for that yet. Not ready for her to hand me the keys and walk away. I'm still learning how to keep the clinic running without it swallowing me whole. I still don't how she manages patients and keeps the business of the practice healthy at the same time.

Tarryn was always the organized one, I muse. The type to label leftovers and color-code school supplies. And how Sadie, who not long ago told me she never wanted to be involved in vineyard life again, now looks like she was born for this.

For a second, I wonder yet again what it would be like if Ginny were here. If she would see that we're not just some family of bullies. If she could sit with us and laugh about cork shortages and member perks. If she could belong here.

Mom seems to think it's possible, but to me it still feels like a dangerous thought, particularly because Ginny doesn't seem nearly as interested in it as I am. I take another sip of wine and glance at Mom. She's watching Tarryn and Sadie too, her lips in a satisfied smile. Dad finally moves closer and joins their conversation. The room is warm, full of life.

And yet for me, something's missing. Something I don't even know if I can have.

After a moment, Mom disappears into the kitchen, and then returns and claps her hands twice. "Dinner's on. Everyone grab a dish and take it to the dining room table."

The smell of a honey baked ham and the cheesy goodness of homemade macaroni and cheese fills the air. Tarryn and Sadie gather their phones and notebooks, slipping back into daughter and future daughter-in-law mode as everyone shuffles toward the table.

We're just settling in when the front door swings open again, and Max storms back in without knocking—because of course he doesn't—and Zach slinks in behind him, looking like he'd rather be anywhere else.

"We just came from block nine," Max announces. "The rows of pinot are worse than we thought."

I look over at Tarryn. Her shoulders go rigid, and the smile she had while talking to Sadie vanishes. "I know," she says. "Elise and I tested the soil yesterday. We're pulling samples from the bordering rows to compare nutrient levels."

Max ignores her and turns to Dad. "It's spreading. Whatever's going on over there, it's not natural. You need someone managing the vineyard who's got a better handle on this."

And there it is. The dig. The not-so-subtle attempt to push Tarryn out and slide Zach in.

Dad doesn't respond right away, and the silence stretches just long enough to make my stomach clench.

Tarryn speaks again, cool and clipped. "We've got it under

control."

Zach clears his throat, fidgeting beside Max. "I've been working with some of the hands-on irrigation calibration. I could help more if—"

"You're not trained in vineyard management," Tarryn cuts in before he can finish. "And with all due respect, we don't need help from someone who nearly poisoned the chardonnay block last spring."

Zach flinches, but Max barrels ahead, unfazed. "It's not about one mistake. It's about direction. This place needs forward thinking—"

"What it needs," I interrupt, "is less politicking and more teamwork."

Max shoots me a look, but I don't back down.

Tarryn doesn't either. Her jaw tightens, and her hands clench. I know that look. She's holding it together, for Mom and Dad and the rest of us. But she's seconds from snapping.

This isn't about vines or water or soil samples. It's about control. About Max pushing Zach into a role he'll never be ready for, no matter how many late shifts he logs. And about Tarryn fighting, again, to prove she belongs here.

Dad finally speaks, his voice calm. "Let's not do this tonight."

Max opens his mouth, but Mom preempts him with a sweet-as-arsenic smile. "Dinner's getting cold. Why don't you and Zach join us?"

With a huff, Max nods, and everyone resumes moving to the table, stuffing the tension down.

When everyone begins to eat, I glance across the table at Tarryn. She's focused on her plate, but I can tell her mind is miles away.

Max shifts in close to Dad, voice low but not nearly low enough. "I still think the Dempseys are behind what's happening to block nine. It's the only place we share a well with them."

In an instant, the tension returns.

Kingston sets his fork down with a sharp clink. "You

really think they have something to do with the crop dying off?"

Max shrugs like he's just asking questions. "Their property lines run close. Their vines are doing okay. They've got motive."

Tarryn gives him a look. "Those are their prize-winning grapes, and they're *not* doing fine. The canes are turning gray. We irrigate differently. They use sprinklers, and that's what saved them from the frost two years ago, but they're having problems too."

Zach, eager as ever to fan the flames, jumps in. "Please. It's obvious. They've always wanted this valley to themselves. Their operation might look pretty on the outside, but they're desperate. They've lost distribution. Their rosé is tanking. And suddenly we've got sabotage on our hands? Come on."

Beckett narrows his eyes. "Seems rather farfetched that they'd ruin their crops just to shut down one of our blocks that's not even producing yet if you ask me. Where is your proof they've done this?"

"We don't have it yet," Zach says, voice growing louder. "But we don't need proof to admit what we already know. That family is toxic. They've always been out to undercut us. They're bitter, petty, and if they had the chance to watch us fail, they'd take it."

My hands curl into fists under the table.

Then Zach drops the bomb. "And maybe we'd already be doing something about it if someone in this family wasn't sleeping with one of them."

The room goes still. Airless. My spine goes rigid. My breath lodges in my throat. I knew this moment might come, but I didn't expect it like this. Not from him. Not here.

I don't move. I don't even blink.

Zach's looking right at me. His smile smug. Cruel. Like he's been saving that one.

Mom turns sharply, her expression hard. Her lips part like she's going to speak, but she doesn't.

I glance at Tarryn.

"I just spent the weekend with Ginny in Vancouver last month," she says, folding her arms. "We were roommates. I think I'd know if she was sneaking off with Ryker. He's not that reckless." Her gaze pins me. "Right?" She knows how I feel about Ginny, but she's giving me deniability.

I hold it. Don't flinch.

Sadie doesn't speak, but she doesn't look away either. Her expression is calm, but I can feel her tension. Ginny is her best friend.

Dad finally breaks the silence. "Is it true?"

"Yes." My voice is steady. The moment I say it, I know there's no walking it back. But I also know it's what I want to do. I've crossed a line, not just with my family, but with history. And this is how it has to be. "Ginny and I are seeing each other. Or at least we were. I don't know right now."

Max scoffs. "Unbelievable."

Zach sits taller, victorious. "Told you."

"She's not like them," I say, ignoring him.

"She is them," Max snaps. "That name carries weight. And not the kind we want attached to ours."

Zach cuts in. "You've been sneaking around with Evelyn Dempsey's granddaughter while the one well we share with them is killing our vines."

"Our vines? There's a problem with Dempsey *and* Paradise vines," I remind him.

"She works for the family business," Zach says. "She's involved. Whether she wants to be or not."

"She wants out," I tell them, though I'm not sure that's actually my news to share. "She's trying to break free. She just hasn't figured out how."

That's what I keep telling myself anyway.

Beckett rubs his jaw. "Even if that's true...how do you know she isn't being used?"

I feel that one in my gut. "I know," I say, "because I trust her."

Zach snorts. "You're too close to see it. That's the problem.

You've let her wrap herself around you, and now, you can't think straight. And while you're busy playing house, we're the ones dealing with the fallout."

Kingston finally speaks up. "You think she's the one sabotaging the well?"

"I think her family is," Zach says. "And she knows more than she's letting on."

"She doesn't," I growl. "You don't know her."

"And you don't know them," Zach shoots back. "They'll ruin all of us."

"I'm not the one poisoning the family from the inside," I say. "You want to talk about loyalty, Zach? Maybe clean up your own messes before pointing fingers."

His face flushes.

"This feud, this stupid, bitter war none of us asked for, it's cost everyone something," I continue. "And I'm done apologizing for something I didn't start."

"Careful," Tarryn warns. "You don't know what you're walking into."

"I do," I say. "And I'm still walking."

"So what now?" Greyson asks. "We just pretend like nothing's happening?"

"No," I say. "But we stop blaming Ginny for the sins of her family."

"Ryker…" Dad says. "You need to be smart. You're falling for someone on the other side of something that's far from over."

"I'm already in it," I say. "And if I have to choose between a history of hate or the possibility of something real with her, I choose her."

Zach shakes his head. "Then you deserve what's coming."

He's always hated that I never had to beg for a seat at this table, that I earned trust while he still fumbles for scraps. This isn't about Ginny. It's about me and the fact that I make everything he wants look easy. Zach's not interested in protecting this family. He just wants to watch it fracture.

Not on my watch, even though the silence after my last

words hangs like smoke over the table — thick, uncomfortable, impossible to ignore. There has to be a way through this. I remind myself that Mom is on my side.

Then Sadie clears her throat.

She sets her napkin on the edge of her plate. "For what it's worth, Ginny is my friend. She has been for a long time. She's going to be in our wedding." She looks over at Beckett. "I think we all need to remember that no family is perfect. Ours included."

All eyes shift to her.

"There are good people and bad people in every bloodline. And sometimes, the worst mistakes come from the people closest to us, not the ones with different last names. So maybe…we don't paint the entire Dempsey family with a single brushstroke, just like we wouldn't want someone doing that to us."

Max leans back, lips pressed tight. Tarryn lowers her gaze to her plate, quiet now. Beckett gives Sadie a small nod.

Then Mom stands. "This is Sunday dinner," she says, looking around the table. "And I won't have it become some battlefield." She straightens her shoulders, adding with a soft sigh, "I'm going to get the tiramisu. And when I come back, I expect this table to remember that we are family. And family should be able to talk, disagree, and still care for one another without letting bitterness run the show."

Tarryn doesn't say anything, but her shoulders drop slightly. She's still upset but not unreachable.

Mom pauses just long enough to let that land. Then she turns toward me. "Ryker, come help me serve."

My stomach drops.

There it is. The summons.

Zach lets out a quiet, low whistle. "Oof. You're in trouble now."

I shoot him a look but don't bother replying. I know better. I push out of my chair, bite my tongue, and follow Mom toward the kitchen.

The kitchen smells like vanilla and espresso, the scent of "Mom's" tiramisu, which she actually buys from the Italian grocer. She moves around the island to retrieve dessert plates, her back to me.

I lean against the counter, waiting.

"I really thought we were past this," she says after a moment. She turns, holding a stack of plates against her hip. "The feud. The assumptions. The ugliness. It's been years since things boiled over between our family and the Dempseys. I thought everyone had matured." She sighs and sets the plates down. "Clearly, I was wrong."

I open my mouth, but she holds up a hand.

"I'm not talking about you. I'm talking about the rest of them. Zach. Max. Even your father, sitting there like it's not his fight to jump into." She shakes her head. "It's disappointing."

I let that sink in. "I'm glad she's not here," I admit.

"I'm disappointed once again," she says, offering a small smile. "But this time you're right."

I chuckle.

She smiles, though her eyes are still sad. "Look, I know it's messy. I know the history isn't easy. But if you care about her, really care about her, then you don't let the family name stop you. I stand by what I told you before."

"I'm trying," I say. "But I know she's catching it from her side too. Her grandmother's already suspicious. And if this gets worse..."

"You'll figure it out," she says firmly. "Because if she's worth it, you'll make it work."

I press a hand to the back of my neck. "It's just...hard to see a future when everyone's telling us we shouldn't have a present."

She rests a hand on my arm. "So let me ask you something. And don't give me the safe answer."

I nod, readying myself, and her question lands like a meteor.

"Do you love her?"

My defense springs to life immediately. I thought I was just scratching an itch. Keeping things simple. My eyes water. But the way I ache to hear from her, the way I'd fight the world just to sit beside her at dinner… There's no other answer but the truth.

"Yes," I say, the word catching in my throat. "I love her."

Mom gives my arm a squeeze, then turns back to the counter like she didn't just watch me unravel.

"Good," she says. "Then we'll figure out the rest."

TWENTY-FOUR

Ryker

Sleep won't come.

The house is still, but my mind is loud, full of ghosts from tonight's dinner, all bearing my last name and sharpening their knives.

I've replayed the evening half a dozen times. Every look. Every accusation. Every time someone glanced my way with suspicion, like I'd let the enemy into the family.

But Ginny isn't the enemy. She never was.

I roll onto my side, staring at the shadows on the wall. My jaw clenches. *Stupid Zach.* He's the first to point fingers, and the last to think about consequences. He's always been good at stirring shit up and watching the rest of us burn. It shouldn't surprise me that he's painting Ginny with the same brush as her grandmother.

I stew on that a moment, and then something occurs to me.

Zach would be especially prone to laying blame elsewhere if it ultimately serves his interests. Tarryn is still watching his shady ass and tracking what he does. And we never have made any sense of that phone call I overheard. He's involved with something, and it's not anything good. But unlike him, we don't just fling accusations around for fun. We're determined to do this right.

In the meantime, though, everything about this sucks. He knew about Ginny. I don't know how, but Zach knew there was something between us. And he made damn sure the whole room turned on me before I could even speak.

Even Tarryn didn't say anything. Not really. She looked at me like she wanted to, but in the end, I guess silence was easier.

I sit up, running a hand through my hair, hot with frustration. Caring about Ginny shouldn't feel like a declaration of war. But tonight, it did. I'm grateful to have Mom's support, but I'm not sure I have her patience and faith. I'm sick of pretending centuries-old grudges should dictate who we love.

I don't accept this idea that who Ginny is related to somehow defines her. I didn't intend to fall for her, but I did. And now, I have to fight my own damn family just to protect what we have?

Someone benefits from keeping this feud between our families alive. And it's not me or Ginny.

I grab my phone from the nightstand. I want to call her. Hear her voice. Remind myself why this is worth it.

But I don't. Because she's already unsure, and she doesn't need the weight of this too. Nothing about what happened tonight would help her feel better about sticking it out with me.

I lie back, arm behind my head, and let out a long breath. Tomorrow, I'll talk to my dad. I'll try to get through to him.

My phone pings.

Ginny: Are you awake?

That changes everything. I call her immediately.

When she picks up, it's not her voice I hear first. It's a soft, muffled sound. A sniff. A shaky breath.

My heart drops. "Ginny?" I keep my voice gentle, even though every muscle in my body tightens. "Talk to me."

"I'm here," she whispers, but she sounds wrecked.

I swing my legs over the side of the bed, ready to — I don't know what. Run directly to where she is? My heart aches hearing her like this. "What's going on?" I ask. "Are you okay?"

She exhales slowly. "I didn't know who else to call. I'm sorry."

"You never have to apologize for needing me," I assure her. "Do you need me to come get you?"

Her breath hitches, and I know something's coming. Something I don't want to hear. "What does your family think about us?" she asks.

"Well…" I hesitate, and that silence says too much.

"I knew it," she breathes, hurt in every syllable.

"It's not that simple," I say. "It came out at dinner before I intended it to, and it was a lot at once. Zach ran his mouth. Max made it worse."

"Zach," she mutters. "Of course."

"But my mom is on board, and the others will come around," I tell her, hoping I sound convinced. "They're just…stuck in the past, clinging to old wounds."

"Yeah, well, my grandmother practically lost her mind tonight," she says, voice cracking. "She was absolutely unreasonable, talking about loyalty and listing things our families have done to each other."

I close my eyes. "I'm so sorry."

"I told her the feud is ancient history. That it has nothing to do with us. But she wouldn't hear it. None of them would." She laughs softly. "You'd think I confessed to murder."

I grip the edge of the mattress. "You didn't do anything wrong."

"We're both doing everything wrong," she whispers. "Aren't we?"

"No," I say firmly. "We're doing something brave."

She goes silent again. Then she tells me something I haven't heard before. "They think you're stealing our water."

I blink. "What?"

"They think your family diverted runoff from the upper watershed, and you're willing to sacrifice your new vines to destroy the vines on our side that produce our best wines."

"You've got to be kidding me."

"I wish I were. Gran has the lawyers reviewing the original agreements, and she's pulling soil samples."

My blood boils. "Jesus. That's way beyond a wild accusation."

"I know," she says, voice weary. "It's the war all over again. And we're caught in the middle."

"I would never do that to your family. My family wouldn't do that."

"I believe you," she says. But then her voice breaks again. "It doesn't matter, though. They don't. And they never will."

I want to argue, though this is remarkably similar to the defeatist spiral I've just been circling in myself. I want to tell her something that will make sure none of it matters. But I hear her trying to breathe through tears, and my mind goes blank.

"This is why we can't be together," she whispers.

"No," I snap. "Don't say that."

"You don't understand. You haven't seen the way they look at me, the way they talk about you. It's not safe." Her breath hitches again. "I'm scared for you. I'm scared of what they're going to do."

"I'm not."

"Well, I am," she counters, and I can hear the panic bleeding into her voice. "I need you to hear me. Please, don't come here. I couldn't handle it. I can't protect you."

I press my fingers to my eyes. Every part of me wants to be with her. To hold her. To take this weight off her and make it mine. But I know she's right.

"Okay, I won't come," I say gently.

Her breath shudders out. "Thank you."

"But do you want to come here? Meet somewhere? I'd love to see you, help you through this."

"I can't risk it right now. Evidently, my cousins have been watching, so for tonight, I think I'll just lie low." She sighs.

"I'm not giving up on you," I tell her. "Not now. Not ever. You mean too much to me."

She doesn't answer right away. Then, in a whisper so soft I almost miss it, she says, "You mean everything to me."

We stay on the phone, breathing in sync across the distance, two hearts breaking quietly in the dark.

"I can't do this," she whispers. But she doesn't hang up. She stays. Needing me even as she pushes me away.

Finally, she murmurs goodbye and the line goes dead. I close my eyes and imagine her here, curled beside me like she used to be.

I want to throw something. Scream. Drive over there and demand that her family stop treating her like some kind of traitor. But I don't. Instead, I text Tarryn.

Me: You awake?

The three dots come to life.

Tarryn: Unfortunately, yes. What's up?

I stare at the screen for a second, then type.

Me: Just got off the phone with Ginny. She says Evelyn is convinced we're stealing their water.

There's a pause.

Tarryn: We're NOT.

Me: I know that. But they think we'd sabotage our own

vines just to destroy theirs. She says Evelyn has lawyers and is collecting soil samples.

Tarryn: That's insane. We're having issues in the same area. Something's off, and trust me, I'm not interested in losing the money or the time invested in those vines just to destroy theirs.

Of course something's off. But we're too busy drawing battle lines to talk to each other like neighbors.

Me: If the families actually talked, we could probably figure it out together.

Tarryn: That would require Evelyn Dempsey to be a rational human being. So…unlikely.

I smirk despite myself.

Me: You're not wrong. She's old. Stubborn. And dangerously good at rallying people around a vendetta.

Tarryn: She's been nursing a grudge since disco was popular.

I sigh.

Me: Zach's also really good at nursing a grudge. That had to be a calculated move at dinner tonight, right? You think he's really that worried about Ginny? Maybe he's just shifting the attention off of himself.

Tarryn: Maybe. I'm still logging the weird things I notice, but so far, there's no smoking gun.

Me: I've got tomorrow off. Want to go out to block 9 and take a look? See if we can figure out what's really going on with

the water?

    Tarryn: Yeah. Meet at the maintenance shed at 9. Dress to get dirty.

    Me: Always do.

I put my phone on the nightstand and let my head fall back against the headboard. What a mess. But at least this is a way to take action. Showing people the truth is going to be the only way they'll stop believing the lies. We have to start untangling this, one acre, one argument, one act of good faith at a time.

TWENTY-FIVE

Ryker

When my alarm sounds in the morning, it feels like I only closed my eyes an hour ago. My limbs are heavy, my mind still fogged with everything that happened last night. But it's time to get started.

I lift my phone and fire off a message to Ginny.

Me: I'm going out with Tarryn this morning to take a look at the vineyard. I'll let you know what we find.

No clue if she's awake yet. Doesn't matter. She'll see it when she's ready.

By eight forty-five, I'm pulling into the barn lot with two cups in hand, the spicy-sweet scent of chai filling my Armada. I spot Tarryn near the equipment shed, arms crossed, ponytail high, looking like she hasn't slept much either.

I hold out her drink as I approach. "Peace offering," I say.

"You trying to butter me up for something?" she asks as she takes it.

"I thought I was already your favorite brother. Or did last night change that?"

"You are my favorite brother," she says, sipping. "Today."

I give her a look.

She sighs. "I'm sorry about last night. I'm having enough problems with Max and Zach. I didn't think getting involved would help."

"I know. I just thought that since Ginny was in the wedding, they'd be further along in forgiving."

Tarryn waves that away. "You do you. Ignore Max and Zach. You have Mom's support, and that's what matters."

I nod, and just as we're about to head out, Elise rounds the corner, hair tucked under a faded baseball cap, clipboard in hand.

"Well, well," she says. "Is this a secret mission or am I crashing something?"

"Not secret," Tarryn replies. "Just early."

"We're going to inspect block nine," I tell her. "I want to get eyes on whatever's happening with the well."

Elise nods. "Smart. I've been hearing complaints from the vineyard crew. Dry patches where there shouldn't be."

"It's affecting vines and causing trouble on both sides of the property line. You should come with us," I suggest.

She nods, and we load into the four-wheeler, Tarryn at the wheel, Elise riding shotgun, and me in the back.

Halfway up the hill, Elise turns slightly. "So, how do you know the Dempseys are upset about this?"

I hesitate.

Tarryn glances at me over her shoulder, then looks back to the road.

I shrug. "Ginny told me."

Elise turns fully this time, eyebrows lifting. "Ginny Dempsey?"

"Yeah."

"You're talking to her?"

"More than talking to her," I admit. "We're in Sadie and Beckett's wedding together, and we've been...seeing each other."

Elise's mouth opens, but Tarryn jumps in before she can speak.

"I like her," Tarryn says. "She's smart. Honest. And she's Sadie's best friend, so she's going to be part of the family whether anyone likes it or not."

That shuts Elise up for a second.

I give Tarryn a look. Where was this energy last night? "Thanks."

She shrugs. "Just stating facts."

Elise hums thoughtfully.

The trees thin as we crest the ridge. The sun catches on the vines' new leaves in the immediate rows, but the ones beyond that are unmistakably off. Plants that should be vibrant and gearing up for maximum growth look sunburned. The soil below them is dry and cracked in spots and overly saturated in others.

Tarryn cuts the engine.

"Well," she says, climbing down. "Let's see what the hell is going on."

Elise walks among the rows slowly, head down, hands on her hips. She crouches near one vine, brushes her fingers through the dry soil, then stands and moves on, expression tight.

"Some of these vines are barely clinging," she mutters. "And this patch over here is soaked. It makes no sense."

She turns the irrigation system on and stands back. "They all seem to be working right."

I'm about to follow her when the crunch of gravel behind us draws my attention.

An old truck kicks up dust as it pulls to a stop near the service path. The doors open almost in unison.

Sera and Josie. Dempsey sisters, sharp as thorns and just as likely to leave a scratch.

Fantastic.

They stride toward us, in jeans and boots, both wearing

expressions like they came to pick a fight.

Sera speaks first. "Interesting that you're all out here, inspecting our problem."

"It's on our land too," Tarryn reminds her evenly. "We're having the same issue."

Josie folds her arms, scanning the vines. "Funny. Yours look a lot better than ours."

"We came out here to see what's going on," I say, stepping forward. "Not to argue. But yeah, I've heard the rumor that you think we're stealing your water."

Sera lifts her chin. "It's not a rumor if it's true."

"It's not true," I say firmly. "We didn't divert anything. That's not how we operate."

Josie goes quiet, focused on a patch of withering vines. Elise, ever the peacemaker, steps in.

"Josie," she calls, "will you come take a look at this? Your eye's sharper than mine when it comes to these younger roots."

Josie hesitates, then nods and walks toward Elise. The two of them lean over the rows, voices low as they huddle.

Sera stands beside me and Tarryn, but her eyes zero in on mine. "So. You and Ginny."

Here we go. "I'm not getting into that," I tell her. "Not here."

"Why not?" she asks. "Because you don't know where I stand? Because you think I'll go running to Evelyn?"

I don't answer.

She scoffs. "That's smart. You're learning."

I turn to meet her gaze. "I care about her."

Sera's jaw ticks, but she doesn't seem surprised. She glances toward Josie and Elise, who are deep in conversation. "She stood up to Evelyn in front of all our cousins for you," she says quietly. "You better be at least half the man she says you are."

Before I can answer, Elise calls out, waving us over. Josie is holding up a clump of soil and shaking her head.

She straightens as we approach, brushing soil off her

hands. "This isn't consistent with runoff redirection," she says. "If you all were diverting water, it'd be a cleaner pattern—one side suffering, the other thriving. What we've got here..." She gestures to the vines. "...is patchy. Erratic."

Elise nods. "Some vines are saturated. Others bone dry. That suggests irregular flow, not manipulation. The irrigation system is working."

Josie walks over to one of the drip-system heads and taps her finger to the water, placing it on her tongue. Her brow creases. "The water doesn't taste quite right."

Elise does the same thing. "I don't know. It's not that bad. I think it's the high-density polyethylene we use for the drip system."

Josie considers that. "Maybe. We don't use a drip system on the hillside. We have a sprinkler system that goes off every morning at four o'clock."

Tarryn crouches beside the trunk Josie just examined. "Could it be a blockage somewhere higher up?"

"Maybe," Josie replies. "But I think it's more likely there's a break or damage in the irrigation line that's creating pooling in some areas and starving others."

"Could it be sabotage?" Sera asks, crossing her arms again.

Josie doesn't answer right away. She looks at me. "Have you had any equipment issues? Vandalism? Anything...off?"

My mind flashes to Zach. He's definitely *off*, but that hardly seems like something I should share with the Dempseys. We don't even have enough evidence to confront him directly yet.

"I don't know," I admit. "But I'll look."

"So," Elise says, "we have erratic water flow with no clear pattern and no proof of redirection." She looks around, and everyone nods.

The wind shifts through the vines as Josie dusts her hands off again and pulls her cap lower. "We'll run diagnostics on our end. Pressure tests. Line inspections. You should do the same."

I nod. "We will."

She gives me one last look. Not hostile this time. Just guarded. It's the first time I've seen her drop her shield, even a little. And for Josie Dempsey, that's as close to an olive branch as I'll ever get. "Tell Ginny to keep her head down," I offer.

She looks at me a long moment, then gives the slightest nod before she turns and walks back toward the truck, Sera falling in beside her.

Tarryn sighs. "Well, that could've been worse."

"Yeah," I agree, watching them go. "But it's still not clear what's going on with the vines. And despite getting through this with no drama, I feel like someone wants this feud to explode."

Just then Josie pauses at the edge of the path and turns back to Elise. "You should come by Black Bear," she says. "Take a look at our rows. Compare conditions. If there's something systemic going on, it's bigger than just your vines or ours."

Elise lifts a brow, surprised. "You sure about that?"

Even Sera glances at her sister, seeming startled by the offer.

Josie nods. "I don't care about the politics. I care about the fruit. And right now, this is our only troubled patch. But if this is just the first patch to have a problem, it will be a disaster."

That gets everyone's attention.

"I'll come," Elise says with a nod. "This afternoon?"

"Works for me. I'll let the crew know," Josie says. "Our families may not like each other, but our vines don't care who owns them. If this problem spreads, no label in this valley will survive it."

I glance at the sunburned vines. She's right, and I'm more than glad to hear her say it. This seems like an entirely reasonable approach. I raise my arm in a wave, and then they're gone, tires crunching as they drive back down the hill.

Tarryn exhales. "Okay. That was unexpected."

"Yeah," I sigh. "But I'll take cooperation over a courtroom any day."

Elise nods, her eyes still on the path where the truck disappeared. "It's a smart move. But it also means this might be worse than we thought."

"So what do you think is causing this?" Tarryn asks.

Elise squats again near a vine, touches the brittle leaves, then brushes her hand through the soil. "If it were a natural blockage or root problem, we'd see a gradual decline. But this? It's targeted. Deliberate. Like someone's toying with the system."

Tarryn raises a brow. "Deliberate?"

"I'm not saying sabotage," Elise replies, "but I'm not ruling it out either. Josie hinted at the same thing. Whoever it is, if someone is doing this, they're clever enough to make it look like a systemic issue, not an attack."

I feel my eyes narrowing. "And whoever it is benefits from keeping both families angry and in the dark."

Tarryn turns to me, —and for a second, just a heartbeat, we share a look. That could be Zach.

She clears her throat. "So what now?"

Elise straightens, brushing her palms together. "I'll head over to Black Bear this afternoon. Having more information about this can only help, and hopefully, there won't be any run-ins in the process."

I nod. "And I'll go over our lines again. Personally."

TWENTY-SIX

Ginny

I've been so good the last two weeks, keeping my distance, keeping things simple. But one look from Ryker and all that resolve crumbled. We were supposed to be helping Sadie and Beckett with wedding stuff last night, not ending up tangled in Ryker's sheets. Now, I'm slipping out of his house all over again like this is some shameful secret. He asked me to stay. I told him I couldn't. I've already been here too long. Tonight was a mistake, even if it didn't feel like one. Not with the way he kissed me like I belonged to him. But this can't be safe for either of us.

When I return, the caretaker house looks peaceful from the outside, porch light glowing like a welcome sign, windows warm with lamplight. But the second I step out of my car, my stomach knots.

Gran's sedan is parked in the drive.

Waiting.

I square my shoulders, force my steps to remain steady as I cross the gravel, but my heart pounds. When I'm halfway up the walk, the driver's door creaks open. She's been standing there. She doesn't look at me. Doesn't say a word.

She just gets in and drives away.

Gravel kicks under her tires, echoing in the quiet night. I watch the taillights disappear up the road until it's just me and the sound of the crickets and the sudden, suffocating weight of dread.

She knows. Of course. I always get caught.

I don't move for a minute. I can't. Eventually, I manage to wrap my arms around myself like that'll hold me together. But inside, everything is splintering. I fumble at the door, pushing inside with shaking fingers and locking it behind me, though I don't know what I'm protecting myself from. It's too late for that.

She didn't yell. Didn't make a scene. The silence said everything. There's going to be hell to pay.

I stand in the kitchen, unsure if I should scream, cry, or pour a drink. My phone buzzes.

Ryker: Home safe? Miss you already.

I don't reply. Instead, I set the phone down and close my eyes for a moment.

I take a shower and crawl into my bed, but I'm not tired anymore. My brain is on overdrive. Every time I close my eyes, I see Gran's car pulling away. No words. No more chances. Just quiet, disappointed judgment in the dark.

Now, something inevitable is coming, and I can't stop it. Hell, it was probably always coming, but now, I can't buy myself any more time.

When my alarm sounds, I haven't slept at all. I go through the motions of getting ready and grab my laptop and jewelry-making toolbox on the way out the door. I may be too nervous to do much work today, but I'll at least be prepared in case there's down time.

I park behind the tasting room and head toward the gift shop, trying to act normal. I don't even make it to the front door before Josie steps out.

She doesn't smile, just tugs the sleeves of her cardigan down her arms and meets me halfway. "She's looking for you," she says softly.

I swallow. "Is she...in a mood?"

Josie's eyes soften. "She's your grandmother. She loves you. No matter what."

Which means *yes*. She's in a mood. The shit is about to hit the fan.

I nod, not trusting my voice, and square my shoulders. One breath, then another. Then I start walking, — past the barrels, past the bottling line, and up the old wooden staircase to the office that's ruled this vineyard for three generations.

I knock.

The door opens, and my mother slips out without a word. She doesn't meet my eyes, just brushes past me like I'm a stranger. I don't let myself flinch. After a moment, I step inside.

Gran is at her desk, fingers laced tightly together. Her back is straight. Her expression is calm, though the air is thick with tension.

She doesn't ask me to sit.

"Where were you last night?" she asks instead.

"I was out with friends," I say.

Her eyes narrow. "Was it Ryker Paradise?"

I hesitate. Then I nod. "We had wedding —"

She holds up her hand to stop me. "You've shamed this family," she snaps, rising from her chair. "After everything they've done to us. After what they've taken. And you—" She jabs a finger toward me. "—you go and warm his bed like nothing matters. Like we don't matter."

My throat burns. "It's not like that."

"Then what is it like, Genevieve?" she demands. "You sneaking around in the dead of night? Lying to my face? You think he cares about you? You think any of them do?"

"I care about him," I say, before I can stop myself.

Her mouth tightens. "Then you can go be with him."

I freeze. "What?"

"You're no longer welcome in this house. Or at this vineyard. Your things will be packed for you at the caretaker house. You are to leave this property immediately, or we'll call the police, and they'll charge you with trespassing."

All the air rushes out of my lungs. "You don't mean that," I whisper.

"I mean every word," she says coldly. "I warned you, and you made your choice. Now, you'll have to live with it." She sits back down. Dismisses me with a wave of her hand. "Close the door on your way out."

I feel something akin to my life flashing before my eyes, but I can't think of anything to say, so I go. And I don't look back.

My feet carry me to the gift shop. I'm desperate now. I need my mother.

The bells above the door jingle as I step inside. Mom is behind the counter, deep in concentration, rearranging a display of cookbooks and wine accessories like the fate of the entire vineyard depends on it. She doesn't look up.

"I thought we were leaving the shop layout the way I planned it," I say gently, for what feels like the hundredth time.

"I like it this way," she answers, still not looking at me. "It's more...functional." She points to a box. "I believe those are yours."

I step over to check, and inside are my jewelry pieces—pendants, cuffs, and wire-wrapped stones I was selling here. Now, everything's tangled in a knotted mess.

I swallow, pulling the worn cardboard box tight against me. "I..." I hesitate and set the box back on the counter.

She finally looks at it. And then at me. "You should've known better," she says. "You always knew how she felt."

I blink. "So that's it?"

Suddenly, I remember how when I was little, Mom used

to braid my hair while I sat on the kitchen counter. How she'd hum without realizing it. That version of her is gone.

"I don't have a choice."

"I have nowhere to go," I whisper.

Her face twists, not with cruelty, but with weariness. Like life has squeezed all the softness out of her. "I can't take you in right now."

"Why not?" My voice cracks.

"Because I can't afford to upset your grandmother." Her hands tighten around a stemless wineglass. "Without her, I have no home. No money. No safety net."

I feel like I've been punched. She doesn't even look at me.

"And I'm what? Disposable?"

She doesn't answer.

I back away, tears hot behind my eyes. "Thanks for the support."

She's my mom, so I hoped for more, but I guess she's right. And I shouldn't lean on my sisters, either. If they try to help me, they'll put their own jobs and places in the family at risk. So I'm on my own now, starting from nothing.

The bells jingle again as I leave. And this time, I don't stop walking until I'm back in my car. But I still have nowhere to go. Ryker would be a comfort right now, but this is not how I want to show up. I don't want him to think I choose him only because I have nothing left. I can't make this his problem as well. No, I need to sort this out first. Find my bearings...

So I drive around town with no destination, no plan. I follow the edge of the lake down to its southern end and the town of Black Bear, named by the indigenous nation and anglicized. I cry until I can't anymore.

That's it. This is the end. I'm cut off. Just like my dad.

Somewhere past the lake, surrounded by nothing but trees and old road signs, I pull over and scream into the silence. Because I've given everything up, and I have nothing left to lose.

TWENTY-SEVEN

Ryker

This is a hospital day, and the text comes just after I finish my afternoon rounds.

Unknown Number: She's out. Excommunicated. No place to go.

My thumb hovers over the reply button as my heart starts to pound.

Me: Who is this?

The number's not saved in my phone. There's no area code clue. Why anonymous? Is someone trying to help without getting caught? Or is someone trying to screw with me?

Me: What are you talking about?

No dots. No typing bubble. Nothing.

My mind spins. Excommunicated? No place to go?

Ginny.

I call her. Straight to voicemail. The second I hear her message begin, my throat closes.

"Hey. It's me." My voice falters. I clear my throat and try again. "I got a text from a number I don't recognize. I don't know if it's true, but Gin, if it is, if something's happened, please call me. Just let me know you're okay. Please."

I end the call and stare at my phone like I can will it to ring.

Panic tingles in my extremities. I knew things were bad between her and her family, but this? Being cut off entirely?

I scrub a hand over my face and pace the length of my office. I don't know where she is. I don't know who sent the message. I don't even know if it's real.

But I know one thing for damn sure.

If she needs me, I'll find her. I don't care what her last name is. I don't care what lines we've crossed. She's it for me. I just keep waiting for her to realize that, to choose me too. But if she's hurting, if she's out there alone, it's an emergency.

Screw this.

I scroll to Sadie's name and hit dial. She picks up on the second ring.

"Ryker? Everything okay?"

"Is she with you?"

"Who?"

My heart sinks. "Ginny. I got this weird text. Something about *she* being out and excommunicated. It was vague and from an unknown number. I can't find her to figure this out."

A pause. Then Sadie sighs into the phone. "It must be her. I can't believe she did that. Fucking Evelyn."

"I don't know for sure. Ginny's not answering her phone, and I have no idea where she'd go."

"Alaric maybe? Her mom's place? And she's always welcome here." Sadie exhales. "I never thought she'd do this. I thought Evelyn wanted control, not total destruction."

"Right? We're not *that* bad," I quip.

She manages a laugh, and we agree to keep in touch and reach out if we hear from Ginny.

I have several patients left on my schedule back at the clinic, but in between I check my phone. Nothing. No calls. No texts. Not even a read receipt.

With my appointments finished, I duck into my office again and scroll to Alaric's name. I want things to be professional between us, but surely, he'll be concerned as well. And right now, I'll take anything that gets me closer to Ginny.

He answers on the second ring. "Paradise."

"Have you heard from Ginny?" My voice is hurried and decidedly not professional.

"No," he says slowly. "Why? What's going on?"

"She's not answering her phone. She hasn't reached out to Sadie. I got this vague text earlier. Someone said she was 'out' and 'excommunicated'. They didn't use her name, but things have been tense with Evelyn. I don't even know what that means, but—" I exhale hard. "I don't know where she is."

He's quiet for a second. "Okay. Breathe."

I close my eyes, jaw tight. *Of course the shrink tells me to breathe.*

"I haven't heard from her," he continues after a moment. "But if this involves my grandmother, Ginny wouldn't want to put me in her crosshairs. She's smart, though. Resourceful. She won't just disappear. If she needs space, she'll take it, but she knows how to land on her feet."

I rub a hand down my face. "If you hear from her—"

"I'll have her call you. Promise."

"I really care about her," I tell him, hoping he understands.

"I know she cares about you," he replies. "There are just some things at play that are out of her control."

"I understand. I'm having some of the same issues."

"Maybe the two of you can be the pair that bridges the

gap."

I should appreciate that vote of confidence more than I'm able to in this moment. "Thanks."

We hang up, and I close my eyes, sending a silent message out into the universe. *Come on, Ginny. Just tell me you're okay.*

TWENTY-EIGHT

Ginny

Eventually, I end up in the parking lot of the Paradise Steaming Mugs. The store windows are fogged from the afternoon caffeine rush, and there's a line inside, but I don't care. At least I can stretch my legs and get some caffeine.

I grab my laptop from the passenger seat and go in. The barista behind the counter gives me a half-smile and a nod, familiar, but not friendly. She probably recognizes me. Most people in town do. Not as Ginny but as a Dempsey. That's how it always is. They know the name, not the person behind it. What I've done, what I haven't. Doesn't matter. The last name speaks louder than I ever could.

I wait in line, and after I have my coffee, I find a table in the corner near the radiator and slide into the chair like I'm trying to disappear. My laptop hums to life as I plug in and connect to the Wi-Fi. Around me, the coffee shop buzzes, but no one pays me any attention. I'm a woman barely holding it together, pretending to work. I open my inbox out of habit, just for something to do.

But then I see it.

Subject: Part-Time Marketing Manager Offer – Black Bear Valley Wine Consortium

My heart skips as I click it open.

It's real.

A clean offer. Bullet points and bold text—position details, start date, hourly rate, projected salary. My name is right there, plain as day.

I can hardly believe it. This is what I wanted. What I worked for. A foot in the door. A job that will finally let me build something for myself, separate from my family's business. My chance to prove I'm more than just a Dempsey.

My heart leaps, but then it comes crashing right back down to Earth. Will my family ruin this for me somehow?

They're bound to find out what's happened. This town is too small. And the consortium is all about prestige and tradition. Hiring someone blacklisted by her own family? That's not exactly on-brand. *Damn it.*

I slam the laptop shut, and a couple at the next table glances over. I don't care. It's too much. I press the heels of my hands to my eyes, willing myself not to cry in public. Not again.

I breathe for a moment, and eventually, I feel a little more solid. I've got to be practical here. There's no reason to panic and assume the worst. That's the Dempsey move, for sure. *And that's what you're trying not to do*, I remind myself.

After a moment, I pick up my phone. I scroll past Ryker's last message—three words I've read a hundred times. *Please call me.* I don't delete it. I just can't. And I also shouldn't ignore it anymore.

Me: Hey…things have fallen apart with my family, and I need some time to sort it out. I'm safe, so you don't have to worry. I'll reach out when I'm ready to talk.

Then I'm back on task. I call Marc Warner and have a rather pleasant conversation about the position they've offered me. I explain as delicately as I can about the change in my other employment, but he seems unconcerned. His main focus is when I might be able to start.

By the time I finish the call and look up again, Steaming Mugs is almost empty. The baristas are wiping down counters, flipping chairs onto tables, and pretending not to notice I've been nursing the same cup of coffee for hours. I should leave. But where should I go? Mom made her position clear, and I won't put my siblings in the line of fire. I understand their dilemma, but I can't say it goes unnoticed that none of them has reached out to me.

I heave a huge sigh. Sadie said she wanted to spend more time hanging out, that she was tired of the wedding being front and center all the time… I chuckle to myself. I guess maybe this is her chance. *Lucky girl.*

In all honesty, she's probably the only person I have access to right now who might understand this disaster. I've been kicked out of my family and my home, and the one person I want to run to is the one I can't.

By the time I make it to Sadie and Beckett's place, my throat burns from holding it all in.

Sadie opens the door, her eyes bright and welcoming. "Hey! What a great surprise! Come in. We were just going over some wedding logistics."

I nod, my lips trembling. "Can I — Do you have a minute?"

"Of course. What happened? Ryker's been looking for you. Are you okay?" She steps aside, pulling me inside and into her arms.

The second she does, my chest tightens, and I start to cry, not the graceful kind, but the raw, ugly kind that makes your shoulders shake.

"Someone dropped off your things this afternoon, and we weren't sure what was happening," she says. "I'm so glad you're here."

Beckett appears behind her. "What's going on?"

Sadie doesn't let go. "Come on. Sit down."

"I'm sorry," I say as I shuffle inside, hugging my purse tight. "I didn't know where else to go."

"You don't have to explain," Sadie says.

"You're welcome to stay as long as you need to," Beckett assures me.

I sink onto the couch and tell them everything because it's boiling in me, and I need to get it out. It can't possibly do any more harm now.

"My grandmother was waiting in my driveway when I got back to the caretaker house late last night. I'd been with Ryker after our planning here." I wipe my eyes. "She didn't say anything, just gave me a look and drove away."

Sadie sinks onto the couch beside me. Beckett stays near the kitchen, arms crossed.

Slowly, I tell them what's unfolded since then, and somehow, I manage not to cry.

Sadie just looks at me for a second when I've finished, then deadpans, "What a fucking bitch."

A stunned laugh escapes me. I sniff and swipe at a tear. "You're not wrong."

"What did your mom say?"

I snort. "My mom is too dependent on my grandmother to cross her. She was in the gift shop, rearranging everything to how she likes it again. She handed me a box of my jewelry on my way out. It was all just dumped in there, tangled like garbage."

Sadie shakes her head and wraps me in another hug. "I want to see your pieces. I can help untangle them. What about your dad? He certainly knows how this feels, right?"

I scoff at that. "He's not really part of my life. Though Sera said he's been living with someone up at Marshall, building a new winery." I glance toward the window, my voice quieter. "I guess there's no reason not to reach out now... Honestly, I knew this was coming. I should have made the choice myself before it came to this. My grandmother's too bitter and volatile to not blow everything up."

Sadie takes my hand. "You're not going back there. Not now. Not ever. You're staying here as long as you need to. And Ginny? You don't owe that woman anything."

I want to say no, that I don't want to be a burden, that I haven't earned this kind of kindness. But the words won't come. And I can't afford to say them anyway.

Beckett clears his throat. "Guest room's ready if you want it. No pressure. Just...you're not alone."

His voice is calm, but there's tension in his jaw, and I can tell he's biting back his opinion.

"Thank you," I whisper.

Sadie studies my face. "What did you do all day? Please tell me you didn't just sit in your car crying."

I shake my head. "No... Well, maybe a little. But mostly I drove. Aimlessly. Up and down the lake, into town, through the hills, and then I sat at Steaming Mugs."

Sadie gives my hand a squeeze.

"But there could be one bright spot," I say, looking over at her. "I got an email from the Black Bear Valley Wine Consortium."

Her eyes widen. "Yeah?"

"I got the job," I say, the words finally starting to feel real. "They want me to develop a marketing plan to bring more visitors to the valley and highlight the success of the local wineries. It's flexible, and it's a fresh start. I called Marc Warner at the consortium after I got the offer and told him I'm no longer employed by Black Bear. Fortunately, he didn't care."

Sadie lets out a delighted squeal and grabs the wine bottle off the coffee table. "Yes! That is amazing. We are so celebrating this. Where's the opener?"

Beckett raises an eyebrow from across the room. "Pretty sure I already opened that bottle."

Sadie grins. "True. Okay, then we'll open another. She may have been fired by a tyrant, but she just landed a job doing something she actually loves. That calls for a proper toast."

I laugh. "You're really good at making everything feel less terrible."

Beckett brings in fresh glasses, and Sadie pours.

"That's what friends—and wine—are for." She clinks her glass against mine. "So here's the deal. Tonight we celebrate. You're free from that vineyard prison, and you're free to date Ryker. He's been frantic to make sure you're okay. Have you contacted him? Someone sent him a text, and he's been worried."

I can finally breathe again. "I let him know I'm okay. I'll reach out again soon." I sigh loudly. "I'm just still psyching myself up. I didn't want to bring this mess straight to his doorstep. I want to come to him on my own terms because I know this isn't going to be easy with your family either." I look at Beckett.

He shrugs. "We've never kicked anyone out, although ask me later about Zach."

That makes me smile.

"Ginny, maybe this isn't the end," Sadie says. "Maybe it's a beginning."

I let out a sharp laugh. "Yeah, sure. Homeless, underemployed, and disowned. Sounds like a dream come true."

She doesn't flinch, just shakes her head. "You've been saying for months that you don't fit in there. That you can't breathe under your grandmother's thumb. All she did was shove you out the door. Maybe that's exactly the push you needed to build something that's yours, not hers."

I open my mouth to protest but then close it again. Her words sting because they're true. Nothing has changed. I've felt this way about my family for years. That's why I left the first time around. The only difference now is that I don't get to hide behind the safety net they offered. It's terrifying. But also...freeing.

We all smile. I feel the tiniest flicker of something that almost resembles hope.

"I don't want to be a burden."

Sadie looks me dead in the eye. "Ginny, you're not. And honestly? Fuck your grandmother."

That makes me laugh, then brings the tears again, but not so many this time.

"How about another glass of wine?" Sadie offers after a moment.

I nod, sinking onto their couch like it might swallow me whole. "Thanks."

She disappears into the kitchen, and Beckett sits beside me, his voice low. "You're safe here. Whatever you need."

"Thank you," I whisper.

Sadie returns with a bottle of red and a sleeve of cookies. "Comfort first, nutrition later," she says, pouring the wine. "Now, tell me more about this new job."

"Well, I start Monday. I won't be able to rent much on what I'm making, but I'll figure something out."

Sadie lets out a triumphant whoop. "See? The Dempseys might've slammed a door, but the universe opened a freaking skylight."

I can't stop the laugh that escapes me this time. I am going to be okay.

We finish a second glass, and then the day begins catching up to me. I thank them again and excuse myself to the guest room. I'm so tired.

But before I go to sleep, I force myself to read Ryker's messages and respond.

Me: I'm sorry for the delay in getting back to you. It's

been a day. I'm at Beckett and Sadie's now, and I am exhausted. Just wanted to let you know. I'll be in touch again soon. Promise.

TWENTY-NINE

Ryker

I'm just looking at Ginny's message when Sadie calls later that evening. The first words out of her mouth are, "She's here."

I blow out a relieved breath. "Yes. She just texted to let me know. Can I talk to her?"

"Just a second," she says.

There's a muffled sound, Sadie calling Ginny's name, and then a new voice comes on the line.

"Hello?"

My heart cracks. "Ginny. Jesus. Are you okay?"

"Eh, I've been better," she says.

"Talk to me. What happened? I got a text from an unknown number, but they didn't mention you by name."

"That was probably Josie." She sighs. "Gran was waiting for me at the caretaker house last night when I got home from your place..."

My hands curl into fists as she tells me the rest of the story. I pace across the room, fury pulsing in my veins. "So she fired you and kicked you out?"

"That's the short of it, yes." Her voice hitches, but she pushes on. "I knew she'd do this eventually."

"Why didn't you call me?" I ask.

"Because...I think I didn't want you to see me like that," she says. "Homeless, jobless, tossed out like trash. I don't want to be your...project."

Project? Why doesn't she understand that I want to be her protector?

"I need to stand on my own as I sort this out," she adds. "Even if I'm falling apart. Especially then."

"Ginny." My throat's thick now. "That's—Jesus, I'm so sorry." I want to throw something. Yell. Do anything to take this pain off her shoulders. "I just want to support you, not take over. I promise."

"I know. Thank you." Her breath catches. "I hated being part of the Dempsey family drama, but I didn't realize how much of me was wrapped up in it until it was gone. I just need time to figure things out. I want to make the choices that are right for me, not act because I have to."

I press a hand over my eyes. "I understand," I tell her. "But I know you can do this. You're not alone."

"Thanks," she says again. "Like I said, I'll be in touch again soon. But this isn't your mess to clean up."

"Ginny, are you sure you—"

"I just need some rest," she assures me. "Things will look brighter in the morning."

"Okay," I say reluctantly, because what else can I do?

But after we hang up, I feel restless, shaky. Like I'm not where I need to be.

I text Sadie.

Me: I'm on my way over. Please let Ginny know I'm

coming.

Sadie: Hold on. It's been a tough day. She hasn't slept, and she's really trying hard to sort all of this out. I think give her tonight and connect with her tomorrow.

That's not at all what I want to hear, but I can't ignore every bit of feedback I receive. Ginny is safe, and she has been clear about what she wants. I need to respect that.

Me: Okay, but if anything changes or if you need anything at all, please be in touch.

I pocket the phone, trying to calm myself. I think of Ginny curled in my bed last night for the first time in so long, her head tucked beneath my chin, her laughter low and unguarded. I know that felt right to both of us.

I have to believe we can be there again. Surely, this is ultimately a good thing for Ginny, even taking our relationship out of the equation. Because the Dempseys, or at least Evelyn Dempsey, cares more about grudges than they do about their own family members.

I press my palm to my chest, trying to calm the storm there.

My family fights loud and loves louder. We slam doors and say things we don't mean, but we always come back to the table. Always. Being cut off? Disowned? It's unthinkable. We don't throw each other away.

I drag a hand through my hair, guilt heavy in my throat. Ginny deserves someone in her corner. Someone who won't just say they love her but will choose her. Every single time. And I do.

I can't fix everything, but I can show her she's not alone. She's mine. I have to show her she's still herself, even without her family behind her. I'll give her tonight, like she asked, but tomorrow is a new day. I'm not letting her walk through this without knowing I'm here for whatever she needs.

THIRTY

Ryker

I'm up bright and early the next morning, and all I want is Ginny. I hate the idea that she feels she can't trust me with this, though I absolutely do understand her needing to do things for herself. I can't come on too strong. She's vulnerable right now.

Finally, after two cups of coffee and a run, I can't wait any longer. But I decide not to just show up at Sadie and Beckett's place. Instead, I call Ginny first.

She picks up on the second ring.

"Hey," I say. "Good morning. How are you feeling?"

There's a pause, then a breath. "Better. Sleep helps — a lot."

She sounds good. "I'm so glad to hear that."

"I spoke with Sera and Josie a little bit ago," she says. "They apologized. Said they didn't agree with what happened."

"Okay, that's good," I agree.

"But they're tied to the vineyard," she continues, "and they're already dealing with my cousins trying to edge them out. So they can be sorry all they want, but it doesn't change anything. They're not about to take a risk like letting me stay with them. Nothing will be different until Evelyn decides to step down. And we both know the only way she'll do that is if she's in a pine box."

"I'm so sorry, Gin. You don't deserve this."

She lets out a tired laugh. "I'm not sure what I deserve, but I should have seen this coming. She did it to all three of her children, and now, she's working on my generation. I think my little sister, Addie, was the smartest of all of us. She pretty much gave Gran the middle finger and walked away."

She sighs. "But I did speak with Marc over at the consortium yesterday, and they've offered me the marketing job. It's part time, but maybe I can get a job at Steaming Mugs to help pay the bills."

"That's great!" I press the phone tighter to my ear. "Are you still staying with Sadie and Beckett?" I ask.

"For now. But I'll figure something out."

"Let me help. Come stay with me, just until you're back on your feet. I would love nothing more."

"No. The last thing you need is to have your family do this same thing."

"They won't," I assure her. "I mean, Max may rant and rage about it, but my mom understands—I told you that—so she'll get my dad on the same page. And you know Tarryn likes you. Please. Stay with me. It's not charity," I add after a moment when she doesn't respond.

"I know," she says. "But I need to do this on my own. I have to. Otherwise, I'm just someone who got kicked out of one family and ran straight to the arms of the enemy."

I bite back a curse. "You and I are not enemies. When are we going to stop being victims of our families' pasts?"

Her voice softens. "It's not just that. I know you want to help. I know you care. But I don't think it's a good idea."

I want her to feel good about this, to feel strong, so I don't push. "I miss you," I say instead.

"I miss you too," she whispers.

I sit up straighter. "Okay, then here's what we're going to do."

"Oh?" she says, sounding wary. "Are we plotting revenge now?"

"Better." I grin. "I'm stealing you for the day."

She laughs. "You? Take a day off? What about your patients?"

"Mom will cover for me. It's just one day. Only fun. No work, family drama, vineyard sabotage, or secrets."

"You're terrible at relaxing," she points out.

I smirk. "Challenge accepted."

She exhales. "Ryker..."

"I'm not trying to take over and fix anything," I tell her. "I just want to give you one good day. You're between jobs. Can you let me do that?"

"Fine," she says eventually, though I can hear her reluctance. So damn hard headed. "But I get to choose the music."

"Deal. I'm on my way. We're starting with a good breakfast."

"On your way?"

"Yep. Just put on comfortable clothes. Don't worry about your hair or your makeup. This is going to be all about us, and I'm warning you, we might get dirty."

It's a quick drive through the neighborhood to Beckett and Sadie's place. All my siblings live either on vineyard property or on adjacent land that's been converted to real estate. I pull into the driveway and kill the engine, giving myself a second before getting out. I don't want to rush her, don't want to spook her. *Play it cool, Ryker. Just give her a chance to relax.*

But the second the front door opens, I lose the thread of every careful plan I rehearsed on the drive over. She's wearing black yoga pants, Adidas Sambas sneakers, a thick hoodie, and her hair's knotted in a messy twist like she didn't even bother to look in the mirror. She looks beautiful. How did I ever manage without her?

"Hey," she says.

I cross the threshold and wrap her in my arms without a word. She sinks into me, head resting against my chest like she's been holding herself together with duct tape.

"You ready for a good breakfast at Dots?" I murmur into her hair.

"Yes." She breaks away. "That sounds like just what I need."

During the short ride over we hold hands, and I don't ever want to let go. But that kind of intensity is not what she needs from me right now. I remind myself again to *chill. Just be supportive.*

Dots smells like bacon and syrup, and I hold the door open for Ginny as she walks in. She's quiet as we slide into a booth by the window, but at least she's agreed to do this.

I hand her a menu she doesn't look at. She just wraps her hands around the mug of coffee the server brings and stares out at Main Street.

"We're not talking about yesterday," I say gently, though she still flinches. "No Dempseys. No drama. Just pancakes, bacon, and whatever ridiculous thing we decide to do next."

Her lips twitch. "Ridiculous, huh?"

"Completely irresponsible. I have a plan. Just you wait and see."

That earns a quiet laugh. "Deal," she says. "One fun day. No emotional landmines."

We order French toast with strawberries and the breakfast scramble, and by the time we're halfway through, her shoulders have dropped an inch. The tightness around her eyes is starting to ease.

She sets down her fork and wipes syrup from her lips. "You know, it's hard to be here and not think about Rosie Kennedy. This was her grandmother's place, and she started working here when her mom moved to Vancouver."

My heart tightens. "She was really a lovely person."

"I agree," Ginny says softly. "She made Sadie promise to do their bucket list. There's a whole notebook full of crazy ideas. Paris in the spring. Dog sledding in the Arctic Circle. Learning how to blow glass." She shakes her head, smiling a little. "She wanted to live big, even if she didn't get the chance."

I nod. "If you could go anywhere — like, right now — where would it be?"

Ginny stares into her coffee for a second. "Greece. Santorini. I want to swim in the Aegean and eat feta that isn't mass produced."

"That sounds perfect." I grin. "I'd pick Patagonia. The lakes, the mountains. Total silence."

"Very outdoorsy of you." Ginny laughs.

"Don't sound so surprised," I protest. "I hike. Occasionally. Under duress."

She laughs again, and then for a little while, we just sit there, sipping coffee and dreaming about blue water, open skies, and the possibility of something good.

We scrape the last bites from our plates, still trading travel dreams, and I toss down cash and grin. "You ready?"

She tilts her head. "Ready for what?"

I smirk. "Go-karts is first on the list, down at Rattle Snake Canyon."

She blinks. "Go-karts?"

"We're racing," I explain. "I need to crush you on the track to restore balance in my universe."

She laughs. "You think you can beat me?"

"Oh, I know I can beat you."

"That sounds like someone who's never seen me take a corner at full throttle."

I shrug. "Then let's find out."

We climb back into the Armada, and as I pull onto the road, she looks out the window for a minute. The hills are lush with grapes, apple trees, peach trees, and blueberry bushes, and the fields rush by as we drive.

"I'm okay," she says finally. "Just…bruised."

She's bruised, not broken. I think I love her even more for that. And I'm so glad she's starting to see it for herself. I glance over. "Yeah?"

She nods. "I'm not an idiot. Gran's never been soft. And I made my choices anyway. But still…it hurt."

"Of course it did. I'm sorry."

She shrugs. "My dad got kicked out years ago, and so did his brother and sister."

I glance over at her. "She kicked out all three of her children?" I knew they'd left, but I guess I was too young to understand that Evelyn helped them to the door.

Ginny nods, still watching the landscape roll by. "Gran called it a betrayal of blood."

I frown. "What did your dad do?"

She looks over at me. "He had an affair with a Paradise — Chereen."

I almost slam on the brakes. *That's why she disowned him?* "Chereen isn't a Paradise. Not by blood anyway. She was just married to Max."

Ginny nods. "She's a Fields, but to Gran, my dad had chosen your family over ours."

"My mom said Chereen and Henry didn't love each other."

She winces. "I don't know. Both of them went back to their marriages, at least for a while. But when my mom told Evelyn what had happened, she cut my dad off completely and he left, just like Chereen did, right? It wrecked both their marriages."

"I only found out about their affair when my mom told me a few weeks ago."

She nods. "No one talks about it. They pretend it didn't happen, that he just 'left.' But he didn't. He got erased."

"What about your aunt and uncle?"

"Neither wants anything to do with the vineyard and Evelyn's anger. I was maybe five when my granddad died, and even I noticed that Gran was particularly miserable to be around after that. My uncle, Franklin, was cut off and has since died, though I don't know how. Georgia, his wife, and my Aunt Eleanor come around when it benefits them or their children."

"I'm not going anywhere," I tell her.

She gives my hand a squeeze. "I know."

THIRTY-ONE

Ginny

By the time we pull into the parking lot of the go-kart track, I've officially stopped trying to figure out Ryker Paradise.

He's a pediatrician who knows the exact number of marshmallows it takes to cheer up a five-year-old and also the guy who insists we handle our emotional damage with gasoline and speed.

I follow him toward the rental counter, trying to control the butterflies in my stomach.

"Admit it," he says, handing me the forms. "You're terrified."

I arch a brow. "Of what? Embarrassing you in public?"

His grin is infuriating and adorable. "Of losing to a Paradise."

I snort. "Please. You drive a luxury SUV with backup

sensors and a pediatric car-seat checklist."

He lowers his voice as he signs the waiver. "Sexy, right?"

"Deeply," I deadpan, though the truth is — God help me — it actually kind of is.

They assign us helmets and cart numbers. I pull mine on and glance over in time to see Ryker adjusting the strap beneath his jaw. He catches me staring and smirks.

"Try to keep up, Dempsey."

"In your dreams, Paradise."

When the first race begins, I gun it off the line and hit the corner like it owes me money. Ryker's fast — I'll give him that — but he underestimates my inner agent of mayhem, the part of me that has absolutely no fear when it comes to tight turns and ridiculous risks.

By the third lap, he's a full cart-length ahead, and I catch his side-eye as I zip past him at the final straightaway.

When the checkered flag drops, I throw my hands in the air.

"Eat my dust!" I crow as we pull into the pit.

He pulls up beside me, pulling off his helmet. "Okay, I might have underestimated your need for vengeance."

I wink. "Consider yourself warned."

We're forced off the track between races so they can refuel and reset, which means we've got about twenty minutes to kill.

Ryker finds the little arcade tucked in the corner of the building and practically lights up. "No way. They've got Pac-Man."

I raise a brow. "Are you about to tell me you're some sort of vintage gaming god?"

He shrugs. "Only one way to find out."

We slide a few coins into the machine, and he insists I go first.

"I'm terrible at this," I warn.

He crosses his arms, a smug little half-smile on his face. "Prove it."

I smack the start button and guide Pac-Man around the

maze, dodging ghosts, grabbing pellets. I do okay until I corner myself near Blinky and die.

"Impressive," he notes. "Truly elite strategy."

I elbow him. "Shut up."

He takes the controls and immediately wipes the floor with my score, eating every ghost in sight like it's his job. At the end of the level, he's still alive, and I'm staring at the screen in disbelief.

"You've done this before." I shouldn't be smiling this much, not when my life is in shambles. But I can still kick his ass at go-karts, so maybe not everything is so bad.

"Gamer reflexes," he says, cocky as hell.

"Is this your seduction strategy?" I ask. "Dominate me in retro games until I fall into your arms?"

He shrugs, still steering Pac-Man through the maze. "It's working, isn't it?"

"Not even a little."

He finally dies just shy of the second level's final round and steps back like he just won Olympic gold. "Your turn," he says. "Let's see if you can last longer than a sneeze."

"You're insufferable."

"And you're adorable when you're losing."

I try again. And again. Each time, I barely beat my last score, and each time, he's right there with a smart comment, laughing under his breath, too close, too warm. He brushes his arm against mine like he's not slowly rewiring my entire nervous system.

When I finally manage to outscore him—by three points— I throw my arms in the air. "Victory!"

He snorts. "That was luck."

"I don't care. A win is a win."

He moves in close, eyes gleaming. "Want your prize?"

"What kind of prize?"

He lifts a single brow, then dips his head like he might kiss me—just for a second—but he stops short, teasing. "Bragging rights. What were you thinking?"

I roll my eyes. "You're the worst."

We walk out of the arcade and back to the track.

The second race begins, and it's soon clear Ryker has learned something. He doesn't make the same mistakes twice. This time he takes the inside track, blocks my best lines, and beats me by a solid two seconds. I give him a dramatic slow clap as we step out of our carts.

"I see the man has a competitive streak."

He slings his arm around my shoulder. "That wasn't competition. That was revenge."

I shake my head. "You're terrible."

He shrugs. "You started it."

We take another break and go to the café, which smells like fryer grease and nacho cheese, but the heat is welcome after the chill of the track. Ryker steers me to a corner booth and insists I sit.

"I'll get us something," he says, walking backwards toward the counter. "Don't go falling in love with me while I'm gone."

I flash him a look. "Try harder."

He grins and turns, leaving me shaking my head. I sink into the booth, pulling my vest tighter around me. I'm not cold exactly, just…raw. It's easier to laugh than feel too much.

A few minutes later, Ryker returns with two frosty drinks and a wooden tray loaded with sliders, onion rings, soft pretzel bites, and something that looks suspiciously like deep-fried pickles.

"I wasn't sure what you'd want," he says, setting everything down. "So I ordered everything they had that wasn't glowing or still frozen."

I raise a brow. "Hoping to impress me?"

He hands me a drink, eyes twinkling. "I figured if I couldn't win your heart on the track, I'd buy it with bar food."

I take a sip. "Good strategy."

He settles across from me, gaze warm. "You eat first. I'll just sit here and nervously hope you like something."

I reach for a slider. "I'm not picky," I say casually. "Otherwise, I wouldn't be seen with you."

He lets out a soft laugh, leaning back like he's been hit and is somehow enjoying it. "Low blow."

"You love it."

"Unfortunately, I do."

We eat for a few minutes. He lets me steal the best onion ring without complaint, which is either love or foolishness.

I glance up. "I start the consortium job on Monday."

"That's great."

"It's only part time," I say, voice quieter. "Enough to stay afloat, maybe. But not enough to get a real place. I'll need something else — maybe freelance marketing or part-time gigs — so I can rent a decent apartment. I haven't been the best about saving. I put all my money into stones and beads for my jewelry business."

He looks at me then, really looks at me, and I feel it before he even opens his mouth.

Don't say it. I pray silently. *Please, God, don't let him say it.*

But he just nods. Thoughtful. Quiet. And doesn't say a word.

I release my breath and pop a pretzel bite into my mouth.

He studies me for a second longer, then grins. "You're ridiculously bad at pretending you don't think I'm about to suggest you move in."

I almost choke. "I am not!"

"You were seconds away from climbing out that window."

"I was preparing a graceful deflection."

"I'm glad I saved you from it."

I smirk, trying to hide the rush of relief. "Don't get any ideas, Paradise."

He raises his drink. "No promises."

We clink glasses.

"You're proud of yourself right now, aren't you?"

"Deeply," he says, biting into a fried pickle with zero

shame. "This is peak boyfriend energy."

Boyfriend. The word clangs around my insides, too heavy and too tempting. I pretend it doesn't rattle me. I raise a brow. "Boyfriend?"

He winks. "Cart-racing partner. Same difference."

I shake my head but don't argue. I'm too busy pretending my heart didn't just skip a beat.

I nibble a fry while Ryker polishes off the last of the onion rings.

"Can I tell you something?" he says, voice low, almost like he's not sure if he should say it.

I set my fry down. "Of course."

He hesitates. "I used to think love had to be perfect to be real. My parents made it look easy. I thought if things got messy or hard or someone disappointed you, that meant it wasn't the right kind of love or they weren't the right person. So I kept waiting for something flawless, something easy." He exhales. "But that's not love. That's a fantasy. Real love...it has cracks. Blemishes. People screw up, they say the wrong thing, they get scared. And you love them anyway. Not because it's perfect, but because it's real."

I blink hard, trying to keep the emotion from spilling over. "You really believe that?"

His gaze holds mine. "Yeah. I do."

I swallow hard. "Was that why you don't do relationships?"

He considers that. "I think I stopped trying for anything that felt permanent. It just seemed safer."

My throat tightens. "Good. Because I'm all flaws. I come with scars and baggage, and I've been kicked out of my own damn family."

He reaches across the table, his fingers curling around mine. "I'll take all of it. Every flaw. Every scar. You don't need to be perfect. You just need to be you." He looks me in the eyes. "I know we can do this."

I feel myself blushing. "You're not easy to walk away

from," I tell him.

That makes him smile.

We sit like that a moment longer, fingers tangled across a table scattered with half-eaten fried snacks. And in the quiet, something shifts. Not loud. Not obvious. Just a small, steady opening, like maybe we're both starting to realize that we could last, even when it's messy.

We leave before the third race. We have other places to go.

THIRTY-TWO

Ryker

I haven't had this much fun in years. We left go-karts and headed to laser tag. It was Ginny's idea, and I couldn't say no.

Her helmet is slightly askew, her vest blinking triumphantly as she saunters out of the laser tag arena like she just conquered a battlefield, and honestly, she kind of did.

I follow, my vest barely lighting up after she annihilated me in the last two rounds. "You didn't even hesitate," I say, pulling off my gear. "You ambushed me behind the fake dumpster."

She grins, cheeks flushed, eyes dancing. "What can I say? You paused to adjust your sensor. Rookie mistake."

I shake my head, laughing. "You shot me in the back."

"You left it unguarded," she says, like that's the only explanation needed.

I toss our gear in the return bin and trail her into the lobby. "Where did you learn to play like that?"

She shrugs, collecting a water bottle from the vending machine. "I grew up as the second youngest in a circus of energy — eight cousins, three older siblings, and a grandmother who turned Easter egg hunts into tactical war games."

My eyebrows lift. "Please tell me that's a metaphor."

She smirks. "She used a whistle. And a point system. Candy was awarded based on performance."

I stare at her. "Jesus."

"She said it built character," she adds, cracking open the water.

"And possibly trauma," I note.

She shrugs again. "When you grow up in a family like mine, you either learn to compete or you disappear."

I watch her for a second, trying to imagine little Ginny Dempsey elbowing her way through a crowd of kids just to get a chocolate bunny and a nod of approval from her grandmother.

It makes sense now, why she's guarded, why she flinches at kindness but comes alive in a storm, why she always seems ready to run, even when she wants to stay. And then there's her jerk of an ex-fiancé who betrayed her trust all over again.

"I like the way you fight," I tell her. "Even when it's against me."

Her eyes soften. "I don't want to fight you."

I take a step closer. "Then don't."

We stand there, breathing the same air, everything between us electric and uncertain.

This day — full of racing and fried food and ambushes in dark corners — feels more real than any of the serious, carefully planned dates I've ever been on. I don't want it to end.

The sky's turning dusky by the time we get back to the Armada, the sunset streaked with orange and purple. The air has that soft, fading warmth of late spring, cool enough to make you think about a jacket, but not cold enough to rush.

Ginny walks a step ahead, her hands in her hoodie pocket.

Her hair's come half loose from its twist, strands brushing her cheeks as the breeze picks up.

She looks over her shoulder as I unlock the doors.

"That was a good day," she says.

I nod. "Yeah. It was."

She hesitates by the passenger side, like she's not quite ready to get in. I stop too, giving her space. Letting her lead.

"I haven't had a day like this in a long time," she adds, not looking at me. "Where everything felt easy. Light."

My throat tightens. "You deserve that."

She finally turns to me. "So do you."

The air shifts between us. Her expression flickers. Then, without a word, she steps forward. One hand grabs the collar of my hoodie and pulls me down. The other finds my jaw. And her mouth is on mine before I can even think.

It's not tentative or careful. It's heat and frustration and something dangerously close to need.

I recover quickly, and my hands find her waist, drawing her in as I taste the salt of her lips. Her fingers curl tighter in my sweatshirt like she's anchoring herself.

By the time she pulls away, we're both breathless. She's not just the girl I want. She's the life I didn't know I could have.

She licks her lips and looks up at me, defiant and flushed. "I told you I fight."

I smile, brushing her hair behind her ear. "I like it when you fight for this."

She opens the door and climbs in, leaving me standing in the parking lot, heart pounding, a stupid grin on my face. I'm completely gone for her.

I circle the car, and she's barely buckled her seatbelt when I glance over and say it, "Come home with me tonight."

She goes still. "Ryker…"

"No pressure," I add quickly. "You don't have to."

She looks out the window, biting her bottom lip. "It's not that I don't want to. It's just… It's been a really big day."

"I know." I pause, watching her profile. "And it doesn't

have to end with us going separate ways. Not tonight."

Her silence stretches long enough that I'm sure she's going to say no. But then she turns to me, eyes narrowed. "We're supposed to be keeping this quiet."

I lift a brow. "Ginny, I think the secret's officially out."

She huffs a laugh and looks away, but I can tell the words hit. It's the truth.

"Text Sadie," I suggest. "Let her know where you are. You don't have to sneak around anymore."

She studies me a second longer, then nods. "Okay."

That one word sends something warm spiraling through my heart.

She pulls out her phone as I start the Armada. Her fingers move fast, thumbs flying across the screen. Then she lets out a quiet snort.

"What?" I glance over.

"She said she won't wait up for me. And added three winky faces. She's the worst."

I grin. "Sounds like she approves."

"She's also threatening to tell Tarryn."

"Tell her I'll bribe her with cinnamon buns if she lets me talk to her first."

Ginny rolls her eyes but smiles. That small, tired, real smile I've come to crave. The one that tells me she's letting her guard down.

As we pull out of the lot, I reach across the console and lace my fingers through hers. She squeezes my hand — quiet, deliberate. Like she's not just choosing to come home with me. She's choosing me.

She wants me. Even with our families bleeding into everything we touch, she chooses me. And I'll burn it all down for the chance to keep her.

I look her direction as I pull into the drive. Her face is half in shadow, half bathed in the warm pink spill of the evening sun. I throw the Armada into park and turn toward her, stopping myself from pulling her across the seat and devouring her.

"You sure?" I ask, even though my body's already decided.

She meets my eyes, defiant and a little breathless. "No reason to change my mind now."

God help me.

We get out, and the warm breeze greets us, sweet with lilac and summer and her perfume clinging to my sweatshirt. She walks beside me up the front path, our hands brushing now and then like they've got their own agenda. The sun's still hanging on, painting the sky with every shade of heat I feel in my heart.

At the door, I pause with the key in my hand. One last chance to do the right thing. "I'm not trying to rush you."

She tilts her head. "Ryker, if I was worried about rushing, I wouldn't be here."

That's it. That's all I need.

The lock clicks, and the door swings open.

Once we're inside, I turn around, and she's right there, looking at me like she already owns me. And maybe she does.

But I don't move.

I want to see her like this, lit by the gold light spilling through the windows, eyes dark with want, lips parted.

I memorize every inch of her—legs, flushed cheeks, the pulse at her throat. My hands twitch at my sides.

"Tell me if you want me to stop," I say.

She doesn't even blink. "I'll tell you if I want more."

With that, I take her mouth like it's mine to keep. There's no easing into it, just heat and hunger and the sound of her whimpering when I slide my hands into her hair and tilt her head exactly the way I want it.

She tugs at my sweatshirt, and her fingers graze my abs as she pushes it up. I groan into her mouth, breaking the kiss long enough to yank it over my head, and then I'm back on her like I've been dying for this. Because I have been.

I trail kisses down her neck, stopping to suck lightly at the spot just below her ear that makes her shiver. She gasps, and I grin, hungry and a little smug because I plan to hear that sound again.

"Still want more?" I murmur, mouth brushing her jaw.

"God, yes."

I scoop her up, and she laughs, a sound that punches the air from my lungs, and I kiss it right off her lips as I carry her down the hall.

The bedroom is bathed in the last light of the day, blush and amber pouring through the blinds. I don't bother with the light. I don't need to see everything to know I want it all.

She's been in yoga pants and a hoodie all day, but damn if she's ever looked better. I lay her on the bed, and the soft cotton clings to her curves as she lands. I follow her down, hands slipping beneath the hem of her hoodie, pushing it up slowly, inch by inch. Then I turn my attention to her leggings until she's squirming beneath me in nothing but a black lace bra and that flushed, breathless look I can't get enough of.

She takes my breath away. "Ginny," I say reverently.

She reaches up, fingers curling at the back of my neck. "No more waiting."

So I give her everything.

We move slowly because we've got all night to memorize every inch of each other. Her fingers tangle in my hair, tugging just enough to make me groan. Her thighs part, inviting me in, and I press forward, the head of my cock dragging through her slick heat before I push deep, burying it to the hilt. She arches beneath me, mouth falling open, and the tight, wet grip of her around me nearly shatters my control.

Her eyes flutter shut, but I shake my head and press a kiss to her cheek. "Look at me," I whisper. "I want to see your face when you fall apart."

Her breath hitches, and then she moans, high and desperate, as her body tightens around me. Her back arches off the bed, head thrown back, thighs anchored around my waist. I feel it, the way she pulses around me, wet and wild and perfect, and my name bursts from her lips like a prayer.

Then I lose it. My hips jerk, rhythm shattered. The heat

inside me coils and detonates. I bury myself inside her, groaning against her neck as I come, everything in me pouring into her as I shake with how fucking good it feels to fall apart with her like this.

Her body softens, pliant and warm, and I collapse over her, breath mingling with hers, sweat cooling between us. I don't pull out. I don't move. I just hold her, still pulsing, completely wrecked.

My forehead pressed to hers, our chests rise and fall together. She's still shaking, body warm and open beneath mine, but it's the look in her eyes that undoes me.

Not the way she kissed me. Not the way she whispered my name. It's the way she looks at me now.

I kiss her again, slower this time. Tender. Careful. Like if I take too much, I'll break this fragile, beautiful thing between us.

She whispers, "I'm not going anywhere."

I trace her cheek with my thumb, pushing back a strand of damp hair, memorizing the curve of her jaw, the way her lashes tremble even now.

"Neither am I," I manage.

Everything in me tightens. Because I know it now. This woman has me. Entirely.

She looks up at me, eyes wide, lips parted, and I feel it coming. Something big. Something permanent. She reaches for my hand.

"I love you," she whispers.

Everything inside me stills. The words hit a place I didn't even know existed. For a second, I freeze. I want to believe her. God, I do. But that voice in my head, that part of me that never thinks I'm enough, whispers that she might not mean it. But then I look at her, and I know she does.

I kiss her again, soft, deep. "I love you," I breathe against her lips. "I didn't know how badly I needed you until you were already in my blood."

Her eyes glisten, and she smiles.

I've never had anything like this.

We move again now, slow and tangled in sheets and truth. Fingers clutching, lips searching, the words we were too scared to say finally connecting us like they'd been waiting all along.

And when we collapse again, wrapped in heat and promises neither of us says out loud, I hold her close. Because she feels like coming home.

THIRTY-THREE

Ginny

It's been a week and a half of bliss and nerves and hiding in plain sight. Ryker and I have been living in a bubble, pretending our last names don't come with baggage or, at least ,that none of it matters. We've cooked dinner together. Slept tangled up. Laughed until our stomachs hurt.

My new job at the consortium is already keeping me busy. I swear I've heard from every one of the two hundred vineyards involved, except Black Bear. Everyone has ideas, demands, complaints, and pet projects they're sure I should prioritize. It's more work than will ever fit into part-time hours, but I love it because this is all mine. Something I'm building on my own, without Black Bear or the Dempsey name.

Ryker has asked me again to come to Sunday dinner with his family. I said no. Just the thought of it makes my stomach twist. The last family dinner I went to at Gran's was a full-blown disaster, and now, the idea of sitting around someone else's table pretending everything's normal? Instant dry heaves. I told him I wasn't ready.

And then Vicky Paradise calls.

I almost don't answer. The number pops up on my screen while I'm elbows deep in a marketing plan I'm presenting to the consortium, and for a second, my heart nearly stops. But I put on my big-girl panties, remember what Ryker says about his mom being supportive of us, and decide to stop running away.

"Hello?"

"Hi, Ginny?" Her voice is warm, soft with the edges of a smile.

I fumble the phone a bit. "Hi, yes, this is Ginny."

"It's Vicky Paradise. Ryker's mom. I hope this isn't a bad time."

Panic bubbles in my throat. Could this be an ambush? What if this is it? The moment it all explodes. The moment she tells me I'm not welcome near her son, her dinner table, her family.

"No, not at all," I manage, brushing a stray hair off my blouse with a shaky hand.

"I was wondering, " she says, and I swear I brace like I'm about to be hit, "if you'd like to come to Sunday dinner."

I blink. "Oh! Ahhh..."

"I think Ryker has mentioned it to you," she continues. "But I thought a personal invitation might be helpful. I'll make my lemon chicken and roasted potatoes. That's Ryker's favorite."

"Oh," I breathe. "That's really kind of you."

"You've been on my mind," she continues. "I know things between our families haven't always been...simple. But you're important to Ryker, so you're important to us. And Ryker..." She trails off for a second, then chuckles. "He's different lately. Softer. Happier. I think maybe you've had something to do with that."

Tears prick behind my eyes.

"I'm not trying to pressure you," she adds, as if she can sense me spiraling. "I know how complicated this probably feels.

I just wanted you to know you're welcome. Always."

It's her tone more than her words that undoes me, so open, so Ryker. Suddenly, I can picture him as a boy, sitting at her table, learning how to be gentle and bold in equal measure.

"I'd love to come," I whisper.

"Wonderful," she says, and I can hear her smile. "Dinner's at six on Sunday night. No pressure to stay all evening, but I'm really glad you said yes."

I smile. So am I. Even if I'm terrified.

Two days later, I'm pacing in the guest room at Sadie and Beckett's, trying not to have a full-blown panic attack.

Sadie keeps swearing it's not scary. She keeps reminding me she'll be there too. "*It only gets heated when Max or Zach shows up,*" she said, like that's supposed to be comforting. As if I'm not already one awkward comment away from bursting into flames.

Eventually, I settle on my favorite sundress — soft cotton, pale yellow, the one I always feel like me in. But even as I slip it on and smooth it over my hips, my hands feel jittery.

Dinner at Paradise Hill. With Ryker's entire family, well, hopefully not Max and Zach.

I look at myself in the mirror and try to breathe. I've already said yes. I'm already going.

Sadie yells goodbye from the other room. She and Beckett are leaving early to meet with his parents about the wedding. I tell her I'll see her soon.

A little while later, Ryker arrives to pick me up. As he steps through the doorway, his mouth curves. "You look beautiful," he says. "That sundress is dangerous."

I laugh, tugging at the hem. "It's just a dress."

"It's *you* in the dress," he counters, brushing a kiss across my cheek. His eyes linger on mine. "You look nervous, but you've got nothing to worry about, Gin. Not with me."

As we drive toward Paradise Hill, my nerves keep climbing like they're strapped to a rocket. My hands are clenched in my lap until I finally blurt out, "We have to stop."

Ryker glances over. "Stop?"

"I'm not showing up empty-handed," I insist. "I may be a Dempsey, but I'm not rude."

He laughs, but I can't tell if it's amusement or nerves of his own. "Ginny, they're not expecting anything—"

"I am," I snap, already pulling out my phone to find the nearest wine shop. "And if I walk in there with nothing, your mom will smile like everything's fine while mentally questioning my manners."

"It's a good thing I love you," he says as he backtracks to town.

He stops at a small boutique next to the liquor store. I make a beeline for the flowers and spot a bouquet of soft pink hydrangeas wrapped in brown paper and twine. They're beautiful and old-fashioned and somehow remind me of Vicky.

I collect them like I'm bracing for war with floral armor. After whipping out my credit card for the flowers, we step into the liquor store. I immediately regret it.

"So many options," I murmur, scanning the racks. "And they're all competitors." I hold up a sleek bottle of Black Bear Chardonnay and turn to Ryker. "This one beat Paradise at last year's International Wine Festival. Maybe I should bring it? See how fast I can get myself banned for life?"

Ryker chokes out a laugh. "Tarryn would actually kick you out. And I wouldn't even blame her."

"Yeah, okay, fine." I smirk, putting it back. "Something less offensive then."

I find my favorite ice wine tucked in the corner—a golden Ontario dessert wine I discovered years ago and always save for special occasions.

"This one," I say. "Sweet. Classy. Non-threatening.

Basically the liquid version of vanilla gelato. Perfect for impressing your boyfriend's mom."

Ryker kisses my temple. "They're going to love it. And they're going to love you."

I nod and try to believe him.

But as we pull back onto the road toward the vineyard, all I can feel is a tight ache inside me and the pressure of every single Dempsey expectation whispering that this is a very bad idea. The flowers are in my lap. The wine's tucked carefully in a bag at my feet. And I still feel like I might throw up.

Ryker reaches over and threads his fingers through mine. His thumb brushes the inside of my wrist, slow and steady, like he's trying to calm a wild animal. "You're going to be great," he says softly.

I stare out the window. The vineyard signs are getting closer. My heart is in my throat. "You don't know that," I whisper.

"I do," he says. "Because I know you."

I glance over. He's watching the road, calm as ever, like bringing me home isn't a risk at all. Like he's not walking a tightrope between the people who raised him and the woman who might ruin everything.

"They already love you," he adds as we arrive. "They just don't know it yet."

He studies me once he's parked, like he knows I'm spinning out and wants to say something more. But then he just squeezes my hand and walks around to the passenger side. When he takes my hand again, I hold on tight.

Paradise Hill looks exactly the same, warm and sprawling, the vineyard stretching out like something out of a painting. But tonight, it feels different. Like I'm taking a pop quiz on a subject I've never even heard of, with all the right answers scribbled in invisible ink.

Vicky and Trace are waiting outside on the front porch. She's in a pale blue sundress, waving like I'm an old friend. Trace is beside her in a crisp button-down, arms folded, a familiar

Paradise smile on his face.

I force a bright expression as we approach, bouquet in hand.

"Oh, these are beautiful," Vicky says, taking the hydrangeas from me gently, like they're made of glass.

"I wasn't sure what to bring," I admit. "But I didn't want to show up empty-handed."

Vicky's eyes crinkle as she looks down at the blooms. "Did Ryker tell you these are my favorite?"

I glance at him, startled. He shakes his head slightly.

"No," I say. "He just said you liked pink."

"Well, he was right," she says with a smile. "And clearly, so were you."

She disappears inside, calling over her shoulder, "Let me find a vase."

I'm still processing that when Trace steps closer and plucks the bottle of ice wine from the bag I handed him.

"I love ice wine," he says, inspecting the label. "Haven't had this one before. I'm looking forward to it with dessert." He gives me a grin. "Might not share it, though. We'll see how the night goes."

I manage a laugh, nervous and high-pitched, but he's teasing, not testing. Still, the knot in my stomach refuses to loosen.

Two down. An entire family and dinner to go.

Ryker takes my hand again as we step inside, guiding me through the front hall toward the kitchen. I hear them before I see them, voices overlapping, laughter bouncing off the walls, someone teasing someone else about overcooking the chicken.

It's loud and chaotic. Not at all what I expected or am used to.

And then—

"Ginny!"

Sadie's voice cuts through everything, and a second later, she's barreling across the room, arms flung wide.

"Oh my God, I'm so happy you're here!" she squeals,

wrapping me in a hug before I can brace myself.

I blink, startled, and let out a laugh that's more nerves than joy.

Sadie pulls back and beams. "You guys, Ryker and Ginny — I mean, come on. Look at them. I called this, like, months ago. You're all welcome." She waves at the rest of the group dramatically. "This love match was brought to you by me."

Ryker groans beside me. "Sadie — "

"Don't ruin my moment." She loops her arm through mine and pulls me farther into the room. "Okay, this is Trinity — Greyson's wife, and basically the nicest human alive, and she's the mother to that adorable little boy on Beckett's lap, Theo. Everyone else you already know, so no need for intros. If they act weird, just assume it's normal and move on."

Trinity offers me a warm smile and a gentle hello, and I manage to squeak out a reply.

The rest of the room is a blur, faces I've seen at fundraisers or walking through town, but never like this. Not this loud, this casual, this close.

My stomach flips. I'm not one of them.

But Ryker squeezes my hand, and Sadie's still talking a mile a minute at my side, so maybe I won't crash and burn after all.

For a moment, I manage to forget who I am and who I'm not. But peace never lasts in this town, not with the last name Dempsey. And the second the front door opens again, the air shifts. Max and Zach have arrived.

THIRTY-FOUR

Ryker

I glance toward the entry just in time to see Max stroll in, Zach behind him like a damn shadow.

They aren't supposed to be here. Mom swore up and down that Max and Zach had other plans tonight. That it would just be immediate family — *"low-key, drama-free."* Those were her exact words.

My jaw tightens.

Ginny stills at my side, then tenses as Max spots her. Surprise flickers across his face before his expression hardens into something sharp and cold.

"Well," he says, stepping into the kitchen. "Didn't realize tonight was open invite."

No one answers. Even Sadie goes quiet.

Max's smile stretches. "What's the saying? Keep your friends close and your enemies closer?" His gaze cuts to me.

"This one must be real close by now."

I feel Ginny's breath hitch beside me, and I slide my hand to her lower back.

"Don't start," I say softly.

But Max moves forward, ignoring the warning in my voice. "You all realize what's happening here, right? This isn't just some date. It's an infiltration. A classic Dempsey move. Burrow in, charm everyone, gather intel. Strike when no one's looking."

Ginny doesn't speak. Doesn't flinch. But I've had enough. "She's not a threat," I declare. "She's my girlfriend."

I don't care who hears it. I need Ginny to hear it. To know I'm choosing her, no matter what it costs me.

That lands like a boulder in the middle of the room.

Sadie's eyes go wide, and even my mom looks like she's trying to decide whether to gasp or intervene.

Max's laugh is short and bitter. "Girlfriend," he repeats. "That's rich." He turns to Dad. "He's signing his death warrant."

"That's enough," Mom announces.

Max takes another step closer. "You think *girlfriend* means something to a Dempsey? Loyalty? Truth? You think she's not running home and reporting every word we say over a glass of wine with her family?"

"Back off," I warn, voice tight.

But Max doesn't. He turns, slow and deliberate, his words like knives. "You think she's innocent? Her great-grandfather killed my brother. He was in love with Mabel Dempsey, and they were going to run away. But he wouldn't have it. He killed them both."

Ginny's fingers curl tighter around mine. But she doesn't say a word. Doesn't move, eyes wide and stunned.

Uncle Auggie. We were raised knowing he'd been killed by James Dempsey for trespassing, but not that he was trying to run away with James's youngest daughter.

Ginny goes still beside me. Seems she didn't know that either.

The room's wound so tight a single word might snap the whole damn thing in two.

And then my mom steps forward. Her voice rings out like a bell. "I invited her, Max. She's my guest, so please keep that in mind."

Max's head jerks toward her, eyes narrowing. "What?"

"I invited Ginny," she repeats. "And I'm glad she came."

Before Max can snap back, my dad steps in. Calm. Controlled. But steel laces every word. "That's enough, Max. If you can't behave like a gentleman, you need to leave."

Max turns to him like he's been betrayed. "You're okay with this?" His voice spikes. "She's a Dempsey. After what they did to our family, you invite one to eat at your table?"

"She's not the one turning this dinner into a battleground," Dad says.

"This is the biggest insult to our family in decades. If you really think this is acceptable, maybe you shouldn't be running the vineyard anymore."

Dad tilts his head. "What are you saying? That seems like a bit of a leap. And yet, somehow, that's always where you end up."

Max shakes his head. "It's time the rightful branch of the family takes over. You've grown soft, Trace. We need someone who actually gives a damn about legacy, loyalty, and history."

Dad smirks knowingly. "You mean you. How convenient."

And just like that, they're ready to go to fisticuffs.

Sadie reaches across the table and grabs Ginny's hand. Trinity moves closer to Greyson, eyes wide. Mom steps away with Theo in her arms.

My muscles coil tight, every part of me ready to jump in.

But Kingston gets there first, stepping in with his quiet strength that always shuts the room down. Greyson's right beside him.

"Back off," Greyson says.

Kingston crosses his arms. "Not here. Not like this."

Then Zach finally moves. He brushes past Ginny and me without a word, slipping in beside his father.

And just when it feels like the whole house is about to explode — *Crash!*

There's the sound of ceramic shattering against the tile floor.

Every head turns.

Mom's voice is sharp, unshakable. "That's enough!"

She stands in the doorway of the kitchen, chest heaving. There's an empty spot on the counter where the serving tray was sitting a moment ago.

"I said enough," she snaps. "This is my home. My table. It's a meal, not a negotiation. And if you can't show basic human decency, you're not welcome." Her eyes blaze as they pin Max in place. "Get out."

He stares like he doesn't recognize her, like the woman who's fed him since she joined this family has turned into a stranger.

"This isn't over," he says coldly. Then he nods to Zach and they walk out without looking back.

A moment later, the front door slams shut behind them, and the room finally exhales.

Theo fusses through the monitor in his nursery, and Trinity gets up to go to him.

"I'm sorry," Mom says to Ginny.

"You have nothing to be sorry for," she replies.

Sadie rushes forward to sweep up the shattered ceramic. I know she's trying to do more than clean. She wants to sweep away the moment. The explosion. The fracture.

Mom slowly lowers herself into one of the chairs, running her hands down the front of her dress like she's trying to erase the last ten minutes. "That was my favorite serving tray," she says softly. "But I didn't know how else to get them to stop."

She looks up blankly, and Dad wraps his arm around her and kisses her temple.

Ginny steps toward the doorway. "Maybe I should go. I

don't want to make this harder for anyone."

Before I can protest, Greyson lets out a dry laugh from across the kitchen. "All the drama's over now. You might as well stay."

Ginny freezes.

Sadie points a finger at Grey. "Not helpful."

I cross the room and wrap an arm around Ginny's waist, pulling her close. "I go where you go," I say quietly, pulling her in tight. "But don't think that's how my family behaves."

She looks up at me, wide-eyed and overwhelmed.

"Please stay," Mom says, the color returning to her face. "This isn't your fault at all. Max has his own demons. Trace and he will figure it out."

Ginny nods. "Okay, then. Thank you. What can I do to help?"

Mom moves to a cabinet and pulls out another serving tray. "Let me get the chicken, and then everyone can grab a dish and start passing to the right."

There's the hesitant start to finding our places at the table. A few half-hearted jokes. It's clumsy, but eventually, it settles.

When Mom returns, the lemon chicken's perfect and the vegetables roasted just right. The rolls are soft and warm.

"Thank you again for inviting me." Ginny spreads a napkin on her lap. "This looks delicious."

"Yes," I add. "Thank you for making my favorite meal."

"Suck up," Beckett mutters. And the tension breaks.

With a chuckle, we start passing the dishes, and soon, forks clink as we eat. Trinity compliments the potatoes. Sadie pours more wine. Tarryn mutters something to Kingston about the barrels in cellar three.

And Ginny floats at the edge of it all. Until she speaks.

"Can I ask something?"

The whole table stills.

Dad nods. "Of course."

She hesitates. "What happened to Auggie? You said my great-grandfather killed him. But no one in my family ever talks about that."

The silence that follows is different, not volatile, but heavy.

Dad stares off like he's reaching for something buried deep. "Auggie was our oldest brother," he says finally. "A charmer. Wild at heart. If there was trouble, he was usually standing in the middle of it, grinning like he'd lit the match himself. Often he had."

I huff out a laugh. That's exactly how I've always heard about him—trouble tied up in a bow.

"He fell in love with your great-grandfather's youngest daughter, Mabel." He glances at Ginny. "That's not as crazy as it sounds. The generations were a bit tangled up, and they were both young. Stupid in that way people are when they think love makes them invincible. Our families had bad blood, but they didn't care. Snuck around for months."

Ginny's throat bobs like she's swallowing something sharp.

"One night," Dad goes on, "Mabel tried to sneak out to meet him. Your great-grandfather caught her climbing out her window and followed her. When he saw Auggie waiting, he fired his rifle. Said he thought it was a trespasser."

He pauses.

"Mabel jumped in front of the shot. She took most of it, but it still caught Auggie in the heart. She didn't survive," Dad says softly. "And he didn't either."

No one speaks.

Ginny's staring at the table, jaw tight. Then she nods. "My family has a...much different version of that story."

Dad nods. "Makes sense that they would." He doesn't sound bitter. Just tired. "Next time you're at the library, pull the story from the newspaper. It happened back in the summer of 'seventy-eight."

She nods. "I will. Thank you for telling me."

I reach under the table and find her hand. She grips mine instantly. I can't imagine what this feels like, hearing something from the other's perspective. Having to sort back through everything you thought was true.

The silence lingers until my mom clears her throat. "Before that things had been getting better with your grandfather," she says. "With Robert."

Ginny looks over at her, eyes wide.

Mom nods. "He and Trace had started meeting, nothing formal, but they were talking. There was a deal in place for a parcel of land down at the south edge of the valley. We were going to buy it. Black Bear was struggling, and…well, Robert had a lot of strengths, but business wasn't one of them."

Dad chuckles. "I'm not sure I'm any better. You've seen the spreadsheets. After watching what Tarryn's doing with the operations now, I wouldn't even hire me."

A small wave of laughter ripples around the table.

"Thanks, Dad." Tarryn beams.

But then Dad's voice sobers again. "When Robert died, Evelyn tore up the deal. The land had been sold and already registered to Paradise Hill, but she insisted we were making it up. I don't know if he never told her, or she just refused to believe, but your family has continued to work it like it's still theirs ever since."

Ginny looks stunned. "What?"

Mom nods. "We never pushed. It wasn't worth the war. We figured maybe one day it could be settled between better people."

Dad looks at Ginny. "Your grandmother saved Black Bear. No question. But in my eyes? She destroyed your family to do it. All the disowning and threats? I wonder if it will be worth it."

Ginny doesn't say anything, but I can feel her unraveling a little beside me. This has to be so hard to hear, to sort through. She looks around the table. Everyone has gone back to their side conversations. Sadie is arguing with Kingston about wine pairings, and Trinity leans into Greyson's side as they murmur together.

"I'm grateful to be here," she says. "Thank you for inviting me. For sharing with me, even when you didn't have to."

Mom squeezes her hand. "You're always welcome at this table."

Ginny's shoulders are tense, her eyes wet, but she's holding herself steady. She's still upright, still soft in a room full of sharp edges. I don't just love her. I've fallen for her, completely.

Later, when we're alone, I'll ask her how she's holding up, how I can help. For now, I just hold her hand and pray she doesn't let go.

THIRTY-FIVE

Ginny

Nearly four months ago now, I left Black Bear, my family, and everything I thought I needed behind. My plan was to stay with Sadie and Beckett until I figured things out, but then Ryker invited me to his place one night. It wasn't supposed to be permanent, but eventually, I stopped leaving.

So now, I'm staying with Ryker, not Sadie and Beckett, though we never made it official. Never had the talk. It just happened. I started keeping a few things at his place. Then more. Eventually, we stopped pretending I didn't live here.

It's the easiest relationship I've ever had—free of performance, pretense, and the need for walking on eggshells.

We just work. He makes me laugh when I forget how. He brings me coffee in the morning like it's instinct. He kisses my shoulder when he thinks I'm still asleep.

And for once in my life, I don't feel like I have to be someone else just to be loved.

Today, Ryker's coming with me to Marshall. It's on the northern tip of Little Black Bear Lake and almost a two-hour drive. It's a long way to go for dinner, but I hope it will be worth the journey.

I haven't seen my dad since he left, though I've talked to him on the phone a time or two, and we reconnected after everything exploded with Evelyn. I figured he would understand, and he has. He's been supportive about what happened, and he knows I'm working for the consortium now. I've been helping promote the boutique wineries and organizing the fall showcase. He's proud, I think. In his way. I'm not sure what going to see him is going to accomplish, but it feels like something I need to do.

As I'm clearing the last few things off my desk for the day, Marc Warner, the director of the consortium, drops into the seat across from me and slides a coffee my way. "You look like you've already run a marathon."

"I'm pacing myself," I joke, taking the cup. "Thanks for this. We've got four events next week. And I promised to finalize the copy for the artisan series before I leave town."

"You're heading up to Marshall, right?"

"Yeah. Visiting my dad. Ryker's coming."

Marc raises an eyebrow. "Good man. You're building something solid."

I look down at my planner, suddenly shy. "That wasn't the plan when it started."

"Plans are overrated," he says. "Besides, I've seen you build more from scratch in three months than most people do in three years."

I give him a half smile. "Thanks for giving me a chance, even after Evelyn decided not to."

He laughs. "Evelyn called me a spineless bureaucrat in front of a full board meeting three years ago. It's practically a badge of honor."

That makes me smile. Marc's been one of the few people who doesn't flinch when the Dempsey name comes up. He seems to see me as Ginny, not Evelyn's granddaughter or a Dempsey problem to manage. And he trusts that I have skills of my own. He's giving me room to figure out who I want to be.

My phone pings while I'm packing the mock-ups.

Ryker: You want me to drive? Or are we pretending I'm just tagging along and you still have something to prove? 😊

I laugh under my breath

Me: You drive. I'll pretend I'm letting you.

Now, I'm grinning like an idiot.

A few minutes later, Ryker is standing at my office door, flipping his keys in his hand. "Let's get a move on. The traffic is going to be a mess."

I roll my eyes. Mess is relative. People here think if you can't drive forty kilometers over the speed limit, there are too many people on the roads. But we do want to arrive before dark, so I finish putting everything in my bag and let Marc know I'll see him on Monday.

The drive takes over two hours, but with Ryker behind the wheel and the windows down, it flies by. We don't talk much. It's just an easy journey of shared playlists, pointed glances, and the occasional sarcastic jab when he skips a turn on the GPS he insisted we didn't need.

When we finally pull onto the long dirt driveway, I sit up straighter. I've never been here before. I knew Dad had land, that he was finally pursuing the dream he'd put off for most of his life, but seeing it in person? That's something else.

Rows of young vines stretch across the slope, still small and a little wild, but perfectly trellised. There's something tender about the whole place, like it's still learning how to become what it wants to be.

"They're maybe two years old," I murmur to Ryker as we park near a collection of buildings. "Still a couple more seasons before the grapes are mature enough for winemaking."

"They're healthy," Ryker says, sliding his sunglasses to the top of his head. "Vines like this...someone's putting in the work."

As if summoned, my dad walks out from the barn, with dust on his boots and a wide grin spreading across his face. He pulls me into a full-body hug that smells like sunshine and fresh earth and home.

"Alaric's been keeping me updated," he says gruffly, arms still tight around me. "But seeing you in person..." He pulls back to look me in the eyes. "It's better."

I swallow hard and nod. "It's good to see you too."

He shakes Ryker's hand, gives him a onceover that's more curious than protective, and gestures toward the vineyard. "Come on. I'll show you around."

We walk for nearly an hour while he talks about his planting schedule, his irrigation system, and the blends he's hoping to try once the grapes come in. He's got five hundred acres—nowhere near the scale of Paradise or Black Bear—but it doesn't matter. That's still a lot of land. He's proud. And that pride is infectious.

"This place... It's yours," I say, imagining what that must be like.

He shrugs, modest as always. "I don't need to be big. Just want to make a wine people enjoy. Something honest."

I glance at Ryker, who's walking next to me, fingers brushing mine. *Something honest.* I know the feeling.

As we head back to the house, a woman steps out onto the porch. She's in maybe her mid-sixties, with silver hair pulled back in a low bun and the kind of smile that makes you feel safe.

"This is Viola," Dad says. "Viola Burton. My partner."

Viola steps down and wraps me in a gentle hug, like she's known me longer than a moment. "So happy to finally meet you. I've heard so many good things."

Her warmth is genuine, and I feel something settle in my chest, some deep, fractured part of me softening at the edges as I introduce Ryker.

We step inside, and Viola brings out lemonade and fresh scones. Ryker charms them both without even trying. My dad keeps looking over like he's memorizing me, and I realize how much I've missed him. How long I've been pretending I didn't need him.

With Evelyn as his mother, I've never understood how he turned out so kind. So sensitive. Alaric has always told me how much he cares about us. But I don't think I fully believed it until today. Maybe Dad's background is exactly why he became the man he is. Maybe he knew what it felt like to be pushed to the edges and decided never to do the same. Maybe he made a silent promise to himself to do better, to love softer, to never let his kids feel the way he once did.

As the sun starts to dip, my dad squeezes my hand.

"I'm proud of you, Gin."

"Thanks, Dad." It's surreal to have someone view my actions in an entirely different way. I want to be brave enough to view them that way myself.

The table is already set, and something warm and buttery is baking in the oven. Ryker and I exchange a glance, and he nods before I can even ask.

Viola has made a mushroom risotto that might be the best thing I've eaten in weeks—creamy, earthy, perfectly salted. She serves it with a crisp white blend from a nearby winery and a simple salad with shaved fennel and lemon. And also fresh bread.

The conversation is light. Easy. My dad tells old stories about me trying to grow grapes in pots on the patio when I was a kid. Ryker listens, engaged, even laughing at the terrible puns my dad can't help slipping in. Viola watches us closely, but not in a suspicious way. More like she's hopeful.

It's all so different from the way I grew up, so much gentler. Then the conversation turns to weddings, specifically

Sadie's.

"We're heading into the final stretch," I say, setting my fork down with a little sigh. "It's coming up fast."

Viola lights up. "You're in the wedding party, right?"

I nod. "Maid of honor. And Ryker's the best man, so we've got front-row seats for the excitement."

"I'm sure it's going to be beautiful," Viola says. "Sadie's the one you were close to growing up?"

"Yeah," I say, smiling. "She's like a sister. And I do think it's going to be lovely. Honestly, she's been the opposite of a bridezilla, but there are just so many details. The rehearsal dinner, final fittings, gift bags, speeches, the seating chart—" I laugh. "I feel like I'm always behind."

Viola squeezes my hand. "You'll get it all done. And if you don't, no one will notice. They'll be too busy watching you all shine."

My dad chuckles. "Caleb and Beckett were always tight. I'm glad he's marrying Caleb's little sister. I remember them as kids—inseparable. It's nice to see how far they've come."

"It really is," I say. "And Sadie deserves this. She's been through a lot."

"What's your dress like?" Viola asks, eyes twinkling.

I grin. "It's simple. A deep wine-colored silk with a sweetheart neckline. Tea-length, fitted bodice. I'm wearing nude stiletto sandals with it."

Viola sighs. "Oh, Ginny, you're going to look stunning. Please tell me you'll send pictures."

"I will," I promise, and it's not a polite lie. I actually want to. "I think the dress is the only part I'm one-hundred-percent ready for."

"I can't wait to see it," she says. "You're going to make that aisle sparkle, maid of honor or not."

I'm not used to compliments without strings, but with Viola, it doesn't feel like an act. My cheeks flush a little, but it's nice. This sort of approval is something I didn't realize I'd been missing.

Ryker nudges me under the table, a smile on his face like he knows exactly what I'm feeling. And maybe he does.

After dinner, I follow Viola into the kitchen to help with the dishes while Ryker and my dad wander out toward the rows of vines with a pair of tumblers and a bottle of something red.

Viola hands me a tea towel and smiles. "He talks about you a lot, you know."

I pause, surprised. "Dad? He does?"

"All the time." She rinses a wineglass and hands it to me. "He's proud. And he's worried. But mostly proud."

My throat tightens. "I haven't exactly made things…easy."

Viola shrugs. "You've been figuring out who you are. That's never easy. But it's necessary."

We fall into a rhythm—washing, drying, stacking—and I find it oddly soothing. Like I'm slipping into a life that could've been mine if things had gone a little differently.

"I've seen Alaric a few times," Viola says after a pause. "He comes by for lunch when he's in town."

I nod. "He's good to Ryker," I say softly. "They don't like each other much, but they respect each other. And that counts for something."

"I think there's a reason Alaric went into psychology. I can tell he's good at it."

"Have you met my sisters?"

Viola hesitates. "Addie. Once. But not Sera or Josie. I think they're afraid to…stir things up."

"They're still under Evelyn's roof. Dad and I are prime examples of what happens when you upset my grandmother."

"It's hard on your dad, but he understands."

"Yeah. They've got too much riding on the vineyard to risk it."

Viola presses her lips together. "That woman casts a long shadow."

I glance out the window to where my dad and Ryker are silhouetted against the last light of day. "Yeah," I whisper. "She does."

"But shadows aren't permanent," Viola adds, placing a hand on my arm. "They shift. And so do people."

I nod, quietly grateful for the way she sees me.

When we step outside to say our goodbyes, the stars are just beginning to show. My dad hugs me tight again. "You're always welcome here."

"Thanks, Dad."

Ryder laces our fingers together like he always does, and I'm glad we came. Evelyn might've cast us out, but Dad and I are still a family. That's something else good that has come from this.

Maybe that's the real truth I've been chasing. Not who I was, but who I get to become. Free. Loved. Home.

THIRTY-SIX

Ryker

A few weeks later, the sun dips low over Paradise Hill's acreage, bathing the rows of vines in a coppery glow. Lights are strung above the courtyard, and for a moment, everything feels still, like time has slowed to let us enjoy Sadie and Beckett's rehearsal dinner.

Guests fill the long tables, the air buzzing with clinking glasses and easy laughter. I've been on my feet since mid-afternoon, helping Ginny wrangle place cards and reworking the seating chart after someone's plus-one turned into a plus-three. But it's finally settling down, and I let myself breathe.

Across the courtyard, Beckett steps out of the crowd, holding two glasses of our family's vintage. He heads straight to me. "Thought you might need a refill," he says, handing me one.

"You trying to get me drunk the night before I give the best man speech?"

He cracks a grin. "You're funnier with a buzz. Less likely to roast me."

I take a sip, watching him. He's quiet for a second, just looking over the crowd. "They're all here," he says, voice soft. "Even Caleb. I didn't think he'd make it."

"He wouldn't have missed it." I bump his shoulder. "You're his brother too."

Beckett nods, but his gaze drifts toward Sadie, who's laughing with Caleb's girlfriend, Katy, and Mom near the dessert table.

"She looks happy," he says. "Like…really happy."

"She is."

He swallows hard, eyes glassy. "I didn't think I'd get this. Mom and Dad set the bar so high. I didn't think I could find something even close. I never thought love would look like this for me."

I shake my head. "Beckett—"

"I know I act like I've got it all under control," he continues. "But I don't. I've spent years trying to make sure everyone else was okay, especially you. And now, I'm the one getting married, and it's terrifying."

"You're allowed to be terrified," I say. "You're doing something big. Something that matters."

He turns toward me. "What if I screw it up?"

"You won't," I say without hesitation. "You've already done the hardest part. You let someone love you. You let Sadie in."

There's something raw in his eyes. "You sure?"

"Absolutely." I step closer, lowering my voice. "Sadie sees the guy the rest of us rely on. You've always been there for me, Beckett. I won't forget that."

For a second, I think he's going to brush it off. Make a joke. But instead, he taps his glass against mine.

"Thanks," he says. "That means a lot."

We stand in silence, two brothers who've weathered enough storms to know this peace won't last forever, but tonight, it's ours.

Then Ginny appears from the patio, practically glowing, her hair twisted up and a soft flush on her cheeks. She spots me and waves, and I feel that pull again, like the Earth shifts a little when she's near.

Beckett follows my gaze and smiles.

"You're in deep, huh?"

"Drowning," I admit.

"Good," he says. "About damn time." He chuckles. "Then I guess it's time I welcome you to the club."

I arch a brow. "The what now?"

He taps his glass to mine again. "The club of men who know they're completely screwed because they've found the one person who makes the world make sense."

I can feel myself smiling. I like that club.

As the last rays of sunlight slip behind the hills, we take our seats at the long dinner tables set up beneath the pergola. The tables are draped in white linen, dotted with wildflowers in mason jars and flickering candles. The wine flows easily, and the smell of rosemary chicken and grilled vegetables wafts in from the nearby catering tent.

Beckett stands at the head of his table and taps his glass with a fork.

"First of all," he says, his voice carrying over the music, "thank you all for coming. I know some of you flew halfway around the world—" He nods to Caleb and Katy, who raise their glasses. "—and some of you just walked across the field. Either way, we're glad you did."

Sadie slips her hand into his. "We wouldn't be here without two very special people," she says, her voice a little wobbly with emotion. "Our best man and our maid of honor, who have done everything from late-night planning texts to emotional triage when one of us"—she glances at Beckett—"decided to stress-organize the entire groomsmen's tie situation."

A ripple of laughter moves through the crowd, but she's

looking only at Ginny.

"Gin, you've been my rock. You've kept me grounded when I started to spin out, and reminded me to laugh. I know this year hasn't been easy for you, but I want you to know, your friendship means the world to me. So…I got you something, and I hope it reminds you how much I love you."

She reaches beneath the table and pulls out a small, wrapped box. Ginny's cheeks flush pink as she takes it and carefully peels the paper back. Inside is a delicate silver vintage jeweler's loupe, not for daily use, but a beautiful, decorative one with a history and an engraved message that reads, "For the one who sees the real me."

Ginny smiles as she holds it up. "It's beautiful," she says, blinking a few times before standing and pulling Sadie into a hug. "You didn't have to—"

"I wanted to," Sadie whispers. "You always make other people feel seen. I wanted to make sure you felt that too."

I should be relieved that someone else sees her worth, but part of me aches. Because I want to be the one who makes her look that way, find that peace. They hold on to each other for a moment, and something in Ginny's face softens in a way I haven't seen in weeks.

Then Beckett clears his throat and turns to me. "And Ryker," he says, shooting me a crooked grin, "my little brother, my best man, and the one who somehow managed to keep this thing on the rails, even when I started checking guest lists at three in the morning."

He's exaggerating, so I laugh, and so does everyone else, but there's real affection in his voice when he continues.

"You've always had my back, even when I didn't deserve it. And I know I'm not always the easiest guy to work with, but knowing you were here—managing the madness, distracting Mom, making sure I didn't forget the rings—that meant everything."

He reaches under the table and hands me a slim, rectangular box. Inside is a custom-engraved pocketknife. Clean, black metal with a wooden handle. My initials are carved into one side, and on the other it reads, "For the one who always shows up."

My throat tightens unexpectedly. It's more than just a gift. It's a reminder that someone sees the weight I carry and chose to honor it.

"Thanks," I say because I can't trust myself with anything more than that. I stand and give Beckett a one-armed hug, then pull Sadie in too. "You two are disgustingly perfect together, and I love you both."

The crowd gives a collective "*aww*," and Sadie fans her eyes to keep from crying again.

They both give a toast to Rosie Kennedy, Sadie and Ginny's best friend from high school who passed away last year.

The rest of the dinner unfolds in waves—soft music, heartfelt conversation, and that warm buzz that only happens when so many people you love are in the same place at the same time. Ginny runs her thumb over the jewelry loupe absently as we sit side by side. Her smile is different now, softer, and freer. She's been through so much, and tonight, she finally seems at ease and truly herself. And damn if that doesn't make me fall a little harder.

Beckett catches my eye across the table and gives me a knowing nod.

I return the nod, then reach for Ginny's hand beneath the table, threading my fingers through hers. Right now, everything's just as it's supposed to be.

As the song ends and the dance floor shifts into something faster, I move close to Ginny's ear. "Come with me," I murmur, scanning the crowd. I want nothing more than to forget the world and just keep her near tonight.

But then I spot Zach standing with Max. The music and laughter cover most of their voices, but I can see something in their faces—the clipped jaw, the stiff gestures, Max radiating that quiet authority that always rubs me raw. They don't look like they're discussing what a lovely party this is.

Zach shakes his head, like he's trying to shove Max off, but Max just presses closer, saying something that makes Zach's whole being tighten. A beat later, Zach mutters something and pushes past him, storming off across the lawn.

Plenty of people come and go at a party, but the way he leaves — rigid spine, fists balled, like he's walking through land mines — sticks with me. It's like I've just watched a fuse catch flame, and I don't know how long it'll burn before it blows.

Still holding Ginny's hand, I spot Tarryn near the edge of the courtyard, talking with one of our cousins. I raise a hand and catch her eye. She frowns when she sees my face, excuses herself, and crosses over.

"What's wrong?" she asks, her party smile vanishing.

"Max just said something to Zach, and he took off with a purpose."

Her expression hardens. "Did you see what direction?"

"Toward the staff lot behind the shed. I don't think he saw me watching."

"Let's go," she says. "Come on."

Ginny looks between us. "Are we — ?"

"We're following him," I confirm. "Because something's not right, and I'm done waiting for the worst to find us."

THIRTY-SEVEN

Ryker

We stick to the edges of the courtyard until the lights from the party fade behind us. We can just barely glimpse Zach up ahead. Then Tarryn leads the way to her truck, parked by the cellar. She yanks open the driver's door and hops in.

I open the passenger side, but there's only room for two.

"Sorry," I say, flashing Ginny a sheepish look. "You're stuck with me."

Her eyes widen just slightly, but she doesn't argue. She climbs in, settling sideways on my lap as I close the door behind her. My hands go to her hips to keep her steady as Tarryn starts the engine.

Ginny glances back. "This truck doesn't have a backseat?"

"Nope," Tarryn says as she reverses hard. "Built for hauling. Not for sneaking around with friends."

Ginny's cheeks flush, and I chuckle under my breath as we lurch down the gravel road.

We turn onto the main service lane behind the vineyard, just in time to see Zach. He's driving one of the four-wheelers that drags a five-hundred-gallon water tank. We watch as he hauls up a plastic container, large and square, and pours it into the water tank. Even in the dim light I can tell he's up to no good. I'm sure it's some kind of chemical. My stomach knots.

"What the hell is he doing?" Ginny whispers as he gets back in the driver's seat.

"He's not going home," Tarryn says, her jaw tight. "That's the path going toward block nine."

"Along with blocks six through twelve," I point out, scanning the direction of Zach's headlights as he pulls out of the lot.

"I know my own damn vineyard," Tarryn counters. "I'm saying he's not headed toward the highway driving that thing. He's going to the back access road, near the block nine pinots. Why would he be watering tonight? We've got to get there first."

"I think we should stay on him," I tell her. "What if he turns off? What if he saw us?"

Tarryn shakes her head. "The truck's too wide for that path on the incline. Plus, he'd see our headlights. Surface streets are faster. And less obvious."

"I don't like it," I mutter.

"I don't care," she snaps, then hits the gas. "If I'm right, we'll beat him there."

Ginny's hand finds mine where it rests on her leg. Her fingers curl tightly.

We fly down the road that surrounds the vineyard. Tarryn knows every dip, every curve, and she's pushing her truck in a way I've never seen her drive.

Still, I can't help scanning the horizon for his lights.

"What if he turned off?" I mutter. "What if we guessed wrong?"

Ginny shifts on my lap to face me more fully. "Ryker, do

you see him?"

I shake my head. "No."

"He's up to no good," Tarryn says grimly. "No one waters at night, particularly in the middle of a family party. And if he's headed where I think, he's not doing maintenance."

I hold on tight to Ginny as Tarryn takes a turn.

She grips the wheel tighter. "He's the one doing the damage. This could finally confirm it."

Tarryn cuts the headlights as we get to block nine. So far no one else seems to be here. Tarryn angles the truck and coasts to a stop beneath a canopy of fruit trees that borders the edge of our vines.

Just a minute or two later, we watch as the four-wheeler lumbers its way up the hill. Tarryn's instincts were spot on. Zach stops by the well. In the harsh glare of a handheld flashlight, we see him crouch beside the old well cap that feeds part of our irrigation system. He disconnects the water drum and takes out a large hose, ready to attach it to the water tank and send whatever he mixed up into the well.

My gut flips. He's going to poison the damn water supply.

"What the hell is he doing?" Ginny breathes.

Tarryn doesn't wait. She throws on the truck's headlights, swings the driver's door open, and storms forward.

"Zach!" she yells. "What the hell do you think you're doing?"

Zach jumps like he's been electrocuted, nearly dropping the flashlight.

"I—I wasn't—" He stammers, scrambling to block the opening. "It's not what it looks like!"

"Oh really?" Tarryn shoots back. "Because it looks like you were about to dump something into the well."

"It's not poison. It's for maintenance! Just to clear out sediment—"

"Cut the crap," I say, stepping forward. I reach past him and grab the hose. He resists for half a second before letting go.

Tarryn makes a call. "Hi, I'm up here at the well off block

nine. Can you grab a chemical kit and meet me here? Ryker, Ginny, and I watched Zach pour something into a water tank, and he was preparing to dump it into the well until we stopped him." She listens. "Okay. We'll be here."

"You want to tell me what's really going on?" I ask, turning back to Zach. "Because if I call the cops right now, you know sabotaging vines is a felony charge you're walking into."

Zach shakes his head rapidly, his face pale in the flashlight beam. "No, you don't understand. I wasn't going to do anything. I didn't pour anything. I swear!"

"Zach, we watched you. What was in that drum?" Ginny asks from behind me, arms folded tight.

"Just water," he says, eyes darting to the trees like he's measuring his chances.

Tarryn steps closer, her voice like ice. "Did Max tell you to sabotage our vines? Or did you just take it upon yourself to poison the section of land we've spent the last two years cultivating?"

"I didn't do anything!" Zach yells, panicked now. "I didn't pour it. I swear to God. It was a warm day. I thought I'd just water tonight. That's it!"

Ryker stiffens. "Why would you do that?"

But Zach doesn't answer. Instead, he bolts. He sprints back to the four-wheeler, jumping in and throwing it into gear. He spins it around and takes off, not down the main road, but through one of the narrow dirt paths that cuts through the vineyard blocks. But he's managed to leave the water drum he hauled up here behind.

"Shit," I mutter, heart pounding as his taillights vanish. I almost chase him on foot—almost. But I know it's too late. He's gone.

Tarryn runs for her truck.

"You won't catch him," I call. "He's not heading toward the barn."

"Damn it!" Tarryn slams her fist against the hood.

We stand there in the glow of the truck's headlights,

listening to the fading crunch of tires over dirt as Zach disappears between the vines.

I look at the well cap, still sealed tight. "He didn't pour it," I murmur. "But he was going to."

Ginny steps up beside me, eyes on the spot where Zach disappeared. "Do you think Max told him to do it?"

Tarryn's jaw clenches. "I have no doubt."

A minute later, Elise arrives in her pretty dress, lugging our chemical box. "What happened?"

We explain how Zach took off, and between the light of the two trucks, she prepares to test the water. She snaps on a pair of nitrile gloves and crouches beside the water drum. She pulls a test kit from her canvas field bag and lines up the vials and strips with quiet precision. She doesn't speak, and silence makes the tension crackle.

She unscrews the drum's lid and winces as a sharp scent wafts out. "God," she says. "That smells like pickles."

She fills a small plastic cup with the liquid, the color murky and slightly brown. Dipping the first pH test strip in, she waits a beat — then two — and pulls it out to compare the color with the chart printed on the side of the bottle.

"Four," she says, frowning. "That's low. Really low."

Tarryn steps closer. "That's acid range, right?"

"Yep. Let me test again."

This time, Elise reaches for a digital pH meter, pops the cap off the electrode, and dips the tip directly into the cup of liquid. The small screen flickers and calibrates for a few seconds before settling.

"Three-point-two," she announces.

"Shit," I mutter under my breath. That's not just low. It's corrosive.

Elise looks up at me. "When you looked at the lines, you told me you saw corrosion. Now, it all makes sense."

She pulls the probe out, rinses it in a small squeeze bottle of distilled water, and sniffs the sample again. Her whole face twists. "It's vinegar," she says, grimacing. "Someone poured vinegar into this. Strong stuff too, not the kind you put on salad."

Tarryn looks sick. "Could he have been putting this into the well?"

Elise nods. "That makes sense. It would absolutely lower the pH, and that explains why our drip-irrigated vines are dying. It's targeted, direct to the root system. Sprinklers like the Dempseys use would turn the leaves. Adding such large volumes of liquid to the water table also explains why the water levels are all over the place."

She packs up her gear but keeps the sample. "I'll take this to the lab and test for residual acetic acid to confirm it's vinegar, but there's no question. This is sabotage to both vineyards."

Tarryn doesn't respond. She just stares into the distance, like she's watching the whole vineyard curl up and die in front of her.

I stand back, hands on my hips, trying to keep my frustration from boiling over. I've known Zach my whole life. He's a screwup, yeah, but this is kilometers over the line.

Tarryn turns away. "I have to tell Evelyn," she murmurs. "She's going to lose it. Those were her award-winning vines. And Dad..." Her voice cracks. "They were his babies."

I walk up behind her, place a hand on her shoulder. "We'll figure it out."

We head back to the vineyard in silence, the water drum towed behind us like some kind of explosive. When we return, the rehearsal celebration is still in full swing—twinkling lights, laughter, music—but it all feels far away now.

I hop down from the passenger side and turn to Ginny. "Stay with Tarryn. I'll get my dad."

She nods, and I jog up the hill toward the main house, weaving through the outskirts of the party until I spot him near the tasting patio, deep in conversation with one of the vineyard board members.

"Dad," I say quietly. "I need you to come with me. Now."

He turns, sees my face, and doesn't hesitate.

We return to the truck, where Tarryn and Elise are now

crouched near the water drum, the fifty-gallon jug we watched him dump into the container beside them. Elise has pulled a portable test kit from her bag and is running a pH test on the jug.

When she stands, her face is pale. "It's completely off the charts," she says. "This is acidic. The levels are consistent with vinegar. No wonder everything that well feeds is dying."

Tarryn's eyes are glassy. She crosses her arms and looks out over the rows of withered vines beyond the truck. "All that work," she whispers. "That was supposed to be my mark. My legacy outside of Dad. And he torched it."

Our father takes the test strip from Elise's hand. He stares at it in silence, then looks toward the empty horizon where Zach disappeared minutes ago. "I want every drop of that water tested," he says, voice shaking with fury. "Every pipe. Every wellhead. I want the entire system flushed and shut down. And I want to know how the hell this happened."

"It was deliberate," I say quietly.

Elise nods. "There's no way this was accidental. Vinegar-level acidity doesn't happen from runoff or algae. Zach did it on purpose."

Dad's hands curl into fists at his sides. "Were the Dempseys involved too?"

"No," Ginny says from behind me, stepping forward. Her voice is quiet but sure. "It was designed to look like them."

Dad exhales hard. "If you hadn't caught Zach tonight, we would've gone to Evelyn without all the facts and likely started a war. Given Zach is a Paradise, it still may start a war. But if we can admit fault and take care of the damages, maybe we can keep this out of the courts and newspapers."

Tarryn's eyes narrow. "Zach's not smart enough to do this on his own."

Dad exhales, jaw tight. "This goes deeper than Zach. Someone's pulling strings."

"Elise," Tarryn says, voice shaking slightly now, "can you send everything to the lab tonight?"

"I already texted the lead chemist," Elise replies. "They'll expedite it."

Tarryn nods but keeps her eyes on the dying vines. She sinks onto the truck bumper, her shoulders curling in. Not in defeat but grief. "We're supposed to be celebrating tonight," she whispers.

"We still are," I tell her, forcing a small smile. "We just happened to catch a criminal act while taking a break."

Ginny gives a soft, dry laugh.

The celebration is still going on down the hill, the music and laughter continuing like nothing's wrong. But tomorrow, after the wedding, everything we thought we knew will shift. Because now we know someone's willing to burn us from the inside out.

THIRTY-EIGHT

Ginny

It's the morning of Sadie and Beckett's wedding, and everything is a whirl of satin, flowers, and nerves. The cottage smells like fresh eucalyptus and garden roses. I've barely slept, but the adrenaline in my veins is doing a decent job of helping me pretend I did.

Ryker and I were up late, sitting in the Armada outside Zach's apartment. We'd hoped for some sign of him, even just lights turning on inside. But the place was empty. No car. No movement. Just silence. We didn't talk much. There wasn't much left to say after everything that happened in block nine.

My stomach twists as I think about facing my grandmother. Evelyn Dempsey doesn't just receive bad news. She weaponizes it. And confirmed sabotage to her prized vines? She'll go nuclear. I can already see the storm in her eyes, the way her jaw will tighten before she blames me, not outright, but in that quiet, scathing way that cuts deeper than shouting ever could. I've survived her disappointment before, but this time feels different. She's done everything to me it seems like she could, but she could still say or do something horrible that costs me Ryker.

In her mind, I'm sure this all circles back to me choosing him, stepping over the line and siding with the Paradise family. It won't matter that I had nothing to do with Zach's actions. To her, loyalty is black and white, and I've already picked the wrong side.

Tarryn and Elise have agreed. We aren't going to ruin this wedding. Sadie deserves this. Beckett too. No family drama, no vineyard sabotage, no betrayal will get airtime during their event. We've shelved it until after they're man and wife.

This morning, Vicky caught us in the hallway on our way to get coffee. She looked tired, her smile more strained than usual.

"Trace didn't sleep," she murmured. *"Up pacing half the night. He can't believe, after all the chances we gave Zach, that he would do something like this."*

We know he didn't do this alone. She didn't have to say it. None of us trusts Max. And if Trace confronts him, Max will lie. He always does.

Still, there's no proof it was anyone other than Zach. No confession. Just suspicion and acid churning in my stomach.

Ryker's fingers brush mine under the table at breakfast, just enough to ground me. He doesn't say anything, but I know we both were hoping Zach would show up.

I catch a glimpse of Max standing beside Trace, laughing like he doesn't have a care in the world. He's all charm and backslaps, the life of the damn party, and for a second, I wonder... What if he's not behind all of this? The sabotage, the well, the vines dying inch by inch? He doesn't seem guilty. If anything, he looks smug, completely at ease.

"Where's Zach?" Ryker asks.

Max scans the room lazily and shrugs. "I haven't seen him

since last night at the rehearsal dinner," he says with a smirk. "He's probably shacked up with some girl. Maybe we should be looking for the missing female instead."

My stomach turns. He's disgusting.

But now is not the time for that.

Now, I get to help Sadie into her dress. I get to watch her marry the man who loves her fiercely. I get to stand up in front of everyone and pretend, for a few hours, that the world outside doesn't matter.

I'd really like to believe that.

A little while later, Sadie stands in front of the mirror in her robe, her hair half-pinned and curls tumbling down one shoulder. She looks beautiful already, even with no makeup on yet. Outside, it's the kind of morning you hope for on your wedding day—clear skies, no wind, everything calm. Yet my insides are anything but.

She watches me in the mirror. "Okay, what's going on?"

I freeze mid–mascara swipe. "What do you mean?"

She turns to face me. "Don't play dumb. You've barely said two words, and you've already dropped your brush twice. Something happened. Did you and Ryker have a fight?"

"No," I say quickly. Then soften. "No, we didn't fight. I swear."

"Then what?" she presses. "You look like you haven't slept."

I force a smile. "Just wedding stress. You'd be surprised how much work it takes to be a bridesmaid."

She narrows her eyes. "I don't buy it."

Before I can offer another flimsy excuse, there's a soft knock on the door and Tarryn slips in, cheeks flushed and eyes urgent. "Hey. Can I borrow you for a sec?"

Sadie lifts a brow. "You're not even trying to be subtle."

Tarryn waves her off. "You're minutes away from being the center of attention for the rest of the day. Let me borrow your maid of honor for five."

Sadie crosses her arms and grins. "Fine. But if she doesn't come back smiling, I'm dragging Ryker in here and making him explain whatever the hell is going on."

Tarryn pulls me into the hallway and doesn't speak until the door clicks closed behind us.

"I've been thinking about how to handle Evelyn," she says, lowering her voice. "We could go with the angle that Elise and Josie discovered the chemical imbalance together. Pretend it was all some unfortunate accident."

I blink at her. "You want to lie?"

She pauses, like she's been wrestling with it. "Only to soften the blow. Ease her into it."

My stomach clenches. "That feels like a mistake. There's no way vinegar accidentally got into the well. It will just raise more questions."

Relief flickers across her face. "God, I'm glad you said that. I think so too."

We both exhale.

"Okay," she continues, "then maybe Dad and I should go to Evelyn and Sera ourselves. Lay it out honestly — everything we found, no spin. We'll take full responsibility and offer reparations for the damage Zach caused. Fall on our swords."

I nod slowly. "I like that idea. A lot." It feels right — honest, accountable, and most importantly, it keeps me out of the crossfire. "When are you going to do it?"

"Probably during the reception," she says. "I don't want to ruin Beckett and Sadie's day, but we don't want to delay. The sooner Evelyn hears it from us, the better."

I nod again. "That's a good idea. And...thank you. For leaving me out of it."

Tarryn gives me a faint smile. "You're Sadie's maid of

honor. You're not part of the Paradise family. Not officially, anyway," she adds with a look. "Go be there for her. We'll handle the mess. But you know some of the blowback may affect you."

I nod, and for a moment, I have to rest against the wall. "Probably. Or maybe I'm already out, so there's nothing more she can do. With Evelyn, you never know. Thank you for telling me."

She touches my arm. "We'll loop you in later if we need to. But for now, go get Sadie into her dress. Make her day perfect. She deserves that much."

I nod, swallowing the knot in my throat. For once, I don't have to play the fixer. I don't have to explain anything or keep any secrets or stand between two families locked in a centuries-old conflict. I just get to be Sadie's friend.

The bridal suite transforms the moment the wedding planner arrives — clipboards, timelines, emergency sewing kits, and a flurry of bobby pins.

"Pictures in fifteen," the planner calls, directing bridesmaids and groomsmen like a general preparing for battle. "We start with the bridal party, then immediate family, then extended!"

Sadie is in her dress now — elegant and classic, all lace and understated glamour. Her veil floats like mist around her shoulders as she turns in the mirror, catching sight of herself with a soft, awed smile.

"I can't believe this is real," she whispers.

"It's real," I say, my throat tight. No one deserves this joy like Sadie.

Photos begin on the front lawn of the vineyard's estate house, where wildflowers spill along the stone path and the lake glitters in the background. There are candid and posed shots, laughter and tears, and more than one moment where I think Sadie might smudge her mascara permanently.

When it's time for the wedding to start, the planner moves us into position. The music plays, and Kingston steps up to the altar as the officiant in a tailored navy suit, looking surprisingly confident for someone who claimed he was feeling ill an hour ago. He smiles at Beckett and gestures for the music with a calm, steady hand.

Once I've reached my place in front, I turn to watch Caleb walk Sadie down the aisle. The moment he places her hand in Beckett's, a smile lights up his face. He's not so much giving her away as passing her into the care of someone he already trusts.

Sadie is radiant, her focus on Beckett like no one else exists. And Beckett... He's not even pretending to be stoic. He reaches up to wipe away a tear.

Something shifts inside me. All this time, I thought loving someone meant risking myself. That letting someone in meant giving them the power to leave. But here, watching Beckett's hands tremble as he holds Sadie's, I see something else. Love isn't weakness. It's strength. The kind that keeps you standing when everything else falls apart.

For so long, I thought I had the Paradise family figured out—wealthy, entitled, emotionally distant. But Beckett's emotion is raw and real. Tarryn's fierce loyalty, Vicky's open heart, even Ryker's tenderness in the quiet moments—they all paint a different picture.

They're not perfect, but they love hard. They show up. And when they give their heart, they don't hold anything back.

A breeze moves through the vines, and I close my eyes for half a second, letting it wash over me. When I open them, Ryker's looking straight at me from the other side of the aisle.

He doesn't say a word.

Just lifts two fingers and blows me the softest, smallest kiss.

My breath catches. It's not just the kiss. It's the look in his eyes. Steady. Unflinching. Like he sees every broken piece of me and still wants in. And I let myself believe that maybe I deserve that. In that moment, I feel like a million bucks.

No matter what storm is coming, I think there's a place for me here.

After the ceremony, the guests move on to the reception, and the bride and groom pose for pictures together.

Then it's time for the Paradise family photo. Beckett's parents, Ryker, Tarryn, Greyson, Caleb, and Kingston gather under the arbor. Wives are included, but Sadie lingers nearby with her bouquet, seeming uncertain, with Beckett at her side.

"Ginny," Vicky calls, waving me over. "Come join the photo."

I blink. "What?"

She's already gesturing to the photographer. "She's part of this family whether she knows it or not. So is Caleb's girlfriend—Katy?"

Katy looks just as surprised as I feel but slips in beside Caleb with a bashful smile. I hesitate for a breath too long, and Ryker takes my hand and pulls me gently to stand with him. His mother smiles like it's the most natural thing in the world. My heart swells. This isn't temporary. This isn't them making room for me out of politeness. This is them choosing me. Over and over again, they've shown me. And now, I'm ready to choose them back.

The photographer gives instructions, Beckett and Sadie take their place, and we all shuffle in a bit tighter.

Before the shutter clicks, Sadie steps in front of the group, her bouquet lowered at her side, her eyes glassy.

"Wait," she says, voice trembling. "Can I say something first?"

Everyone goes still, and the photographer nods.

Sadie turns toward the group, blinking rapidly. "When my parents died, I knew I still had Caleb. He was my anchor, the one thing that kept me from falling apart. But I didn't realize until recently how much I missed having a family. A real one. Loud and messy and opinionated and so full of love it knocks the air out of you sometimes."

She pauses. "I just want to say thank you to all of you. For taking me in, for making room for me. For making this day feel like more than just a wedding. It feels like coming home, not just to Beckett, but to all of you."

Beckett is beside her in seconds, wrapping an arm around her shoulders and kissing her temple. Tarryn's already dabbing her eyes. Caleb pulls Katy closer. Vicky sniffles quietly and rests against her husband.

And I feel Ryker's hand curl around my waist like he doesn't plan to let go anytime soon. The ache in my heart eases.

After a few more photos, the photographer calls it a wrap, and we all start making our way toward the vineyard's reception site, a gentle slope overlooking Black Bear Lake. The sky is a brilliant sweep of blue, and the sun's warm but not harsh, with just enough breeze to rustle the golden leaves clinging to the edge of summer. It's perfect.

The emcee introduces the wedding party, and I find my seat at the table beside Ryker, who gives my hand a squeeze. After a moment, glasses clink in a chorus, and the room quiets.

Ryker rises from his seat, a glass of bubbly in his hand and a lopsided grin tugging at his mouth. The light catches in his hair, and there's a flush to his cheeks—part pride, part nerves.

"I know it's tradition for the best man to give a toast. But I told Beckett I wasn't going to do it. I didn't want his giant head to get any bigger," he begins, glancing at Beckett, then Sadie. "But Beckett threatened to put a picture of me in footie pajamas in the slideshow if I didn't say something, so here we are."

The room chuckles, and Beckett smirks, raising his glass like he might have that picture in his pocket.

Ryker takes a breath, and his grin softens. "Growing up, it was always the four of us—Kingston, Greyson, Beckett, and me. But the teams were clear. Kingston and Greyson were the serious ones. Responsible. Mature. Probably born with a five-year plan and a spreadsheet. And then there was us."

He gestures between himself and Beckett. "Beckett and me, we were the chaos. The noise. The bruised elbows and half-baked plans. We built forts and broke windows. Got in trouble, usually together. It was loud and messy, and honestly? It was the best place in the world to grow up."

His voice dips into quiet. "I know we don't say it enough, but I admire you, Beckett. You're calm when the rest of us are losing it. You listen when most people talk just to hear themselves. And even though you fight dirty — seriously, Sadie, he's sneaky — you're also loyal. Fiercely. Relentlessly. If you're lucky enough to have Beckett in your corner, you never have to face anything alone."

Sadie dabs at her eyes.

Ryker lifts his glass. "To Sadie and Beckett. May your marriage be a little chaotic, a little messy, and the best place either of you has ever called home."

The room erupts into claps and cheers as glasses rise around the tables. Beckett stands and gives Ryker a hug.

And when Ryker sits again, his fingers find mine under the table. I squeeze them. Because tonight feels like everything good — honest, open, and completely ours.

As the applause fades and people settle back into their seats, the room shifts. Faces turn. Eyes land on me.

Someone calls out gently, "Ginny?"

Oh. It's time. Ryker's hand tightens around mine under the table, and then I stand slowly, heart fluttering somewhere between my ribs and my throat. I don't even know if my voice will work, but then I look at Sadie.

She's glowing, bouquet resting in her lap. Her eyes meet mine, and suddenly, I know exactly what to say.

I lift my glass. "I wasn't sure if I'd be able to get through this," I begin. "But here goes."

The room stills.

"When I think about high school, I don't remember the classes or the boys or the drama. I remember Sadie. I remember sleepovers on Friday nights and skipping class to drive up to the lookout with gas money we didn't have. I remember her dragging me through heartbreak, bad haircuts, and one particularly regrettable spray tan incident."

Laughter ripples across the room. Sadie covers her mouth, eyes shining.

"But the truth is," I go on, "I've never been good at goodbyes. Or hellos, for that matter. I build walls and call them boundaries. But Sadie? She never let me disappear, not really. I wouldn't have survived any of it without her. And coming back here after all these years... She welcomed me without hesitation, no judgment, just love."

I glance around the room—at the twinkle lights, the decorations, the people who have slowly, without me realizing it, become part of my story again.

"She's been here for me through everything. And Beckett, that makes you one of the luckiest people alive."

I shift toward him, smiling. "You're marrying up."

The room laughs again—bigger this time—and Beckett doesn't miss a beat.

"Fully agree," he says, lifting his glass. "No argument here."

I raise my glass a little higher. "To Beckett and Sadie. May your life together be filled with laughter, loyalty, and a love that never stops showing up."

The clinks ring out again, a soft chorus of celebration.

Vicky catches my eye from the table and gives me the smallest nod. Warmth blooms in me all over again.

As I sit down, Ryker kisses the side of my head, whispering, "That was perfect."

I smile back at him and realize that for once I'm not bracing for the fall. I'm letting myself hope.

THIRTY-NINE

Ryker

Ginny's already sitting up when I crack my eyes open the next morning, squinting against the slice of light bleeding through the curtains. She's still, her knees pulled to her body and her eyes on something I can't see.

"Did you sleep?" I ask as I raise my head, though I already know the answer.

She shakes her head. "Not a second."

I groan and flop back into the pillow, instantly regretting it. My skull pulses like I've got a jackhammer wedged behind my eyes. My mouth tastes like the wrong end of a whiskey barrel. "God. Why did I do shots with Caleb?"

Ginny doesn't answer, just reaches for the coffee she's set on the nightstand. She hands it to me silently, and I grunt a thanks before taking a sip.

"Remind me not to toast your toast again," I mutter. "Too much tequila. Not enough sense." I sit up, rubbing a hand over my face. "Hey. I didn't mean to ruin your night. Sorry you couldn't sleep."

She waves it off. "It's fine. I just couldn't shut my brain off. I kept thinking about what's coming."

Right. The meeting. The one we all agreed to postpone until after the wedding to keep from ruining Beckett and Sadie's day. Dad and Tarryn tried to see Evelyn during the reception, but they couldn't get in.

Which means today's the day.

I drag in a breath and swing my legs over the side of the bed. "Elise is bringing her test kit. I guess I'm tagging along since I caught Zach with the drum."

Ginny nods, still hugging her knees. "Vicky is going to try to talk your dad out of going since every time he and Evelyn get together it ends in a screaming match. Tarryn and Elise are going to be the ones to tell Evelyn. No pretending, no spinning the story. Just the truth."

That surprises me. "Not softening the blow?"

"Nope. Tarryn considered floating a lie—have Elise and Josie 'discover' the issue together—but she asked what I thought, and I told her it felt wrong. She agreed." Ginny finally looks at me. "So now they're falling on their swords."

"When did you talk to her?"

"Before the wedding."

I nod, trying to focus through the pounding in my skull. "It's probably smart. The vines are already dying. Might as well get it over with."

Ginny exhales. "I told her thank you for leaving me out of it. But it seems I'm the only one who can get them inside."

My gaze sharpens. "I'm sorry. You shouldn't have to deal with this."

"Yeah, but I think I do." She stands and walks toward the window. "When this comes out, Evelyn's not going to care who poured what. All she'll see is that I'm still with you. Still on the wrong side."

I don't have a good answer for that. I just walk up behind her and wrap my arms around her waist, pressing my forehead to the back of her shoulder.

She relaxes into me, just for a second. "I need you to remember that she's not me. She may say terrible things, but that doesn't make them true. I don't want to lose you."

"You won't lose me, Ginny. There's nothing she could say that would change my opinion of who I know you to be."

She turns to look at me. "Thanks."

I hug her close, and then we both let go. *Let the fireworks begin.*

We meet Tarryn and Elise at my parents' house and drive over to Black Bear Winery in my Armada.

Elise double-checks the box of soil samples in her lap while Tarryn scrolls through something on her phone. Every pothole slows us down. Ginny watches the road like she's willing it to be straighter, smoother, anything but this rutted mess.

The tasting room comes into view, and the parking lot is mostly empty, except for a few trucks and delivery vans. Black Bear isn't open for tours today, but a few staffers are moving around, and they pause mid-task as we pull in. No one says anything, but the stares follow us all the way from the gravel lot to the front steps.

Ginny texted Sera to tell her we were coming, and Sera's waiting just outside the door, her face tight. Her eyes widen slightly as we come walking up, but she nods and opens the door without comment.

"Gran is in her office," she murmurs, stepping aside so we can pass. "Josie's with her."

Ginny leads us through the tasting room, past rows of empty wine barrels and polished counters. Every footstep echoes loudly. People stare. Their eyes track Ginny, wide and unblinking, like she's grown a second head.

My heart pounds, but I keep moving. Ahead I spot Monica, and I want to tell her what she's done to her daughter, but I can't stop. Not now.

When she sees us, she freezes for a split second before turning to duck down a side hall without a word.

Coward, I think bitterly. But the sting fades fast. What else do I expect? She's relied on Evelyn most of her adult life. Choosing silence over conflict isn't cowardice. It's survival.

Ginny slows at the carved oak door of Evelyn Dempsey's office and glances back at the three of us behind her. Tarryn gives her a small nod. She knocks once and doesn't wait for a reply, just swings the door open.

Evelyn Dempsey looks up from her desk with the kind of expression that makes grown men forget how to breathe. Her sharp blue eyes cut through the air like blades.

She doesn't stand. Doesn't speak.

She just waits.

Tarryn breaks the silence, stepping forward like a general entering enemy territory.

"We've found the source of the sabotage," she says. "The well on the eastern edge of the property—the one our families share—has been tampered with."

Evelyn's gaze sharpens, but she stays silent.

Tarryn continues. "It was our cousin Zach."

The name hangs in the air like a gunshot.

"We caught him two nights ago," Tarryn continues. "He poured fifty gallons of vinegar into a five-hundred-gallon water pony. We stopped him as he was preparing to put it into the well."

Evelyn's pen drops from her hand and clatters against the desk.

Her jaw tightens. "Where is he?"

"We confronted him," I tell her. "And he ran."

Evelyn's eyes flick to mine, and I see it—shock, fury, maybe even a flicker of fear. But it's gone just as quickly, masked behind a wall of granite resolve.

She stands slowly, placing her hands flat on the desk. "You're telling me," she says carefully, "that a Paradise boy was caught red-handed poisoning the only remaining water source on that slope, and now, he's vanished?"

"He was acting alone," Elise adds quickly. "We believe he had his own agenda. We don't think the rest of the Paradise family knew anything about it."

"That's convenient," Evelyn snaps, eyes darting toward Ginny, then me. "Very convenient."

"He's Chereen's boy," Tarryn says, as if that explains something. Maybe it's something Evelyn can understand. She does seem to register it.

I take a breath. "We're not here to use him as a scapegoat. We're here to tell you the truth. To stop this before it gets worse. Before someone gets hurt."

"That level of acidity could've destroyed both our vines permanently if left untreated," Elise continues. "Zach wanted to cause lasting damage, not only to our land, but to our relationship."

Tarryn steps in. "Paradise Hill will replace any vines that were destroyed. We will also compensate you for the loss of revenue over the next five years while our vintners work together to fix the soil and grow healthier vines."

Evelyn stares at Tarryn, her mouth set in a hard line. "You think this is going to fix everything? That I'll just forget?"

That stings. But what else can we do? Rebuilding trust takes time. Especially when at least one party doesn't want to.

There's a long pause. Josie's frozen by the window, Tarryn lingering near the doorway, both of them looking like they're not sure if they should jump in or run.

Then Evelyn looks at each of us and turns slowly back to Ginny. "You said caught. Did you witness it?"

"We found the vinegar drum and a funnel, and then Ginny, Ryker, and I caught Zach with a hose near the well cap," Tarryn explains. "His fingerprints are on the containers. And there's security footage, though it's grainy."

Evelyn lets out a breath through her nose. "I want that footage," she says. "And I want the full report. If you find him before I do, you bring him to me."

If Evelyn Dempsey gets to Zach first, she won't be asking any questions. She'll be burying the answers.

Tarryn speaks again, her voice firm but respectful. "We'll take responsibility for what was done. There doesn't need to be any blood loss."

Evelyn looks at Tarryn a moment and then nods. Josie's head jerks toward her in surprise, but Sera places a hand on her arm.

"I'll work directly with you," Tarryn continues, her gaze moving between the Dempsey sisters. "Sera, Josie, I'd like to coordinate efforts. You know this land better than anyone."

Evelyn's lip curls slightly, but she doesn't argue.

Tarryn squares her shoulders. "I also want to be your contact at Paradise moving forward. Leave my dad and Max out of this."

My heart thuds. Evelyn's expression falters, not in anger, but recognition. Tarryn's not just speaking for us. She's leading us. And maybe that scares Evelyn the most. Tarryn doesn't play by the older generation's rules.

Evelyn's eyes narrow. She stares at Tarryn, assessing, then slowly nods. "Fine. We'll start there at least."

"We'll send you everything we have," Elise says. "Footage, soil tests, fingerprints — everything."

I nod and turn for the door, Tarryn and Elise behind me.

Ginny moves to come with us, but Evelyn's voice stops her cold.

"Ginny. Stay."

My stomach drops. I glance at Ginny, and she gives me a nod.

"I'd like Ryker to stay with me," she says.

Evelyn's shoulders drop. "Really?"

"Yes."

Tarryn closes the door behind her, and we're left alone with the woman who's ruled this family with an iron will and a ledger book for as long as I can remember.

She sits down again, folding her hands on the desk like she's preparing to dissect me.

We stare at each other for a long beat. And then she says, "You're in love with my granddaughter."

It's not a question. It's a statement.

"Yes."

She exhales through her nose, like that one word confirms every fear she's ever had. "Do you understand what that means?"

"Yes," I say again. "I'd do anything for her."

Silence stretches between us.

Then, with a voice like gravel, she mutters, "Be careful what you pledge. That cost me my sister-in-law, not to mention my children. Every generation has its tragedy when our families cross lines. You will be yours."

I take a breath and step closer. "I'm not asking for permission. But I am asking for peace."

Her stare is arctic. "Peace isn't part of our legacy."

"This family has been at war for longer than I've been alive," Ginny says. "I'm done fighting battles I didn't start and I'm not letting them decide my future." With that, she turns and walks out.

I watch her go and turn back to Evelyn. "I think that tells you where we stand. I love Ginny. And loving her might cost me, but losing her would cost me more."

And that's the difference between us, I add silently. I'm willing to take a risk for something real. Evelyn's only ever fought to keep what she controls from falling apart.

She waves me off with a flick of her wrist. "Go."

I hesitate. "Evelyn —"

"Go before I say something I'll regret."
So I do.

FORTY

Ginny

A couple weeks later, the end-of-season crush party at Paradise Hill Estate Vineyard doesn't end so much as it unravels.

One by one, the last people filter out — laughing, hugging, drunk on celebration and wine. Beckett and Sadie left in a blur of sparkles and confetti, hand in hand, disappearing into their own beginning. They stuck around for two weeks after their wedding, but now, they're off to Paris to work on Rosie's bucket list during their honeymoon.

The field hands have been working hard these past few days, collecting the last of the grapes off the vines. Each box has been carefully marked with the block, row, and type. Elise and Josie have been saving what they can in the damaged blocks. It will be a long haul before the water is good.

Tarryn and Trace went to the police to file a report about Zach, but he's vanished—no calls, no sightings, not even a whisper through the vineyard grapevine. It's like he stepped off the map.

Max is furious, swearing up and down that Zach's being framed, that this is all some elaborate setup. But the more he insists, the more I wonder who he's really angry at—the people accusing Zach or whoever might be behind this. And I still wonder if it's him. There's a sharpness to Max lately, like he's guarding more than just his pride.

The air around the vineyard feels charged, like we're standing on the edge of something. Zach might be gone, but the trouble he's tangled in is still here, wound tight around the family like a trellis vine choking the roots. Whatever this is, it isn't over. And when the cracks form in Paradise, the fallout has a way of finding the people least prepared for it.

Fairy lights twinkle in the distance, and the cleanup crew is packing up chairs and carnival games. But out here at the edge of the lake, the cool night air brushes over my skin. My clothes are wrinkled, my hair's falling out of the twist Sadie insisted on, and my feet are throbbing from a day spent constantly moving.

But I've never felt lighter.

"I figured I'd find you here," Ryker says, his voice curling around me like the breeze.

"You followed me."

"Always," he says simply, walking barefoot down the dock. He's rolled up his sleeves, and the moonlight paints him in silver and shadow. Even now, when I should be used to it, he steals my breath.

He settles beside me, our shoulders brushing. "You okay?"

"I think so. I can't believe the season's over. It's taken a lot to get here."

Ryker chuckles. "It wouldn't be Paradise if everything went smoothly."

I glance over at him. "Do you think Beckett and Sadie will

be okay?"

"I do," he says without hesitation. "They've been through the fire. They chose each other. That counts for something."

My heart swells a little. Because so have we.

He reaches for my hand. "What about us?"

"What about us?"

His thumb brushes across my knuckles. "Now that everything's out in the open—your family knows, my family knows, the sabotage is discovered… What do you want?"

I look out at the dark water. "Honestly? I just want peace, mornings without the knot in my stomach, without wondering who's going to explode next. I want to be with you without looking over my shoulder. A life that's ours, untouched by everyone else's battles."

Ryker nods slowly, and then reaches into his pocket. "I think that is an attainable goal. I hope you do too."

My breath stalls. "Ryker…" My heart hiccups. Not because I didn't hope, but because suddenly it feels real. Like the ground is shifting beneath us.

"I've been carrying this around since your dad granted me permission to ask. I wanted to make sure at least one Dempsey would approve," he says, pulling out a small velvet box. "I've been waiting for the right moment."

He shifts to his knee in front of me, and the moment expands around us, thick with moonlight and meaning.

"I didn't plan a speech," he admits. "But I know this. Loving you hasn't always been easy. It's been messy and terrifying. But it's also been the most honest, incredible thing I've ever done." He opens the box.

The ring is stunning, unconventional with a sapphire center stone and two perfect diamonds, and so completely me.

"I want to build something real with you," he says. "Will you marry me?"

Tears well instantly. I nod, barely breathing. "Yes."

His smile breaks wide as he slides the ring on my finger. Then I launch into his arms, almost knocking us off the dock.

We laugh into a kiss. It's messy and happy and full of every promise between us. Eventually, we lie back on the dock, side by side, staring up at the stars.

"You nervous?" I ask, glancing at him.

Ryker laces our fingers. "Terrified."

"Of me?"

"Of losing you."

"You won't," I whisper.

His voice is quiet but certain. "I know."

We stay like that a little longer, talking about nothing and everything—who we'll tell first, whether we'll live at his place or find something new, how pissed Evelyn will be when she finds out.

Eventually, Ryker's phone buzzes. He checks it and smiles.

"What?" I ask.

He holds up the screen. It's a song. He hits play and sets it down. A soft acoustic melody fills the air.

"Beckett and Sadie sent this. Dance with me."

"Here?"

"Why not?"

I laugh but let him pull me up. We sway on the weathered dock, the lake beside us, the stars above us, and nothing but possibility ahead.

As he bends in to kiss me again, I realize something simple and true. There was a time I thought love had to hurt, that it came with expiration dates or conditions. But this is different. This is what forever feels like —soft, fearless, and finally ours.

And it's just beginning.

EPILOGUE

Ginny

Three months later

The morning sun has barely touched the edge of our bed when Ryker's mouth finds my neck, hot and possessive, like he's branding me before the day begins. His hand slides beneath the sheets to caress every inch of me. And after everything we've been through, I've stopped pretending I don't crave him like air.

He's already hard, already pressing into me from behind. "Morning," he murmurs.

"Mmm… You're insatiable," I whisper, hips arching into him.

"And you're mine," he growls, his hand sliding between my legs, drawing a gasp from my lips.

There's no slow build. Not this time. It's all heat and hunger.

We don't talk. We don't have to. Our bodies do the speaking, fast and frantic, like we've been starved for days instead of hours. He rolls me onto my back and thrusts inside, deep and deliberate. I gasp, clinging to his shoulders, his name a whisper I can't hold back.

Every time with him feels like the first. Like something sacred.

And when I come apart beneath him, the look on his face makes me believe in forever.

After, we lie tangled in the sheets, his fingers tracing lazy circles on my bare hip.

He kisses me like it's the only thing keeping him alive, deep and consuming, his tongue sliding against mine as his hips start to move again.

Slow at first. A tease.

I breathe his name, and he swallows the sound, one hand braced beside my head, the other gripping my thigh and hiking it higher around his waist.

"More," I whisper.

He gives it to me, each thrust deeper, harder, angled to hit the spot that turns my bones to water. My back arches off the bed, nails dragging down his back, and he groans like he's unraveling with me.

"Look at me," he says, voice rough.

I do.

Everything in me tightens as his rhythm builds, driving me closer with every stroke. I'm not even sure where I end and he begins anymore. There's only the heat, the tension, the way he's inside me like he's trying to stay.

"God...I'm right there," I gasp, clutching him tighter.

He shifts just enough to send me tumbling over the edge, my climax hitting hard. I cry out his name, head falling back, and he chases me over with a growl that vibrates against my skin. He pulses inside me, hips stuttering, and then collapses, his forehead pressed to mine, our chests heaving in sync.

"Still insatiable," I manage, breathless.

He chuckles, voice raw. "Only with you."

I used to think this would end. That we'd burn bright, then out. But here we are, still tangled up in each other, still reaching for more. This is what real love looks like. Not perfect. Just persistent.

We stay like that for a minute—skin to skin, hearts still racing, breaths tangled in the hush of the morning.

He brushes damp hair from my forehead. Then his thumb grazes my cheek. "I don't think I'll ever get over you," he says softly.

My heart stutters. "That's the point, right? You're not supposed to."

He shifts to his side, gathering me close, his leg sliding between mine. "I still wake up and think I'll open my eyes and you'll be gone. Like all this was something I dreamed."

I press my palm to his chest, right over his heart. "I'm not going anywhere."

He nods. "Good. Because I don't know how to do this life without you anymore."

"I don't want you to," I whisper.

His hand slides to my belly, then lower, over the curve of my hip. "You ever think about what comes next? Like, after the wedding? After all the festivities?"

"All the time," I admit. "I think about mornings like this. Making coffee in our kitchen. I think about…a quiet kind of happy."

He smiles against my temple. "You and me and that quiet kind of happy. Sounds like a dream worth chasing."

I close my eyes, wrapped in him, the world outside forgotten.

His fingers trail over my spine, drawing slow, invisible shapes. I'm about to pull him in for another kiss when my phone buzzes behind me and his phone pings on the nightstand.

Ryker groans. "Ignore it. It's probably spam."

"Nope." I check the screen, my smile fading.

He catches it instantly. "What is it?"

"Tarryn," I say, thumb hovering over the message preview. "She never texts this early."

"Everything okay?"

I read the message out loud, a chill curling my spine.

Tarryn: Call me. It's about Zach.

She sent it to both of us. My stomach lurches.

Our phones sound again before we've even had a chance to reply.

Tarryn: Actually, scratch that. I'm coming over. Be there in ten.

"She's on her way." I set the phone on the nightstand like it might burn me. "She didn't even wait for a reply."

"So much for naked breakfast."

I arch a brow. "What do you think she wants?"

"Maybe they found him and he's been arrested," Ryker says.

That gets my attention.

Ryker's jaw ticks. "That would be good, wouldn't it?"

"I don't know," I whisper.

He draws a long breath, pushing the worry from his face with effort. "You think we should get dressed?"

"Probably."

"Damn shame." He shoots me a lopsided smile.

Despite the nerves knotting in my gut, I laugh because this is Ryker. He makes me laugh even when everything feels uncertain.

Ryker leans in, brushing a kiss beneath my ear. "We could sneak out the back."

I snort. "Where would we go? We live here."

His fingers drift lower. One calloused thumb circles my nipple, slow and deliberate. "Fine. Then we take a risk. Lock the door. Pretend we're not home. Let her catch us mid round three…"

My breath hitches, hips arching instinctively. "You're incorrigible."

"I'm inspired," he murmurs, tongue tracing my collarbone. "But I'm also practical."

I blink. "Since when?"

"She has a key."

That sobers me. I pull back, meeting his eyes. "You gave her a key?"

Ryker grins, hand slipping away with one final teasing graze. "Don't worry, baby. I'll make it up to you."

He gets up, heading toward the bathroom. "At least three times this afternoon," he calls over his shoulder. "Starting the second we get rid of my sister."

I shake my head, lips twitching despite the nerves in my stomach.

A sharp knock rattles the front door.

Ryker groans and changes direction. "She knocked. That's new."

I grab my robe. "It's a warning shot."

He smirks over his shoulder as he disappears down the hall. "Shower now. I'll stall."

I sprint to the bathroom and let the water scald away the distraction still pulsing through me. By the time I emerge in fresh clothes and damp hair, Ryker's in the kitchen serving coffee.

Tarryn's sitting at the island, one perfectly arched brow lifted. "Sorry to interrupt this morning."

I roll my eyes, trying to play it cool as I steal Ryker's mug and take a sip. "What's going on? Did they arrest Zach?"

"I was dropping off a delivery at the tasting room this morning. Before sunrise. And I swear..." Her voice lowers. "I saw him."

My spine straightens.

Ryker's gaze hardens. "Are you sure?"

She nods but then pauses. "Not completely. But the build, the walk— It looked like him. He was near the loading docks, and by the time I parked, he was gone." Tarryn folds her arms. "I thought he'd left town."

I shake my head. "No one's seen him for the last three

months."

"So what if it's him?" she asks. "If he's still here?"

I glance out the kitchen window toward the vineyard.

"Then we can figure out who's pulling his strings."

Authors note: Thank you for reading *Dr. Ryker*. If you aren't done with Ryker and Ginny, check out this bonus content here.

Thank you so much for reading *Dr. Ryker*! I hope you fell for Ryker and Ginny the way I did. I always wanted to write a story that is rooted in the Hatfield and McCoys and this continues the Dempsey and Paradise family generational feud. Their story means the world to me, and I'm so grateful you came along for the ride. Up next is *EMT Declan*, and let's just say things are about to get even more complicated (and a whole lot hotter) when Tarryn Paradise reunites with the man who broke her heart returns to Paradise and he's ready to be the only gift under her Christmas tree...

EMT DECLAN SNEAK PEEK

Unedited — so it's bound to be changed a little bit.

Tarryn

The smoke wakes me.

At first, I think it's part of a dream — thick and acrid, curling into my lungs like a warning. But then I cough, hard, and my eyes snap open.

It's real.

I sit up, disoriented, heart thudding in my chest as the room swims. The scent hits stronger now — burning wood, melting plastic, something sharper beneath it all. My throat scratches with every breath.

"Elise!" I shout, stumbling toward the door of my bedroom. "Elise, wake up!"

Her door swings open at the same time mine does. Her eyes are wide, hair a mess, voice tight with panic. "Tarryn? There's smoke. There's a fire!"

"It's downstairs. We have to go. Now."

I grab my phone off the nightstand and nothing else — no wallet, no charger, not even the knit blanket at the end of my bed. Elise already has her coat halfway on as we both race for the front door. My lungs burn. The stairs are thick with haze, and the smoke alarm — where is the fire alarm?

"Elise, the fire alarm — why didn't it go off?"

"I don't know — just move!"

We burst out into the cold night air, coughing and shivering on the gravel drive, the cottage glowing an unnatural orange behind us. Through the windows, I can see flames licking up the back wall of the living room. It's spreading fast.

I fumble with my phone and dial 9-1-1. My hands shake as I give them the address. "It's the guest cottage at Paradise Hill Vineyard. There's a fire — it's inside the house — we're out, but it's bad. Please hurry."

The dispatcher promises they're on their way. I hang up and immediately call my parents. "It's the cottage," I rasp. "There's a fire. We're okay. But you need to come."

They live just up the hill. Not even a full minute passes before I hear the crunch of tires on gravel. Headlights sweep the driveway. My dad's truck skids to a stop, followed by my mom's car, hazard lights flashing.

They run toward us.

My mom wraps me in a blanket she must've grabbed on her way out the door. "Oh my God, baby. Are you hurt? What happened?"

"I don't know. We were sleeping and — there was smoke, it just —" I can't even finish the sentence.

My dad's already barking questions. "Was something left on? The stove? A candle? Did you leave the lights on on your Christmas tree?"

I shake my head. "No. Nothing."

The fire is visible now through the windows — wild and unforgiving. Elise stands beside me, coughing quietly, her arms wrapped around herself. We watch helplessly as the flames race along the ceiling beams like they're chasing something.

Sirens scream in the distance. Red lights pulse in time with the panic in my chest.

The first fire truck swings into the drive, followed closely by the ambulance. A crew jumps out and rushes to unspool hoses. Firefighters shout commands, racing toward the blaze.

Then I see him.

Tall. Broad. Stepping out of the passenger side of the ambulance like he belongs here.

Declan Conner.

I blink, stunned. My heart lurches.

What the hell is he doing here? He moved to Vancouver. He broke my heart, left without warning, and never looked back. Almost two years gone. And now he's here—just casually walking back into my life while my home burns?

Before I can process anything more, he spots me.

He stops cold, oxygen tank slung over one shoulder, and for a heartbeat we just stare. The past, the pain, the what-the-hell-is-happening of it all—it clogs my throat more than the smoke.

Then he's moving.

"Tarryn," he says, urgent but calm, kneeling beside me. "Are you okay? Are you breathing all right?"

I nod stiffly, but he doesn't take my word for it.

He fits the oxygen mask gently over my face, his fingers brushing my cheek, warm despite the night air. The contact sends a shiver down my spine. His eyes lock onto mine—concerned and something else—something that makes my stomach twist.

God help me, I forgot how blue his eyes are.

I forgot how easily he could look right through me.

"Breathe normally," he says softly, keeping the mask steady. "Just let it flow."

Elise sits beside me on the tailgate of my dad's truck, arms wrapped around herself, still shivering.

Declan glances over. "Anyone having chest pain? Trouble breathing? Dizziness?"

We both shake our heads, but he still runs through the

protocol. No shortcuts.

He steps closer to Elise first. "I'm going to check your vitals, okay?"

She nods.

He clips the pulse oximeter onto her finger and watches the numbers, then takes her wrist and counts. "You've got a little smoke inhalation, but your oxygen levels are holding. You cold?"

She gives a tight laugh. "Freezing."

He turns and waves to one of the other EMTs, who quickly brings over an extra blanket and foil wrap. "Here," he says, wrapping it around her shoulders. "You need to keep warm. Shock can creep in quiet."

Then he moves back to me.

His hands are confident, practiced, as he gently takes my wrist and checks my pulse. "You're fast," he murmurs. "Adrenaline."

"Gee, you think?" I mutter behind the mask.

The corner of his mouth twitches.

He crouches, one hand steadying my knee, the other lifting the sleeve of my coat to feel along my forearm. "Any burns?"

I shake my head.

"Smoke exposure?"

"I woke up coughing," I say. "But it wasn't thick upstairs. I didn't pass out or anything."

He nods, already moving on to the next check. He unzips the top of my coat just enough to inspect my neck and collarbone. His touch is clinical, impersonal. But my body doesn't seem to get the message. It reacts anyway.

"Lift your foot," he says gently.

I do, and he tugs my boot off, checking for burns or blisters on my bare skin. My toes are already turning pink from the cold.

"God, you didn't even grab socks."

"Didn't exactly have time to pack."

He exhales through his nose. "Of course not." He signals to another EMT who brings over a warming pack, which he tucks under my blanket and guides toward my lap.

"You're going to be okay," he says, eyes catching mine again. "You both got out fast. That matters."

I hate how steady he sounds. How gentle. Like he didn't leave me in pieces the last time we stood this close.

My parents hover nearby, my mom wringing her hands, my dad staring grimly at the cottage as flames spit from the windows.

Beckett and Sadie have arrived now. Ryker and Ginny, too. They're talking to the fire chief, assessing, asking questions, already moving into damage control mode. The family reflex.

But I can't move. Not yet.

Because Declan Conner is back in Paradise.

And somehow, the first hands to touch me after the flames… are his. And for one brief, stupid moment, I let myself forget that he did.

Then I remember.

"You're back," I say, voice muffled by the mask. "You're really back."

His jaw tightens. "Yeah."

Before I can ask more, Beckett and Sadie arrive, followed by Ryker and Ginny. I don't know who called them, but suddenly we're surrounded. Familiar voices, rapid-fire questions, worried eyes scanning the flames.

Beckett talks to the fire chief. Ryker stands watch, his jaw clenched, always scanning the perimeter like he's expecting this to be something more.

Sadie rushes to my side and wraps an arm around my shoulder just as Ginny mirrors her, looping an arm through Elise's. Their warmth is instant and grounding.

"My God, are you okay?" Sadie asks, brushing my hair back and tucking it behind my ear like I'm one of her kids.

Elise nods slowly. "We got out just in time."

"Your dad called," Ginny adds, pulling the foil blanket tighter around Elise's shoulders. "Said there was a fire. We came right over."

Sadie leans in close, eyes searching mine. "Tell me everything. What happened? Was it electrical? Did you leave a candle burning?"

Once. Just once I left a candle burning when I was thirteen and it started a fire that we didn't even call the fire house over. Dad doused it with a glass of water.

"I—I don't know," I say. "We were sleeping. I woke up coughing. The smoke was already in the hall upstairs."

Elise adds, "We didn't see flames until we ran out the front door. But it spread fast."

Beckett glances over from his conversation with the fire chief, his attention catching on our words. Ryker steps closer, crossing his arms over his chest.

"Why didn't the smoke alarm alert you?" Beckett asks. "Did it wake you?"

"No," I say, shaking my head. "That's the weird part. It never went off."

My dad, who's been pacing just behind us, stops mid-step. "That's impossible. I had those alarms checked and the batteries swapped six months ago."

"I'm telling you," I say. "Nothing. Not a beep."

Elise looks at me, then them. "It wasn't even chirping. Just nothing."

A beat of silence falls over us, the only sound the pop and crackle of burning wood and the hiss of water as the fire crew hoses down what's left of the back half of the cottage.

My father's expression darkens. "That unit was up to code. I had it inspected last spring. Our insurance requires it."

Sadie exchanges a glance with Beckett. "You think something was tampered with?"

Beckett doesn't answer. He just shifts his weight, eyes narrowing on the cottage like it might confess something.

Ryker turns toward the vineyard. "If the wind had shifted, it could've jumped into Block Fifty-Eight."

We all turn to look at the dark slope behind the cottage. Row after row of dormant vines stand like ghostly sentinels in the moonlight.

"That's a strong block," Beckett says tightly. "Some of our best merlot grapes."

My stomach sinks. "I didn't even think—"

"Don't," Ginny cuts in quickly, giving Elise's arm a squeeze. "This isn't your fault."

"But if the fire started downstairs..." Elise begins, her voice trailing off.

"We'll figure it out," Beckett says. "They'll investigate."

"Block Fifty-Eight's safe for now," Ryker adds, but the set of his jaw says he's not convinced we're in the clear.

Declan reappears at my side, his gaze sweeping the group before resting on me. "Fire's under control. It didn't breach the tree line."

"And the cause?" Beckett asks, voice cool.

Declan shakes his head. "Too early to say. Chief's already called in the marshal."

My dad mutters something under his breath and stalks away toward the fire captain.

Elise and I just sit there—huddled together, dazed, shivering under our blankets. Our home is still smoldering, the air thick with ruin. And despite the crowd around us, I feel exposed. Raw. Like everything I've built outside of the family walls is going up in flames.

And standing at the center of it all is Declan—steady, silent, watching me like he's seeing something I haven't said yet.

Like maybe he still knows how to read me.

I look toward the vineyard, terrified the flames will jump the fence. The vines are dormant for winter, but dry. It wouldn't take much. If we lose even a few acres...

Ryker's already there, flashlight in hand, talking with one of the firefighters and surveying the slope like he's preparing for war.

I clench the blanket tighter.

Then I look back at the cottage.

Or what's left of it.

The roof's half gone. The back wall is caved in. We see the flicker of flames as smoke pours through every broken window like the house itself is exhaling one final, choking breath. It's almost entirely gone.

My throat tightens. All the little things — my handmade mugs, the stack of sketchbooks I've filled over the years, my grandmother's quilt on the reading chair, the silly gingerbread house Elise bought me because we needed something in the cottage that looked like Christmas — all of it, burned.

Ash now. Gone in minutes.

I swallow hard, but the ache won't leave. My chest feels hollow. Like someone took the one space that was fully mine and carved it out without warning.

"I didn't grab my laptop," Elise says suddenly, her voice small. "It was charging on the kitchen counter."

I close my eyes. My own computer was on the desk, right by the window. I remember seeing it as we ran out. I didn't even hesitate.

"It's okay," I whisper, but I don't believe it.

Beckett hears us and steps over, still in full big-brother mode. "It's not a big deal," he says, calm but firm. "Everything's backed up to the cloud, right?"

I nod slowly.

"Good. Then I'll make sure you both have replacements by tomorrow. Don't worry about it."

I nod again, but it doesn't soothe the sting. It's not about the files. It's the feeling — like the life I'd built outside the family safety net just got scorched down to the studs.

All I can do now is sit there, wrapped in a scratchy blanket that smells like smoke and fear, and try not to fall apart.

Declan fades into the background, eclipsed by the smoke and devastation still rising from what used to be my home. This isn't about him — it's about everything I've lost. The smell of burning wood. The blackened outline of a life I was still building. The sickening realization that safety is a myth, and even the walls you create for yourself can be reduced to ash.

Answers can wait.

What matters now is why the alarms stayed silent.

How the fire took hold so quickly.

And whether someone, somewhere, struck the first spark.

And I want to know who, if anyone, lit the match.

Available in December 2025 Preorder/Download **at here.**
https://www.amazon.com/dp/B0FRDLSZR9

THANK YOU

This book was made possible by...

Early-morning writing sprints, bottomless mugs of coffee, endless cups of Earl Grey, and plot twists that showed up uninvited but refused to leave. (Plus, a few ugly-cry moments I totally blame on my characters.)

It was fueled by half-filled notebooks, entire chapters sent to the recycle bin, and those rare sentences that landed so perfectly they gave me goosebumps.

It was rescued by:

Readers who review, recommend, and remind me why I keep telling stories. Your words are the spark that keeps the pages turning.

My husband, who has patiently survived every draft, every meltdown, and every "just one more chapter." You are my biggest plot twist—and the only one I'll never delete.

My boys, who roll their eyes at "Mom's swoony doctor books" but still cheer me on anyway. Your quiet support is everything.

Jessica Royer Oken, my genius developmental editor, who takes my messy drafts and somehow makes them shine. I don't know how you do it, but I'm forever grateful.

Courtnay, Linda, Iris, Nancy, and Diana, my typo-fighting dream team—you make sure no rogue comma dares sneak past. Any others that snuck by, are my fault.

This book was also brought to you by stubborn persistence,

reckless amounts of hope, and the unshakable belief that love stories are worth every word.

Thank you for coming along for the ride.

With love and gratitude,
Gracie

BOOKS BY GRACE MAXWELL

Men of Mercy
Doctor of the Heart (Paisley & Davis)
Doctor of Women (Nadine & Michael)
Doctor of Sports (Eliza & Steve)
Doctor of Beauty(Laine & Jack)
Men of Mercy Box Set

Mercy Medical Emergency
Doctor Delight (Tori & Griffin)
Doctor Bossy (Amelia & Kent)
Doctor Rebel (Lucy & Chance)
Doctor Enemy (Ava & Roman)
Previously released as *A Doctor for Valentines* **in "Love is in the Air, Vol 3"**
Doctor Tyrant (Hailey & Christian)
Mercy Medical Emergency Box Set

Brothers Paradise
Dr. Greyson (Trinity & Greyson)
Dr. Beckett (Sadie & Beckett)
Dr. Ryker (Ginny & Ryker)
EMT Declan (Tarryn & Declan)

www.ingramcontent.com/pod-product-compliance
Lightning Source LLC
Chambersburg PA
CBHW072343020726
47506CB00004B/979